## THE ABDUCTED

Never had she been so vulnerable, so completely powerless. Even in her parents' house on that August night twenty-three years before, she'd been able to take action, fight for survival.

The noise in her throat was a choked moan.

Erin prayed that her sister wasn't with her. Prayed that the voice over the intercom had been only a trick, and Annie was safe at home.

She wanted one of them, at least, to survive this night.

# BLIND PURSUIT

# BLIND
# PURSUIT

## Brian Harper

A SIGNET BOOK

**SIGNET**
Published by the Penguin Group
Penguin Books USA Inc., 375 Hudson Street,
New York, New York 10014, U.S.A.
Penguin Books Ltd, 27 Wrights Lane,
London W8 5TZ, England
Penguin Books Australia Ltd, Ringwood,
Victoria, Australia
Penguin Books Canada Ltd, 10 Alcorn Avenue,
Toronto, Ontario, Canada M4V 3B2
Penguin Books (N.Z.) Ltd, 182-190 Wairau Road,
Auckland 10, New Zealand

Penguin Books Ltd, Registered Offices:
Harmondsworth, Middlesex, England

First published by Signet, an imprint of Dutton Signet,
a division of Penguin Books USA Inc.

First Printing, January 1997
10  9  8  7  6  5  4  3  2  1

PUBLISHER'S NOTE
This is a work of fiction. Names, characters, places, and incidents either are the
product of the author's imagination or are used fictitiously, and any resemblance
to actual persons, living or dead, events, or locales is entirely coincidental.

I look back on my life like a good day's work;
it was done and I am satisfied with it.

—Grandma Moses

## ACKNOWLEDGMENTS

Special thanks to my editor, Joseph Pittman, whose detailed commentary shaped the final draft; to my agent, Jane Dystel, who has diligently guided my career for a decade; to associate publisher Michaela Hamilton and publisher Elaine Koster, for their support and commitment; and to all the marketing and sales personnel, who do the heavy lifting that gets the books into the stores.

—BRIAN HARPER

# 1

In darkness, the urgent buzzing of an intercom.

Erin Reilly surfaced from sleep, blinking alert. Propped on one elbow, she studied her bedside clock's digital display, luminous in the night.

2:16 A.M.

From the living room came another prolonged buzz, insistent as a stabbing finger.

One of her patients? At this hour?

Like any psychologist, she occasionally received post-midnight phone calls and beeper messages from anxious or depressed people in need of help. But an unscheduled visit to her apartment was something new.

She'd never even released her home address, and she wasn't listed in the phone book. So how . . . ?

As the intercom blared again, she kicked aside two layers of blankets and swung out of bed.

The hardwood floor was cold. Her toes curled reflexively.

A pair of slippers lay somewhere nearby, but she didn't take the time to hunt them down.

Barefoot, she hurried into the living room. Carpet in there, thank God. Warmer.

Again and again the intercom blatted at her, bursts

of angry noise, distressing as a baby's wail. She groped for the controls. "Hello?"

The voice that crackled over the speaker was familiar, the most familiar voice in her world, but startling now: "This is Annie."

*"Annie?"* Not a patient with a problem. Her sister, and her best friend. "It's after two a.m. What are you doing here?"

"I'm in trouble. Please. Need to . . . talk."

In the oddly halting quality of her speech, Erin thought she heard suppressed sobs.

"Of course," she said instantly. "Come on up."

She was already holding down the Enter button to release the lock on the lobby's security door. After a count of eight she let go.

Agitated, she unlocked her own door and flipped the wall switch. A brass torchiere and two end-table lamps threw crisp ovals of light on the white walls.

She drew a breath of comfort from the pristine orderliness of her home and, by extension, her life. No muss and clutter, no untidy loose ends.

The white sofa, glass coffee table, and teakwood entertainment center were objects of minimalist design and spare, elegant simplicity. They mirrored her soul no less exactly than the careful notations in her appointment book, the crisp lines of her signature, her manicured hands, the styling of her hair: swept back from her forehead, trimmed short at the nape.

She returned to her bedroom and, without switching on a light, found her slippers and robe.

Her apartment was on the top floor of a four-story building, a high-rise by local standards. The bedroom windows framed miles of moonlit rooftops and brush-choked vacant lots. In the distance the lights of downtown Tucson flickered faintly, cupped by the dark humps of mountains and canopied with stars.

Beyond the rows of carports at the side of the building, traffic hummed past on Pantano Road, and a dry wind shivered through the fronds of palm trees.

Erin shivered, too, as she left the bedroom. Forty-five degrees tonight—chilly for southern Arizona—though the temperature would climb to eighty by mid-afternoon.

The desert in springtime was an environment of extremes—cold nights and hot days, long stretches of aridity punctuated by brief bursts of punishing rain, prickly pear cacti and ocotillo costumed overnight in garish floral blooms.

Living here in this season ought to teach a person to be prepared for abrupt changes, for the constant certainty of surprise.

But Erin had not been prepared to hear her sister's voice over the intercom.

Admittedly, Annie did tend to get emotional about things. But she'd never disturbed Erin so late at night, not even with a phone call.

Something must be really wrong.

*I'm in trouble,* she'd said.

Whatever trouble it was, it must have just come up. Annie had sounded fine on the phone a few hours ago, when Erin had called her to make a lunch date for tomorrow.

*Not tomorrow,* she corrected herself, remembering the time. *Later today.*

She paced the living room, running through a mental checklist of possible crises.

Pregnancy? Unlikely. Her sister knew enough to take precautions, and she hadn't dated seriously in a while.

Illness? She'd given no hint of any problems.

Death in the family? Impossible; they had no family left except each other now that Lydia was gone.

Annie ran her own business, so she couldn't have

been fired; and her shop was doing well, so she wasn't bankrupt.

Drugs, alcohol, something criminal? No chance.

Well, Erin would find out as soon as Annie arrived at her door.

It was taking her a long time, though. The elevator was slow, but not this slow.

What if Annie was afraid to face her for some reason? Afraid to disclose this secret of hers?

Unthinkable. The two of them had been close—more than close, inseparable—for their whole lives. Holding something back would be completely out of character for Annie, wouldn't be like her at all.

But coming to Erin's place at this hour, desperate and mysterious—that wasn't like her, either.

And she still wasn't here.

"Damn," Erin murmured to the stillness around her. "I'd better see if she's downstairs."

She found her purse, the shoulder strap looped over the back of a dining room chair, and took out her keys. Briefly she wondered if she ought to slip on some clothes—embarrassing to be caught roaming the building in her robe.

Oh, forget about it. At this hour no one else would be up.

She scanned the hallway—deserted—then shut and locked the apartment door behind her. Rows of closed doors passed by as she walked quickly to the elevator, her slippered feet padding on the short-nap carpet, the terry-cloth robe gently swishing against her pajamas. She punched the call button.

Hum of cable. Squeak of gears. The doors rattled open.

No Annie inside.

Erin got in, pressed Lobby. The elevator descended, groaning.

Third floor. Second. She jangled her keys nervously. Lobby.

The doors parted. She stepped into the building manager's fantasy of potted ferns and saltillo tile.

The exterior door was closed. A glass door: Annie was not visible outside it.

Near the elevator was the manager's glassed-in office, dark. No one in there, either.

But it made no sense. There was only one elevator, and Annie hadn't been on it.

Had she taken the stairs? Why would she?

More likely she'd lost her nerve, gone away. If so, she must be badly upset. Must be—

Behind her, a rustle of movement.

Erin turned. "Annie?"

Froze.

Not Annie.

Her heart kicked. Breath stopped.

The man was tall and heavyset, red-bearded, an uncombed shock of scarlet hair spilling out from under a baseball cap, the bill cocked low over his eyes. On the fur collar of his winter coat lay a bristle-toothed leaf, deposited there by the sword fern in the alcove where he had lain in wait.

His hands were gloved. In his right first, a gleam of metal.

She almost screamed, and then his left hand shot out, seized her shoulder, slammed her up against the elevator doors.

The impact winded her. She had no breath, no voice.

Thrust of his right arm, the metallic thing digging into her stomach below the breastbone, two sharp prongs pinching her skin through the robe and pajama top.

From a yard away she stared into his eyes, blue and cold.

His forefinger flexed.

Pain exploded in her. Her jaws clicked shut and her vision blurred as the pain went on and on, singing in every nerve ending, a single high note held unwavering at its peak.

Blindly she lashed out with her fists, trying to drive him back. The blows fell like flower petals on his chest.

Whistling static rose in her brain. She wanted to cry out, shout for help, but her mouth wouldn't work.

Her knees loosened. Her arms flapped spastically.

The static rose to a steady, hissing roar, and Erin was gone.

Everything was gone.

# 2

Annie Reilly, sleepless in the dark.

Her bed creaked with each restless change of position. She lay on her left side, her right, prostrate, supine, under the covers, on top of the covers, the pillows pressed to her cheek, flattened under her stomach, discarded on the floor.

Hell.

She couldn't sleep.

Beyond her windows, higher in the foothills, a choir of coyotes lifted their voices in piping, ululant wails. A ghostly serenade.

Normally, Annie liked hearing those distant cries, the leitmotif of a desert night. She appreciated the reminder of her distance from the city, her closeness to the weathered peaks of the Santa Catalina range, rising like stone spires and broken battlements against the expansive sky.

But tonight the songs disturbed her. She pictured a coyote band, lean and scruffy and ravenous, heads lifted as they sang of strange hungers and gnawing needs.

Blood songs. That was what they were. Songs that were the prelude to a kill.

A slow current of dread rippled through her like a fever chill.

She'd never envied Erin's apartment over on the east side of town. Never wanted to live amid the strip malls and the auto lots. Preferred her town house in the lap of the Catalinas, remote from traffic and distraction.

But in town, at least, the desert's wildness was held at bay.

Erin must be sleeping soundly now. No nocturnal predators sang to her.

Erin. Predators.

Her foreboding sharpened. It was less a thought than a taste, the bitter flavor of fear at the back of her mouth.

Her hand fumbled for the nightstand. She didn't know what she was reaching for until her fingers closed over the plastic shell of the telephone.

Call Erin? In the middle of the night?

Crazy.

She released the phone, climbed unsteadily out of bed. In the kitchen she poured a glass of milk.

There was a phone in the kitchen. Again she felt the irrational impulse to call.

*What are you going to say? That you had a premonition of danger, so you decided to wake her up at two-thirty?*

Too bizarre.

The milk was cold and foamy. It relaxed her. A little.

Funny how she couldn't shake her unease, though.

Of course, insomnia was nothing new to her. For most of her life she'd suffered occasional nights when she couldn't sleep at all. More frequent were the nights of interrupted sleep, when nightmares would startle her awake; she often spent an hour or more chasing away their ugly afterimages before she dared shut her eyes again.

The bad dreams were always the same, always a replay of the worst night of her life, the pivotal trauma of her childhood.

Tonight, however, was different. Tonight her anxieties were not focused on the past.

It was Erin she was afraid for, though she had no idea why.

Well, they would laugh about it at lunch. Maybe Erin would offer some Freudian interpretation of her anxiety attack. Something to do with sex. It all had to do with sex.

Annie smiled, but the smile faded as another coyote call split the night.

She became aware of eyes watching her. Green eyes like her own, but unlike hers these were luminous in the moonlight. They studied her with an owl's unblinking attentiveness.

"Can't sleep either, huh, Stink?"

The colorpoint shorthair wound sinuously around her ankles, his fur ermine-soft.

"Those mean old coyotes keeping you up? They're not after *you*."

Stink didn't answer.

"Maybe you want some milk. That it? Does Annie have milk and you don't? Unfair, you say? You have a keen sense of justice, Stink."

Stink did not really stink. His malodorous appellation commemorated a kittenish habit, fortunately now outgrown, of throwing up at the least excuse.

Annie fixed a saucer of milk for the cat. Stink sniffed it, sniffed again, almost declined the offering, reconsidered (perhaps out of politeness), and lapped the dish dry.

Finished, he nuzzled her leg in gratitude. She bent to caress his neck, his back. When he purred, he sounded like a very small person snoring.

Stroking him, Annie thought about the animals outside in the night, not safely sheltered like Stink, but huddling in dark burrows or flitting anxiously from one brushy hiding place to the next.

Bad to be alone and unprotected in the dark, with the coyotes keening.

Again she thought of Erin, though there was no reason for it.

Erin . . . and nocturnal hunters, stalking prey.

# 3

Sprawled on the lobby floor, she twitched and flopped.

He peeled off a glove, thumbed her carotid artery.

Heartbeat weak but regular.

She would live. For now.

The Ultron stun gun went into his coat pocket. A top-of-the-line model, complete with safety trigger and double shock plates. The battery would produce 150,000 volts when the trigger was squeezed.

On past occasions he had struck from behind. Curled a gloved hand over the victim's mouth, rammed the gun into the nerve center of the base of the spine, and discharged the current. For some technical reason, explained by the Ultron's manual but incomprehensible to him, the voltage could not pass into his own body even when he was in physical contact with his adversary.

This time he'd had no chance to grab her until after she'd spun around. Then he had delivered a five-second pulse directly to her solar plexus. The resulting disruption of her nervous system should keep her immobilized for at least ten minutes.

It was his first face-to-face encounter. He had found it interesting to watch her eyes roll up white in the sockets.

Despite everything, he had to admit that in the past he had enjoyed this phase of his activities. Using the stun gun, then exploring a woman's body with his hand while she lay unconscious and unresisting ... It had given him a shameful, furtive thrill of pleasure, had made him feel—for once—fully alive.

What had come later ...

No pleasure then, only a compulsion he couldn't override.

He pushed aside these thoughts. Must get moving. Someone might enter the lobby at any moment and find him here.

Kneeling by her, he scanned the tiled floor. A key ring lay near her jerking hand. Car keys were included in the set. Good.

The keys disappeared into another pocket. Then he lifted her in his arms. She was reasonably tall, perhaps five-eight, but slender, no more than 125 pounds. Slung over his shoulder, she was easy to carry, and the reflexive spasms trembling through her muscles created the pleasing illusion of a futile, panicky struggle against his superior strength.

He caught the scent of her hair as he lugged her to the side door. Faint fragrance. Not perfume. Bath salts.

The door opened on the parking lot that served the complex. Rows of automobiles, pickup trucks, and motorcycles were arrayed under metal carports. Fluorescent bars cast a pale, glareless glow on steel and fiberglass.

In the doorway he paused, surveying the area.

The moon, a waning crescent, hung low over the horizon, hooked in a mountain's clawlike peak. It washed the asphalt in milky light. Anyone watching from a window or balcony would see him once he exited.

Fortunately, the blue Taurus was parked in one of the more desirable assigned spaces, only a short distance from the door.

He took a breath and carried her there, staying clear

of floodlights. Behind him, the apartment building loomed dark against an icy spray of stars. On Pantano Road, safely screened from the parking lot by colonnades of oleanders in white bloom, cars shot by like comets, and a motorcycle whined past, mosquito-quick.

If a car should turn into the lot . . . if he should be pinned in the headlights . . .

He walked faster. His breath became hoarse and ragged, loud over the clicking of unseen insects.

Only once he was under the carport roof, concealed from any likely observer, did he again feel safe.

Fumbling the key ring out of his pocket, he unlocked the trunk and popped the lid. Gently he deposited her inside, placing her on her back.

From a utility pouch clipped to his belt, he removed cut lengths of rope. Bound her ankles first, then her wrists. To further restrict her movements, he lashed her wrists to her right thigh.

Good. Very good.

A roll of heavy electrician's tape was also among the contents of the pouch. He tore off a six-inch strip and prepared to seal her mouth. Hesitated, studying her face. His first opportunity to look at her, really look at her, up close, in the flesh.

Dangerous to indulge himself like this, under these circumstances. Still, he could not turn away. She held him fascinated.

Of the women he had taken, she was by far the most beautiful. By far.

He admired her as a connoisseur of art would admire a fine painting, attentive to every detail. It was an undiluted pleasure to study her lovely face as minutely as he liked, with no risk that she would return his gaze or challenge his absolute control.

She was thirty years old, balanced at that delicate equilibrium point between youthfulness and full maturity. Her skin was smooth, powdered with faint freckles; a light suntan endowed her with a pink, scrubbed look, wholesome somehow. Offsetting these girlish features were her strong cheekbones and blunt jaw, which gave her face a squarish shape, and her wide, serious mouth, not a child's mouth at all.

Her auburn hair, combed away from her forehead, shone even in the carport's wan fluorescence. A stray lock lay along her temple like a spiral of sewing thread, reddish-gold.

Peeling back her eyelids, he stared into gray eyes, smoky and mysterious.

He parted the flaps of her robe. Removed one of his gloves so he could stroke her white pajama top, feel its softness. Satin.

The clean lines of her neck, the bare skin stretched taut over her thin collarbones, the scatter of reddish freckles on the margin of her cleavage, cupped in the buttoned neckband . . .

He reached for the top button, wanting to see her breasts—

No.

He jerked his hand away as if slapped.

His mouth twisted. A noise that was both grunt and gasp hiccuped out of him. Its echo hopped like a frog among the metal stanchions of the carports.

Dirty. Unclean. Corrupt.

Quickly he taped her mouth, then clawed a blindfold out of his pants pocket and snugged it over her eyes, knotting it in the back of her head.

Helpless now. Deprived of mobility, speech, sight. She was a free agent no longer. She was his.

Erin Reilly was his.

The Ford's trunk thumped shut like a coffin lid.

# 4

Her keys gave him access to her apartment. Strange to be here, in another person's living space, and in a home so different from his.

No dull glaze of dust on the tables and fixtures. No soiled spots in the carpet, long ignored and now permanently set. No brittle carapaces of dead insects lining the baseboards, shiny in the lamplight.

His own apartment was a ground-floor unit, cramped and airless, the windows staring blankly at the stucco wall of the building next door. Erin Reilly's place conveyed a sense of openness and freedom, with its views of the city and mountains, its promise of light and air, its immaculate floors and whitewashed walls, its silent testimony to the serenity of a well-ordered life.

He almost hated Erin for having all of this around her—and then he remembered that she would have it no longer.

In the bedroom closet he found a set of three valises, small, medium, and large. He chose the medium-size suitcase. Opened it, then began pulling random clothes off hangers and stuffing them inside.

No. Random was wrong. He forced himself to concentrate on selecting items that went together as outfits. It must look as if she had done the packing.

What else? Footwear. He tossed in a pair of fringed western boots.

Undergarments. They were neatly folded in a bureau drawer.

Toilet articles. In the bathroom he collected them. Toothbrush. Toothpaste. Shampoo. Deodorant. Comb. Hairbrush. Other things, including some feminine products he'd never seen before and couldn't identify.

Stationery. His gloved hands rifled the drawers of a mahogany desk in the den. He found a bundle of pale olive envelopes and matching sheets of writing paper that bore her letterhead.

The suitcase was bulging when he zipped it shut.

As he toted it to the front door, worry nagged him. He was certain he was forgetting something.

Of course.

Slung over a chair in the dining room was her purse. He rummaged through it, taking inventory of its contents:

Wallet, thick with credit cards and currency.

Compact. Lipstick. Eyeliner.

Appointment book.

Spiral-bound memo pad and pen.

Bottle of pills, nearly empty—birth-control, he assumed without reading the label.

Miscellaneous other items, none of significance.

He pocketed the cash, then shrugged the purse's strap over his shoulder.

Leaving her apartment, he turned off the lights. It was something she would do.

He avoided the elevator, afraid of encountering one of the tenants, took the stairs instead. The suitcase felt heavier at each landing, heavier still as he lugged it outside.

The parking lot remained empty of people. He put

the suitcase in the Ford's backseat, then opened the trunk.

Erin was beginning to stir as the effects of the stun gun wore off. It was preferable to keep her unconscious as long as possible.

He took out the Ultron, pressed the switch. Lightning flickered between the two electrodes in a blue crackling arc, the noise too faint to be heard from the building.

He shoved the gun into her chest, held it there for a full five seconds.

She was twitching again as he withdrew the gun. Briefly he worried that with her mouth taped, she might choke on saliva.

Oh, nonsense. She would be fine.

He climbed behind the wheel, adjusted the driver's seat to fit his longer frame, then started the car.

Out of the parking lot. Two blocks east on Broadway. Then onto a residential side street, an older subdivision of tract homes, ranch-style brick houses landscaped in cactus and yuccas.

The moon had set. Stars burned pinholes in the sky. A false dawn, the russet glow of the city's ambient light, faintly brightened the horizon.

He slowed the Taurus and parked at the curb behind a gray Chevy van.

His van.

It was a 1988 Chevrolet Astro, a cargo model with bucket seats up front and no seating accommodations in back. He'd bought the vehicle used; the previous owner had logged nearly 100,000 miles on the odometer while putting dents in the fenders and side. The price had been reasonable.

The Astro had come equipped with an optional heavy-duty towing package that permitted it to haul up to six thousand pounds. That feature, which had made it possible for him to hitch a U-Haul trailer to the van not long ago, would now come in handy again.

Quickly he hooked the van's towing bar to the Ford's front end, stringing safety chains on either side. He keyed the Ford's ignition to the "accessory" position, shifted the transmission into neutral, checked to confirm that the parking brake was released.

Somebody's dog began to bark. The racket might draw attention to the street. Better hurry.

The Astro had both a sliding side panel and dual rear doors. He opened the latter and looked in on the windowless, uncarpeted cargo compartment, empty except for a small huddle of items draped by a tarpaulin. Under the tarp were two red canisters, a coil of rope, a mallet, and a pair of metal stakes.

The stakes were meant for putting up a badminton net, but he had found another use for them.

He opened the Ford's trunk and transferred Erin to the rear of the van. Checked again to confirm that the rope and blindfold were knotted tight.

"You're not going anywhere," he muttered as he swung the doors shut, "Dr. Reilly."

He slipped into the driver's seat of the Astro, started the engine. A V-6, 150 horsepower. Noisy as hell.

The van rumbled like an unmuffled Harley as he steered it away into the night.

He drove for two and a half miles, heading east on Broadway, past the lighted islands of shopping plazas and the dark, rustling stretches of undeveloped land.

At Houghton Road he turned south. He was near the outer edges of town now. Rare horse ranches and isolated patches of tract housing were all he saw around him.

By the time he passed Escalante Road, more than two miles south of Broadway, even these proofs of habitation had largely vanished. His surroundings were a great starlit expanse of mesquite trees and cactus, rippling like some strange ocean, extending in every direction to the mountains outlined against the blue-black sky.

He was outside city limits now. A psychological barrier had been crossed, and irrationally he felt safer. Driving with one hand, he removed the baseball cap, red wig, and false beard.

Without the disguise he was a balding, moon-faced man of forty-six, his pale cheeks as smooth as a child's.

In profile his chin was weak, and his nose, badly broken in a long-ago fight, was flat and shapeless. Tufting his scalp were scraps of hair, straw-colored once, now prematurely gray.

The lights of the dashboard played on his face, gifting him with the illusion of expressiveness and life; but the light did not touch his eyes. They lay in shadowed hollows under thin, feminine brows.

The job, he thought, had gone flawlessly so far. Better than expected. Surpassing all hopes.

He nodded, satisfied, but he did not smile.

Harold Gund never smiled.

# 5

Erin regained consciousness and found herself in the dark, the absolute dark of a nightmare, and she couldn't move, *she couldn't move.*

*Seizure,* she thought in blank confusion. *Had a seizure, and now I'm paralyzed somehow.*

But that couldn't be it. She hadn't had an epileptic episode since she was fifteen. And besides, she was forgetting something, something vitally important, something that had happened to her just a short time ago.

The lobby.

Man in a baseball cap.

Electric pain shocking her body.

Kidnapped. Not a seizure. She'd been kidnapped.

A scream of blind terror welled in her throat but found no release. Her mouth wouldn't open. Her lips were sealed.

She twisted wildly, found her legs lashed together at the ankles, her wrists tied.

And her eyes—heavy cloth was stretched tightly over them, imprisoning her in darkness.

Bound. Muzzled. Blindfolded.

Helpless.

The pounding drumbeat of her heart, the choked

grunts behind her closed lips, the snorts of breath flaring her nostrils—these were the only sounds in her world, her only reality.

He could do anything he liked with her, anything at all, and she was powerless to defend herself. At this moment he might be standing over her with a knife or a gun, might be preparing to slice her throat or put a bullet in her, or something worse, inflict some variety of slow torture, and there was nothing she could do about it, no way out, no chance for her, no hope—

*Stop it.*

The voice in her mind, firm and authoritative, was her own.

*Stop it, Erin, come on now, stop it and think.*

Think. Yes. She had to think, because thinking was the only recourse left open to her. Had to think and understand.

With trembling effort she forced down panic, struggling for calm, directing the splintered chaos of her thoughts into straight-line patterns.

First question: Where was she?

She lay still, listening hard. Over the violent rhythm of her heart she heard the throb of an engine.

A vehicle. Was she in the trunk of a car?

No, she sensed somehow that the space around her was bigger than that. And the cold metal surface beneath her, vibrating with the engine, felt like the uncarpeted floor of the cargo compartment in a truck or van.

Moving pretty fast, she'd guess. Maybe forty or forty-five miles an hour. No stops for traffic signals. On a highway, but not an interstate. The road was too rough. One of the older highways that led out of town.

Out of town . . .

Into the desert? There could be reasons for taking her to an isolated spot, far from buildings and people.

Fear rose in her again, squeezing her heart in its cold grip. She thought she might pass out.

No. She had to remain conscious. It was her only chance.

There was a possibility he would unseal her lips at some point, if only to hear her scream or plead. Should he do that, she would reason with him, try to establish contact. Dealing with irrationality was her daily business. There ought to be some way for her to get through.

Then she remembered his eyes, so blue, so cold.

Well, she could try, anyway. If he let her talk at all.

And if for some reason he untied her? What then?

She would have to fight.

The idea was not entirely desperate. Three years ago she'd taken a class in tae kwon do, the Korean form of karate, as part of a training program designed to help therapists defend themselves against violent patients.

She was by no means a martial-arts expert—she'd earned only a yellow belt, qualifying her as barely more than a beginner—but if she could deliver a snap kick to her abductor's kneecap or a palm-heel strike to his throat, she might be able to drop him to the ground long enough to flee.

In practice sessions, at least, she'd done well enough. Annie, a suitably impressed spectator, had dubbed her Erin-san, the Irish Ninja. But then, what could you expect from a woman who'd named her cat Stink?

Annie . . .

The voice over the intercom. Annie's voice.

Oh, God, did he have her, too?

Erin wished she hadn't been gagged. Wished she could call out Annie's name, learn if her sister was somewhere nearby. Perhaps trussed and silenced as she herself was, sharing the nightmare.

Would he have wanted them both? Why? They had no enemies. It didn't make sense.

Who was he, anyway? She'd seen his face only briefly; it had seemed utterly unfamiliar. That thick red beard and shock of carrot-top hair . . .

But perhaps the beard was a disguise. If so, he could be nearly anybody. One of her patients, even.

Any therapist could become a target. That was why she'd been careful to keep an unlisted address, and why she'd chosen to live in a security building.

Three of her current patients had shown occasional violent tendencies. Nothing like this, though. And none of the three had those chilly blue eyes.

Well, maybe he was someone she'd treated years ago, during her internship at a psychology clinic downtown. Or one of the numberless transients she'd met while doing pro bono work at the local shelters—sad, lost men whose faces she never would remember, because they were all alike.

Her speculations led nowhere. His identity was unguessable, and without knowing who he was, she couldn't know his intention in abducting her. But on that point she had to assume the worst.

Had to assume he meant to kill her.

Twisting her wrists, she tried to loosen the cord that secured them. The bristly scrape of the binding against her skin told her that he had tied her hands with rope. Thick, stiff rope lashed around her wrists in multiple coils, python-snug.

She had seen a calf trussed once at a rodeo, its hooves bound with a cowboy's lasso. Though she had pitied the bleating animal, she had never imagined one day sharing its fate.

Even its ultimate fate? To be led to slaughter, to sag under a butcher's saw?

The sticky stuff sealing her lips was tape. If she

could lift her hands to her face, she could untape her mouth, then chew at the rope on her wrists until possibly the knot came undone.

But her arms wouldn't move. They were pinned to her right thigh by another loop of rope, knotted so tightly it threatened to cut off the circulation in her leg. She was unable to work it loose.

Bending at the waist, she tried to bring her head closer to her hands, close enough that she could at least raise the blindfold.

No use. She would have to be a contortionist to do it.

Never had she been so vulnerable, so completely powerless. Even in her parents' house on that August night twenty-three years ago, she'd been able to take action, fight for survival.

The noise in her throat was a choked moan.

Erin prayed that her sister wasn't with her. Prayed that the voice over the intercom had been only a trick, and Annie was safe at home.

She wanted one of them, at least, to survive this night.

# 6

The van's high beams splashed white light across a blur of macadam and roadside mesquite shrubs as Harold Gund sped south on Houghton Road.

He wondered if Erin was alert yet. The others had recovered quickly from the incapacitating shock. All three had been fully conscious when he'd carried them into the wilderness and hammered the stakes into the ground.

The memory of those women, of what he had done to them in the woods, made him feel . . .

But he didn't know how he felt.

His hands gripped the steering wheel, the knuckles squeezed bloodless. From this clue he surmised that what he felt was fury.

Fury at himself? Or at the women, for having been so damnably easy to abduct? Or at a world that could make possible a thing like him? And what kind of thing was that?

He had no answers to these questions. Introspection was unknown to him. When he looked inside himself, he saw only darkness, as deep and still as the desert gloom.

His turnoff was coming up shortly. He cut his speed a bit and leaned forward, eyes narrowed. The unmarked side road would be easy to miss, especially in this dark landscape devoid of variation, this infinite sweep of sameness.

He wondered how many little lives were fated to be snuffed out tonight in the expanse of brush and weeds around him. How many cactus wrens would be plucked from their nests, how many rabbits would perish in their burrows? Even now, among the gnarled trees and glistening cacti, warm blood was being spilled, moist flesh tasted.

He was not so different from the rest of creation. Perhaps it was the safely civilized members of the human species who were unnatural, not he.

Or perhaps not.

He shook his head, defeated, as always, by the enigma of himself.

Sometimes he listened to the TV specials that promised to explain men like him, hoping for insight. So far he had been disappointed.

The experts consulted by the police and the media were fools. Possibly they knew something about others of his kind, but of him they understood nothing.

He recalled an interview with one such specimen, described as a psychological profiler. The man wore a gray suit and a red telegenic tie. He sat behind his office desk, haloed in diplomas, buttressed by shelves of books. His opinions were stated with the blunt obviousness of a factual report.

*The typical serial killer, or lust murderer as he is more accurately identified,* the man explained in a bland, professorial tone, *views murder as a substitute for sex. He attains sexual release by spilling his victim's blood or by abusing the body afterward. For him, killing is a form of intimacy, the only intimacy he knows.*

The interviewer asked if such a man might experience twisted feelings of love for his victim. *Oh, yes,* the expert replied. *Love or at least erotic desire. Often the woman is a surrogate for someone who rejected him or hurt him—a particular woman from his past.*

He killed strangers to avenge a past wrong? *That's right. And to give a purpose to his existence. The only organizing principle of his life, the only order and structure imposed on it, is his cyclic pattern of violence. He lives solely to kill.*

Would he ever stop? *Never. He doesn't want to. He feels alive while killing, feels powerful and whole. This is not a tormented person. This is a man who's quite comfortable with what he does . . . and what he is.*

Gund closed his eyes briefly.

Jackass.

Less than a mile north of Interstate 10, he turned onto a narrow side road. The yellow sign warned NO OUTLET.

The road was a mere strip of rutted dirt, a foot wider than the van on either side. Palo verde trees, blooming yellow, lined the road, casting windblown blossoms on Gund's windshield. Abruptly the trees on the left side vanished, replaced by a barbed-wire fence, rows of knotty strings gleaming white in the starlight.

Beyond the fence, ramshackle buildings slouched in crooked silhouette against the mountainous horizon. No lights burned in the windows.

Centered in Gund's high beams was a gate, hinged on posts that straddled the road. A padlocked chain kept it shut—an unnecessary precaution, since nobody ever came here.

Nobody but him.

# 7

The vehicle slowed.

Erin perceived the gradual abatement of engine noise, felt the transmission shudder through a change of gears. The ride, which had been rough for several minutes, became rougher still.

Dirt road? Felt like one.

The brakes sighed.

Dead stop. Motor idling.

Creak of a door swinging open. Pause. Clunk: the door slammed shut.

Moving again, but only at a crawl. The chassis lurched and jounced, shock absorbers squeaking like mattress springs. Had he driven off the road altogether?

Whatever was happening, one thing was clear: He had reached his destination.

Her heart ran like a rabbit in her chest. She could be dead soon. Her private universe, extinguished.

Her parents, both strict Irish Catholics, had given her the beginnings of a religious upbringing, which Lydia Connor had carried on; but college had bled a lot of that out of her. She wasn't sure if she could believe in a life beyond this one. It was a problem she hadn't expected to face with any urgency for years. For decades.

Never got married. Never had a kid. Never took that

trip to Ireland to look for the original Reillys and Morgans. Never, never, never; and now, maybe, she never would.

*Stop that. Stay focused.*

Again the vehicle was slowing. It rumbled to a stop. For the second time a door groaned open.

Footsteps on dirt or gravel. Closer. Closer.

He was coming for her.

Fear soared toward blind panic; she fought to ground her emotions before they carried her away.

To struggle would be pointless as long as her hands were bound. For the moment her best hope was to feign unconsciousness. If he thought she was still out cold, he might get careless, give her an opportunity to strike.

She made herself go limp, drawing long, rhythmic breaths.

Turn of a key, rattle of a sliding door. Double thump as he climbed up into the rear of the vehicle where she lay.

He planted his feet directly before her. She smelled shoe leather.

"Still asleep?" he murmured, sounding puzzled.

She inhaled, exhaled, the slow cadence of her breath playing in counterpoint to the jackhammer pounding of her heart.

Creak of a knee as he crouched down. When he spoke again, his voice was very close.

"Well, not for much longer."

What did that mean? Nothing, forget it, concentrate on breathing in, out, in, out, no break in the pattern, nothing to give herself away.

Hands.

Large hands, rough-textured. Stroking her hair, her face.

Was he going to rape her? Mustn't think about that, mustn't think about anything.

His touch was clumsy yet tender, almost loving, but the word that issued from his mouth was uttered like an obscenity: *"Filth."*

Abruptly she was lifted. Surprise nearly jostled a gasp out of her. She felt her body tensing reflexively. With an effort of will she relaxed.

He draped her over his right shoulder, supporting her with one hand, and rose to his feet. She heard no grunt of strain. A big man, powerful. She remembered that he had looked tall and heavyset in the lobby.

How could she ever hope to fight him even if she got free? He must outweigh her by a hundred pounds.

She replayed the few words he'd spoken, tried to remember if she'd heard his voice anywhere before. It was distinctive enough—gravelly and breathy at the same time, deep but not resonant.

Not one of her current patients; she was sure of that. Nobody she'd ever treated, as best she could recall.

A stranger, almost certainly. Yet he seemed to have strong personal feelings toward her, both positive and negative, an unsettling blend of desire and hostility.

Scary. Scarier by the minute.

He was climbing down out of the vehicle now. A brief pause as he bent and hefted something, apparently in his left hand. It swung in time with the rhythm of his stride, rubbing against his pants leg; she heard the whisper of friction.

He carried her through yards of musty enclosed space, then out into the open. Night breeze on her face, chillier than it would be in town. The wind blew unobstructed here, in the desert's open spaces.

His shoes crackled on dirt and dry brush, then on what sounded like gravel.

He stopped. Metallic tinkle. Keys.

He was unlocking a door. The hinges mewled as he pushed it open.

Inside.

Smell of dust and neglect. Drumbeat of his footfalls on a hardwood floor.

She heard him panting now. So he was human, at least. He was showing fatigue. Perhaps if he slipped up, she'd have some kind of chance against him.

The sound of his footsteps altered. Not the hollow crack of contact with wood, but a more solid thud, suggestive of concrete. It took her a moment to realize that he was going down a flight of stairs.

Cellar? Must be.

The implications of a cellar weren't good. A hidden place, a place for buried secrets and suppressed desires. Bodies had a way of turning up in cellars.

She tried hard not pursue those thoughts.

At the bottom now. His breath puffed in short bursts. Lugging her all this distance had worn him out. If she sensed any opportunity, she would take it.

Keys again. Another door, easing open.

This new space felt smaller. The air was stale, spiced with unclean smells.

Soft thump as he set down whatever item he'd been carrying in his left hand. Then he shrugged her off his shoulder, deposited her carefully in a chair. It creaked and wobbled. Wooden chair, not new.

The rope around her ankles came loose.

He was releasing her. She had only to continue her rag-doll charade a minute longer. Then with her hands free—attack.

He fumbled at the rope securing her wrists to her thigh. If he had a knife, he would simply slice through the knot. No knife, then. And the high-voltage weapon he'd used—one of those stun guns, obviously, the kind she'd seen in TV news clips—was probably tucked away in his pocket, not instantly accessible.

She would not wait for him to raise the blindfold. She could do that herself, as soon as he had freed her hands.

As part of her tae kwon do training, she'd learned to do push-ups on her fists, a habit she had maintained even after discontinuing the class. Her wrists were strong, her knuckles toughened.

In a karate-style punch, executed with the first two knuckles projecting from the fist, she could damage her abductor's larynx or dislocate his jaw. After that, a knee to the groin or an elbow to the ribs, and he would be immobilized.

Except in harmless classroom sparring, she'd never used violence against another person. But she was certain she could do it. In defense of her life, she could do whatever was necessary.

Hesitation, squeamishness—these were weaknesses she couldn't afford. Once she sprang, she would be in a fight for survival, as savage and unforgiving as any struggle of animals in the wild.

She was ready. Ready to kill or die.

Her hands were fully untied now, no longer lashed together or pinned to her leg. But he had not let them go.

He held them in her lap, stroking her fingers, palms, wrists. . . .

His grip tightened. His thumbs squeezed her wrists hard.

"So," he hissed.

She stayed limp, breathing deeply, deeply, her eyes open wide behind the blindfold.

"It's no good, Dr. Reilly. I know you're awake."

No, he couldn't know that. It was a bluff. Had to be.

"You gave a good performance. Extremely convincing. But I'm afraid your pulse rate has given you away."

His thumbs dug deeper into the veins of her wrists.

"It's at least one-twenty. Much too fast for a person who's genuinely unconscious."

Still she gave no response, tried to brazen it out.

"You've been playing possum for a reason, I imagine. You were planning to try something. Well, let's get one thing straight between us right from the start."

Abruptly he clamped her wrists together, clutching them in one hand, while with the other he jerked the tape free of her mouth.

Pain seared her lips as the adhesive pulled away. Involuntarily she let out a sharp cry.

"You don't toy with me, Doc. Not ever. No tricks, no scams. Understood?"

Though it was pointless to try fooling him now, she couldn't bring herself to answer. Her throat seemed paralyzed.

He shook her by the shoulder. The rickety chair legs squeaked.

*"Understood?"*

Had to respond or he might turn more violent. No predicting what he would do.

Weakly she nodded. "I understand."

The hoarse rasp of her own voice startled her.

"Good," he breathed, still holding her wrists. "I'm gratified to see that you take me seriously. But I'm not entirely certain you've learned your lesson." Rustle of clothing. "Maybe this will make you a better student."

Inches from her face, a faint electric crackle.

"No," she croaked. "Please don't. Not again."

She hated to beg, because she knew begging—helpless submission—was what he wanted. But she couldn't face the prospect of more pain, and worse: another blackout, when she would be utterly defenseless and he could do whatever he liked.

"Don't," she said once more, her body rigid in expectation of a new jolt of agony.

The stun gun sizzled angrily for a moment longer, then fell silent without touching her.

"I'll cut you a break this time," he said.

An involuntary shudder of relief trembled through her.

"But," he added coldly, "any more nonsense, and you'll learn what pain really is." He released her wrists. "Now sit still. Don't move a muscle till I tell you to."

Footsteps, receding. The door clicked shut.

"All right, Doc." His voice, muffled, came from outside the room. "Remove the blindfold. And take a look at your new home."

# 8

The blindfold was snugged tight over her face, and she had to undo the knot before she could remove it. The task was made more difficult by the nervous trembling of her hands.

Finally the cloth slipped free. She blinked against the sudden glare.

An unshaded lightbulb hung from the ceiling by a chain, providing the room's only illumination. Not more than a hundred watts, but dazzling after her long interval of darkness.

She let her vision adjust to the light as she rose from the chair and slowly surveyed her surroundings.

Not a torture chamber, not a crypt. Merely a dusty cellar room, ten feet square, with walls of unpainted brick, lightly mildewed, and a floor and ceiling of concrete.

A sill cock sprouted from one wall at knee level. When she turned the handle, water drooled out in a thin, warm stream, puddling on the floor.

The only furnishings were the chair he'd put her in, a similar chair facing it, and a five-foot foam pad partly covered by a cotton blanket.

Her bed, apparently. For how many nights? Better not think about it.

The room had no ornament or decoration of any kind. No windows, and only one door, of wood. Not a hollow door, she was certain; it had to be solid mahogany. It looked disturbingly impregnable, though a small peephole fitted with a fish-eye lens had been cut in it at a height of six feet.

He must be staring through that lens right now, studying her as she explored her surroundings. She felt like a gerbil in a cage.

Near her chair was a medium-size suitcase. One of her own. Resting on top of it, her purse. Those items must be what he'd been carrying in his left hand.

Apparently he had raided her apartment after zapping her. She wondered why.

The cash was gone from her wallet, but otherwise the contents of her purse were untouched. She spent a long moment looking at the bottle of pills.

Unzipping the suitcase, she found some of her clothes and toiletries haphazardly stuffed inside. She made a show of sorting out the items while considering what she knew or guessed about her abductor.

It was clear that he had carefully planned both her kidnapping and her confinement. Detailed preparation was inconsistent with schizophrenia or other acute psychosis. The person whose thoughts were a tissue of illogical associative leaps was largely incapable of orderly, methodical reasoning.

From their brief dialogue she gathered that he was relatively calm, not manic, not desperate, in control of the situation and of himself. That was good. He was less likely to do something impulsive if he was somewhat relaxed.

His speaking voice, in fact, was reassuringly normal in most respects. She had detected no hint of the pure sociopath's affectless monotone or the would-be suicide's listlessness and despair.

She didn't want him to be suicidal. The line between suicide and murder was easily crossed.

He seemed intelligent, articulate, fairly knowledgeable; not only had he noticed that her pulse was fast, he'd estimated the rate. And the kidnapping had been skillfully executed, by no means the work of an incompetent.

She wondered just how smart he was. Smart enough to outthink her? To counter any strategy she could devise?

*Hope not,* she thought grimly. *If so, I'm in major trouble.*

As if she wasn't, anyway.

She finished examining the things he'd brought from her home. The oddest items were a bundle of envelopes and a sheaf of writing paper, both from her desk drawer. She had no idea what he would want with those.

The only other object in the room was a large, lidless cardboard box. She inventoried its contents also.

Canned goods, bananas and apples, dried fruit, loaf of bread, jar of peanut butter.

Picnic plates, paper cups, plastic utensils. Paper napkins and towels. Manual can opener. Pail, sponge, washcloth.

Roll of toilet paper, sealed in plastic shrink-wrap. Empty milk jugs and coffee cans—for bathroom purposes, she realized.

Two last things: a ballpoint pen and a manila folder stuffed with what appeared to be yellowed newspaper clippings.

Frowning, she reached for the folder.

"Not yet, Doc."

His voice again, from the other side of the door. She caught her breath, startled.

"You can look at that stuff later," he added. "You'll

have plenty of opportunity. You'll be spending a good deal of time in this room. All your time from now on, in fact."

She turned toward the lens in the door. It glinted at her like a single, unblinking eye.

"How long can I expect my stay to last?" she asked, trying to keep the question safely neutral.

"As long as required."

"I'm not sure I understand." Keep it light, not challenging, not defiant.

"Everything will be explained shortly. First, you've got a job to do. You see the pen I've provided, the writing paper and envelopes in your suitcase?"

"Yes."

"You're going to write a letter—a very brief letter—to your sister."

Annie. She must be okay, then. He wouldn't want a message sent to her if she'd been kidnapped, too.

"All right," Erin said casually. "What should the letter say?"

In the momentary silence that preceded his reply, she considered the most probable scenarios.

Ransom demand. That would almost be a relief, an indication of a comprehensible motive.

General complaint against the psychological profession. Perhaps he'd been hospitalized against his will sometime earlier in his life and had developed a hatred of all mental-health practitioners.

Personal complaint against her. It was possible she'd treated him briefly at some early point in her internship, perhaps for only one or two sessions, and he held some kind of grudge.

The last would be the most dangerous development, and perhaps the most likely. It was not uncommon for a disgruntled patient to set out to destroy his therapist's reputation and career. Many frivolous malpractice suits were prompted by nothing more than personal animus.

Of course, shocking your shrink into unconsciousness and carting her off to a secret hideaway showed considerably more determination than filing a lawsuit.

She waited.

"The letter," he said finally, "will state your decision to go away for a while, on your own. You need some time to yourself. Your sister shouldn't worry—everything is fine—but she may not hear from you for an indefinite period. Got it?"

Bad. Very bad.

He didn't want money for her, and he wasn't interested in making a statement, general or personal.

He simply wanted her to disappear. Indefinitely.

"Got it?" he said again.

She managed a weak smile. "No problem."

"A word of warning, Doc. I'll peruse that letter extremely carefully. Any deviation from the content I outlined—any clues, any hints—will not pass unnoticed. Or unpunished."

*Peruse,* he'd said. Hell, his vocabulary was better than her own.

"I won't drop any hints." She hoped her shrug looked sincere. "I know when it pays to be cooperative, and this is one of those times. Anyway, it's fairly obvious you've been one step ahead of me all along."

"You're working so hard to establish a rapport with me, lull me into a false sense of complacency. See how well you've succeeded?"

*Oh, sure,* she thought bleakly. *I've got you right where I want you.*

Seated in the chair, a sheaf of embossed paper balanced on her knee, she composed the letter in a few sparse lines. There was no suggestion of her own personality in the message. A robot could have written it.

Annie would never believe any of this garbage, of course. Each of them knew the other far too well to fall for such an obvious trick.

Possibly, however, the letter was intended not to deceive Annie, but to defuse any police investigation that might be under way. Tucson P.D. could hardly pursue a missing-person case when the person in question had expressly stated that she'd left town voluntarily.

And if no one was looking for her, she would never be found.

"Make out the envelope, too," he ordered as she put down the pen.

Writing the address, she had an idea. A sizable risk for a minimal gain, but she would dare it.

Annie lived at 509 Calle Saguaro. Erin wrote 505, carefully rounding the fives.

SOS.

Would Annie notice? Would it matter even if she did? Impossible to say.

"Now place the letter and envelope on the other chair, and put on the blindfold again."

Knotting the cloth in place, blacking out her world, she tried another conversational ploy. "I'm glad you want me blindfolded. That way your identity will be safe."

"It will be safe, anyway—if I kill you."

A frighteningly logical answer, which raised an all-too-obvious question.

*Well, ask it, then. Be direct.* "Is that what's going to happen?"

"Not necessarily. You're right about the blindfold, Dr. Reilly. As long as you haven't seen my face, you've got a chance of surviving our relationship."

*Our relationship.* She supposed she should be glad

he'd phrased it that way, implying a connection between them.

This time she didn't hear the door open, but somehow she knew the precise moment when he stepped
into the room. His presence chilled her like a cold draft
from an unseen window.

The other chair protested as he sat down. He must be
facing her across a distance of six feet. She waited
through a long silence, thinking hard.

This would be their first extended encounter—very
likely a period of maximum danger. She was something new in his world, destabilizing, threatening. It
was possible he'd never been alone in a room with a
woman before. He was almost certainly under more
stress than his outwardly cool manner would suggest.

How to handle it?

Even though he'd seen through her efforts to form a
bond between them, she had to keep trying. It was im-
perative that he not be allowed to objectify her, to re-
duce her to the status of a mere symbol. She had to be
a person in his eyes, preferably a person who mattered
to him.

Best to be agreeable, cooperative—but not overly
friendly, or he would sniff out the lie.

He was perceptive, not easily deceived. He would
know she had to be angry and scared. There was no
need to conceal those feelings completely, even assuming she could. But she needed to tone them down,
feign a comfort level she hadn't achieved, and perhaps
soothe his own anxieties also.

"Very good," he said finally. She heard the crinkle of
folding paper. "The letter, I mean. You were smart not
to try anything clever. I would have used the Ultron on
you for sure. Or done something worse."

Proper response: subdued or combative? She chose a
middle course, hoping to distract him while he slipped

the letter in the envelope. She didn't want him to notice her pitiful SOS.

"You really don't have to keep emphasizing your control over me," she said mildly. "It isn't necessary."

"Isn't it? I take it, then, that my control is understood."

Acknowledge his power—a subtle compliment to him. "You've got the stun gun."

"I've got more than that." The chair scraped the floor. Two quick footsteps. She felt him near her. "Hold out your hand."

Hesitantly she obeyed. Touched something smooth and cylindrical. The barrel of a handgun.

"It's a nine-millimeter." He pulled the weapon away. "Fully loaded. I can kill you at any time, Doc. I can put a bullet in your heart"—click of a safety's release—"or in your brain."

"I told you, it's not necessary—"

She tasted metal. The muzzle of the gun, thrust between her teeth, blocking speech.

"Bang," he whispered.

Breath stopped, she sat rigidly, hands gripping the edges of the chair.

If he pulled the trigger, she would never even know it. That thought scared her worst of all.

"I don't like you lecturing me on what is or is not necessary." Fury clawed at the polished smoothness of his voice, shredding it at the edges. "And I don't need to hear any of that crap about 'control.' I'm simply trying to establish guidelines for our relationship. Rules for you to live by. Literally."

The gun withdrew. The pounding violence in her ears was the racket of her own heart.

"From now on, I—and I alone—will determine what's necessary and appropriate. That's acceptable to you, isn't it, Doc? Or would you prefer to suck my pistol till it comes?"

The ugly sexual imagery, the explicit connection drawn between violence and intimacy, frightened her worse than the gun itself.

*Show contrition now. No trace of defiance, nothing to set him off.* "I'm sorry . . . really . . . if I said the wrong thing."

"That's better."

He sat down again. She fought to suppress the tremors shivering through her body. The dampness on the inside of the blindfold was a sprinkle of tears.

"I honestly don't mean to hurt you." He spoke in a gentler tone. "I will if I have to, but that's not the way I want things to work between us. See, I have plans for you."

His pause solicited a question. She obliged. "What plans?"

He didn't answer directly. "I have a problem, Doc."

This time she waited, asking nothing.

"A problem," he said again, gently. "I guess you'd call it a compulsion. I've yielded to it more than once."

"What sort of compulsion?"

"I kill people. Women. I kill women."

*Don't lose it now. Come up with a response. Something noncommittal, until you know what he wants you to say.*

Erin held her face rigidly composed. "I see."

"Three women so far. Three over a period of fifteen years." The chair creaked as he leaned forward. "You probably think I enjoy it. That violence gratifies some twisted desire of mine. But it's not true. I don't kill for fun. I get no pleasure from what I do. It makes me sick."

His voice dropped with each of the last four words, ending in a whisper.

"I do it"—he spoke so softly she had to strain to hear—"because I can't stop myself. I've tried. But I can't. I swear I can't. I hold off as long as I can, and then I cruise the streets and . . . and I do it again."

"You weren't cruising the streets tonight," Erin said slowly. "You targeted me specifically."

"Because I need you."

"What for?"

"You're going to treat me, Doc. Cure me. Fix it so I don't have to kill anymore. You're going to set me free."

# 9

Erin let the echo of his words settle in the room's stillness. Though she knew what she had heard, somehow it seemed unreal to her, a ridiculous joke.

"That's why you brought me here?" she said finally.

"Yes."

"For . . . therapy?"

"It was the only way."

"If you were to turn yourself in, you'd receive comprehensive treatment—"

"*No.*" She'd pressed one of his buttons. *Watch it.* "I've got no intention of ending up in the nuthouse or on death row. I'm sorry for what I've done, but I'm not willing to submit to . . . punishment."

His voice quavered on the last word. Erin wondered what sort of punishment had been inflicted on him in the past, and by whom.

"Anyway," he added, "it would be unfair."

Careful now, no hint of judgment: "Would it?"

"Of course. I told you, I can't help what I do. It's outside my control. So why should I be held accountable?"

Pointless to argue. Better to change the subject, reinforce the connection he was looking for.

"And you feel I can help you," she said.

"You're a shrink. You've got the training. And unlike the so-called experts on TV, you won't be engaged in armchair analysis. You'll be working with me directly. Besides, you have specific qualifications for treating me."

"Do I?"

"I've read your articles. Some of them, anyway. The one in the *Journal of Consulting and Clinical Psychology* was particularly interesting."

How had he gotten hold of that? The *Journal* was a scholarly publication, not available at newsstands.

The university library carried it, though. Was he a professor? A part-time student?

"I'm not certain," she said cautiously, "that my writings suggest any particular expertise in the area of . . . multiple homicides."

"You'll see things differently once you've read the details of my case. It's all there, in that folder you were so curious about."

She remembered the sheaf of newspaper clippings. His résumé, apparently. The public record of his crimes.

"Anyway," he added coolly, "you don't want to convince me that I picked the wrong person for the job. That would be counterproductive from a survival standpoint."

Nice way of putting it. "You're right."

"Okay, then. Here are the terms of my deal with you. I'll come in every night, for as many hours as necessary—intensive psychotherapy." Every night. Presumably he had a day job. "You'll get to the root of my problem and help me resolve it. After that, I'll let you go, unharmed. You haven't seen my face, don't know where you're being held, so you won't be able to lead the police to me. It *is* possible for you to live through this . . . if you can cure me."

"I see."

"But try any funny business—any more nonsense like that possum act—and you'll pay for it. You'll pay very dearly."

"I won't try anything."

"Even assuming you cooperate fully, you'll have to get results. If the treatment goes nowhere . . ."

The chair squealed like an untuned violin under the restless shifting of his weight.

"Let's just say I've been feeling it again the past couple of months. Stronger and stronger. My . . . compulsion. I've found myself making preparations, buying certain equipment, without even realizing it. Just like all the other times." He took a breath. "My point is, I don't know how long I can hold off doing what I've done three times before."

She didn't need to ask who his fourth victim would be. "How much time do I have?"

"I'm not sure."

"You can't expect immediate results."

"Don't tell me what I can or cannot expect."

"I'm just trying to be realistic. Therapy normally doesn't work overnight."

"Well, you'll have to speed up the process, won't you? Push the envelope. I'd say you've got a powerful incentive."

"I'll do my best," she said quietly. "There is, however, one potential . . . complication."

She hated to raise this issue, but she had no choice.

"Complication?" His tone was a blend of skepticism and impatience.

"You looked in my purse. You must have seen the little bottle of pills I carry."

"Birth control. So what? You aren't pregnant, are you?"

"They aren't birth control. They're carbamazeprine—brand name, Tegretol. Two hundred-milligram tablets."

"None of that means anything to me."

"Prescription medicine . . . for epilepsy."

"Hell." Disgust in his voice, and anger at the unplanned, the unanticipated. "You're not going to start pitching fits on me, are you?"

"I haven't had a seizure since I was in high school. I've been on medication ever since. Nearly all cases of grand mal epilepsy can be controlled pharmaceutically."

"So you've got your pills. What's the problem?"

"The bottle is almost empty. I've got enough for twenty-four hours, but that's it."

"You mean—oh, Christ—you need to refill your prescription?"

"I already did. The new bottle is in my medicine cabinet at home. I see you took some things from my bathroom—but you didn't take that."

"What happens if you run out of this—this . . . ?"

"Tegretol."

"Right. What then?"

"I'd have a serious problem. To go off the maintenance dosage overnight would almost certainly bring on a seizure. Possibly something worse than a grand mal episode."

"I thought grand mal was as bad as epilepsy gets."

"No, there's what they call status epilepticus. It means a prolonged seizure that doesn't end naturally. It can continue for hours, even days. If it's a violent episode, it can kill you."

"Shit." He fell silent, and she let him think.

It was a risk, telling him this. He might conclude she was more trouble than she was worth. Might dispose of her and find another psychologist to do the job.

But she wasn't lying. The danger of renewed seizures, even of a sustained status episode, was all too real.

"Well, what can I do about it?" he asked finally.

She was grateful for the question, which implied that he wanted to keep her alive. "Get me the other bottle."

"In your apartment? Go back there?"

"It's the only way."

"I can't take that kind of chance. You want me to get caught. That's what this is all about, isn't it? You're trying to trick me—"

"Look at the pills in my purse if you don't believe it. Check the label. Tegretol. I'm *not* playing games."

Another long beat of silence.

"All right," he whispered. "I'll get your damn medicine. How long will the new prescription last, anyway?"

"A month."

"That'll be more than enough time. One way or the other." The legs of his chair scraped on the concrete floor with a raw, throat-clearing sound. He was up. "You catch my meaning, Doc?"

"Fully."

She listened as his footsteps receded.

"I'll bring your meds this evening," he said from what had to be the doorway. "That's when our work together will start. And, Doc . . . you'd better be real good at what you do."

Slam, and she was alone.

# 10

A long-held breath shuddered out of her. She sagged in the chair, fumbling weakly at the blindfold until it came loose.

On the other side of the door, a key rattled in a key-hole. A moment later, footsteps thudded up the stairs. Creak of floorboards overhead; the distant closing of a door.

The house was empty. She waited, straining to hear, until faintly the growl of an engine reached her from far away. It grew slightly louder, perhaps as the vehicle pulled out of the garage, then quieter again; seconds later, it was gone.

Her abductor didn't live here, it seemed. His home was somewhere else, and this place was simply a hold-ing pen for her.

She stood, then sat again, surprised at the loose, wa-tery trembling of her knees. Silently she counted to twenty, drawing slow, measured breaths. When she felt strong enough, she crossed the room to the door.

No doorknob on her side. The smooth sheet of wood mocked her.

On tiptoe she looked through the peephole. The fish-eye lens revealed only darkness.

Crouching, she examined the clearance between the

door and the jamb. It was wide enough to expose part of the bolt drawn into place by the turning of the key.

A dead bolt? Or a latch bolt, the kind with a beveled edge?

A latch bolt could be defeated with a credit card. There were some in her wallet. The cash had been removed, but not the plastic.

She tamped her MasterCard out of its acetate pouch, then knelt by the door. Her heart kept up a hard, steady beat as she inserted the rectangle of plastic into the crack between the door and the frame.

The MasterCard's leading edge slipped past the gain of the faceplate and bumped up against the bolt. She pushed, trying to make the card flex. The trick was to snake it along the angle of the latch bolt, between the faceplate in the door and the striker plate in the jamb. Pop the latch, and the door would open.

"Come on," she breathed, jiggling the card. "Come on, *please,* just do this for me, and I'll never complain about the finance charges again."

Nothing.

The card wouldn't do the job. She removed her laminated driver's license from the wallet and tried that. It was thinner than the MasterCard, more flexible, but it had no greater success.

Finally she gave up. The door must be secured either by a dead bolt or by a latch bolt with the diagonal edge facing away from her. Regardless of which was true, loiding the lock was impossible.

She wasn't surprised, really. The man holding her prisoner was smart—too smart, possibly, to leave the charge cards and license in her wallet if they could be useful in opening the door.

There was a way of defeating a dead bolt, though. She had learned of the technique years ago, while living in a low-rent district near the university, earning her graduate degree. The other unit in her duplex had been broken into, her neighbors' place cleaned out. She remembered the T.P.D. detective at the scene explaining how the dead bolt on the front door had been released.

*Simple enough,* he'd said. *They just pried the bolt open with an ice pick. Happens all the time.*

All she needed was an ice pick. Too bad she didn't happen to have one available.

Of course, any long, needlelike tool would do. She searched her purse, her suitcase, the box of foodstuffs.

The item nearest to what she needed was the ballpoint pen. But it was too big to fit between the door and the frame.

She unscrewed the pen's metal casing, thinking that perhaps the ink cartridge inside might work, but although the tube was narrow enough, it was made of cheap, flexible plastic that would afford her no leverage.

One last point of attack presented itself. The hinges. Could she lift the pivot pins out of the barrels and simply detach the door from the wall?

The pins were in tight. Their caps were smooth and featureless, offering no grooves in which to fasten the tip of a screwdriver, even assuming she had one. If she could grip the caps with a pair of pliers, she might be able to tug the pins free. Pliers, however, were another item her abductor had neglected to leave in her possession.

Could she smash the hinges? They were old and rusty, vulnerable to a sharp hammer blow. She searched the room for a blunt instrument, found none. The sill cock would make a powerful weapon, but she saw no way to liberate it from the wall. A loose brick would serve almost equally well; frustratingly, a thorough patting of the walls established that all the bricks were mortared firmly in place.

Hopeless.

The bolt could not be loided or picked. The hinges could not be disassembled or broken. Unless she could flatten herself to the thinness of a pancake and ooze under the door, she was stuck.

It crashed down on her then—the full weight of her captivity. Strength left her. She sank to her knees, planting her hands on the floor to keep from falling prostrate.

Head lowered, eyes squeezed shut, she felt her shoulders shake with soundless sobs.

The patter of dampness on her knuckles was a steady rainfall of tears.

To lose her composure like this was humiliating, entirely unlike her, but she couldn't help it. Her life, her world, her daily routine, so carefully ordered and meticulously maintained—all of it had exploded like a bomb, and screaming chaos was the aftermath.

What she wouldn't give right now to be safe at home in her comfortable, familiar apartment, enclosed by walls that were not a prison, locked behind a door to which she held the key.

Her eyes burned. She heard herself sniffling miserably and dragged a hand across her nose.

"Help me," she whispered to the unhearing room, the empty house, the vast stillness around her. "Help me, somebody. Help me, please."

# 11

Harold Gund drove slowly through Tucson's dark streets, seeking a mailbox.

Best to get Erin's letter in the mail as soon as possible. Once Annie received it, her fears would be allayed, and any preliminary police investigation into her sister's disappearance would be terminated.

Still, mail delivery was slow. It might take three days for the letter to reach Annie's residence. A lot could happen in three days.

Unless he delivered it personally.

There was no particular risk in doing so. Annie would simply assume that Erin herself had delivered the letter in the middle of the night, avoiding the pain of a phone call or a face-to-face encounter, before departing on her mysterious sabbatical. Unusual behavior, but not implausible under the circumstances.

All right, then. Do it.

In less than twenty minutes he reached the Catalina foothills. He guided the van into a town house community off Pontatoc Road.

Dangerous to park in the open. He pulled behind an unfinished row of town houses near the entrance, killed the headlights and engine, and pulled on his gloves before handling the letter again.

On foot he walked along a curving street, illuminated only by low-wattage bulbs above the mailboxes at the head of each driveway.

The development, like most places in the foothills, had no sidewalks. His shoes crackled on scattered dirt at the side of the road.

Annie's place was just ahead, a single-story home with a red tile roof and desert landscaping, which shared walls with the units on either side. Gund slowed his steps.

Abruptly it occurred to him that if anybody happened to see him here, he could be linked to the letter and thus to Erin's disappearance.

Then he shook his head. Ridiculous. No one would see him. It was nearly four-thirty in the morning. Everybody in the complex was asleep.

Annie lay on her living room sofa, staring into the dark.

For the past couple of hours she'd snatched brief intervals of slumber, never quite finding the perfect zone of dreamless oblivion that would have lasted until first light. Every random noise woke her: the creak of the house settling, the rustle of mesquite branches outside her windows, the coyotes' shrill, distant cries.

She wondered what was really keeping her up, what obscure worry nagged her just below the threshold of awareness.

*You're getting to be like Lydia,* she chided herself half seriously, remembering her aunt's nervous disposition, her medicine chest stocked with antacids and headache remedies and sleeping pills. *Before you know it, you'll be pacing the floor all night long. . . .*

Through the living room windows, a sudden orange glow.

The porch light had snapped on.

Annie sat up, blinking.

The light was wired to an electric eye beamed at the driveway. It was a system installed by the town house's previous owners; personally she'd never felt much need for such protection in this part of town.

What would make the light come on now?

An intruder seemed unlikely. In the three years she had lived in this neighborhood, there had never been a break-in.

A coyote was more probable. Or a band of javelinas. The hairy desert pigs sometimes ventured out of the dry washes in search of food.

She swung off the sofa and pulled aside the curtains, peering out at the driveway and the front walk.

Nothing was there. The light shone on her mailbox and the tangled clump of cholla at its base. The cholla's needles glowed like moonlit fur.

If there had been an animal, perhaps it had continued down the street. She walked to the door, intending to look, then paused.

Suppose it wasn't an animal. Safe as this neighborhood was, a trespasser was always possible.

Her nose wrinkled in irritation. She was scared of her own shadow tonight.

Decisively, in defiance of her fears, she opened the door and stepped outside.

Faintly she heard the crunch of gravel. Footsteps, retreating fast.

Coyote. Had to be. Scared off by the light.

They were timid creatures, despite their unwarranted reputation for aggressiveness. To her knowledge, none had attacked an adult human being.

She padded along the driveway, slippers scuffing the macadam, and peered down the street in the direction of the noise.

Nothing. And the footsteps were no longer audible.

Must have just missed him. Too bad. Encounters with desert animals were among her prime reasons for living on the outskirts of town.

Oh, well. Next time.

She returned to the house. As she was about to shut the door, another sound reached her. The rumble of an engine.

At first she thought it belonged to some passing vehicle on Pontatoc Road. But no, the source was closer than that. Within the town house complex.

She listened as the noise diminished, the vehicle—a truck or a van, it sounded like—speeding off into the night.

Maybe what she'd heard hadn't been a coyote, after all. Maybe it had been the vehicle's driver, taking a brisk predawn walk before heading to work. Nothing unusual about that.

So why was she afraid?

She couldn't say. She knew only that the muscles of her shoulders and back were flinching under the caress of a sudden chill.

*Erin,* she thought abruptly. *Please be all right. I'm scared for you . . . for both of us . . . and I don't know why.*

# 12

Erin delayed looking at the contents of the manila folder as long as possible. She was quite sure she wouldn't like what she would find.

Finally curiosity won out over apprehension. She picked up the folder, seated herself, and opened it.

The first clipping had been ripped from an inside page of the *Milwaukee Sentinel,* dated February 16, 1980. An article headlined *Stevens Pt. Woman Reported Missing* disclosed the disappearance of Marilyn Vaccaro, twenty-four, last seen leaving a midnight church service. A photo showed a smiling dark-haired woman with large, alert eyes.

Erin stared at that photo for a long time. *What did he do to you, Marilyn?*

Slowly she turned to the next article in the file.

*Hikers Find Skeletal Remains.* Subhead: *Victim May Be Missing Stevens Pt. Woman.*

The date was June 3, 1980. Marilyn had disappeared in February. Erin thought of the hard winter her relatives and friends must have endured, awaiting this grim news.

She hoped the woman's death had been quick, at least.

The article, bare of details, didn't say. Yet odd hints

suggested the worst: "apparently ritualistic murder . . . evidence of sadism . . . even veteran investigators are shaken."

A rustle of paper, and she froze, staring at the third clipping.

*Stevens Pt. Woman May Have Been Burned to Death, Authorities Say.*

Burned to death.

"No," Erin whispered. "No, not that."

Fire was her greatest fear—hers and Annie's. Had been ever since that August night in 1973.

She could face any danger, any threat, any form of torture, but not fire. God, not fire. Please, dear God.

Panic welled in her, the same blind, screaming panic she had known when she'd awoken in the dark, bound and helpless.

He killed with flame. Killed women. She would be next. And the local papers would report it in their cold, factual accounts. *Tucson Woman Found Burned Alive.* People would read the story as they sipped their morning coffee. *How terrible,* they would mutter before turning to the sports pages and the movie reviews.

No, that couldn't happen. She couldn't die like that, for Christ's sake. Could not, could not, could *not!*

*Stop.*

Teeth gritted, she refused to lose control. Refused to let terror break her.

She would deal with this. She would be strong. She had faced other crises. Even as a small child, she had confronted death and survived.

She hugged that thought, drawing comfort from it. If she had kept her composure when she was only seven years old, she could do no less now.

With the back of her hand she wiped her eyes dry, then returned her attention to the article.

Through dental records the remains had been identified as those of Marilyn Vaccaro. Charred bones, disarticulated and slightly scattered by scavengers and blowing snow, were all that was left of her. The clearing in which they had been found was still fire-scarred; according to arson experts, gasoline had been liberally poured. Above and below the blackened skeleton were two metal stakes, hammered into the frozen winter ground.

She had been tied hand and foot to the stakes, soaked in gas, and burned.

*That's how he'll kill me, too,* Erin thought. *Stake me to the ground and pour gasoline.*

A wave of nausea shuddered through her. She clutched her stomach and fought back the impulse to retch.

The next two articles filled in additional details. Although Marilyn Vaccaro had been kidnapped in Stevens Point, she had died more than a hundred miles northwest of town, in the Chequamegon National Forest near Lake Superior.

Erin remembered her own ride earlier tonight, her utter helplessness and pounding terror. Marilyn's ride had lasted longer—two hours or more.

Perhaps she had been unconscious most of the time. Or perhaps not.

The next article, culled from the *Grand Rapids Press,* was dated July 27, 1986. Six years had passed since Marilyn's death.

This time the victim was Sharon Lane, thirty-one, of Holland, Michigan, abducted the previous night and discovered only a few hours later, dead in a wooded area near Rose City in the eastern part of the state.

She, too, had burned. In the dry, hot summer night the fire had spread, consuming acres of forest before firefighters controlled the blaze. Damping down the hot spot, they had stumbled on Sharon's body.

Again there was a picture of the victim as she had looked in life. The article said Sharon was a young mother; she had been taken from the parking lot of a shopping mall after dark.

Another gap of years, and then, on October 4, 1991, a minor article in the *Minneapolis Star Tribune* reported the disappearance of Deborah Collins. The nineteen-year-old had vanished after finishing her night shift at a downtown donut shop.

The following September, her body was found in the woods near Thief River Falls. Like the first victim, she had spent months in snow and rain, her bones worried by scavengers and carpeted in moss. But the telltale metal stakes remained in place, warped by heat and oxidized by flame.

Nothing else in the folder. Deborah Collins had been the last. The killer had been quiet since.

Until now.

She wondered where he would do it when her time came. There were no woods in the immediate vicinity. Would he drive her into the forested mountains, or simply burn her in the desert under the open sky?

*Shut up,* she told herself angrily, though she hadn't spoken aloud.

She flung the folder to the floor. Stood and paced the room.

Now she understood why her abductor had been intrigued by her journal articles. All of them had focused on the pathology of fire-starting. It was a subject that had haunted her since childhood.

Even so, she wasn't certain her specialized expertise actually did apply to this man. He was by no means a typical pyromaniac.

No doubt some of the same compulsions motivated him, however. Nearly all violently antisocial behavior had roots in unresolved conflicts and unconscious hostilities. At least initially, she would have to concentrate on those aspects of the case, the ones she could treat.

Slowly she shook her head. The case. Already she was thinking of him as a patient.

Well, she had better think of him that way—if she wanted to live.

And if she failed to connect with him, failed to help him in time . . .

Scorching heat. Bitter smoke.

She would die hearing the crackle of her own skin as it peeled away from her bones. Die writhing like a snake with a broken back.

With a shudder she forced these thoughts away. Couldn't contemplate her own future tonight. It was too much to absorb, and her mind was sore with use, and she was tired, suddenly more tired than she had ever been.

Wearily she stretched out on the foam pad in the corner, draping herself in the cheap cotton blanket. The pad was eight inches too short for her; she shifted into a fetal position, tucking her right arm under her head.

Rest was all she intended, not sleep. Sleep was out of the question. Though fatigue had numbed her body and blanked her mind, agitation and residual fear would keep her awake all night.

No, she could never hope to sleep. Not here, in this brick-and-concrete dungeon. Not if she remained a captive for ten years.

But at least she could close her eyes, shut out the sight of those bare walls lit by the bare bulb. Close her eyes and breathe easy, easy.

Never sleep. Not tonight. Maybe not for the rest of her life.

Never sleep. Obviously.

Never . . .

Erin slept.

# 13

In a haze of light Gund treads a familiar path through a dry wash. Steep embankments rise on both sides, crawling with twisted palo verde trees rooted in the powdery soil.

Javelinas have been here recently; he smells their skunklike odor. The strong scent, the crunch of loose pebbles under his sneakers, the filigree traceries of sunlight on a fallen saguaro's exposed ribs—all of it is vivid and distinct, more real than reality.

The experience is by no means new to him. He knows every detail intimately, anticipates what he will see even before he reaches the narrow end of the arroyo, before he takes hold of a palo verde's green trunk and climbs the crumbling rise, before he reaches the top and lifts his head above the rim.

Beyond a waving stand of bitterweed in yellow bloom, under the blue expansive sky, she lounges in a recliner. Posed like a model: head thrown back, arms relaxed at her sides, long, tanned legs glistening with lotion. She breathes, and the hills of her breasts rise and fall, their movement fascinating.

She wears denim shorts and a cotton shirt, partially unbuttoned, showing inches of smooth flesh.

The tingle in his groin tells him he is getting hard

and stiff down there. Though he hates the feeling, he cannot turn away.

Abruptly she sits up, turns her head from side to side, eyes masked behind sunglasses. Always he worries that she's sensed his presence somehow; she never has. She is merely confirming that she's alone.

Her hand moves to her shirt and undoes the remaining buttons one at a time.

The shirt opens. He has lived this moment a thousand times, yet the sight of her bare chest still robs him of breath.

Squirt of suntan lotion into her open palm. Her hand creams the oil over her cleavage, her breasts. She rubs harder, fingering her nipples. Her legs flex as her head lolls. Glint of sunlight on her mirrored lenses. One hand caresses her breasts while the other drifts lazily down to the zipper of her shorts. She wears no underpants. Lotion on her finger. The finger curling inside . . .

Gund woke.

His breathing was loud and labored above the pounding of his heart.

Blinking, he registered a smear of morning light caught in the window curtains. He must have kicked off the covers during the night. Naked, supine, he lay motionless, arms and legs splayed.

Beside the bed, an upended apple crate supported a gooseneck lamp and dime-store alarm clock. The short and long hands of the clock were at seven and three: 7:15.

He'd awoken fifteen minutes before his alarm was set to go off. Strange.

After dropping the letter in Annie's mailbox, he'd come directly home, arriving at five in the morning. He had shed his clothes—the outfit from last night lay scattered on the floor like a trail of clothes left by a melting man—and collapsed into bed, falling instantly asleep.

That had been only two hours ago. He would have expected to sleep straight through.

Perhaps a residue of excitement over last night's successful enterprise had roused him. Or the nagging sense of urgency, the awareness of a looming deadline, which had been with him for the past two weeks.

He studied the wall opposite the bed, bare of ornament save for the single decorative item found in his apartment: a calender showing scenes of America's national parks. Today's date was April 17. A Tuesday.

It had been April 3 when he purchased the two cans of gasoline that now lay under the tarp in the rear of his van. Three days later he had bought a badminton set at a toy store. The net, shuttles, and rackets had gone into the trash; he had wanted only the metal stakes used to put up the net.

They were hidden under the tarp also.

Funny how he had done these things without quite permitting himself to know where his actions would lead. Oh, he did know, of course, but in some peculiar way he seemed able to block out that knowledge and operate on automatic pilot, making his purchases and preparations with no conscious planning, no definite intentions.

It was always that way. But this time things would be different. This time he had Erin Reilly to help him.

If she could.

And if not . . .

Then the stakes and the gasoline would be used for her.

His mouth twisted, and a groan shuddered out of him, thick and wheezy.

He wondered how much time he had before the compulsion became irresistible. A month? Two weeks?

Perhaps not long enough for Erin to do her work. But it had to be. For his sake and hers.

Therapy. The prospect simultaneously frightened and intrigued him. He supposed she would ask him about his childhood, his sex life. Those appeared to be the standard avenues of inquiry.

Some evasion would be necessary in both areas. There were things he wouldn't reveal, secrets he meant to keep.

Dreams. That was another topic sure to arise. Well, there was only one dream that mattered, the dream that had visited him on so many nights, the dream that would not let him go.

A frown crossed his face. The dream . . .

That was what had woken him ahead of the alarm clock. Of course.

Slowly he raised his head and, for the first time since opening his eyes, looked at himself. He preferred never to see his unclothed body. His pale white flesh, thick around his waist, repelled him, and he found the hairy swatch of his genitalia troubling in some obscure way.

Still, he looked, then released a relieved sigh. His penis was soft, flaccid. He did not have an erection. Good.

Erections scared and disgusted him. Pain and shame were inextricably intertwined with any reminder of the sexual act.

He thought again of the dream. Lotion on her finger; her finger between her legs . . .

The stream of images would unwind in his mind throughout the day, persistent as a migraine, unless he did something to push the memory away.

He knew what was necessary. The photo. His special picture.

Quickly he rose from bed and threw on a robe, belting it to hide his body from himself. Barefoot, he left the bedroom and proceeded down the hall to the den at the far end.

The den contained just three sticks of furniture: a writing desk he'd salvaged years ago from a retiring professor's office, the desk's swivel chair, and a steel file cabinet. Dust dressed everything in a dull gray coat.

At the back of the file cabinet, in an unlabeled manila folder, he kept the photograph.

Carefully he took it out, then sat in the desk chair and studied it in a band of light filtering through a gash in the curtain.

The photo's corners were dog-eared, the edges worn from repeated handling. It had been crisp and new when he'd obtained it. But since then, nearly every night, he'd found himself drawn to the picture, gazing at it sometimes for hours.

The picture calmed him, as it always did. He lost himself in it and felt the world slide away.

Relaxed now, the dream banished, he could examine his own feelings more objectively.

Yes, his ugly impulses were stirring. But he could control them. He could hold off the need to take action. He could refrain from taking Erin outside the ranch, to the arroyo. He could stop himself from ending her life in a shout of flame.

He was certain of it.

Almost certain, anyway.

# 14

Late.

Annie checked her watch for the fifth time.

She sat alone at a table for two, a menu in her hands, the table's umbrella unfolded to shelter her in shadow. Around her, bright noon sunshine fell in ribbons of glitter through a scrim of fluttering banners and rippling leaves, the sun rays shifting with the wind.

Voices murmured over the clink of silverware. At a table across the courtyard, half a dozen women in power suits laughed at a shared joke. Nearer to Annie's table, two men pursued an intense discussion of the upcoming NFL draft.

Pleasant here, in this courtyard restaurant in the heart of Tucson's downtown. Ordinarily, Annie could relax in a place like this as easily as slipping into a warm, soapy bath.

Today, foreboding overlay her impressions of the restaurant, the bright sun, the blue sweep of sky. Foreboding—and a memory of her insomnia last night.

She had sensed danger to Erin. A premonition, irrational and no doubt groundless. Yet even now she couldn't shake it.

And Erin was late.

The two of them had made a lunch date for twelve

o'clock. Annie had been waiting fifteen minutes already, and she'd arrived ten minutes late to begin with.

Her sister was maniacally punctual, always had been. Whichever gene was responsible for tardiness had been omitted from her complement of chromosomes. For her to be this far off schedule was simply unheard of.

Possibly an unexpected crisis had come up in her practice. Suicidal patient, say.

Or maybe something had ... *happened* to her.

Traffic accident.

Random violence.

Medical emergency.

Hell, anything. Anything at all.

Really, though, it was silly to get all worked up. The simple truth was that Annie had almost certainly misunderstood the arrangements she and Erin had made. Probably she'd gotten the time, the date, or the location wrong—very possibly all three. She'd done it before.

Her sister could remember every detail of her schedule without strain. Annie had trouble enough just remembering to get up in the morning.

Most likely Erin was still at her office, expecting to have lunch at one o'clock—or she was waiting at a different restaurant entirely and wondering how scatterbrained Annie had managed to screw up again.

Of course. It had to be something like that.

*I'll just call her office,* Annie thought, *and—*

"Still waiting?"

The male voice startled her. She looked up from the menu held indifferently in one hand, and her waiter was there, a blond kid with Malibu surfer looks, incongruous in the desert.

"Uh, yeah." Annie put down the menu. "I may have been stood up. Is there a phone around here?"

"Right outside the rear entrance."

"Thanks." She pushed back the tubular chair. "If a woman comes in—redheaded like me, but a lot better looking—please tell her I went to make a call."

"I'll tell her. But she won't be better looking."

The compliment lifted a surprised smile to her lips. The smile lingered as she left the cafe.

Nice to be admired by a younger man. Of course, he probably had no idea how much younger he was. Most people took her to be about twenty-five, but she and Erin had both turned thirty last month and had commiserated together.

Erin. The smile faded.

A telephone kiosk, fortunately not in use, was just where the waiter had said it was.

Though she had dialed the switchboard at Erin's office countless times, the number was gone from her memory. Hardly an unusual occurrence—she had no head for figures, and she wasn't good with names and faces either.

The number was in her address book, and her address book was somewhere in the chaos of her purse. She pawed through a clutter of key rings, tissues, cosmetics, coupons, scribbled notes to herself, Life Savers, breath mints, pens, business cards, loose coins, and out-of-date lottery tickets before she found the booklet.

Then she fed a quarter into the phone and punched in the number.

The receptionist answered. "Sonoran Psychological Associates."

"Hi, Marie, this is Anne Reilly. Is my sister—"

"*Annie.* I've been calling your shop."

Tension in the words—alarm, even. Fear pounced on her like a tiger. "You have? Why?"

"You didn't get my message?"

"No, I've been out, I'm *still* out, what message, what's going on?"

"It's Erin. We can't find her."

"You can't *find* her?" She felt stupid repeating the words.

"No one knows where she is. She missed her ten-fifteen, and her eleven o'clock, too." A truck rattled past the pay phone, and Annie had to strain to hear. "I've called her home three times; her machine keeps answering. Tried calling you forty minutes ago, left a message with your assistant—"

"I was already on my way downtown. For lunch with Erin. She hasn't shown up here either."

Unthinkable for Erin to miss even one appointment with a patient, let alone two. The world would end before she would permit herself that kind of irresponsibility.

Could she have had a seizure? Terrible thought. Erin's last epileptic episode had occurred in high school; since then the prescription medicine she took had kept that problem completely under control.

Still, it was possible. If she'd suffered convulsions while driving to work—or fallen in her apartment and struck her head . . .

"Okay," Annie said, holding her voice steady. "I'll take a run over to her place and see if she's there."

"Let us know—"

"I will, I will. Thanks, Marie."

She hung up and drew a shallow, shaky breath. For a panicky moment she couldn't think straight, couldn't recall where she'd parked her car. Then she remembered: the county parking structure, a couple of blocks from here. Yes.

She walked swiftly to Alameda Street. The main branch of the public library rose on her right, a handful of taller buildings assembled behind it. None stood higher than thirty-five stories.

For the most part, downtown Tucson could have been downtown Des Moines or Tulsa or Toledo, any small city that had begun as a few square blocks of brick and concrete. Outside the small historic district, there was little in the town's business section that was distinctive. The area retained none of the Wild West flavor of Tucson's outlying horse ranches and saguaro forests; it owned no particular charm or glamour, save perhaps for one evocative street name, Broadway, said to have been the inspiration of a visiting New Yorker at the turn of the century.

Though big-city magic was absent here, so were the worst excesses of urban blight. A few transients slept in El Presidio Park, and some spidery graffiti clung to alleyways and street signs, but otherwise downtown remained remarkably orderly and clean.

Whitewashed walls gleamed in the strong sunlight. Patches of grass made squares and crescents of green. Mulberry trees sighed, lovesick, in a gentle breath of breeze.

Annie barely noticed any of it. Her mind replayed the phone conversation, hunting among Marie's words for some overlooked clue, finding none.

This was bad. Really bad.

Erin was in trouble. Might be injured.

Even . . . dead.

Ugly thought. A shiver skipped over her shoulders.

"No way," she said firmly, drawing a stare from a vendor at a sandwich cart.

Erin couldn't be dead. Annie refused to so much as consider the possibility.

People died all the time, but not her sister.

# 15

The radio came on when her car started, a blast of Billy Ray Cyrus exploding from the speakers.

Annie punched the on-off button, silencing Billy Ray, and swung the red Miata out of its parking space. At the exit-ramp gatehouse, money and a receipt changed hands, and then she was on the street, hooking north on Church Avenue and east on Sixth Street, heading for Erin's apartment complex at Broadway and Pantano.

The little sports car was fun to drive, but Annie was too agitated to have any fun now as she cut from lane to lane, bypassing slower traffic, running yellow lights. Normally she didn't drive like a maniac—well, not this much of a maniac, anyway—but the apprehension that had been building in her for the past twelve hours had reached fever pitch. She had to know if Erin was all right.

Tension set her teeth on edge. She rolled down the window to feel the rush of air on her face.

At Campbell she cut over to Broadway. Vermilion blooms of mariposo lily and purple owl clover blurred past on the landscaped median strip. Despite worry and preoccupation, she greeted the spring blossoms with a smile.

The sight of flowers always pleased her. Flowers, she often thought, had saved her life.

For weeks after that night in 1973, she had been lost, disoriented, a seven-year-old girl with the face of a shell-shocked soldier. The flowers in Lydia's garden had brought her back. Watering them, plucking weeds, tending to each bud as if it were her precious child, she had found a way to ground herself, to reconnect with reality.

Her sister had spent her teenage years educating herself in the mind's darker recesses, struggling to understand madness and evil. Annie had never wanted to understand. She had wanted only to escape life's horror. In gardens and nurseries and florists' shops, she did.

It took her years to realize that she loved flowers less for their beauty than for the simple fact that they could not hurt her.

Even a tame dog could bite. A kitten could scratch. A loving father . . .

But flowers were safe, always.

Almost in Erin's neighborhood now. The older, more crowded part of town was receding, replaced by newer shopping plazas on larger lots. Developments of tract homes and condos occupied curving mazes of side streets with ersatz Spanish names. The mountains slouched on all horizons, their outlines sharp against a sky scudded with shredded-cotton clouds.

Pantano Fountains, Erin's place, glided into view. Annie parked outside the lobby and walked briskly to the front door.

She fingered the intercom, buzzed Erin's apartment. No reply.

Fumbling in her purse, she found the set of duplicate keys Erin had given her. Opened the door, entered the lobby.

The manager was on duty in her glass-walled office, talking on the phone, her words muted by the glass. A white-haired lady with a proud, lined face; Annie had met her several times when visiting Erin on weekends.

What was her name? Mrs. Williams. Right.

Might be necessary to talk with her later, but for now Annie simply sketched a wave through the glass as she hurried to the elevator. She pressed the call button, and the doors parted at once.

As she was traveling to the top floor, she realized suddenly that she should have checked the carport to see if Erin's Taurus was in its reserved space. That way she would already know if Erin was home.

But of course Erin wasn't home. She hadn't answered the intercom, after all.

Unless she couldn't answer.

A seizure would pass in a few minutes, Annie reminded herself. And it wouldn't be fatal.

But suppose Erin had been in the shower when she collapsed—suppose her prone body had obstructed the drain, and she'd drowned in six inches of water. Suppose . . .

The elevator let her off on the penthouse floor. She ran for Erin's apartment, propelled by panic.

At the door she hesitated, then knocked loudly.

"Erin?"

No response.

She inserted the key—no, wrong, that was the lobby key, try the other one. Got the door open finally and peered in.

Again: "Erin?"

Still nothing.

Slowly she stepped inside.

The lights of the apartment were off, the windows darkened by drawn curtains with blackout liners to hold back the desert sun. She found the wall switch and brightened the living room. It looked orderly and normal, almost magically clean, as always—and Erin was nowhere in sight.

From the bedroom, a faint sound. Music. Some classical composition. Rippling piano keys and a weeping violin.

Annie darted into the bedroom, briefly thrilled by hope—a thrill that died when she found the room similarly unoccupied, the clock radio on the nightstand playing to no audience.

The alarm feature was set to switch on the radio at 7:15. Apparently there was no automatic shut-off. Strange, though, that Erin hadn't turned it off herself before leaving.

The bed was unmade, another oddity. Erin, the neatness freak, invariably fluffed her pillows and smoothed the bedspread upon arising. Loose, tangled sheets were not part of her world.

Her purse was gone, but nothing else of value that Annie could see.

In the bathroom, she found the shower stall dry. She fingered the towels on the racks. They were dry, too.

Into the kitchen, where a few plates soaked in the kitchen sink under a lacy film of liquid soap. Dinner dishes, streaked with tomato sauce and spotted with the remnants of salad greens. No cereal bowl, no spoon.

Den, balcony, hall closet—nothing. No signs of intrusion or disturbance, no furniture or valuables missing, and no Erin anywhere.

She'd left no note, and the only messages on her answering machine were from Marie at the clinic, asking Erin where she was.

Still no answer to that question, and now Annie was finding it harder to shake the cold fear that clutched the base of her spine.

Erin had to be all right. Annie simply wouldn't permit her to be injured or sick or—worse.

"It's not allowed," Annie said softly, as if in challenge to the empty rooms around her. "You hear me,
Erin? You're not allowed to be in any trouble."

There was still the parking lot to check. Annie
locked the apartment and descended to ground level.

At the side of the building, under one of the carports, she found Erin's assigned parking space. Empty.

The Taurus was gone. Erin *had* left.

In the strong sunlight Annie stood unmoving, oblivious of heat and glare, thinking hard.

The bed had been slept in, and her purse taken. Presumably, Erin had gone to work as usual.

But why had she been in such a hurry? Why hadn't
she found time to shower, eat breakfast, make the bed,
even switch off the radio?

There was another possibility. Suppose a patient had
phoned her in the middle of the night with an urgent
problem. It happened. Erin would have gone to her office for an unscheduled session. That scenario would
fit the facts quite well.

But where was she now?

Had she been in an accident on the way to or from
the office? Jumped by a mugger? Attacked by her own
patient?

Crazy, she thought as she went back inside the building. Just crazy to think that way.

Mrs. Williams was off the phone by now. She rose
from behind her desk, uttering the first syllable of a
welcome. The greeting died when she saw Annie's
face.

"Miss Reilly. What's the matter? Nothing's wrong,
is it?"

Reflexively, Annie smiled. She wondered why her

mouth would do that when she knew of no reason to be cheerful.

"Oh, no," she said in a light tone that matched her careless grin, "nothing's wrong, except Erin's sort of hard to find today."

"Hard to find?"

"You haven't seen her, have you?"

"Why, no."

"Her car's not around. She's not at work. It's funny, isn't it?"

Annie knew it wasn't funny, but she couldn't erase the witless smile of denial from her face.

Mrs. Williams seemed to see beneath that smile. "Maybe you ought to telephone the police."

"The police. What for?"

"See if there's been any problem. A traffic problem. You know."

*Accident,* she meant to say, but couldn't. Annie nodded. "Yes. I guess I should do that."

Mrs. Williams took out a phone book and found the number of the police department's Traffic Enforcement Division. Annie was about to dial when she realized she couldn't remember Erin's license plate.

"We have it on file," Mrs. Williams said, opening a cabinet drawer. "Have to ensure that our tenants park in their reserved spaces."

Annie reached a traffic-division sergeant, who took down the car's make, model, and license number, then put her on hold. She waited through an internal of silence, shifting her weight and wishing she could make her damn mouth shed its idiot grin.

*You are no good in a crisis, Annie, no good at all.*

If this was a crisis. But it wasn't; it couldn't be.

In her mind she heard the sergeant's voice, oddly tentative. *Ms. Reilly? I'm sorry, ma'am, but your sister was in a crash earlier today. . . . Hit by an oncoming truck, a Mack truck, big one . . . She's dead, ma'am.*

*She's in a coma, ma'am.*

*She's paralyzed, a quadriplegic.*

*She's—*

"Hello?" The sergeant again. The real sergeant, not her fantasy tormentor.

"Yes?" Fear throbbed in her chest, and she felt the spiraling onset of light-headedness.

"I've checked. There's no report of any accident involving the vehicle you described."

Annie put out her free hand to grip the edge of Mrs. Williams's desk. "I see. Well . . . that's good, isn't it?"

"Ma'am?"

"But then—where *is* she?"

The sergeant cleared his throat. "Excuse me?"

Annie blinked. "Nothing. I just . . . nothing. Thank you very much for your help."

Her fingers continued to grip the handset even after she had set it down in its cradle.

Mrs. Williams regarded her with worried eyes. "No traffic accident?"

"No."

"I'm glad to hear that, at least."

"Yes. So am I."

"Do you have any idea . . . I mean . . . Has your sister ever disappeared before?"

"She *hasn't* disappeared," Annie snapped.

Mrs. Williams said nothing.

Annie lowered her head, bit her lip. Her knees were trembling.

"Sorry," she whispered. "I guess . . . I guess she has."

# 16

"Anybody there? Can anybody hear me?"

Fists hammering the cellar door. Shock waves of sound echoing in the room.

"If you hear me, please answer! *Please!*"

Nothing.

Exhausted, Erin turned away from the door and slumped against the wall.

She had expected no response. Her abductor was too smart to hide her in a place frequented by other people. She doubted there was another habitation within a mile of this one.

Still, there was always a chance someone would pass by, near enough to hear her—a mailman on a rural route, a child playing in a forbidden yard, a gas-company meter reader. Anyone.

That was why, several times since waking, she had battered at the door and strained her voice in futile cries.

She assumed it was now noon or shortly after; without a wristwatch or other timepiece, she could judge time only by her schedule of meals. She'd already eaten breakfast—a banana and an orange, accompanied by her next-to-last Tegretol, washed down with luke-warm water from the sill cock—and she was beginning to think about lunch.

The rest of her morning had been spent keeping busy. The dirt and mildew in the room had offended her; she'd set to work with paper towels, scrubbing and cleaning, until the worst of the grime was gone. Next she'd organized the contents of her suitcase, straightened and smoothed the futon's cotton blanket, dusted the chairs.

Those chores done, she'd stripped off her pajamas and robe, given herself a sponge bath, washed and combed her hair, subjected herself to the humiliating exercise of urination with the help of one of the empty milk jugs left for that purpose, and finally dressed.

She'd started with underpants and a bra, slipping them on with distaste bordering on revulsion. *He* had handled these items, these most personal garments. Feeling them against her skin had been almost like . . . like feeling his hands on her body.

Mustn't think about it, she'd told herself. Anyway, he had probably worn gloves while packing the suitcase.

Looking through the other clothes he'd brought her, she had selected a cotton shirt, denim shorts, and boots.

The shirt was beige—an optimistic choice. It would blend in with the sere tones of the desert should she find a way to escape.

Escape. Sure.

She might as well have put on a bright red shirt with a target painted on it for all the difference it made. She wasn't getting out of here.

With that thought, they began to prick at her again— vague and tentative manifestations of claustrophobia, which had been teasing her all morning. She paced the room, fighting to dispel the groundless fear.

Well, of course it was groundless. Utterly irrational. She ought to know; she treated phobias all the time.

The walls were awfully close, though. She could

cross from one end of the room to the other in four strides.

Back and forth, back and forth, her perambulations ticking like the strokes of a pendulum.

Low ceiling—she had to dodge the hundred-watt bulb on the chain. The room's only source of light—if the bulb failed, she would be sealed up in darkness.

*Don't think about it.*

She didn't want to, but the awareness of confinement was getting to her, accelerating her heartbeat, clenching the muscles of her abdomen.

Trapped here in this underground chamber—it was like being buried alive.

Suppose her abductor never returned. No one would know where she was.

The meager provisions he'd left would soon run out. The bulb would flicker and fail. In the dark she would starve slowly; deprived of her medicine, she would suffer seizures. Eventually she would die.

But first she would surely go insane.

"Don't," she snapped at herself, but the ugly thoughts would not leave her alone.

She sat in her chair and closed her eyes. Willed herself to relax, to go limp. She had done it last night when she was being carried to an unknown fate; she could do it now.

But the stiffness in her neck and shoulders wouldn't abate, and her breathing still came fast and shallow. She was starting to hyperventilate.

*Go away, Erin. Go away to some peaceful spot far from here.*

She had visited San Francisco last year. Muir Woods, northwest of the city, had fascinated her. She hadn't seen such dense stands of trees since her early childhood in California.

Now she pictured herself among the dizzying redwoods, in a place of birdsong and cool shadows and rustling greenery, misty in early morning, the air pregnant with droplets that tingled on her face.

So different from the heat and aridity, the vast spaciousness of the desert. Here in the forest she could see no more than a few yards into the tangled groves. The sun, low over the horizon, was hidden behind thick walls of foliage. Canopied branches shut out the sky, locking the woods in perpetual shade.

Colonnades of tree trunks, scrims of leaves . . . all of it close—too close—hemming her in. The moist air, clogging her lungs. Hard to breathe—

Damn.

She stood, her heart hammering against her ribs.

So much for visualization exercises. What was another strategy to control phobic panic?

Distraction.

She had tried that already, when she cleaned her cell. Hopeful of spotting something else to tidy up, she scanned the floor, but the place was immaculate save for two small rectangular cards lying near her suitcase.

Her driver's license and MasterCard. She'd pocketed them in her robe last night after failing to slip the latch on the door; they must have fallen out when she folded the robe this morning. She picked them up and put them in the side pocket of her shorts.

No other litter to collect, no mess to deal with. No TV or radio to offer a diversion. No reading matter save the file of newspaper clippings, and she hardly expected those to ease her mind.

Nothing, then. Nothing for her to do, except pace and worry, until her abductor returned.

If he ever did.

When she lifted her head to survey the room again, the walls seemed closer than before.

# 17

"I'd like to report a missing person." Annie sat rigid at her desk in the office at the back of her shop, clutching the telephone handset, fighting for calm.

"Adult or juvenile?" the T.P.D. desk sergeant asked with mechanical perfunctoriness.

"Adult. My sister. She—"

"Please hold."

Silence. She stared at a green spray of rhododendron, blooming pink, and hoped she could keep her voice dry of tears.

What time was it, anyway? After three o'clock. Three hours had passed since she'd learned Erin was missing.

*Should have called her last night,* Annie thought. *Should have trusted my intuition. Now it may be too late.*

A murmur of voices bled through the door. Someone in the front room—customer or supplier or delivery person—talking with her assistant. She hoped nothing had come up that required her supervision. There had been enough interruptions as it was.

Since returning from her abortive lunch date, all she had wanted to do was pursue her strategy for finding Erin, carrying out a desperate quest via telephone, but there had been constant distractions.

First, she'd had to sign for a delivery of flowers and greens from a local grower; she made such purchases every day to keep her inventory fresh. Then an importer had called to inquire about her need for exotics. Precious minutes had been wasted talking to him.

At two o'clock a local restaurant, one of her regular customers, had faxed an order for a grand arrangement to serve as a centerpiece at a private dinner party tonight. Though it had been hard to concentrate, she'd had to design the bouquet herself, a complex mingling of spring flowers: azaleas, star magnolias, grape hyacinth, Passionale daffodils, and the quintessential seasonal bloom, the primrose.

Through it all a stream of customers had flowed into the shop, many with requests requiring her personal attention. Ordinarily she would have been happy to hear the cash register ring with such exuberance. Today she had other things on her mind.

"Walker, Detective Division."

The male voice, quietly authoritative, matched her preconception of how a cop should sound.

"Detective? My name is Anne Reilly. I want to report a missing person. My sister, Erin."

"How long has she been missing?"

"Since this morning, at least."

"This morning? That's not a great deal of time. Normally we wait twenty-four hours—"

"No, you can't wait that long. She's in trouble. I . . . I know she is."

*Oh, good, Annie. Very composed. Why not just burst into sobs and throw yourself on his mercy?*

"Take it easy, Ms. Reilly."

She was grateful for his understanding tone. "Call me Annie."

"All right, Annie. I'm Michael. Michael Walker. Now tell me, how old is your sister?"

"My age. Thirty. We're twins."

"Identical twins?"

"No, not identical. We don't even look that much alike. She's tall, I'm short, she's beautiful, I'm not—we're opposites." She realized she was babbling and shut up.

"Is Erin dealing with any personal difficulties that you know of? Depression? Dissatisfaction with her job, her social life?"

"She was feeling fine. I talked to her just yesterday. We made a date for lunch. She never showed up. And she's not in her apartment or her office—"

"What sort of work does she do?"

"She's a psychologist. She's missed all her appointments today. Her car is gone, and nobody knows where she is."

"Have you been to her home?"

"Yes. She's not there."

"Perhaps you could try contacting some of her friends—"

"I've done that. I've been doing it all afternoon. I took her Rolodex with me when I left her apartment building. For three hours I've been on the phone. I called all her friends, her doctor, her dentist, her ophthalmologist, the service station that works on her car, her travel agent, the shelter where she does pro bono work on the weekends, the clinic where she interned, the U. of A. professors she's kept in touch with, the president of the local branch of the American Psychotherapy Association—"

"What about relatives?"

"We don't have any."

"No family at all? Not even out of state?"

"None anyplace."

"I see." Walker sounded uncomfortable, as if sensing he'd raised a painful issue. "Her patients, then?"

"One of her associates at work has been making those calls. It has to be handled delicately—you know, not to alarm these people. They depend on Erin."

"Of course. You realize it's possible she's tried to reach you by phone and couldn't get through. It sounds as if the line has been tied up for hours."

"I'm using my private office line. If she wanted to talk to me, she could call my shop's listed number. Or my message machine at home. She hasn't. I've been checking my messages every fifteen minutes."

"Does Erin have any medical problems?"

"Epilepsy."

"Frequent seizures?"

"No. She takes medication. She hasn't had a seizure since we were teenagers."

Walker hesitated. "There are other possibilities—"

"Like a car accident? I thought of that. Called the Tucson P.D. traffic division right away. Later I tried the highway patrol, the sheriff's department, even the tribal police on the reservations. Nothing."

"Hospitals—"

"Phoned every one in the county. Gave them Erin's name and description. She's not there. She's not *anywhere*."

"All right, Annie. It sounds as if you've been very thorough, but there are a few avenues I can explore before we proceed any further. Give me a description of your sister and the car she was driving. Then let me have ten or fifteen minutes, and I'll get back to you."

Annie supplied the information, left her number with him, and hung up. Immediately she called Erin's apartment again. The message machine answered. She thumbed the phone's reset button, waited for a dial tone, then used the memory feature to call her own home number.

An irritatingly chipper voice—her voice on tape—greeted her.

"Hi, this is Annie. I'm not home right now, so if you're a burglar, I'm in trouble. If you need to leave a message, please wait for the tone and then talk. Bye."

She punched in a two-digit code that activated the playback mechanism. Three beeps answered: no messages.

Annie cradled the phone, then paced the office. Out front, a customer—it sounded like Mrs. Garcia—was saying something about forsythia. Annie thought she really ought to go out and help; Mrs. Garcia was notoriously demanding and it seemed unfair to let her assistant handle the order alone. But she was unwilling to leave the telephone unattended for even a minute, afraid of missing Walker's call . . . or Erin's.

Ten or fifteen minutes, Walker had said. She flipped through Erin's Rolodex, hunting for any likely name she might have overlooked. No, she'd called them all.

It didn't make *sense*. A car accident, a seizure—horrible though it was, an explanation of that kind was comprehensible. But for Erin to simply vanish, car and all, without a word or a trace—

The phone rang. Instantly she snatched it up. "Yes?"

"Walker here. I'm afraid the couple of things I tried didn't pan out either."

"What did you do?"

"Called the supervising officer of the MAC team—that's M-A-C, Mobile Acute Crisis. They respond to reports of disturbed or disoriented individuals. Mostly transients, but sometimes you get a person who's suffered a seizure or a stroke. Anyway, they haven't encountered your sister. Then I tried the city and county jails—"

"The *jails*?" That idea never would have occurred to her.

"Anything can happen. But Erin isn't incarcerated. And you'll be relieved to hear that the coroner's office knows nothing about her either."

"Thank God." The morgue was another possibility she hadn't considered, or perhaps hadn't wanted to consider.

"You said she doesn't suffer from chronic epileptic fits? That it's been years since the last one?"

"That's right."

"She hasn't reported being harassed or stalked?"

"No. Nothing like that."

"And you saw no indication of depression?"

"She was fine, like I told you. What are you saying, anyway? You think she committed suicide?"

"I haven't suggested anything of the kind."

"She isn't suicidal. Erin's tough. A fighter. She always keeps it together, never lets things overwhelm her, get the better of her. Unlike me."

"What's so objectionable about you?"

"I'm not exactly a cool head in a crisis . . . as I guess you've noticed."

"I'd say you've handled yourself exceptionally well. You've done everything I would have done in your place."

The compliment buoyed her, but she couldn't quite bring herself to accept it. "You wouldn't have been fighting back tears the whole time."

He didn't answer that. "You said you looked in Erin's apartment. I take it you've got a key."

"Sure."

"Her place is a rental unit? Manager on duty?"

"Till five-thirty."

"Why don't we meet there? I'd like to check it out for myself. I don't have a warrant, but if your sister gave you free access, and the manager approves—"

"She will. She's as worried as I am. Well, almost."

"Can you get to Erin's place in half an hour?"

"Yes. The address—"

"I already know it. I punched up her D.M.V. file. I'll meet you there at four-fifteen."

Click, and a dial tone buzzed in her ear.

Half an hour would be just enough time to get there. She had to hurry.

Mrs. Garcia had already left when Annie entered the front room. Just as well; Annie had no time for one of the woman's interminable monologues on the health and well-being of her dachshund, Snoops.

Despite her haste and worry, she took a moment's pleasure in the familiar clutter of her shop. It was a small place, what most people would refer to as a hole in the wall—but it was *her* hole in the wall, brought into existence out of her imagination, investment, and work, and she loved it more dearly than anything in her life, except Erin.

Hanging plants in wicker baskets dangled from ceiling hooks, trailing long leafy stems. Barrels of silk flowers and other artificial greenery flanked the counter, setting off displays of dried flowers in bunches and wreathes. In a walk-in cooler along one wall, bouquets and nosegays sprouted from glass and ceramic vases. Scattered around the room, half hidden in a jungle of green, were odd treasures: teddy bears, chocolates, dried fruits, greeting cards.

But what she cherished above all were not silk flowers, not dried flowers, not flowers tucked away in a humidified and refrigerated cabinet, but living blossoms in the open air, fragrant and alluring, inviting every customer to smell and touch. The shop was crowded almost to bursting with blue dwarf asters, sweet violets, orchids, bell-like lilies of the valley, carnations in rainbow assortments, painted daisies, towering stalks of hollyhock. The perfumes of countless blooms mingled in an aromatic medley.

Breathing in those scents, Annie remembered an evening, five years ago, when she had stood outside the storefront in the late summer twilight, gazing up at a gaudy canopy, newly installed. SUNRISE FLOWERS, it said, a reference to the store's location in a suburban shopping plaza on Sunrise Road and, less prosaically, to the wordless sense of hope that always seemed to rise in her with the sun.

Hope had been all she'd had at the beginning, and not very much of it either. From the start she had feared that the enterprise was doomed. Surely she was too much of a scatterbrain to run her own business.

She'd had a plan, though, a way to set her shop apart from the competition. Though she'd offered all the conventional merchandise and services provided by any florist, she had gone a step further by specializing in a variety of exotic plants, hard to find in this part of town.

From the beginning her ads in the newspapers and the Yellow Pages had featured bonsai trees, large-bloom South American roses, and a wide selection of especially beautiful blooms imported from Holland, Japan, and the tropics. None of these items came cheap, and she had worried that she wouldn't attract a sizable clientele willing to pay a premium for quality.

Her worries had proven to be entirely unfounded. Sunrise Flowers had struggled for only a few short months—months that hadn't seemed so short at the time—before word of mouth brought a stream of customers to her door. Though Annie would never be rich, she seemed unlikely to starve. She had made it. She was her own boss, and prospering.

Success had proved infinitely more shocking than failure would have been. Perhaps, she sometimes thought, a guardian angel—one with a firm grasp of accounting principles—was watching over her.

She hoped an angel, or somebody, was watching over Erin right now.

Her assistant, cutting roses and soaking them at a worktable behind the counter, looked up as she came in. "Any news?"

"I've got to go back to her apartment. A police detective is meeting me there."

"A detective . . ."

"Yeah, well, I thought it was time to get the professionals involved. Look, I'm sorry you had to handle Mrs. Garcia on your own."

"She's not so bad. Don't worry about it."

"It's already three forty-five. I'll be involved with this for the rest of the day. Why don't we close up now, and you can deliver the centerpiece to Antonio's?"

"Antonio's doesn't need it till seven. I'll close the shop at six-thirty, as usual, and drop it off on my way home."

She was touched. "You don't have to do all that. I mean, it's beyond the call of duty and everything."

"Just leave me the keys and get going. You've got more important things to do than talk to me."

"Well . . . okay." She dropped the key ring on the counter. "Look, if any other local deliveries come up, use the messenger service. It's better than leaving the place unattended."

"I know, I know."

"And if Euro-Flora calls again, tell them I double-checked the invoice, and I did order tulips."

"Right."

She hesitated. "You're sure it's no problem, running the store by yourself?"

"It's a flower shop, Annie. Not a nuclear reactor. Now go."

"I appreciate this. Really."

As she was turning to leave, he said softly, "She'll be okay. You'll see."

Caring words. She smiled at him.

"Thank you, Harold. Really. Thank you so much."

He nodded, but he did not smile in answer.

That was the funny thing about her assistant.

Harold Gund never smiled.

# 18

Michael Walker hated cases like this.

He glanced at Annie Reilly, standing stiffly at his
side in the elevator of the Pantano Fountains, watching
the numbers change. He had a good idea of what he
would be required to tell her before long.

In his thirteen years with the Tucson P.D., first as a
young uniformed cop fresh from college, then as a detective working robbery-homicide, Walker had fielded
countless missing-person reports. He knew every step
of the dance he and Annie were in the midst of performing . . . and how that dance would end.

He only hoped she would understand. The barely
controlled anxiety that had frozen her in a pose of unnatural rigidity was not cause for optimism.

Unobtrusively he studied Annie's reflection on the
polished inner doors of the elevator. She was slender
and petite, her skin glowing with a light suntan. A pale
green dress accented her eyes and made a pleasing
contrast with her loose red hair.

Standing beside her in the reflected image was a
man in a brown, slightly rumpled suit jacket and a
crooked gray tie, a man with close-cropped sandy hair
the color of desert soil.

People told Michael Walker he looked like a native

Arizonan, a true desert rat. He was long-boned and lean, and he moved with unhurried ease. His face was carved into the flat planes and sharp angles of a movie cowboy's classic features, the skin stretched drum-head-tight over the bones. His unconscious tendency to squint produced a cluster of faint creases at the corners of his eyes.

Though he shaved every morning, by midday a shadow of beard stubble invariably would emerge, becoming obvious by late afternoon. Once aware of this, he had bought a cordless shaver, which he stowed in his desk or car, but on busy days like today, he found no opportunity to use it.

A cowhand, folks thought when they took note of his lanky form and narrowed eyes. One of the originals. Last of a dying breed.

Untrue. He was no great outdoorsman. Didn't even like the desert's summer heat and dryness, tolerated those conditions purely for the sake of the comfortable winters. Born and raised in Chicago, he had suffered through his share of ice storms and blizzards. His intention was never to shovel snow again.

So after four years at Chicago State, he'd moved west, ending up in Tucson. But a cowboy? Horses made him sneeze.

The elevator doors separated. "Her apartment is this way," Annie said eagerly, leading him down the hall.

"Nice building." Walker observed fresh paint on the baseboards, new carpet, polished fixtures. A luxury residential complex in a desirable east-side location. A top-floor unit here wouldn't come cheap. "Your sister seems to be doing quite well."

"Psychology pays. There are a lot of screwed-up people out there. Yours truly being a prime example."

"Do you always put yourself down like that?"

Annie stopped before a closed door and fished a set

of keys out of her purse. "I don't mean to. It's just that I've always felt that Erin and I are sort of a yin and yang. She's everything I'm not, and vice versa. And she's got her head on so straight, mine feels crooked by comparison."

Walker smiled. "Well, it looks okay to me."

Before exploring the apartment, he took a closer look at the front door. There was only one lock, a dead bolt. He saw no scratches on the jamb or faceplate, no indications of tampering.

Following Annie inside, he surveyed a spacious living room, tastefully furnished and exceptionally clean.

"Did your sister leave the lights on?"

"No. That was me. I must've forgotten to turn them off. Maybe I shouldn't have even come here, huh? I might have contaminated the crime scene."

Walker smiled at that. "We don't know if it is a crime scene," he said gently, "or even if there's been a crime."

He circled the room. The furniture and decorations appeared undisturbed. The entertainment center, stocked with expensive electronics, was untouched.

A sliding door framed a balcony. Locked. The glass intact.

Annie watched him expectantly, as if imagining that any moment he would release a shout of triumph and deduce her sister's whereabouts.

No, he was not looking forward to the conversation they would be having in a few minutes. Not at all.

On the mantel was a framed photo portrait: two women, both redheaded, arms around each other's shoulders, laughing at the camera. One was Annie; the other, whom he recognized from her D.M.V. photo, was Erin.

Both were attractive but in different ways. There was an austerity, a cool and level seriousness, to Erin

Reilly, despite her smiling face. Annie, by contrast, appeared mischievous, playful, something of a rascal.

Walker had seen her smile only in this photo. A pleasant smile. He remembered her saying that Erin was beautiful and she herself was not. He disagreed.

"That's us," Annie said, stepping to his side.

"Was it taken recently?"

"Last November. Around Thanksgiving. I remember we posed for it at lunchtime. The photographer kept coming on to us, and we pretended to be interested. We were in . . . kind of a silly mood. . . ."

Her voice trailed off as she came back to the present: the empty apartment, the missed appointments, Erin gone.

In the den, Walker found a potted schefflera, shelves of psychology books and periodicals, a computer and laser printer. There were no printouts in the tray.

"Does she use the computer exclusively for business?" he asked Annie, who stood attentively in the doorway. It occurred to him that he sounded like an IRS agent.

"Mostly. She keeps a journal on it, though."

"A personal journal?"

"I think so. I'm not really sure, actually."

"Well, you might want to consider booting it up. Not now—when you're alone. There could be some clue to her state of mind."

"State of mind? You mean you think she ran off on her own? Voluntarily?"

"People do."

"Not Erin."

It was too soon to be talking about this. Walker didn't press the point.

The bathroom was clean and scrubbed. "Her towels are dry," Annie said from her vantage point in the hall. "The shower too."

Walker had observed both details. He was more interested in the medicine cabinet. Two of the glass shelves were nearly empty. From what was left, he could make a good guess as to which items had been taken: toothbrush, toothpaste, comb, hairbrush, deodorant.

Not things a burglar would want. But Erin Reilly would take them if she were going on a trip.

On the top shelf, among the aspirin and the cold remedies, was a bottle of pills labeled TEGRETOL. He showed it to Annie. "Erin's epilepsy medicine?"

"Yes. That's what she takes."

"I'm surprised she doesn't carry it with her."

"I thought she did. In her purse. Maybe this is an extra bottle."

He checked the label again, then replaced the pills on the shelf. "Yes, it's a recent refill of her prescription. She probably hasn't run out of the previous batch yet."

Bedroom next. The bed was unmade, sheets sagging in broken ridges like a cake's melted icing. Nothing damaged, no sign of a struggle.

The jewelry box on the dresser was still crammed with necklaces and earrings. Two hundred dollars in emergency cash remained in the most obvious, even proverbial, of hiding places: the sock drawer. Her wristwatch lay on the nightstand.

"I hadn't noticed that," Annie said when Walker pointed it out.

"Does she have another watch?"

Annie stared at the small gold-plated Armitron. "Not that I know of. And she *always* wears a watch whenever she goes anywhere. She's ... she's very punctual."

Walker digested this information without comment.

The windows were shut. Heat pressed against the panes. The locks had not been forced.

Last, he checked the closet. Empty hangers, many of them. Nothing in the laundry basket.

Slowly he nodded.

Annie observed the brief incline of his head and was instantly alongside him. "Find something?"

He saw it in her face, in the wide green eyes and pursed lips—the desperate hopefulness, the intense need for answers.

This was when she expected him to make his brilliant deduction, prove his criminalistic skills. *Do you see this speck of dust, Annie? It's found only in the forests of southern Romania—thus proving that your sister was kidnapped by Gypsies.*

Something like that.

He didn't answer at once. He took a moment to peer into the back of the closet, where two items of luggage were stored. A carry-on bag and a large suitcase. There was a space between them where another suitcase, apparently of intermediate size, had stood.

"How familiar are you with Erin's wardrobe?" he asked.

"We trade clothes all the time."

"Can you take a look at what's here and get some idea of which items, if any, are missing?"

Annie registered disappointment. This was hardly the stunning breakthrough she'd anticipated. "Sure. I can do that."

He waited while she took inventory.

"As best I can tell," she said finally, "three outfits are missing." Puzzlement had replaced worry in her expression for the first time.

"Items suitable for spring?"

"Two skirts and, I think, a pair of shorts. Three

blouses, all short-sleeve. Oh, and a pair of boots. I don't see her robe either."

"Pajamas? Slippers?"

"She's got several pair of each. I can't be sure."

"Some things were taken from the bathroom also. Toothbrush, comb—toiletries. And there's a suitcase missing from her luggage set."

Annie sat on the bed, her features suddenly slack. "You're saying she packed a bag and left."

"Looks like it."

The slow shaking of her head was oddly mechanical, a robot's programmed routine. "She couldn't. She wouldn't. I mean—it's not like her at all."

He stood near the bed, looking down on her, the red curls thick on her shoulders, her hands steepled in her lap. "In my experience," he said, "no matter how well we think we know someone, there's always a surprise lurking somewhere."

"Not this kind of surprise. Not with Erin."

"I'm sorry, Annie. But everything points to the conclusion that your sister went away on an unscheduled trip."

"Without telling me—or anyone? Without even leaving a note?"

"It happens."

"But she didn't take her Tegretol. Or her watch."

"She probably has enough of the medicine left from the last refill of her prescription. As for the watch ... Maybe she bought a new one you don't know about. Or maybe she just forgot. Or she wants to get away from schedules and deadlines for a while."

"Schedules and deadlines are her *life*." He heard despair in her voice.

Walker hesitated, then sat beside her. The mattress springs creaked, and the Smith .38 in his armpit holster rubbed against his ribs.

"Maybe," he said slowly, "she needs a temporary break from her life. All of us do now and then."

"She flipped out? *Erin?*"

"That's putting it a little strong. Look, Annie, it sounds to me as if your sister subjects herself to a lot of pressure. A place for everything and everything in its place. Never late for an appointment, never irresponsible, never out of control. It's hard to maintain that kind of discipline day after day."

"Not for her. That's just the way she is."

"Then there's this to consider. She's a psychologist. The mental-health professions have among the highest rates of"—*suicide,* he nearly said, but checked himself—"burnout. Dealing with other people's problems all day can get pretty grim. Erin simply may have needed some time off."

Annie looked at him, and he saw stripes of wetness on her cheeks. "I talked to her on the phone yesterday. We made a lunch date. She didn't sound depressed or overworked or stressed out. She was fine."

"You don't know what she might have been hiding."

"We don't hide stuff from each other."

"Everybody hides something."

"Not us." Anger flashed in her eyes. He thought of gemstones catching the light. "We're close. We've always been. Ever since . . ."

The spark died then, and her eyes were glassy and cold.

"Since . . . ?" Walker prompted.

She gazed at her restless hands. "Since we were seven years old. We lost our parents, you see. We were orphaned together."

Gently he touched her arm. "How did that happen?"

"Fire." The word a whisper.

He didn't know what to say. The question that came

out of his mouth was safely factual and meaningless. "Was this in Tucson?"

"No, in California. Small town called Sierra Springs, where we were born. We moved to Tucson after the fire. Our aunt adopted us. Aunt Lydia."

"Your mother's sister?"

"Yes. She lived here in town."

He picked up on the singular pronoun. "Alone? No husband?"

Her gaze ticked toward him, then away. "Lydia's husband . . . died." Peculiar hesitation there. "Years before. So Lydia had to raise us on her own. She worked two jobs. It was rough on her."

On her. Walker almost smiled at the way she put it. "I'd say you and Erin were the ones who really had it rough."

"Yeah, well . . . it was a long time ago."

The unnatural pause in her statement about Lydia's husband intrigued him. *Lydia,* he thought. *Lydia what?*

"Did you take your aunt's last name?" he asked casually.

"No. Reilly was our father's name. Albert Reilly. We wanted to keep it. Even though . . . I mean . . ." She swallowed. "We just wanted to keep his name, that's all."

Defensiveness in her tone, which he didn't understand.

"Our aunt was Lydia Connor," she added. "You might have heard of her."

He frowned. "I don't think so. What makes you say that?"

"Just because . . . Well, she was local, you know. Lots of people knew her." Evasiveness now. Strange.

"I take it your aunt is no longer living."

Annie blinked. "She passed away six years ago. Cancer. How did you know?"

"You told me on the phone that you had no family."

"Oh. That's right. No family . . . except Erin. She's all I've got left." She brushed a wisp of hair from her forehead and fixed him with her green gaze. "You're not going to help me, are you, Detective?"

"Michael."

She would not be charmed. "You haven't answered my question . . . Michael."

Here was the bad part. The words he hated having to say.

"Let me explain the situation," he began slowly. "In order for Tucson P.D. to initiate an investigation of a missing adult, certain requirements have to be met." He disliked talking this way, as if quoting from the rules-and-procedures manual. "If the person is believed to be mentally unstable, or is elderly and easily confused, then we have a basis for pursuing the matter. Or if there's some evidence of foul play or suicide or accident." He showed her his hands, palms out. "In other words, there has to be a justification for the use of police resources."

Frustration smoldered in her face, rising slowly to a white heat of fury. "And in this case there isn't?"

"I don't see any reason to suspect that a crime has been committed or is likely to be. It's not illegal for an adult to pack up and leave town. It may be irresponsible, inexplicable, but it's not a crime."

"Damn it, she's *disappeared*!"

Abruptly she was on her feet, glaring down at him from a sudden advantage of height. Her small hands were balled into fists at her sides, the knuckles squeezed white.

"I *told* you Erin isn't irresponsible or impulsive or emotional. *I'm* the emotional one, for God's sake. I get moods, I get crazy—but *not Erin*. She'd *never* walk out on her patients or . . . or on me."

Her rage died with the last words. As she turned her back to him, he saw fresh tears tracking down her face.

He rose, put a comforting hand on her shoulder. She was a small woman, perhaps five foot two; at five-eleven he all but towered over her. But there was strength in her, wiry strength in her thin, sinewy arms, and a nervous tension that held her body stiffly upright even now, in this storm of feeling.

He watched her face, blushing with the shame of un-censored emotions, and her hands, fingers interlocked and twisting, knuckles and tendons rippling under the smooth, taut, lightly freckled skin—he watched, and he wished for something to say, some reassurance he could give.

Then, looking at him from behind a skein of mussed hair, she whispered, "Please, isn't there *anything* you can do?"

He hesitated, avoiding her gaze like a coward. "Officially . . . no."

"But unofficially?"

His caseload was crowded enough as it was. This woman, Erin Reilly, obviously had left of her own vo-lition. Ridiculous for him to offer any assistance—certainly not this soon, when less than twenty-four hours had passed.

But Annie was still watching him, the anguish in her eyes not easy to look at.

"Unofficially," Walker said quietly, both angry and amused at himself for softening his resolve, "I can do a little more. Not much. But a few things."

"Like what?"

"I can contact airport security, have them look for her car in the parking lots. It she left it there, we know she took a flight out of town. Same with the bus and railroad stations."

"What else?"

Walker gave her credit for persistence. "Does she have any favorite places to visit, any particular hotels she likes?"

Annie thought hard. "She goes to conferences in Phoenix fairly often. Stays at the Crown Sterling up there. And she went to San Francisco last year. What hotel was it? The Fairmont. She said she wanted to go back someday."

"The clothes she packed were a little skimpy for San Francisco in April, but it's a possibility. Any chance she would return to the town where you grew up? Sierra Springs?"

"I doubt it. Wouldn't be hard to check, though. There's only one motel there. The Sierra Springs Inn on Route Forty-nine."

"I'll fax Erin's D.M.V. photo to all three places."

"Can you put out an A.P.B. on her?"

"I'm afraid not. She isn't wanted for anything. As I said, leaving town's not illegal."

Annie frowned. "It ought to be."

Walker squeezed her arm. "Later, if she doesn't contact you or resurface within a reasonable time period—say, forty-eight hours—there might be more I can do. Start tracking her credit card purchases, for one thing. That may lead us right to her."

"Or to whoever's using her cards."

"There's no reason to keep assuming the worst. Your sister will be fine. You'll probably hear from her soon. For all we know, she may have called your office within the last hour to explain."

"I don't think she *can* call. And I don't believe she left of her own free will."

"Then somebody went to a lot of trouble to make it appear that way."

"Yes." Annie's face was grim. "Somebody did."

Walker knew of nothing he could say to that.

# 19

Erin was opening a can of tuna fish for dinner when the idea came to her.

Slowly she disengaged the manual opener from the rim of the can and lifted it toward the light. The cutting blade was sharp. It could serve as a file.

Last night she'd concluded that her only hope of defeating the bolt on the cellar door was to pry it open with an ice pick or similar tool. Now she wondered if she could make what she needed.

Rummaging in her suitcase, she found her comb. Eight inches long, with a hard plastic spine the color of tortoiseshell.

Might work. Just might.

Did she dare try it now? She still had no clear idea of the time, but to judge by her appetite, it must be at least seven o'clock.

Her abductor had said he would be back in the evening. He could return at any moment.

Or not for hours. Or not at all.

Risk it.

Gund arrived at Erin's apartment building at 7:15.

He'd closed the flower shop forty-five minutes earlier, dropped off the floral centerpiece at Antonio's

Restaurant, then grabbed a fast-food meal at a drive-through window. Eating as he drove, he'd headed south to Broadway, then east toward the edge of town.

The ranch wasn't far. He would get there by eight at the latest. But first he had to retrieve Erin's epilepsy medicine.

He parked the van and got out. Briskly he walked to the lobby door, the same door Erin had buzzed open last night. Her own keys let him in this time.

The lobby was empty. He ducked into the stairwell and hurried up the four flights of stairs, encountering nobody along the way.

On the top floor he peered into the corridor and saw a man in a business suit unlocking an apartment door. Gund waited until the hall was empty, then left the stairwell and proceeded directly to Erin's apartment.

Key in the hole, twist of the knob, and the door swung open.

The living room lights were on. Annie must have neglected to turn them off.

Unless—disturbing thought—unless she was still here. But she couldn't be. Her meeting with the police detective had been scheduled for 4:15. It couldn't possibly have lasted three hours.

Even so, he paused in the doorway, listening for voices within the apartment.

Silence.

Down the hall the elevator pinged, signaling someone's arrival. The noise prodded him into the apartment. Softly he shut the door.

Safe. And unobserved so far.

Now just get the medicine and depart.

Despite his haste, residual caution made him pad quietly through the living room to the apartment's interior hallway. To his right were Erin's bedroom and, next to it, the den.

He froze.

In the den—Annie.

She sat at Erin's desk, hunched over the computer keyboard, reading text on the amber monitor.

Her back was turned to him. She hadn't seen or heard him yet, didn't suspect she was not alone.

But if she did discover him . . .

No way he could talk his way out of it. He would have to kill her.

His pistol and stun gun were in the van. But he could do the job with his bare hands. Grasp her by the chin and give her head a swift sideways yank—

He could almost hear the crackle of snapping bone.

No. It wouldn't come to that.

All he had to do was get what he'd come for and leave. Annie would never know he'd been here.

The bathroom was to his left. He crept inside, grateful that the overhead light had been left on. Soundlessly he eased open the mirrored door of the medicine cabinet and scanned the shelves.

There. Top shelf. Small plastic bottle, white label.

Leaning against the counter, he reached up and closed his fist over the bottle.

Tegretol. Two hundred milligrams.

He pocketed it, turned toward the hall, and from the den there came the sound of a footstep.

Annie shut off the computer and stood. Pain jabbed her temples; stress and fatigue had brought on a headache.

Long after Walker's departure, she had lingered in Erin's apartment.

No reason to stay, except she'd felt a desperate need to be close to her sister. Pointlessly she had wandered through the neat, uncluttered rooms, touching the walls, reading the titles of books on the shelves, smiling briefly as she fingered a carved ironwood turtle she'd given Erin as a birthday present a few years ago. The smile had seemed to hurt her mouth; she'd found herself biting her lip as if in pain.

"Erin," she'd said to the lonely space around her, "where *are* you?"

The ticking of a clock had been the only reply.

In the den she'd noticed Erin's computer, the keypad covered by a dust shield. Erin kept a journal on the hard disk. Walker had recommended reading it for clues to her state of mind.

A waste of time, most likely; still, no option could be overlooked. And Annie had known of nothing else to do.

Sitting at the desk, she'd booted up the word processing software. With a vague feeling of guilt about invading her sister's privacy, she'd begun to read the journal. The earliest entries were dated two years ago; the file was forty pages long.

She'd assumed the journal was personal, but quickly discovered she'd been wrong. It was concerned almost exclusively with the progress of Erin's patients. Little about her private life was included.

Even so, Annie had read it all. She'd sat there staring at the amber monitor for two hours. And she'd learned nothing.

In Erin's notes there had been no hint of any intention to stop work or leave town. Quite the contrary, in fact. The last entry, dated April 16, had concluded: *Tony still resisting; try sentence-completion Wed.*

Wednesday was tomorrow.

No, Erin hadn't been planning to abandon her patients. But Annie had already known that.

Grimacing, she rubbed her forehead.

Aspirin. She needed aspirin. Major headache coming on.

Wearily she wandered down the hall, into the bathroom.

The door to the medicine cabinet hung open. Funny. She thought she remembered Walker closing it.

She looked inside. Allergy pills, antacid tablets, antibacterial ointments . . .

Then she frowned, suddenly alert, headache and exhaustion forgotten.

Where was the Tegretol?

The new refill of Erin's prescription had been kept on the upper shelf. Walker had studied it, then put it back—and now it was gone.

But it couldn't be gone.

Had Walker only pretended to replace the bottle? Had he taken it for some reason? No, ridiculous. Removing property from the premises without permission must be illegal. Anyway, why would he want it?

She looked through all the items on every shelf of the cabinet. No Tegretol.

The bottle had disappeared. And the cabinet had been left open. . . .

As if someone had been here. As if someone had taken the pills.

Crazy thought. She'd been in the apartment the whole time. Nobody could have broken in without her hearing it.

But maybe there'd been no need to break in. Maybe the intruder had used Erin's keys.

Maybe it had been Erin herself.

No, impossible, unthinkable. She was imagining all this. Of course she was.

Yet even as she told herself as much, her gaze crept to the far end of the bathroom, to the shower stall and the blue shower curtain hanging limply from the rod.

The curtain was translucent, but the glow of the ceil-

ing light barely reached into the stall. Someone could
be hidden behind it.

And suddenly she felt with unnatural certainty that
someone was.

"Erin?" she whispered. "Erin, are you there?"

She took a step toward the curtain.

Every instinct shouted at her not to touch it, not to
draw it back and expose whatever—whoever—might
be concealed on the other side.

Another step. She was within reach of the blue
plastic folds.

Her hand closed over the edge of the curtain.

*Don't,* a panicky internal voice warned.

A jerk of her shoulder, and she threw aside the curtain.

Hooks scraped noisily on the rod. The curtain accor-
dioned against the tiled wall.

No one was there.

Annie exhaled a slow sigh.

Nerves. That was all it had been. Just nerves getting
the better of her.

She turned away from the shower, then glanced back
to reassure herself that it was empty. A soft chuckle
briefly startled her before she recognized it as her own.

Nobody had come here to steal the Tegretol. The
stuff was missing for some perfectly ordinary reason.
Perhaps it simply had fallen off the shelf to the floor,
then rolled out of sight.

She stooped, looking under the sink and behind the
door.

Nothing.

But in a corner a blue-green sparkle caught her attention. A small turquoise stone, catching the light of
the overhead lamp.

The stone bothered Annie, though she wasn't sure
why. She picked it up, studying it with a frown.

Then she realized what was troubling her. Erin never wore turquoise. Disliked it intensely, in fact. Always had, ever since childhood, despite the gem's ubiquity in Arizona.

So what was it doing here?

Well, other people had used the bathroom. Friends, neighbors, anyone who'd dropped by for a visit. Presumably one of them had lost the stone, which might easily have fallen free of a gem-inlaid boot or purse.

The missing Tegretol was a mystery, but in all likelihood the turquoise was of no significance at all.

Even so, before leaving the apartment, Annie wrapped the stone carefully in a tissue and put it in her purse.

# 20

Gund didn't relax until he had pulled out of the parking lot onto Broadway. When Erin's apartment building shrank to nothingness in his sideview mirror, he began to breathe normally again.

He had avoided an encounter with Annie by a dangerously thin margin. If he hadn't heard movement in the den and left the bathroom immediately, ducking into the living room with a heartbeat to spare, she would have come face to face with him.

And now she would be dead.

His grip on the steering wheel tightened. He pictured himself squeezing her slender neck. Choking, strangling . . .

Bad thought. He didn't want to kill her. Didn't want either of them—Annie or her sister—to die. Of course he didn't.

Of course.

At Houghton Road he hooked south, heading for the ranch.

It took Erin a half hour, by her estimate, to make the tool she needed.

Carefully she had cracked off the fine teeth at the

narrow end of the comb until that part of the spine had been stripped naked, a spindly, mangled finger.

Then, rubbing the comb against the can opener's blade, back and forth, back and forth, she had scraped away layers of plastic. Tortoiseshell shavings had accumulated on the floor.

The thought had occurred to her that a witness to her behavior would conclude that she'd lost it. *Poor thing,* a sympathetic voice had clucked in her mind, *she's cracked under the strain.*

There was method to her madness, though. At least she hoped there was.

After two hundred strokes the comb's narrow end was as sleekly tapered as a stiletto, its tip nearly as keen.

Not an ice pick. But close.

She wondered if she still had time to use it. Maybe safer to wait until after her abductor had come and gone.

But she was only guessing at the time, after all. It might be hours earlier than she imagined.

Before proceeding, she took a moment to swallow her last Tegretol. The bottle was empty now. If her abductor didn't return and she was unable to break free, then within twenty-four hours the first withdrawal symptoms would develop. Status epilepticus. A bad way to die.

Quickly to the door, heart drumming.

The doorframe had warped slightly with age, leaving considerable clearance between the door and the jamb. Erin inserted the modified end of the comb into the crack, pressing its sharpened tip against the side of the bolt at the point where the small movable bar sank into the socket in the striker plate.

The comb slipped off the bolt the first time she levered it sideways. No good. Maybe if she held it in place with one hand while manipulating it with the other . . .

That did the trick. She only wished her hands weren't so damp, and that they would stop trembling.

She could do it, could bust out of this joint, run away before her jailer returned.

Smiling fiercely, she imagined his shock at being outwitted, his rage at having failed in this ultimate test of control.

"Very sorry, sir," she whispered in the tone of an efficient receptionist as she began prying at the bolt. "I'm afraid the doctor is *not* in."

For some reason this struck her as much funnier than it was, hilarious even. She giggled, soft, manic laughter rising from her throat, until she realized she was displaying symptoms of incipient hysteria.

"Cut it out," she ordered, focusing her undivided attention on the job at hand.

She worked the comb left, right, left, right. It flexed with each twist of her arm, each calculated increase in pressure, but it did not break. The plastic spine seemed sturdy enough to withstand the demands she was making.

*There.*

The bolt had moved. She'd felt it. She was sure she had.

An inconsequential victory, a slippage of the bar that could amount to no more than a trivial fraction of an inch, but it was something, anyway.

And the bar had not jerked back. That meant it was a dead bolt, not a spring latch. Good. Had the bolt rested on springs, it would have fought her every step of the way.

This was going to happen, she realized with a surge of exhilaration so intense as to be almost disorienting.

She was Houdini, she was Papillon; no locked cell could hold her.

She wedged the tip of the comb in deeper—it definitely was finding purchase now—and wrenched the tool sideways.

Again.

Again.

With a faint muffled rasp, the bolt retracted another hairbreadth.

She'd almost gotten it. She was nearly free.

The tip of the comb scrabbled eagerly, desperately.

Sweat, beading on her eyelashes, dripped onto the bridge of her nose. A muscle in her neck twitched, taut with nervous tension.

Just a little more. Another quarter of an inch to go. That wasn't asking so much, was it? A lousy quarter inch . . .

From the bolt, a thin squeal of complaint, as welcome to her ears as a newborn's first squalling cry.

Good God, she'd done it, done it, *done it.*

Triumph thrilled her. She knew, even before squinting through the crack for confirmation, that she had pried it completely out of the socket.

The door was unlocked.

All she had to do now was ease it open, not a simple task when there was no doorknob on her side. With her fingertips she gripped the edge of the door and tugged.

The damn thing was heavy—solid mahogany—and inertia held it motionless for a long, frustrating moment.

It seemed unnecessarily cruel for anything to impede her progress now. In a more benevolent world the door would have opened by magic as soon as the bolt was retracted.

Of course, in a more benevolent world she wouldn't have been held prisoner in the first place.

She pulled harder. With a reluctant sigh of hinges, the door yielded.

Slowly it swung inward under her hands . . . halfway clear of the jamb now . . . completely clear . . . a half inch of space between door and frame—

It stopped.

Though she pulled desperately, the door would open no farther.

Crouching, she peered through the narrow aperture, and her heart twisted.

A chain. Her abductor had installed a security chain.

"Damn it," she whispered. "Oh, damn it, that's not *fair*."

The chain links, heavy and thick, would challenge even a good-sized bolt cutter. No way she could hope to snap them.

She curled both hands around the edge of the door and yanked at it. If the screws securing the chain weren't imbedded too deeply, she might be able to jar them loose.

After straining every muscle in her arms and shoulders, she concluded that the screws were fastened immovably to the wood.

Defeat the chain, then. There had to be a way. If she—

Outside, the rumble of an engine.

She recognized that sound. The motor of the van or truck that had transported her here.

He was back.

*Oh, Jesus, close the door, close the door!*

She closed it, but the bolt was still retracted. He was certain to notice that.

The engine was silent now. The vehicle had been parked.

She jabbed the narrow end of the comb into the clearance between the door and jamb. Pried at the bolt, trying to reverse what she'd done a minute ago, dig the bar out of the faceplate and insert it in the jamb socket again.

Upstairs, the creak of a door.

Footsteps on the ceiling.

The bolt slid partway out of the latch assembly, but still it was not engaged in the socket.

The footsteps now directly above her.

She pressed harder. The spine of the comb curved.

*Thump-thump-thump:* she heard him descending the cellar stairs.

Frantically she levered the comb, the pointed tip scratching like an agitated pencil. The bolt eased forward another fraction of an inch, just enough to sink into the socket in the striker plate . . .

And the comb snapped.

Its narrow end, broken off, slid down the crack, disappearing under the door, out of reach.

A double thud of footfalls. He was in the cellar, approaching the door.

Just in time she remembered the peephole.

She pushed herself upright and retreated to the rear of her cell.

The single percussive beat startled her. She needed a second to identify it as the rap of his hand on the door.

"I'm back, Doc." The familiar raspy voice, muffled by two inches of solid mahogany.

Half of the comb was still in her hand. As casually as possible, she turned slightly, concealing it from his view. "I heard." Her voice was steady, betraying nothing.

"Put on the blindfold."

"Yes. Of course."

She leaned over the cardboard box and made a show of rummaging through it as she hid the comb inside.

Her gaze traveled from the box to the floor nearby,

where there was a small, telltale pile of tortoiseshell shavings.

"Can't you find it?" he demanded.

"Yes. Yes, here it is."

She took out the blindfold, then stepped away from the box. With a nonchalant scuff of her shoe she scattered the shavings.

One problem taken care of.

But when he opened the door . . .

Her heart kept up a frantic staccato rhythm. The palsied shaking of her hands made it difficult to knot the blindfold in place.

When he opened the door, he might see it. The piece of the comb under there.

Impossible for her to explain away the tool as anything innocent. If he noticed it, she was dead.

"Hurry up," he ordered.

Quickly she finished fastening the cloth over her eyes. She groped for the chair, found it, and sat.

"Ready," she called. The chilly finger tickling the base of her spine was a trickle of sweat.

Rattle: a key. Clunk of the bolt retracting. Rasp of hinges.

Footsteps in the room.

The chair opposite hers scraped the floor, then protested as he sat.

He hadn't seen the comb. Thank God.

She might live a little longer, then.

She'd lost her best chance of escape and broken the tool that had made it possible, broken it probably beyond repair, but at least, this night, she wouldn't burn.

"Excited, Doc?" he asked softly.

"What makes you say that?"

"You seem . . . on edge."

"I'm always a little tense when I'm working." The

lie came fluently. "That *is* why you're here, isn't it? To start our work together?"

"Of course it is." His chair creaked as he leaned forward. "As of this moment, Doc, our first session has officially begun."

# 21

*Our first session.* The words stirred a cold queasiness in the pit of her stomach.

She wished she could see the man before her, read his face. Difficult to analyze him without the nonverbal clues that often spoke louder than even the most candid testimony.

Well, she would manage. Would have to.

With effort she forced her mind into clear focus. He would judge her skills by her performance in this encounter. If she was found wanting, she might not get a second chance.

"All right," she said slowly. "I've read the newspaper stories you left me. I'd like to discuss what it was like for you when you did those things. What you were feeling each time you . . . kidnapped a woman."

"Burned one, you mean. Kidnapping was merely an unavoidable preliminary."

"Burned one. Yes."

"Don't be afraid to speak plainly. I can take it."

He sounded relaxed, almost cheerful. That state of mind was unlikely to last.

Therapy was not fun. Though it might seem like a game in the beginning, it quickly turned serious and, often, uncomfortable. Her style of analysis was aggressive, probing; to save time, to compress months of work into hours, she made intuitive leaps and challenged the patient to keep up. It was a method that got results, but it didn't always make for restful exchanges.

She wondered how he would react when the first nerve was struck.

"I'll try to refrain from euphemisms in the future," she promised. "Now tell me about this compulsion to kill. Does it come on gradually or all of a sudden?"

"Gradually."

"How does it start?"

"With physical sensations. Coldness in my fingers. Heat at the back of my neck."

"Do your fingers get numb?"

"No. They tingle."

"Painful?"

"Disturbing, that's all."

"Any other symptoms?"

"Sometimes . . . I hear a sort of chiming. Distant. Like ringing in the ears but more elusive. Hard to describe."

She frowned. The symptoms he'd described were suggestive of the aura phase that marked the onset of an epileptic seizure. She'd experienced similar reactions in childhood.

The notion that an epileptic might imitate Frankenstein's monster, blindly wrapping his hands around a terrified maiden's throat, was an irresponsible myth. But in the case of a profoundly disturbed individual, someone already showing homicidal tendencies, a prolonged status seizure of the partial or focal type—a fugue state—might permit his suppressed aggressive feelings to rise uncensored to the surface.

It was possible. But she didn't intend to raise that hypothesis with him, at least not yet. If he believed that a pill could cure all his problems, he wouldn't need her anymore.

"Other than physical sensations," she asked, "are there any other feelings—emotions, moods—that you associate with the murders?"

For the first time he hesitated. She heard a series of soft pops and realized he was cracking his knuckles.

"I don't feel anything when I do it," he said at last.

"No emotions at all?"

"None."

"Any special dreams?"

"No."

"Do you ever dream? At any time?"

"I . . . Sometimes."

"Erotic dreams?"

His chair squeaked with a shift of his weight. "I knew you'd get to that."

"To what?"

"Sex. And dreams. They're unavoidable, aren't they?"

She didn't respond directly. "Tell me about your dreams."

"They're erotic, like you said."

"In what way?"

He cleared his throat. "Nothing special. I mean . . . they're dreams, that's all."

His first apparent resistance. Briefly she considered backing away from this subject if it was agitating him. But under other circumstances she would never do that. When the patient showed discomfort, that was the time to drill deeper, penetrate to the root of the problem.

If she didn't use the techniques that worked for her, if she didn't allow herself to function as a therapist, she would guarantee her own ineffectiveness. And the man before her already had made clear what he would do to her if she didn't get results.

Probe, then. Push.

"You seem reluctant to talk about this," she said carefully.

"I don't see that it's relevant."

She ignored that. "What's your role in the dreams? What do you see yourself doing?"

"I don't do anything. I just ... watch."

"What are you watching?"

"Not what. Who."

"A woman?"

He flared up. "Of *course* a woman. What are you implying?"

"I'm not implying anything."

"I don't want to talk about the goddamn dreams, anyway. I already told you they're not relevant. They have no significance, none at all."

Abruptly she had an insight into him, an insight born at the gut level where the best analysis was done, and though she knew she shouldn't press him further, something within her would not let the thought die unspoken.

"You hate it," she said quietly. "You hate the feeling of arousal, of sexual need. Don't you?"

A short silence. When he spoke, his voice was small, muted. "It's ... *sick.*"

"What makes you say that?" No reply. "Everybody has sexual feelings, you know."

"This isn't what I want to talk about."

"It may be related to your problem—"

"It's not. I told you, I don't feel anything when I kill. It's not sexual. Not sadism. I don't do it for pleasure, any kind of pleasure. I *told* you all that. So just change the subject."

"I still think we need to understand—"

*"Change the subject!"*

The lion cough of his command froze her. For a bad moment she was certain she'd pushed too hard. She sat motionless, listening to his hard, steady breathing above the throb of her own heart.

"Change the subject, Doc," he said at last, his voice flattened into a dangerous monotone.

"All right," she answered evenly. "Let's talk about the killings themselves."

The pattern of the murders clearly reflected a subconscious obsession at the heart of his psychosis. Comparable examples were familiar to her: the man who compulsively washes his hands because he harbors a secret guilt that makes him feel unclean; the woman forever double-checking the locks on her doors, motivated by buried memories of a molesting parent's midnight visits to her bedroom.

"All three of your victims were young Caucasians."

"True." The faint tapping sound was the nervous drumming of his fingers on the side of his chair.

"Why did you pick those particular women?"

"No special reason."

"There wasn't anything that drew you to them; it was totally random. Is that what you're saying?"

"Well, what do *you* think, Doc? What's your brilliant theory?"

He was still exhibiting hostility. She wasn't sure how much she ought to say.

"I don't have a theory." She picked her words with care. "But I wondered if there might be someone in your past, someone you were thinking of when you cruised the streets."

"You mean my long-lost fiancée, the one who jilted me at the altar when I was eighteen and left me emotionally scarred for life? Sorry, Doc, only kidding.

Afraid I can't wrap it up that neatly for you." His jocular tone was obviously defensive.

"Perhaps it's some other feature of those women that you focused on," she said. "Let's take the first one, Marilyn Vaccaro. She was Italian, dark-haired, dark-eyed—"

"So?"

"Would that description fit a woman who means something to you? A girlfriend, a sister? Your mother?"

"Ah, the other shoe drops. The mother complex. Sex, dreams, and mama—the basic ingredients in every Freudian recipe."

Humor again, stiff and forced. Clearly it was a defense mechanism characteristic of him.

She would not be put off. "*Was* your mother dark-eyed? Dark-haired?"

"No on both counts. Her eyes were blue. As for her hair, it was red—just like yours, Doc."

Blue eyes, red hair. Erin saw it then. The link between the first of his victims and his past. "Was your mother Irish?"

In his startled silence she heard the answer he didn't want to give.

"Catholic?" she pressed.

This time he spoke, his reply drawn out of him with painful slowness. "Yes."

"Marilyn Vaccaro was kidnapped after attending a midnight church service." He said nothing. "If you saw her leave that church, you must have known she was Catholic. That's why you chose her, isn't it?"

"I . . . don't know."

"I think you do."

"No, I mean . . . It wasn't a conscious decision on my part. I never realized . . ."

He sounded genuinely astonished to have discovered this unsuspected facet of himself.

"Do you realize it now?"

"Yes. *Yes.*"

"Why do you suppose you focused on her religion?"

"I can't say. Really."

"Do you have something against Catholics?" No response. "Do you?"

"Why would I?"

"You tell me."

"I've got nothing against them." He coughed, a nervous sound.

"Don't hide things from me, please. Not if you want my help." He wouldn't speak. "I'm Catholic, you know. Irish Catholic, like your mother. Did you pick me for that reason?"

"No. No, it was those articles you wrote, the ones on fire starters."

She wouldn't be sidetracked. "Are you a practicing Catholic?"

"Of course not."

"Why of course?"

"I just . . . I could never accept it. An afterlife. Eternal punishment."

Punishment again. The idea that had set him off last time. Plausible enough that he would hate and fear a religion that held out the prospect of damnation for his sins. But somehow his answer struck her as too facile.

"What else do you object to about the Catholic faith?"

"I don't know. I haven't thought about it. I'm not a theologian."

"You don't need to be a theologian in order to have an opinion. Did your mother raise you as a Catholic?"

"Yes."

"You must have learned some tenets of the religion. What turned you off?"

"It's crap," he said with sudden vehemence. "All of it—everything they believe."

"What about it is crap?"

"All of it, I said."

"What, specifically?"

"Abortion." The word was blurted out, and she knew she'd penetrated to the heart of the matter.

"The church doesn't permit abortion," she said quietly.

"No."

"And it ought to?"

"Yes."

"Why?"

"Some people shouldn't be born."

His answer chilled her.

"Like you?" she whispered.

"I didn't say that."

"Do you wish your mother had aborted you?"

*"I didn't say that!"*

Perilous to ride him any harder, but she had to. She couldn't let it go.

"Do you hate her," she asked with quiet insistence, "for bringing you into the world? Is that why—"

"No, God damn you, *no!*"

He was up now, and close—must have leaped out of his chair. She could picture him standing over her, balled fists shaking as he contended with the impulse to lash out and stifle her questions forever.

A long, crackling silence passed while she waited to learn if she would die tonight.

Sudden footsteps circled away from her, toward the door.

"I brought you the Tegretol," he said from a distance, his voice empty of feeling. "You'd better be sure to take it, Doc. We wouldn't want anything to jeopardize your health."

The door did not slam. It clicked shut politely.

She heard the rattle of a key, then a receding drumroll as he climbed the stairs.

*Our first session,* she thought as her trembling hands groped for the blindfold's knot.

She was by no means certain she would survive a second one.

# 22

Erin waited, her gaze fixed on the closed door, until the rumble of the truck or van had faded into the night.

Then she stood, thighs fluttering, and surveyed the room. On the chair opposite hers was a small plastic bottle. She picked it up: her Tegretol.

He had taken a considerable risk to bring her the pills. Absurdly she felt almost grateful to him. The feeling worried her; it was not unusual for hostages to bond with their captors.

She warned herself not to Stockholm. If she started to identify with him, she would lose any hope of resistance.

There appeared to be no immediate danger of losing her perspective on the man who had kidnapped her and continued to threaten her life. Still, she found it hard to condemn him as unequivocally evil.

On the one hand, he did seem to genuinely regret his crimes and to desire liberation from his pathological compulsion; and that compulsion might well be a by-product of an epileptic fugue state in which he was not fully responsible for his actions.

On the other hand, though he had taken three innocent lives, he refused to submit to punishment—or even to treatment on any terms except his own.

Like the classic criminal personality, he was child-ishly oblivious to the needs, rights, or interests of others. Even the murders appeared to trouble him less for the tragic waste they entailed than for the inner turmoil they had generated. That turmoil, at least, implied the nascent stirrings of a conscience, but it was a conscience freakishly stunted and barely viable.

Did she hate him or pity him? Maybe both. Still, as long as she was trapped in this nightmare, facing death in their every encounter, hate would be the dominant emotion.

Well, perhaps she wouldn't be trapped much longer. Perhaps she could complete the escape aborted earlier.

From the cardboard box she retrieved the wide end of the comb. Kneeling, she inserted it in the crack under the door, probing for the other half.

It had to be within reach. Unless her abductor had unwittingly kicked it clear as he stormed out. If so, it could be yards away, irrecoverable.

Slowly she swept the comb back and forth until it brushed against a small, hidden obstacle.

She drew both items toward her. The beaklike tip of the comb's narrow end slid into view.

"Thank God," she whispered.

Then she frowned at herself, ashamed of allowing a mere scrap of plastic to mean so much.

Either end of the comb was, by itself, too short to allow her any leverage. There had to be a way to effect a repair job.

Cleaning the room this morning, she'd found the strip of tape that had sealed her mouth. Her abductor had yanked it off—she winced, recalling the shock of pain as the adhesive tore free of her lips—and let it drop to the floor.

The tape was now part of the small, tidy pile of soiled paper towels and litter that she'd left in a corner of the room. She dug it out and touched the gummed side. It was still sticky enough to be of use.

Carefully she put the comb back together, then wrapped the ragged juncture of the two pieces with the tape, winding it tightly.

To test the comb, she flexed it slightly. Though less stable than before, it ought to hold.

*Just call me Miss Fix-it,* she thought with a smile, then corrected herself, remembering her Ph.D.: *Dr. Fix-it, that is.*

Her brief flush of pleasure, rare in this dungeon, faded as she turned her attention to the double barrier before her: the dead bolt, the chain lock.

Frowning again, she set to work.

Gund was raging, raging.

Outwardly calm as he steered the Chevy Astro onto Houghton Road, heading north. But inside . . .

Bloom of flame. Thrash of limbs. A woman's scream yodeling giddily toward the stars.

Erin's scream.

He wanted to burn her, burn the bitch, soak her in gas and flick a lit match into the puddle—*whoosh*—and watch her smooth skin crisp and peel.

For a long time there was nothing in his world but the hum of the road, the engine's steady grumble, the red petals of fire unfolding like a night-blooming flower.

His jaws slid slowly in a painful grinding motion.

So easy to kill her, and so good.

Part of him had wanted to destroy her all along. Last night he'd very nearly pulled the trigger when the pistol was in her mouth.

He hadn't kidnapped her for that purpose, however. He'd taken her prisoner in order to help himself, *save* himself.

At least that was what he liked to believe. Perhaps it was only a convenient lie. Perhaps his true intention always had been to feed her to the flames.

Even now he could hear her final agonized shrieks, smell the mingled odors of gasoline and charred meat—

*No.*

The wheel spun under his hand. The Astro skidded off the road onto the dirt shoulder and shuddered to a stop.

He killed the engine, listened to the clockwork tick of its cooling parts. Around him was a vast silence and darkness, a waveless sea faintly foam-flecked with starlight.

Dry wind, unusually warm for an April night, gusted through the open window. The air had a velvet texture; it wrapped him like a winding sheet.

Sitting motionless, hands resting on the wheel in the ten o'clock position approved by driving instructors, chest expanding and contracting with slow, metronomic breaths, he struggled to marshal calmness and strength.

The fantasy of Erin staked out, drenched in gas— banish that.

He could afford no such thoughts and images. He was too likely to act on them, to make them real.

A chill passed through him as he understood how near he was right now to surrendering to the secret, deadly side of himself.

But he would not yield. Not tonight.

A long, slow exhalation shuddered out of him, leaving him limp.

He was nearer to the critical stage of his cycle of violence than he had realized. But still in control, for a short while longer anyway. Some time was left to him—and to Erin. Some, but not much.

He wondered if there was any chance he could hold off disaster. Perhaps he could. Perhaps.

Even in their abbreviated session tonight, Erin had offered some unexpected insights. The connection between the three women and his past—he had not been consciously aware of that. Yet as soon as she had identified it, he'd known it to be true.

He *had* selected the first one, Marilyn Vaccaro, because he'd seen her leaving a Catholic church. But at no time then or since, until tonight, had he permitted himself to recognize that fact or to consider its implications.

Though Erin's probing questions had disconcerted him, objectively he had to concede that she'd been doing only what he'd asked her to do, and doing it well. Already he felt fractionally less mysterious to himself, felt that there was logic, of a kind, underlying his dark urges.

She was helping. She really was.

Whether or not she could free him, he didn't know. But one thing was certain: If he killed her, or if he walked out every time she aroused his anger, he would never be cured.

To profit from her skill he had to do the work, ride out the emotional fever that such close interrogation brought on; and he had to be honest with her . . . as honest, at least, as he could permit himself to be.

All right, then. He would go back. Go back and try again, while there was still time.

He restarted the engine, guided the van onto the road, and executed a sloppy U-turn. The headlight beams scared a loping jackrabbit out of the southbound lane.

Flooring the gas pedal, he accelerated to sixty, retracing his route.

# **23**

Erin spent long minutes of sweaty effort prying the dead bolt out of the socket again. Twice the taped-up comb threatened to snap. Perhaps her prayers held it together.

She pulled the door toward her until the chain was taut. The half-inch opening was too narrow for her hand. The comb fit through and easily snagged one of the links, but the chain resisted her efforts to lift it.

Frustrated, she pocketed the comb, then considered the problem more carefully.

It did her no good to hook the chain at its midpoint. The end of the chain was what mattered—the end soldered to the sliding bolt that held it in place.

She had to find a way to hook one of the end links, then lift the bolt free of its slot in the door jamb.

To do that, she needed a flexible tool, which could be angled sharply. Wire would be ideal.

Wire . . .

In her purse was a memo pad, spiral-bound.

Her fingers trembled with barely controlled excitement as she worked the wire free of the punched holes. She pulled it straight, then bent it at a ninety-degree angle and curved one end into a fish hook.

Now all she had to do was tease the chain out of its

slot. She guided the hooked end of the wire through the opening, then rotated it, probing blindly for the jamb plate.

The hook seemed to catch on something, but came free when she started to lift it.

Keep trying.

For a second time the hook caught. She drew the wire toward her, seeking to give the tool a better grip, then slowly raised it. The chain rose also; she heard a faint rasp of movement, the scratching of the slide bolt in the slot—

The hook lost its grip, and the chain fell back in place.

Disappointment stabbed her. Teeth gritted, she tried again.

The hook clawed at air, scrabbled at wood, and then, with a faint metallic jangle, snagged the chain once more.

Careful now.

She drew up the chain slowly, heard the dull scrape of the bolt sliding along the slot.

Higher. Higher.

The chain stopped abruptly. At first she thought it had caught on some obstacle. Then she realized that the bolt must have reached the top of the slot.

Ease it free. Gently . . .

On the other side of the door, there was a soft chink, then a louder rattle, and the chain fell away.

The wire dropped from her hand. She grabbed the door, pulled it toward her, and this time nothing prevented it from swinging fully open, exposing the flight of concrete stairs that led upward into darkness.

She was *free*.

Gulping air, she emerged from the cellar room, planted a foot on the staircase, almost fell—her knees were weak, her head spinning—then mastered her emotions and climbed the stairs, gripping the wooden banister.

The light from the cellar receded. The stairs dimmed. She had to feel her way, one arm outstretched to grope in the dark.

Her fingers touched wood.

A smooth sheet of wood directly before her, stone walls on either side.

A door.

She found a knob. It would not turn.

Locked.

At the top of the cellar stairs, a locked door, *another* locked door.

"No, that can't be right." Her voice quavered dangerously close to hysteria. "Can't be, just *can't* be right."

She had never heard her abductor shut this door or open it. Had never suspected its existence.

Desperately she jiggled the knob, determined to make it turn; but her hand merely slid over the smooth, rounded brass.

Fingering the knob, she felt a small button of metal at its center, like the bull's-eye of a target.

The latch's manual release. Of course.

She pressed it, then tried the knob again, but still it wouldn't respond.

"What's the *matter* with you?" she demanded of the stubborn mechanism, raw anger shredding her self-control.

She punched the button a half dozen times, but the lock remained frozen.

The latch release, goddamn it, had been disabled somehow.

Well, it didn't matter. There had to be some way to open the door. She couldn't be stopped now. Not now—

Engine noise. Outside.

He had come back.

A moan warbled up from the pit of her throat. *"No . . ."*

Had all her efforts been wasted for a second time? Would she have to retreat to the room, lock herself in once more?

Lock herself in . . .

But she couldn't. There was no way she could secure the chain lock from inside the room. Working blind, she could never guide the slide bolt into the slot. Lifting it out had been difficult enough; dropping it back in would be impossible.

Panic seized her. She was stuck, trapped, unable to advance or retreat.

The engine was silent. Or maybe she simply couldn't hear it over the hammer-and-anvil racket of her heart.

Either way, he would be here in seconds.

Her hand dived into her pocket, found the driver's license and credit card she'd transferred there after changing out of her pajamas and robe.

If the latch was a spring mechanism, and if the beveled end faced toward her, she could loid it with one of the cards.

Had to work. Had to.

She tried the credit card first. No good. The clearance between the door and jamb was too narrow, the fit much tighter than that of the door below. The card wouldn't go in.

Driver's license, then. Thinner, more flexible.

She jabbed the license into the crack in the doorway, found the bolt, pressed hard against it.

Nothing.

She withdrew the card slightly, tried again to slip the latch. Still no response.

The ragged chuffs of her breath, the sweaty strands

of hair dipping into her eyes, the ache in her wrists and fingers—this was all there was for her—this, and the card's fitful probing.

From somewhere close by, the groan of a door.

He had entered the house.

Little time left. He would be at this door very soon.

With a last furious effort she drove the laminated card forward, flexing it at a sharp angle, prying madly at the bolt, and this time—thank God—the latch sprang back.

She jerked the knob, and the door swung away from her.

If the hinges creaked, he would hear and come running.

The door opened as silently as a door in a dream. No wonder she'd never heard it from the cellar.

Nearby, footsteps on hardwood. Approaching.

She slipped out of the doorway and found herself at the end of a narrow hall, dimly illuminated by a wash of ambient light from the front of the house.

To her right, the tramp of shoes.

To her left, a single door, two yards away.

She padded to it, gripped the knob, turned. The door opened an inch, letting in a rush of night air, then stopped.

Jesus, what was it this time? Another chain?

No, not a chain. A padlock, fastened to a steel hasp.

The footsteps, closer.

She shut the door again. No getting out that way. The original lock must have been faulty, so the paranoid son of a bitch had padlocked the door from the outside.

Turning, her eyes wild, heart racing, she stared down the hallway and saw no exit, no hope. She was trapped in a dead end. The only escape route would bring her face to face with her abductor when he turned the corner five seconds from now.

*Think, Erin. Think or die.*

The cellar door. Hanging open at a thirty-degree angle to the corridor wall.

The space between door and wall could serve as a temporary hiding place, the kind of nook a child might use in a game of hide-and-seek.

In three quick, soundless steps she ducked behind the door.

He turned the corner. She felt the floorboards quiver with his approach.

Hugging the wall, straining not to breathe, she waited.

His footsteps quickened, then stopped abruptly a yard away in time with a grunt of surprise.

He was standing at the top of the stairs, on the other side of the door. An inch of wood separated her from him.

*He'll hear my heart,* she thought insanely. *Hear it knocking in my chest.*

She remembered childhood nightmares, dreams that had visited her after the summer of 1973, terrible dreams in which she would flee through a labyrinth of darkness, pursued by some shapeless horror. Always the dreams would end with her huddled in a cubbyhole, breathless and rigid, while the beast prowled close by, snuffling nearer, ever nearer, the odor of gasoline on its breath.

This was like that. Except tonight there would be no waking up. And in this nightmare, unlike the others, the beast would not wear the face of her father.

"How could you do this?" he breathed, his voice impossibly close. *"How could you leave me?"*

Fury in his words, and something more: a threat of tears.

Then a cold click of metal, the release of a pistol's safety catch.

He had the gun with him. And this time he would use it.

She waited, grimly certain he was on to her, sure that at any moment he would slam the door shut and reveal her pinned helplessly against the wall.

Stamp of feet on the stairs.

He was descending to the cellar.

Relief weakened her. He hadn't thought to look behind the door, after all. He wasn't omniscient, wasn't infallible. He could be beaten at this game.

All right, time to quit the congratulations and get going. No, hold it.

Balancing first on one foot, then the other, she removed her boots. Clutched them in her left hand, the leather warm against her fingers. Her footsteps would be muffled now.

*"I'll kill you!"* he shouted suddenly, his voice more distant than before. He had entered the cellar room.

She eased the door away from the wall and stepped out from behind it.

Do it. Now, while he was preoccupied.

She took a breath, then darted past the doorway. Dared a glance toward the bottom of the stairs, saw his huge, distorted shadow crawling on the brick wall.

Then she was beyond the doorway, padding barefoot down the hall and out into what had to be the main room of the house.

# 24

The room was large and musty and unfurnished save for a potbelly stove squatting troll-like on the floor. Starlight filtered through dust-coated windows, the panes webbed with cracks. A beamed ceiling, the rafters silvery in the subtle light, hung overhead like rows of leviathan ribs.

Moving cautiously, aware that footsteps could be heard in the cellar, she crossed yards of semidarkness to the front door.

It opened, promptly and fully, as all doors should— no improvised tools, no desperate prayers, simply a twist of the knob.

Air on her face. The oily smell of greasewood. Click and buzz of nocturnal insects.

Quietly she shut the door, then put on her boots and sprinted across a gravel court to the gate.

It was wrapped in multiple coils of chain, secured with a rusty but formidable padlock.

Climb over? No, impossible. Wicked barbed wire was strung across the top. And on both sides of the gate, barbed-wire fence extended along the roadside— five bands of wire, the lowest a foot from the ground, the highest just above her head, knotted to wooden posts driven into the ground at four-foot intervals.

She couldn't get through that fence or over it, not without slashing herself to tatters and leaving a trail of blood.

She turned and surveyed the area. The place was a ranch of some kind, the main house a one-story wood-frame structure, flanked on the left by a modest barn with a fenced paddock attached. Against a waning crescent moon, the barn's weathervane and cupola were etched in stark silhouette.

Something was missing from the scene. She looked closer at the house, took note of the carport extending from a side wall.

Empty.

Where was the vehicle she'd heard?

Dimly she made out tire tracks in the gravel at her feet, curving toward the barn. The big double doors were shut to conceal her abductor's truck or van, parked inside.

And perhaps to conceal her Taurus also.

He had made her write to Annie, saying she'd gone away. The ruse would fool no one if her car was still sitting in its reserved space at Pantano Fountains.

She sprinted for the barn, leaving the gravel behind, crossing yards of stiff, dead grass. The big double door loomed before her, the old wood ragged with strips of peeling paint. The barn must have been green once, with a white roof and red trim—unusual color scheme for a desert ranch.

One of the doors swung open easily in response to her brief tug. She crept inside and pulled it nearly shut, allowing only a pale fan of starlight to bleed through the crack.

Standing motionless, she waited impatiently for her eyesight to adjust to the gloom.

The place smelled of must and age, and not of hay.

No provender had been stored here for years, for decades.

A central feed passage, trough, and manure gutter bisected the barn. The left side was lined with stalls, the half-doors ajar. Horse stalls. This had been a horse ranch once.

No stalls on the right side, only an open space, filled now with a gray Chevrolet Astro van and, beyond it, faintly visible in the barn's recesses, her Ford Taurus.

"Oh, baby," she whispered. "Sweet baby, am I ever glad to see you."

He had taken the keys from her purse. But unless he was supernaturally prescient, he could not have known about the other car key she carried, the duplicate key reserved for emergencies.

And if her present situation didn't qualify as an emergency, nothing ever would.

Pulse racing, she ran to the car, then crouched low and frisked the underside of the chassis. A moment of frightened groping, just long enough for her to fear that he'd found it or it had fallen off somehow—and then her hand closed over a small magnetic case.

She detached it, snapped it open, and the spare key dropped like magic into her palm.

Exhilaration at getting this far competed with naked terror at the thought that she wasn't safe yet; she could still be stopped.

The key in her pocket, she crossed the barn to the main doors, prepared to throw them wide—

Her heart chilled.

The distant thud she had heard was the slam of a door.

Crunch of gravel, then of weeds.

Through the crack she glimpsed a bulky figure covering ground in long strides, a gleam of metal—the handgun—bright at his side.

He was coming here. Coming to the barn.

Silently she eased the door shut.

Total darkness now.

She had to find an escape route. Hunt down a side door and use it.

Sightless, she groped her way along the wall, feeling for a door, finding none.

Too late she realized she shouldn't have closed the main doors so tight. The blackness around her was absolute, impenetrable, making her progress dangerously slow as she crept forward.

Her questing hands brushed the rear of her car. She could hide inside it—lie on the floor, hope he didn't see her—but the risk of discovery was too great.

Better to keep going, find some way out. There had to be another door somewhere, *had* to be.

Past the car, and now she was at the rear of the barn, under the hayloft, she believed.

He would be here any second. And still there was no exit, only empty space, yards of black void in every direction.

Frantic now, she flailed about wildly, searching for a door or cubbyhole, any sort of hiding place.

With a gasp she blundered into something wooden and rickety.

A ladder.

Propped almost vertically, leading upward to the loft.

If she could get up there, hide in shadows . . .

Her best chance. She didn't hesitate. Already her boots were planted on the lower rungs, and she was gripping the side rails, climbing fast, oblivious of the wood splinters chewing her palms, ignoring the sway of the ladder as it wobbled under her, precariously balanced.

Halfway up. Not far to go. She set her foot on another rung—

*Crack.*

Rotten with age, the rung collapsed.

She plunged down, the impact of her descent shattering the next rung in line, and the next, and the next.

Her fists closed over the side rails and broke her fall. She dangled briefly, then found an unbroken rung and stood on it, straining for breath.

She had not screamed. That was something, at least.

But she was still trapped, still hopelessly exposed, and now the ladder was unusable. She couldn't reach the loft.

An eddy of wind. Brightening glow behind her.

The barn door, opening.

He was here.

She dropped to the ground, hoping the brief storm of dust stirred up by the wind could cover the soft thud of her fall.

Crouching low, she gazed toward the front of the barn.

In the doorway he was silhouetted against a gray sweep of desert and a sprinkling of stars. A large, stoop-shouldered figure in long pants and a short-sleeve shirt, his head oddly bulbous, curvilinear as a bullet.

He hadn't seen her yet. She was cut off from him by his van and her car and yards of distance; the light from outside hadn't touched the farthest reaches of the barn.

Sinking to all fours, she scrambled behind the front end of her Ford and huddled there.

His shoes crackled on the dirt floor as he advanced inside.

"Burn you, bitch." His voice was a sleepwalker's

slurred monotone. "Pour the gas down your lying throat. Choke you with it before I light the match."

The low chuckling noises that followed were not any human form of laughter.

Soundlessly she stretched out on her stomach and wriggled under the Ford.

The driver's door of the van canted open. The Chevy rocked on its springs as he swung inside. He climbed out a moment later, and a strong white light winked on, dispelling the barn's shadows.

Flashlight. Must have gotten it out of the glove compartment.

The beam swept over the car, then explored its interior. She pressed herself snug against the ground, terrified that he would examine the underside of the vehicle next.

He studied the car a moment longer, then directed the beam upward at the hayloft.

Safe for the moment. But would he notice the broken ladder? Her footprints in the dirt?

Apparently not. The flashlight beam passed over the ladder without pausing, the beam seeking out the doorway of a small room at the rear of the barn. A tack room, long unused, empty save for a built-in sink. Had she found that room and tried to hide in it, she would be dead now.

Next, the horse stalls. The flash probed them one by one, looking for any uninvited occupant.

Finally he seemed satisfied. The beam was angling toward the floor at his feet when a gust of wind blew the main door shut.

The sharp slam, like an amplified handclap, startled him.

He dropped the flash.

It hit the ground, intact, the beam shining directly at her from ten feet away.

She stared, paralyzed, into the cone of light. Fear closed her throat. She couldn't breathe.

"Hell," he muttered.

He took a sideways step to pick up the flash, and kicked it accidentally.

It rolled—God, no—it rolled *under the car.*

He would have to see her now. The flashlight lay between the Ford's front wheels, less than a yard from her head. She was impaled in its beam.

Past the haze of light, her abductor grunted as he got down on his knees.

Erin felt wetness in her eyes and a sick, feverish trembling in her lower body. The nightmare was back, more real than ever.

She hoped, despite what he'd said, that he wouldn't burn her. Death by fire was her worst fear, had been since childhood.

The gun would be better. Easier.

His hand reached for the flash.

He had to see her now. Couldn't miss her.

Except . . . he wasn't looking.

He hadn't bothered to lie prostrate and poke his head under the chassis. He was still kneeling, groping blindly.

His fingers brushed the flashlight's metal casing. The flash rolled again, and for a heart-twisting second Erin was sure it would roll out of his reach, and he would have no choice but to belly-crawl after it.

Then he clamped a firm hand on the flash, pulled it toward him, and rose to his feet.

Rattle, slam, and he was out of the barn, intent on hunting her in the night.

Erin pressed her face to her forearm and lay very still as tension sighed out of her in a hissing stream.

Close one.

Very close.

# 25

Gund still had no idea how the bitch managed to free herself from the cellar, and he didn't much care. All he knew, all that mattered to him, was that he would track her down, and then she would pay.

He had never been so angry. She'd *left* him. Wrong of her to do that, so very wrong, unforgivably wrong.

He could have killed her last night, but had he? No. She was special to him—still was, despite her betrayal—and he had treated her accordingly. He'd cleaned up the cellar room, stocked it with food and other necessities, even gone to the trouble of installing a foam pad so she could sleep in comfort. He hadn't chained her to the wall, as he easily could have. Hadn't shackled her feet or manacled her hands.

Right from the start he'd been good to her. He'd treated her with consideration and respect. And this was how she'd responded, the ungrateful little whore, the goddamned filth.

His breath came hard, partly from the exertion of frantic activity but mostly from sheer, towering rage.

The good thing was that she couldn't have gone far. He'd been away for less than a half hour, and it must have taken time for her to defeat the two locked doors.

He was guessing she had left the house only moments before his return.

Her car keys were in his pocket, so unless she could hot-wire an ignition, the Taurus was useless to her. Penned in by barbed wire, she had two options: to hide on the grounds of the ranch, or to circle behind the house in search of another way out.

Pausing at the side of the barn, he beamed his flash into the grain bin and fuel shed. Both were empty.

The flashlight guided him as he loped across yards of scorched, bristly grass. A flattened, S-shaped thing—a dead gopher snake—was briefly visible amid a patch of purple weeds.

Behind the house was a utility shed. He looked inside. Nothing.

He didn't expect her to hide, anyway. She would run. And he knew where she was likeliest to go.

Two hundred feet beyond the shed, his property ended in a line of barbed wire, silver in the starlight. Just before the fence was an arroyo.

The wide, dry streambed, carved by seasonal flash floods, ran west to Houghton Road, with no gates or fences along the way. Though Erin couldn't know the wash's destination, she was sure to see that it offered the only means of exit from the ranch, and like any local resident, she would know that arroyos were the natural roadways of the desert, ideal for easy hiking.

He sprinted for the wash, certain the flashlight would reveal her footprints.

Once he picked up her trail, all he need do was track her, a coyote stalking prey.

Erin groped in the dirt by the ladder, hunting among the scatter of broken rungs until she found a nail.

In darkness she fingered it. A two-inch nail, slightly rusty but still sharp.

Just what she needed.

She had been ready to climb behind the Ford's steering wheel when the idea occurred to her. Her abductor was sure to hear the engine as soon as she started it. He would give chase in his van.

Unless the van had been sabotaged.

He couldn't drive it on four flat tires.

Fumbling blindly, wishing he hadn't shut the barn doors when he left, she touched the side panel of her Ford. Its smooth surface guided her as she crept forward in a half crouch, one hand patting the car, the other upraised before her, searching for obstructions.

Deprived of sight, she found her other senses temporarily heightened. She could hear the faint creaks of the barn walls, aged wood shifting under the wind's caress. The smells of rot and fecal decay blended with the closer, more pungent odor of her own sweat.

The car ended, giving way to empty space. Memory directed her to the Chevy Astro, dead ahead in the blackness.

Something skittered past her right foot. Involuntarily she kicked at it with a gasp and heard a small, outraged squeak. Patter of rodent feet, diminishing, gone.

*Just a mouse, Erin. Don't start getting hysterical on me, okay?*

Oddly, the reassuring voice in her head was Annie's. Erin was irrationally glad to hear it, grateful for even the illusory comfort it provided.

Her probing hand found the van's hood. She searched lower and discovered a flat metal disk. Hubcap. The front wheel on the passenger side.

All right, then. First deflate this tire, then the others. Shouldn't take longer than two minutes, and she would buy herself infinitely more time to make her getaway.

If she could do it at all. Having never tried to puncture a tire, she had no idea how thick the rubber might be, how difficult to penetrate.

Only one way to find out.

Clutching the nail in her fist, the point extending from between two fingers, she tensed her arm, took a breath, and struck.

The nail slammed into the tire and punched through. She had time to congratulate herself on the successful execution of the first phase of her plan, and then an alarm went off.

For a startled second she couldn't identify the source of the sudden noise and glare. All she knew was that the darkness was banished, the barn abruptly lit by a yellow stroboscopic light, the silence shattered by a foghorn's furious blatting that went on and on.

Then she understood that the van was equipped with a burglar alarm, and by attacking the tire she had tripped the system.

"Jesus," she hissed, the word lost in the insane racket howling and whooping around her.

That bedlam would be audible for a thousand yards in any direction. It was as good as a searchlight pinpointing her position.

She left the nail imbedded in the tire and sprang to her feet.

Ran for her car, now clearly visible in beats of yellow radiance from the van's parking lights, flashing in distress.

Misjudged the distance, banged her thigh on the Ford's bumper—sparkle of pain down her leg.

Reached the driver's door. Locked?

No, not locked. She flung herself behind the wheel, fumbled the key out of her pocket, fingers sweaty and trembling.

The key slipped from her grasp, fell somewhere on the floor of the car.

Find it, *find it*.

Frantically she searched the car's dark interior, running her hands over the floor mat.

The key was gone. Had disappeared. But that wasn't possible.

"It *has* to be here!" she heard herself scream over the alarm's continuing squall.

Under the seat, maybe. It could have bounced under the seat.

She thrust her hand into the narrow space between the floor and the seat assembly, scraping her knuckles on the rough metal framework, and there it was, the key, almost out of reach. With two fingers she snagged it, slid it forward, then closed her fist over the key and raised it into the light.

Shaking, she jabbed the key at the ignition cylinder, missed the slot twice, found it on the third try.

The engine coughed, coughed again, refusing to turn over.

She wrenched the key clockwise, floored the gas—an ugly screeching sound—and finally the motor caught.

It chugged fitfully for a moment, then ran smooth.

Headlights on, gear selector thrown into reverse, she was set to go. But with the van blocking her, she had less room to maneuver than she'd thought.

Had to back and fill, back and fill, turn the car at an angle. Now she was in the lane between the van and the barn wall, a narrow lane, just enough clearance.

Her foot on the gas, the Ford reversing.

Crunch of impact.

She'd plowed into the van's fender. Not enough clearance, after all, but there was no time to straighten out, not with the alarm still shrieking, its banshee cries pulsing in sync with the heartbeats shaking her like spasms.

She floored the gas and forced the car to continue in reverse. Nails-on-chalkboard screech as she scraped the Chevy's side, the two vehicles grinding against each other like shifting jaws, the Ford shuddering, bucking, retreating in fits and starts, then popping free of the van and skidding backward.

The barn doors, still closed. She rammed them with her rear bumper. They exploded open, and she was outside.

Spin of the wheel, a clumsy U-turn, her headlights sweeping toward the barbed-wire fence yards away.

In the rearview mirror, a man with a flashlight, sprinting toward her.

Gunshot. The rear window blew apart in a shower of tempered glass.

She gunned the engine. The Ford plowed over weeds, over gravel, and slammed into the fence.

The impact uprooted the posts on either side, snapped the wires. The Ford fishtailed onto the road, straightened out. She sped away from the ranch as her speedometer needle climbed.

Looking back, she saw her abductor disappear inside the barn.

The road was narrow and rough. Pebbles clicked and pinged against the chassis, making tuneless music.

She kept pushing her speed—fifty, then fifty-five, then sixty. Dangerously fast for a pitted desert road lit only by her high beams, a road that at any second might coil into a cul-de-sac or dive into a flood-control depression.

Dangerous, yes, but not as dangerous as caution would be.

Behind her, headlights.

The van.

Her high beams splashed across a dotted yellow line

perpendicular to the road she was traveling. Intersection.

She spun the wheel, veering to the left.

Now she was on a major thoroughfare, smooth and well maintained, but empty of traffic at this hour. No lights of houses or stores were visible along the roadside, only bleak miles of desert and, in the distance, the jagged humps of mountains, a dark, broken line against the blue-black sky.

She thought she could identify the mountains to her right as the Sierrita range, west of the city. If so, she was heading south.

Flare of headlights behind her. The van again, swinging onto the main road, frighteningly close.

Ahead . . . the interstate.

She saw the elevated roadway rippling with distant lights.

Get on there, and she would be safe. With other people around, her abductor couldn't do anything.

But the highway was at least a half mile away. And the van was pulling close to her tail.

In the rearview mirror she saw him at the wheel. Blurred face, hairless scalp. No beard—the red one he'd worn in the lobby must have been fake.

Her speedometer needle was pinned to eighty-five. She might be traveling faster; the gauge only went that high.

His headlights flooded the Ford's interior with their harsh white glare, brightening steadily. The car rocked with an impact from behind.

He had rammed her. The car wobbled drunkenly. She gripped the wheel to steady it, and then he butted her again.

"Stop," she muttered, teeth clenched, knuckles bloodless.

The twin globes of his lights expanded as he

punched the gas pedal a third time. She manhandled the wheel, and with a scream of tires the Ford veered into the other lane.

The van accelerated, trying to pull alongside her. If it did, the driver could shoot out the side windows, kill her in a hail of ammunition.

She ground her foot down on the gas pedal, straining for every increment of speed the motor could deliver. The road dipped, descending at a steep grade, and at the bottom of the hill a service station came into view.

An Exxon station, near the interstate's on-ramp, its illuminated sign bright against the night sky, the service court floodlit, fuel islands gleaming.

Open for business. Had to be.

The van hooked sideways, crunching her rear passenger door, chewing metal like a hungry mouth.

The pavement slid out from under her. The Ford skidded onto the shoulder, plowing up a spray of gravelly earth as the steering wheel jerked and ticked under her hands.

She had almost regained control of the car when the van mashed her again, its fender gnawing at the front door on the passenger side, the door buckling in its frame, the window shattering as the frame bent, and for a wild hysterical moment she was a diver in a shark cage, and a great white was chomping insatiably at the steel bars, crushing them out of shape, forcing its huge head deeper inside—

Rows of mesquite bushes flew past on her left, branches whacking the windshield, scraping the doors. She was screaming—she couldn't help it—screaming as the van plowed her sedan off the shoulder into an untended stretch of cacti and weeds.

The car bucked like a skittish horse, her seat lurching wildly forward and back, her hands slapping the horn.

*Should have worn your seat belt,* a voice in her head admonished irrelevantly. *Most accidents occur on trips of less than one mile.*

A massive columnar shape materialized in her high beams. Saguaro cactus, huge, multi-armed like Shiva, armored in needles and leather-tough skin.

She had time for one more scream before the Ford slammed head-on into the saguaro at full speed.

# 26

The windshield exploded. The hood popped open as the Ford's front end caved in. That hideous grinding noise was the sound of the van punching into the passenger side like a mailed fist.

Erin was conscious of none of it. Her sole awareness was of white, a field of white, endless white, expanding before her, swallowing her up with a lover's sigh.

The airbag, erupting out of the steering wheel to cushion the collision's impact.

It caught and held her. Dazed, she lay in its soft folds, a captured insect in a napkin.

A heartbeat later the bag automatically deflated. She fell back against the headrest, blinking at a whirl of stars.

She wasn't dead. Didn't think she was even hurt. The airbag had saved her.

Did the van have an airbag?

Her gaze ticked to the rearview mirror.

The van's front end loomed impossibly close. A zigzag crack bisected the windshield. Behind the glass, movement. Her abductor, pulling himself upright.

He'd been thrown sideways in the crash, but he wasn't dead, wasn't even unconscious.

Why couldn't he have cracked open his head on the

dashboard, flown through the windshield, broken his neck? Something, anything, it didn't matter what, just so he'd been stopped and she could be safe.

No time to dwell on that. He'd survived, and now he was groping on the floor of the van for some item he'd dropped.

The gun, of course.

Couldn't miss her at this range.

She fumbled at the door handle, wrenched the door ajar, pulled herself out. Light-headedness made her stumble.

Loose desert soil sank under her boots. She staggered forward, slipping and sliding on scattered rocks strewn like ball bearings in her path.

Steam hissed from under the sedan's folded hood. She nearly fell again, caught herself by grabbing the car's front panel, then jerked her hands away. Hot.

Behind her, movement in the front seat of the van. He was leaning out the side window, the pistol in his hand.

*Down.*

She flung herself on hands and knees at the front of the car, then froze, waiting tensely for the pistol's report.

Nothing happened. She'd ducked in time. He couldn't hit her with the wreckage of the car blocking his aim.

Gasping, she clambered over the saguaro, prone in the glare of the Ford's one remaining headlight, its arms outstretched as if in a silent plea. The hundreds of spiny needles encrusting the fallen giant poked and jabbed her, spotting her legs with pinprick dabs of blood.

Then she was half running, half crawling toward the road, afraid to rise fully for fear of making herself a target, afraid to stay on all fours because her progress that way was too slow.

At the edge of the road she dared a backward glance, expecting to see the man with the gun racing after her out of the gloom.

Astonishingly, he was still in the van. She saw him pushing on the driver's door with no response. The frame must have buckled slightly, wedging the door shut.

He gave up on trying to open it and began to slide over to the passenger side.

For the moment he was distracted, and she was probably out of his range.

*Run.*

She sprinted across the empty road, toward the Exxon station two hundred yards ahead.

Whoever was in there must have heard the crash. Might be on the phone already, requesting an ambulance.

She didn't need an ambulance. She needed cops.

*"Help!"* Her lungs strained to find the air necessary for a shout. "Police! Call the *police!*"

When she glanced over her shoulder once more, the van's passenger door was swinging open.

Where was the attendant? How long did it take to phone 911, anyway? A man on the night shift ought to have a gun behind the counter, ought to be out here now, protecting her.

She reached the asphalt court of the service station. The office was straight ahead, separated from her by two floodlit fuel islands.

One of her boots trod on a cable near the full-service island. Inside the building, a bell rang.

She cut between two of the gas pumps, avoiding a tangle of hoses that threatened to trip her up. As she sprinted for the self-service island, she risked another look over her shoulder.

He was sprinting after her now, the gun in his hand. She glimpsed a flash of metal in the waistband of his pants—another pistol? How many guns did he have?

Across the second island. Glass door ahead, framing a lighted snack shop.

She nearly flew into the door, slammed her palms against the glass at the last second to stop herself, then grabbed the pull-bar and jerked it violently.

The door didn't open.

Locked.

No, not again, not *another* locked door.

Her fists hammered the door. The ghost image of her reflection, caught in the glass and staring wild-eyed at her, was a mask of frenzy and terror and despair.

"Let me in, he's going to kill me, *let me in!*"

But no one let her in, and abruptly she realized that no one would.

The station was closed. Despite appearances, it had been shut down for the night.

Through the glass she could see the self-contained world of the snack shop, invitingly safe and friendly. Candy carousels, magazine racks, maps and map books, microwave oven, coffee maker—everything neat and orderly and heartbreakingly normal, but not a human being on duty anywhere.

Nobody had heard the crash, and nobody had called for an ambulance, and nobody would open the door, because nobody was here. The lights had been left on by mistake or activated by some timer mechanism's glitch.

The reason didn't matter. What mattered was that she was alone, utterly alone, and her abductor had reached the edge of the service court.

She ran.

There was no place to go, nowhere to hide, but she ran anyway, thinking wildly that she could give him the slip somehow, duck into a rest room or huddle behind a trash bin—crazy thoughts, hopeless, everything was hopeless and she was certain to die.

She rounded the corner of the building, then stopped short, staring in amazement at what was simultaneously the most unexpected and the most obvious thing in the world.

A pay phone. Well, of course. Every gas station had one.

For a moment, shock made her stupid. She dug in her pants pockets for some change, knowing she didn't have any. Then she remembered that a 911 call required no deposit.

She yanked the handset off the plungers, heard a dial tone—it worked, actually *worked*—then stabbed the push buttons with a shaking finger.

Even as she dialed, she wondered what the hell she was doing. Response time to her call would be a minimum of four minutes.

Ringing on the line.

True, the police couldn't arrive fast enough to save her. But perhaps they didn't have to. If she gave her name, said she'd been kidnapped, described the van and the approximate location of the ranch, then her abductor couldn't hope to avoid identification and arrest.

A second ring. Still no answer.

Was he sufficiently rational to refrain from killing her merely because he couldn't hope to get away with it? Only one way to find out.

Third ring.

"Come on, answer!"

Scuff of shoes nearby. He was closing in.

By all logic she should abandon the phone and run.

But she couldn't hope to outdistance him, and somebody *had* to answer soon.

Fourth ring.

He turned the corner. His silhouetted figure, looming huge against the starry sky, expanded to fill up her world.

The pistol—at least she thought it was the pistol—came up fast, the muzzle thrust at her face.

She spun away, nearly dropping the phone, and a coolly dispassionate female voice spoke into her ear. "Pima County Emergency Services."

*"I've been kidnapped, my name is—"*

Agony in her neck. Blinding pain. Her mouth wouldn't work. Her breath was frozen.

Shot. She'd been shot. Oh, Christ, he'd shot her in the neck—

Then she heard the sizzle of electricity, felt the pinch of metal, voltage singing in every muscle and nerve.

Not the pistol. The stun gun.

Her jaws clamped shut. The handset fell from her grasp.

A buzzing roar rose in her brain, and she was gone.

# 27

"Ma'am?"

The voice on the other end of the line repeated that word insistently.

"Ma'am? Are you there, ma'am? Hello?"

Gund ripped out the handset and cord, dropping both items on the ground.

He had to hurry. Every 911 call was instantly traced. No doubt a sheriff's department cruiser was being dispatched to the area at this moment.

Erin lay unconscious at his feet. The Ultron had done its job. She would be out for ten to fifteen minutes, long enough to get her back to the ranch.

If he could get away at all.

He'd meant to kill her when she fled the ranch. The pistol shot fired at her car had targeted her head.

Even after the crash he would have shot her, had she not used the wrecked sedan as cover.

Now he was glad he hadn't ended her life with a bullet. He knew another way, a better way, to punish her for disobedience.

A stitch jabbed at his ribs as he ran to his van. He reached it, then paused with a muttered curse.

The front tire on the passenger side was slowly going flat. A nail was imbedded in it: the bitch's work.

With the hole largely plugged by the nail, the tire wasn't losing air too fast. It should stay partially inflated for a few minutes longer.

It would have to. He had no time to change the tire now.

He climbed in through the passenger doorway, slid over to the driver's seat. The door frame on the left side had been slightly bent in the collision; he would have to hammer the damn thing back into shape. Later.

Twist of the ignition key, and the engine let him hear its reassuring growl.

In reverse, he pulled free of the wrecked Ford, then parked directly in front of it. Removed the towing equipment from the van. Secured the bar and chains.

A noise down the road. Patrol car? No, only the wind. Next time it would be a cruiser, though. *Move.*

Shifting into low gear, he hauled the sedan out of the roadside ditch. The crushed saguaro lifted the car like some oversized speed bump.

Towing the Taurus, he drove to the side of the Exxon station, where Erin lay unmoving near the ruined pay phone. The glare of his one remaining headlight washed over her as he pumped the brake pedal.

Out of the van, quickly. The motor idled, purring like a large somnolent animal, as he threw open the Astro's side door, then hoisted Erin in his arms and dumped her roughly inside.

Time to go.

No, wait. An idea.

From his glove compartment he removed a black felt-tip marker. Spent a couple of seconds leaning over the phone, pen in hand.

Behind the wheel again. At the rear of the building he executed a wide U-turn, the captured Ford rattling and jouncing, and then he was back on Houghton

Road, heading north, punching the accelerator pedal, speeding away from the scene.

Deputies Davis and Smoke arrived at the Exxon station at precisely eleven o'clock.

They found the lights on, a situation unusual but hardly unheard of. Foster Tuttle, the station's owner, was getting on in years. He was known to be absent-minded about such details.

The pay phone had been torn apart. The handset and cord lay in the dirt.

Davis beamed his flashlight at the phone assembly and saw fresh graffiti scrawled over its metal casing.

COPS SUK ME.

He worked up a goodly mouthful of saliva with the help of the wad of Bubblicious he was chewing, then threw back his head and hawked a shining gob of spit into the night.

"Kids," he said in disgust.

Deputy Smoke nodded. "Kids."

For no particular reason Davis retrieved the handset. The armored cord dangled from his hand like a dead snake, the plating bright in the starlight.

"This damn town's getting more like L.A. every damn day," Davis muttered.

"More like." Smoke had learned never to argue with his partner. Besides, it was true, what with the gangs and the drugs and the Mexicans.

"Every damn day," Davis said for emphasis as they sauntered back to their car.

Before pulling away to resume patrol, Deputy Davis added another stick of Bubblicious to his growing wad, and Deputy Smoke got on the radio to report an act of vandalism and a phony 911 call.

# 28

The pianist was playing "For Sentimental Reasons," the rippling chords occasionally overlaid with his hacking smoker's cough. Behind the bar a color TV, volume muted, showed basketball highlights; a game-winning three-point shot elicited a listless sigh of approval from a row of patrons nursing drinks.

Walker leaned back in the corner booth, settling into the imitation-leather banquette, and checked his watch.

Eleven o'clock. Gary should arrive at any minute.

Sipping his scotch, letting his gaze wander from the TV to the pianist and back, he thought about Annie Reilly.

Her sister obviously had left town on a whim. No doubt she'd get in touch with Annie before long, clear everything up. None of that was what preoccupied him.

It was the small glitch in their conversation, the moment when she said, "Lydia's husband . . . died."

Why the hesitation?

She'd asked if he had ever heard of Lydia Connor. Peculiar thing for her to say. There was no reason for him to have heard of her. So what if she had been a local resident? The population of the Tucson metropolitan area was roughly three-quarters of a million the last time he checked.

No, Annie was hiding something. The mystery intrigued him.

Then he smiled at himself, amused by his self-deception. Impersonal curiosity alone would hardly have prompted him to call Gary with a request for information, or to respond so eagerly to his friend's invitation, a half hour ago, to meet at this tavern and review what he'd learned.

He was . . . interested in Annie Reilly. True, he barely knew her, had hardly seen her at her best, and probably hadn't come off too well in her eyes, either. Even so, he was interested.

The date of birth in her D.M.V. file was March 12, 1966. She had just turned thirty. Could pass for twenty-five.

Walker himself was thirty-five, and he was aware that he came off as older than his age; cops often did.

No particular reason to think it could work between them.

Still . . .

In the photo portrait she had been smiling. She did have a lovely smile. And her green eyes, mischievous and alert—he much preferred them to Erin's cool gray gaze.

He supposed he'd agreed to look into Erin's disappearance a little more deeply for the simple reason that he wanted to see Annie again.

Most cops were extroverts, but he had always been rather shy around women, especially women he found attractive. Shy and slow to act. Sometimes too slow.

Rotating his glass, watching chips of ice twirl like glass fragments in a kaleidoscope, he thought back to a party he'd attended last year. In the crush of people, mostly strangers to him, he'd bumped into a dark-haired woman with a quick smile and an intensely perceptive gaze. Her name was Caroline.

They talked for a while, first shouting above the din of conversation, then retreating to a quieter part of the house. Walker was reasonably sure she wanted him to ask her out, but something made him hesitate. Then they got separated, and later in the evening she left with another man.

He heard nothing further of her for months, until the friend who'd thrown the party reported casually that Caroline—*You remember her, don't you, Mike?*—had gotten married. *She meets the guy at my party, and next thing I know, I'm watching them exchange vows at the altar. Go figure.*

Sometimes in the lonely post-midnight hours, Walker thought of Caroline. He wondered what would have happened if he'd been quicker to act on his feelings that night.

Nothing, probably. It was ridiculously romantic, an adolescent delusion, to think that if she'd left the party with him, she would be his wife today.

But how many similar opportunities had he missed? How many relationships had failed because he hadn't stated his feelings, hadn't risked intimacy, hadn't said *I love you* when the words were clearly called for?

He didn't want to make that mistake with Annie. Didn't want to add her name to the roll of lost chances and might-have-beens. Didn't want to think of her, with regret, on sleepless nights alone.

"Hey, Mike."

He looked up from his drink and saw Gary Kendall slide into the banquette opposite him.

"Gary." Walker reached across the table to shake hands. "Hope this hasn't inconvenienced you too much."

A sunny shrug. "No problem, my man."

As usual, Gary looked like a recent arrival from L.A.: chinos, baggy Lakers T-shirt, mirrored sunglasses tipped back on his forehead. People sometimes mistook him for a tourist.

In fact, however, he had never lived in L.A.—or anywhere outside of Tucson, for that matter. He talked of relocating to The Coast, as he called it, but there was no chance of that; he liked his job too much to leave it.

For the past two years he had been associate metro editor of the *Tucson Standard,* and though the stories he covered rarely involved more than car accidents and labor disputes and the endless controversy over the quality of the city's water supply, he seemed to regard himself as a true journalistic crusader, some mythical amalgam of Woodward and Bernstein or, better yet, Redford and Hoffman.

"Truth is," Walker said, "it's probably not that important. I'm not even sure why I thought it was worth pursuing."

"A hunch, maybe? The kind that TV cops are known for?"

"Could be."

"Well, if so, good buddy, you just may have qualified for your very own series."

Walker blinked at him. He was about to ask what that meant when the waitress stopped at the table.

"Get you something?" she asked Gary.

"Beer."

"We got Bud, Coors, Heineken, Amstel Light—"

"Corona." He'd heard they drank a lot of that in L.A.

When the waitress was gone, Walker leaned forward. "You were telling me my hunch paid off."

"Big-time." Gary removed two folded sheets of paper from his pants pocket. "I visited the morgue, looked up the relevant articles. All that stuff is on microfilm, natch. I mean, we're going back a long way."

"How long?"

"Nineteen sixty-eight. That's when Lincoln Connor offed himself."

"Lydia's husband?"

"Right. They lived in the area. Look, I'd better start at the beginning."

Before he could, the waitress returned with a bottle of Corona and a glass. Gary paid with a bill. "Keep the change."

Pouring the beer, then sipping it, he told the story. Across the room, the pianist played "How High the Moon" and soothed his sore throat with a cigarette.

"Lincoln and Lydia had a son, Oliver Ryan. In 1968, at age eighteen, Oliver ran away from home. It made the paper because he stole a neighbor's car to do it. His parents confirmed there'd been a family fight. That was in July.

"Few days later, stolen car turns up in the mountains near Prescott. Still no word on Oliver. But three weeks after that, a Tucson dentist, friend of the Connor clan, is in the Prescott area on vacation, and he spots Oliver. Kid's joined up with a tribe of hippies camping near Granite Mountain.

"The dentist goes up to Oliver, tells him his mom's worried sick and he ought to come home. Oliver gives what the *Standard* described as an unprintable reply."

"Wasn't the kid wanted for auto theft?" Walker interrupted.

"Yeah, but the dentist is hardly in a position to make a citizen's arrest while surrounded by hostile anti-Establishment types in the woods. Once he makes his report, some local deputies go looking for Oliver, but by then the counterculture crowd has cleared out.

"Now here's the interesting part. Four days later, *Lincoln* disappears."

"The father?"

"Right. Turns out the dentist wasn't exaggerating when he said Lydia was worried sick; she had a nervous breakdown right after Oliver ran off, has been recuperating at Tucson Medical Center for nearly a month. Friends say Lincoln's irrationally angry at Oliver. He blames his wife's condition on the boy, says Oliver's brought disgrace on the Connor family. So the supposition is that Lincoln's gone off to find his son and drag him home to face the music.

"Finally, the climax of our little drama. I printed out this article. Read for yourself."

He unfolded one sheet of paper and pushed it across the table. Walker picked it up.

MURDER-SUICIDE IN PRESCOTT NATIONAL FOREST

Prescott—The bodies of two individuals tentatively identified as Lincoln Connor, 46, of 100 E. Ravine Road in the Tucson area, and his son, Oliver Ryan Connor, 18, were found yesterday in an isolated part of Prescott National Forest near Iron Springs, local authorities said.

Edward Winslow, chief deputy coroner of Yavapai County, said that both victims apparently died of shotgun blasts to the head. A Remington Model 870 12-gauge shotgun with a sawed-off barrel, a weapon known to belong to the elder Connor, was found in Lincoln Connor's hand, he added.

"It appears that Lincoln Connor first killed his son, then turned the gun on himself," Mr. Winslow said. "No suicide note has been recovered."

Friends of the family report that Lincoln Connor had expressed hostility and rage toward his son since Oliver ran away from home on July 10, allegedly stealing a neighbor's 1962 Buick Roadmaster.

The exact reason for Oliver's disappearance is unknown, though Mr. and Mrs. Connor acknowledged having an argument with their son on the night he left.

Oliver's departure reportedly contributed to a rapid deterioration of his mother's health. Lydia Connor remains under medical care at Tucson Medical Center.

A hospital spokesman declined to state whether or not Mrs. Connor had been informed of the loss of her husband and son.


Walker looked at the article for several minutes, long after he had absorbed its contents. He thought of Annie and Erin, orphaned in a fire at the age of seven, adopted by their Aunt Lydia.

How long had it been before they learned of the ugly tragedy in their foster mother's past? Did Lydia hang photos of Lincoln and Oliver around the house? Did she display keepsakes of them on the shelves? Were the girls forced to hear stories of the foster brother who'd died when they were two years old, and had they justifiably concluded that the whole world was insane?

No wonder Annie clung so tenaciously to her sister . . . and jumped instantly to the worst conceivable explanation for her disappearance.

He had told her that Erin had just run off, he reflected grimly, draining his glass. Had she remembered Oliver when he'd said that? Oliver, who'd run away on impulse—and never had returned?

Sure, Annie was being paranoid. But it looked as if she had every right to be.

"Thanks, Gary," he said finally. "This is . . . helpful."

Gary shrugged. "As you can see, it was a big local story at the time. I was too young to know about it, but if you'd been living here, you would have heard."

"That's why she thought the name Connor would mean something to me," Walker mused. "Probably took me for a native. Everybody else does."

"Just like everybody takes me for an Angeleno. And I'm a Tucsonan born and bred. Go figure." Gary's smile faded. "There's one loose end I didn't mention."

"In the Connor case? What?"

"Well, the police tracked down those hippies and asked them when was the last time they'd seen Oliver. They said he went for a walk in the woods one evening with a friend from the camp, and neither of them ever came back."

"The friend vanished?"

"That's right. Never turned up. The other kids couldn't help much. Gave a pretty vague description— you know how it was, they were stoned most of the time. They didn't even know his full name. First name only."

"Which was?"

"Harold."

"You think Oliver and Harold were together when Lincoln showed up?"

"Could have been," Gary said. "Maybe Harold got away and was so scared he just kept running."

"Or maybe he was shot, too, and for some reason his body wasn't found." Walker shrugged, dismissing the issue. "Anyway, it doesn't matter now."

"I suppose not."

Walker noticed the other slip of paper still folded in Gary's hands. "Got something else?"

"One last item. Not directly relevant. Doesn't involve Lincoln Connor or Oliver, just Lydia."

"What about her?"

"In 1973 she took in two young nieces, named, let's see . . . Erin and Anne Reilly. Her sister's kids, seven-year-old twins, originally from Sierra Springs, California."

Walker nodded. He tipped the glass and let a piece of ice slide into his mouth, then pushed it around his cheek with his tongue.

"I knew that part," he said. "They'd been orphaned in a fire."

Gary frowned. "A fire, yeah. But not *just* a fire."

Walker chewed the ice and swallowed it. "What does that mean?"

"You *don't* know the story."

"I guess not. Can't be as bad as the first one, though."

Gary shook his head slowly. "You're right. It's not as bad. It's worse."

Walker set down the glass with a soft clunk.

"Tell me," he said softly.

Gary told him.

Even after Gary was done speaking, Walker remained silent. The waitress stopped to ask if he wanted a refill of his scotch, and Gary had to answer for him, because he didn't hear.

# 29

Erin surfaced from unconsciousness to the sound of hammering.

Blinking, she focused her vision. Above her hung a brilliant scatter of stars, bracketed by steep embankments tufted with ocotillo and mesquite.

She was stretched supine at the bottom of an arroyo, arms over her head, wrists pinned together.

Her abductor knelt at her feet, swinging a mallet, driving a metal post into the ground. She tried to move her legs, couldn't; rope lashed her ankles to the post.

He was staking her out like Marilyn Vaccaro, like Sharon Lane, like Deborah Collins.

Panic struck her like a fist. All breath and heat left her body in a rush, and abruptly she was winded and clammy and more afraid than she had been in her life, more afraid than she had been as a small child in a blazing house, more afraid than she had been in the rear compartment of the van last night.

In her mind she could hear it: the crackle of flame, the hiss of steam, the slow crisping and peeling of her own flesh.

No. No. *No.*

Had to stop him. Had to.

Her one hope was to communicate, find a way to

make contact, get in touch with the nascent conscience deep within him that understood remorse.

But she couldn't speak. Something was wedged in her mouth, a scrap of cloth, secured with another strip of fabric wound around her head.

The noise she made was a whimper, a beaten-dog sound.

"Awake, Doc?" He swung the mallet again, and the stake descended another half inch. "Good."

She whipped her head from side to side, fighting to loosen the gag. Words, eloquent words, words that could save her life, bumped up against the wadded obstruction between her teeth and died there unexpressed.

The gag would not come free. He had knotted it tight.

*Don't let him do this, make him change his mind, I'm scared, oh, Jesus Christ, I'm so scared . . .*

He put down the mallet, stood up slowly. The moon had set, and only strong starlight illuminated his face. She saw a smoky suggestion of a flat nose and receding chin. His big hands flexed at his sides.

"You've been a bad girl, Doc. I'm extremely disappointed in you."

Her choked groan was the feeble protest of an animal in a trap.

Flashback: the bedroom of her parents' house, Annie shrieking, smoke everywhere, red glow in the stairwell, and the pungent smell of gasoline—

She would smell it again when he soaked her in gas.

Not fire. Anything else: the gun, a knife, a noose— but not fire, *not fire!*

He crouched near her. Laced his fingers in her hair. His touch was tender, but the expression on his face was a twisted caricature of self-torture, a ham actor's exaggerated display. Eyes narrowed in a painful squint.

Lower lip thrust out like a pouting child's. Stripes of wetness banding his cheeks.

She stared up at him, pleading with her gaze. Could he read her thoughts in her eyes, and would it matter if he did?

"God damn you." His breath, coming fast and shallow, was hot on her face. "I came back to finish our session. Thought you'd be able to help me."

But she *could*. She wanted to scream the message at him. If he would just give her another chance, she would help him, treat him, do whatever he wanted.

He stood. Oddly he seemed to have heard the words she could not speak. He answered her with a slow shake of his head.

"I'm sorry, Doc. I wish this hadn't become necessary. But it has."

She watched through a prism of tears as he trudged toward the embankment.

When he returned, he would have the gasoline with him, and then there would be only the final moments of helpless, racking terror as he drenched her with it and lit the match.

She hadn't known her heart could work so hard, hadn't known it was possible for each separate beat to shake her like an inner explosion, hadn't known a human being could endure this extremity of fear.

He reached the embankment and started to climb.

Desperately she pulled at the ropes, knowing her efforts were wasted, knowing it was over for her, everything was over, and she would never see Annie again, or a blue sky, or her own face in a mirror.

Useless to resist. Death by fire was her destiny. As a child she had cheated fate, but not this time.

This time—she moaned again, pressing her cheek to the dry earth—this time she would burn.

# 30

Sunrise brightened the windows of Annie's living room, spreading a limpid film of light over the glass. She sat up on the sofa and rubbed her bleary eyes.

Last night she had snatched less than four hours' sleep. A nightmare had shocked her awake—some confused memory of the fire in her parents' house, as usual. This version of the event, however, had been strangely different from her previous dreams in two respects.

First, in the nightmare she and Erin had been not children but adults, planted incongruously in the bedroom they'd shared as young girls. Second, while Annie had escaped, somehow Erin had been left behind in the infernal smoke and heat.

And she had burned.

Annie shuddered, reliving the nightmare for the hundredth time since waking. The image that haunted her was vivid and surreal, some detail out of Dali or Bosch. Irrationally she shut her eyes to block out the sight—a useless defense when the vision was imprinted not on her retinas but on her brain.

It was Erin she saw, Erin clothed in flame, hair writhing, skin blistering, limbs thrashing, mouth stretched wide in an endless scream.

That terrible fantasy lingered in her mind as she took her morning shower. She stood under the hot spray for many long minutes, letting the needles of water numb her, until the nightmare finally had been banished.

Then she changed into clean clothes and ate breakfast, barely noticing the taste. Stink received a saucer of milk, in which he displayed his usual perfunctory interest.

Already the day was getting warm. The announcer on the news-talk station predicted unseasonably high temperatures for the rest of the week.

Twice Annie phoned Erin's apartment from her living room. She no longer expected her sister to answer. The calls were a senseless ritual now.

It didn't occur to her to check her own message machine in the study until after eight o'clock. The red LED was flashing excitedly—three bursts, endlessly repeated—three messages.

Had Erin called?

Annie fumbled with the controls, rewound the tape, listened to the playback. Slowly her hopes dimmed, then finally died.

None of the messages was from Erin. All three were from friends Annie had phoned yesterday afternoon, when she'd been trying to track down her sister.

"Jeez, Annie, hope I didn't wake you—this is Darlene—I'm awfully worried . . ."

"Sorry to call so early, but Greg and I wanted to know if there's been any word . . ."

"Did you find her? Oh, sorry, uh, this is Rhonda, it's about seven. So did you? Call if there's any news, or if you want to talk . . ."

All of them must have phoned while she was in the shower, letting the water wash away the sleepless night.

She would have to return these calls and update

some of her other friends also. No doubt most of them were equally concerned but had wanted to keep the line clear.

Well, she could call from work. No chance she was going to be able to concentrate on selling flowers today, anyhow.

There was a time when running her shop had seemed important to her—exciting and even glamorous. Was it as recently as yesterday morning she'd felt that way?

Now the shop was only a distraction. Still, even a distraction would be welcome in the absence of any productive avenue of inquiry she could pursue.

At eight-fifteen she raised the garage door with her remote control and backed the red Miata into the driveway, blinking at the bright sunshine. Under other circumstances she would have thought it was a beautiful day. Dark-boled mesquite trees and slender, pale eucalyptus rustled their tresses of leaves, green against the deep blue of the sky.

At the end of the driveway, she stopped the car opposite the mailbox. It hadn't occurred to her to check her mail yesterday. She got out and lowered the lid.

Bank statement, credit card bill, news magazine, advertising circular, and a business-size envelope.

Her breath stopped, heart froze. For a baffled instant, she didn't know why.

Then her conscious mind registered what her subconscious already had identified.

The envelope was made out in Erin's handwriting.

"Oh, God," she whispered.

Embossed on the envelope was Erin's return address. But there was no postmark, no stamp. Her sister must have personally delivered the letter.

With shaking hands she opened the envelope and extracted a single sheet of pale olive paper.

*Dear Annie,*
*I need some time to myself, so I've decided to*
*go away for a while.*
*Don't worry about me. Everything is fine.*

*Take care,*
*Erin*

Annie stared at the letter for a long time. She read it more than once, read it until the simple message had been committed to heart.

Then she replaced the other items—bank statement, credit card bill, magazine, circular—and shut the mailbox lid. She slipped into the car again, holding the letter and envelope, and then she just sat there, gazing at the words her sister had written, her vision muddy with tears.

A couple of years ago she had submitted an article to a gardening magazine, a brief, humorous piece on ladybugs. The rejection slip that accompanied her manuscript by return mail had been more heartfelt than this letter in her hand.

Incredible to think that Erin could treat her this way. *I need time to myself*—what the hell did that mean?

To abandon her patients, her friends, and Annie herself—and then write a damn letter that didn't even say why, didn't say *anything* . . .

How could Erin do this?

Abruptly her tears stopped. She lifted her head and gazed out the windshield, striped with morning glare.

"She couldn't," Annie whispered slowly. "That's how she could do this. She *couldn't.*"

Erin would never, never, *never* be so thoughtless, so unfeeling, as to write this letter under these circumstances.

A tortured six-page confession maybe. But not these

two paragraphs, these three meaningless sentences, the cheery *Take care* tacked onto the end like the punch line of a bad joke.

The letter was a fake.

Oh, Erin almost surely had written it. The handwriting, unless forged by an expert, was unmistakably hers.

But she had not composed the letter of her own will. She had been forced.

The heat of the sun was beginning to bake her in the car. Annie rolled out onto the street and left the complex, heading south on Pontatoc Road, thinking hard.

At a red traffic signal, she took a second look at the envelope.

The street address read 505 Calle Saguaro. Annie lived at 509.

Erin knew the correct address, obviously. She'd made a deliberate error in writing 505.

Peering closely at the number, Annie saw that the fives were rounded. Erin didn't normally write that way. Her script was jagged, sharp-edged.

These fives looked more like letters than numbers.

Of course. Not 505.

SOS.

Behind her, a driver tapped his horn. The light had changed.

Annie headed east on Sunrise, driving fast.

Harold Gund's gray van was parked outside the flower shop when she arrived. She pulled alongside it and saw Harold unlocking the front door, using the set of keys she'd given him yesterday.

She left the Miata's engine idling as she ran up to the doorway.

"I've got to go somewhere," she said breathlessly. "I'm sorry."

Concern in his round face, his startling blue eyes. "Something happen?"

"Letter from Erin."

Puzzlement now. "She's okay, then?"

Annie shook her head. "No. She's not okay. I'll explain later." She forced herself to focus on work for a moment. "I've got two shipments coming in today—Pacific and Green Thumb. You're authorized to sign for both. . . . We need roses for the Strepman wedding on Saturday. Call Julio, tell him to send Blue Girls and Caribias, same quantity as our last wedding order. Make sure we get the bulk discount. . . . We're running low on gift baskets. Better order a dozen from Marasco's. Half with dried fruit assortments, half with those fudge things. . . . And balloons; we need more balloons, assorted colors; at least two bags' worth. The big bags."

"Got it."

"Don't leave the shop to make deliveries. Use the courier service for anything local. Did you get the centerpiece to Antonio's before seven?"

"With time to spare. Closed up at six-thirty, and—zoom—I was there."

"I owe you some overtime."

"It took five minutes. Forget about it."

"How'd the centerpiece go over, anyway?"

"They loved it. Said they may put in another order today."

"Great," she said without enthusiasm. "If they do, I'll put it together as soon as I get back. If you have a chance, cut some foam for me. The green foam. And soak it."

"I know what to do," he said gently.

"Right. Sorry. Gotta go."

"Good luck, Annie," he called after her.

As she pulled out of the parking lot, she saw Harold still standing in the doorway, one arm lifted in a wave.

# 31

Gund watched Annie steer the Miata through a squealing U-turn and race onto Craycroft Road, speeding south.

The letter hadn't fooled her, as he'd hoped. If anything, it had reinforced her suspicions.

But he doubted that the police would view it in the same light. An overworked detective would seize on any plausible excuse to discontinue the preliminary investigation into Erin's disappearance.

Annie, of course, had failed to think of that. Her mind didn't work that way. She was not devious. To her, the phoniness of the letter was self-evident; naively she assumed that others would agree.

She was in for a disappointment. Well, there would be a worse disappointment yet to come. Because Erin was never coming back.

Gund entered the shop, flicked on the lights. Stuffed animals and garish piñatas peeped at him out of the foliage like huddled creatures in a forest.

He wondered how Annie would deal with it, how she would react as it became clear to her—clearer each day, each passing week—that her sister was gone forever, her fate a mystery never to be solved.

The loss would age her, surely. Kill her, even.

He frowned, lips pursed. No, he decided. It would not kill her. She was strong. As strong as Erin, though she probably didn't know it.

She would live through this.

Unless, of course, Gund should find it necessary to—

*No.*

That never had been part of the plan. Erin's . . . disposal . . . always had been an option, albeit one he'd preferred not to exercise. But Annie wasn't part of this. Annie need not be touched.

"Need not," he whispered, rubbing his hands together. "Need not."

He set about drawing the blinds, dusting the counter, sorting currency in the cash register. These were things he could do automatically; his mind was still on Annie.

In her haste and agitation she hadn't even noticed the damage to his van, though she had parked directly beside it.

Last night he'd replaced the flat tire with a full-size spare, then hammered the door frame on the driver's side back into shape so the door would open and shut. The rest of the damage would require the services of an auto-body shop.

The front quarter panel on the driver's side had been crushed like a beer can. One headlight was gone. Ugly grooves were etched in the passenger-side panel where Erin's Taurus had scraped the van in the barn.

Gund carried no collision insurance. That little bitch had cost him a bundle.

Well, he'd seen to it that she paid for her disobedience. She would never give him any trouble again.

He nodded grimly. Never again.

Though he hadn't heard a weather report, the morning

seemed warm, the shop stuffy. He found the thermostat and turned on the air conditioning.

The sudden whir of the duct fans, a dull, throbbing burr, reminded him of the roar of flames.

# 32

Annie found Walker at a desk in the detective squad room, eating a cruller and sipping black coffee. Crumbs littered his desk blotter.

He stood, wiping his mouth self-consciously, as she approached him. A smile brightened his face, then faded as he saw her obvious distress.

"What is it?" he asked.

"I heard from Erin."

He remembered courtesy. "Sit down."

She seated herself before the desk. Walker took his chair again, then leaned forward and studied her in the wan fluorescent glow.

"Was it a phone call?" he inquired gently.

"Letter." She almost handed it to him, then hesitated. "Do you think it ought to be tested for fingerprints?"

"Fingerprints? Is it some kind of ransom note?"

"No, but . . ."

"Don't worry about prints. Let me see it, please."

He read it carefully, taking more time than he needed.

Other men in suit jackets hurried in and out of the room. It occurred to Annie that all of them, and Walker, too, had guns concealed beneath their jackets, sleek pistols or bulky revolvers. The thought struck her as obvious and, at the same time, somehow bizarre—

like a child's first realization that people were naked under their clothes.

Finally, Walker put down the letter. "This is your sister's handwriting?"

"Yes."

"Well, then . . . it's good news. Isn't it?"

She'd hoped he would see instantly how stilted and unnatural the phrasing was. Now she wondered, with a flutter of doubt, if she could convince him.

"No," she replied, speaking carefully. "It's not good news at all. It's a trick."

"A trick." Though he said it evenly, not giving the words the inflection of a question, she heard his skepticism.

She swallowed. "I know it sounds . . . far-fetched. But Erin wouldn't write this. I mean, she wouldn't write it this way." Was she making any sense? It had seemed so clear to her on the way over, but now she couldn't find the words to express her thoughts. "I mean, she'd never be so impersonal and cold. It's totally out of character for her."

"So is running away."

"She didn't do that, either."

"What you're saying is that your sister was kidnapped and coerced into writing this letter."

Hearing her theory stated so coolly in this orderly place, this place of gray metal desks and pea green filing cabinets and men with guns, Annie thought it sounded preposterous, absurd.

Gamely she stood her ground. "That's exactly what I'm saying." A pause, then a shrug: she might as well play the full hand she'd been dealt. "There's this, too."

She showed him the envelope. He examined it with cursory interest. "The address is wrong," he said.

That surprised her; she hadn't thought he would notice. "Yes. I live at 509, not 505."

"I know. I booted up your D.M.V. file along with Erin's."

"You did? Why?"

"Just gathering information," he replied vaguely. "So what are you telling me? That Erin couldn't have filled out the envelope? You already said the handwriting is hers."

"Yes, it's hers. She wrote the wrong address on purpose." She took a breath, fully aware that she was about to make a fool of herself in his eyes, plunging ahead anyway. "The fives are written to look like S's. See? SOS."

To his credit, Walker showed no reaction to her suggestion. His face remained politely impassive as he did her the courtesy of appearing to consider the idea.

"Yes, well," he said at last, "it could be seen that way."

Hopelessness swallowed her. "You think I'm a paranoid lunatic, don't you?"

"I haven't said that."

"No, you haven't. You're a nice guy. Too nice to tell me how you really feel. But the thing is, I *know* Erin. I know how her mind works, how she *thinks*. This SOS signal is exactly what she would do. She must have thought it up on the spur of the moment, and gambled that her kidnapper wouldn't catch on."

"Or she may have made a small slip of the pen while she was preoccupied with getting out of town. Evidently she wasn't thinking very clearly. She addressed the envelope with the intention of mailing it, but there's no stamp or postmark; she must have hand-delivered it to your home."

"*Someone* delivered it by hand," Annie said. "I don't think it was her."

"We have no reason to suspect otherwise."

He wasn't buying it, as she should have known he

wouldn't. Still, there was one more angle of attack she could try. "The Tegretol is missing."

It took him a second to find a context for the remark. "From the medicine cabinet?"

She nodded. "I stayed at Erin's apartment yesterday evening, reading her journal—there's nothing in it that indicates any intention of leaving, by the way—and when I went to get some aspirin, I noticed the Tegretol wasn't there."

"What are you suggesting?"

"Maybe . . . whoever kidnapped her went back to the apartment and took the bottle."

"While you were still there?"

"He could've gotten past me. I was preoccupied."

"Why would he take that kind of risk just for the medicine?"

"Because Erin needs it."

"You mean her kidnapper is keeping her alive somewhere?"

Annie grasped that this was what she did mean. The realization that Erin very likely was still alive lifted her like a cresting wave.

"Yes," she said, holding her voice steady. "Yes, that's right. He abducted her and forced her to write this phony letter, and then later he returned for the Tegretol because, without it, she could die."

There. She had said it. Even to her it sounded grossly implausible, but she was grimly certain it was true.

Walker shut his eyes. Suddenly he looked tired. "Annie . . ."

She waited, refusing to make things easier for him by anticipating what he wanted to say.

"How much sleep did you get last night?" he asked finally.

She saw where this was leading. "Five or six hours," she lied.

"That much?"

Oh, hell. She'd never been a decent fibber. "More like three or four."

He nodded. "How about the night before? Did you sleep well then?"

"What makes you think I didn't?"

"You had circles under your eyes yesterday. You seemed kind of wired, as if you were operating on adrenaline."

"Okay. I had insomnia that night, too. So what?"

"So you've been functioning on virtually no rest. You're distraught. Your imagination is overacting."

"I hallucinated not seeing the Tegretol. Is that it?"

"Under the same circumstances I might have overlooked it, too."

Frustration and anger boiled up inside her. She thought about opening her purse, showing him the turquoise wrapped in the tissue—*Did I hallucinate this, you son of a bitch?*—but rationally she knew the stone proved nothing.

She took back the letter, folded it in the envelope, put the envelope in her purse. Her hands were shaking, and her knuckles were white.

"So," she said stiffly, "that's it, I guess. Case closed. Nothing more you're willing to do."

"I just don't see any basis on which to proceed."

"Sure. Of course." She was on her feet, the chair scraping the short-nap carpet. A detective at a nearby desk glanced up at her, his attention drawn by the implied violence in her body language.

"Annie—"

"I understand." Tears burned her eyes. "Really."

He was rising, reaching out to her. She turned away.

"I understand," she said again, and then she was out of the squad room, fleeing blindly down the hall.

# 33

Walker hesitated only a moment, long enough to remember Caroline and the other chances he'd missed. Then he went after Annie.

He caught up with her in the visitors' parking lot, unlocking her Miata.

"Annie, wait."

He could see from her face that she was tempted to tell him to go to hell. But after a moment her features softened, and her shoulders slumped.

"What is it?" she asked, fatigue in her voice.

"Take a walk with me."

"I have to get back to my shop."

"Just for a few minutes."

She frowned, and he thought she might still refuse; but with a shrug she relocked the car door and pocketed her keys.

Wordlessly he led her down a side street toward the sprawling community center, a short distance from the police station. Sunlight burned on car windshields, on a fire hydrant, on a crumpled cellophane wrapper in the dirt. The day was warming up. Walker defied departmental regulations by loosening his tie.

"I was wrong," he said quietly. "I shouldn't have

suggested that you were mistaken about the Tegretol. If
you say it's not there, then it's not."

She wasn't mollified. "And how can you explain
that?"

"I've been assuming Erin left town. Suppose she
didn't. Suppose she stayed in Tucson and went back to
her apartment to get the pills."

"She wouldn't have sneaked around while I was
there."

"People in distress do a lot of uncharacteristic
things. Look, her car isn't at the airport, the bus station, or the railroad terminal. She didn't check into the
Phoenix Crown Sterling, the Fairmont, or the Sierra
Springs Inn. My guess is she's hiding out in a local hotel."

"I don't believe it," Annie said firmly.

"It does make sense, though. The only way she
could have delivered the letter in person is if she was
still in the area. It's the one explanation that fits all the
facts."

"But it doesn't fit *Erin*. Was this all you wanted to
say?"

"Walk with me a little farther."

He escorted her across the street, into the community
center, a puzzle of shaded walkways, shops, restau-
rants, meeting halls, and auditoriums. At noon the center would be crowded, but at this hour few people were
in sight.

Walker liked it here. Green trees lined the branching
footpaths. The clusters of stores and eateries were
dressed in southwestern colors: pink stucco, turquoise
molding, red-tile roofs.

He stopped at a fountain, the water foaming over art-
fully arranged rocks into rectangular blue-tiled pools.
Pigeons cluttered the ground, pecking at somebody's
spilled popcorn.

For a long moment he and Annie just stood together and watched the surging carpet of water. Then Walker took a breath and said it.

"I talked to a friend at the *Tucson Standard* last night. He told me about Lincoln and Oliver Connor. And about the fire."

Beside him, Annie stiffened. "You mean you had your friend look it up in the morgue, or whatever they call it?"

"Right."

"Why?"

"You'd aroused my curiosity."

Her startled glance told him that she was wondering, for the first time, if curiosity was all she had aroused. "Did I?" Quickly she looked away. "I would have told you, if you'd asked."

"I understand now why you're so worried about Erin."

"As if I need an excuse."

"She wrote you a letter. A lot of people would let it go at that. You keep assuming the worst. I think the fire is the reason."

No answer to that. She moved away, and Walker followed.

He stayed just behind her, watching as she hurried along, aiming at no destination, her head down, arms folded, purse swinging roughly by its shoulder strap. He thought the back of her neck was pretty.

When she slowed her steps, he eased alongside her. She was not crying, but her face was drawn tight in lines of concentration and pain.

"Maybe you're right," she whispered.

He took her arm, and she did not pull free.

"How much do you remember about the fire?" he asked gently.

"Everything. It's engraved in my memory. I wish it

weren't." Through the light contact of his fingertips on her arm, he felt the sudden trembling of her body. "God damn him."

He knew whom she meant. "Your father."

"God damn him," she said again.

Her knees shook, and her face was pale. Quickly he led her to a tree-shaded bench near a nineteenth-century gazebo, then sat at her side. Annie stared into the distance, at the blocky modernistic shapes of the superior courts and administration buildings, their checkerboard facades smooth and flat like cutouts.

Walker waited. In his line of work he'd interviewed many people: suspects, witnesses, victims, tipsters, cranks. He knew better than to prompt Annie to talk. She would speak when she was ready.

After a minute or two, she found her voice.

"Albert was good to us in the beginning." She used her father's first name, as if reluctant to acknowledge his paternity. "A little stern, maybe too much of a disciplinarian—his family, like our mother's, were all strict Catholics, probably a bit too strict at times. But basically he was kind and ... loving."

The last word nearly caught in her throat.

"He would read us bedtime stories. He'd tuck us in and read *The Wind in the Willows* and *Black Beauty* and that one about the pig and the spider."

*"Charlotte's Web."*

"He did different voices for all the characters. And sound effects. He was ... he was a good man."

Walker said nothing. From what Gary had told him, he knew that Albert Reilly might have begun as a good man, but he hadn't finished that way.

"And then," Annie went on, her voice lowering to a whisper, "he changed. He went crazy."

"Just like that? All of a sudden?"

"It seemed that way. But maybe Erin and I were too

young to pick up on the change until it was obvious. All I know is that he stopped reading to us, stopped tucking us in, stopped kissing us good night . . . stopped loving us."

"Couldn't your mother talk to him?"

She shook her head violently. "He *hated* Maureen."

"Had they been close before?"

"Oh, yes. It was a good marriage; I'm sure it was. Aunt Lydia had some photo albums: our parents' wedding, Maureen and Albert with the two of us as babies, a trip to Yosemite they took on their first anniversary. In the pictures they always look happy, Albert especially."

"Do you have any idea what changed him?"

"Not really. But I've always thought . . . well, I know it sounds odd, but maybe religion had something to do with it."

"What makes you say that?"

Annie looked away, toward rows of flower beds humming with bees. A child scampered past, trailing a balloon.

"I told you he was strict in his beliefs. One night Maureen and Erin and I were together in the living room when he came home. This was a couple of weeks after he'd changed. He was still living with us—he had nowhere else to go—but he was sleeping on a sofa in the den. He'd been sullen and angry for days, but that night he'd stopped at a bar after work, had too much to drink, and his face . . ." The memory touched her like a ghost, raising a shiver. "His face was wild."

"Was he violent?"

"Not in what he did, not then. But the things he said to us . . . the words he used . . ." Her eyes squeezed shut. "He called us abominations in the eyes of God. That's why I think maybe it was some kind of religious

mania or something." She said it again, thoughtfully.
"Abominations in the eyes of God."

Walker was silent.

"Erin and I were too little to know what an abomi-
nation was, but we knew it must be something bad,
something really dreadful. Maureen pleaded with him
to calm down; he slapped her. I can still hear that
sound, like a gunshot. He pointed at her, then at Erin
and me"—she swallowed—"and he said, 'You'll burn.
All of you. *Burn.*' "

Walker didn't know how to respond. This was much
worse than the sketchy details in the newspaper story
Gary had dug up.

"How long afterward was the fire?" he asked slowly.

"The very next night. August eighteenth, 1973."

He nodded. He'd known the date from the article.

"What woke us," Annie said, her voice soft as the
whisper of thought, "were the screams. Screams from
the master bedroom at the other end of the hall. My
mother's screams."

She swallowed, finding strength within her. When
she continued, her voice was suddenly raw, as if she
herself had been screaming.

"Erin and I sat up in our beds and listened. There
was a sharp crack; Albert was in there, and he'd
slapped her again. The screams stopped, and she
started to beg. She said *please* over and over. 'Please,
please, please . . .'

"Then she screamed again, but it was worse this
time. It was the worst sound I'll ever hear.

"From the hallway came a dry crackle, like crinkling
newspaper, then a funny odor, a burnt-toast smell:
smoke. That was when I knew the house was on fire
and my mother was burning to death."

"How did you get out?"

"It was—" She stopped herself and swallowed whatever words she'd intended to say. "I don't know. Luck, I guess. The flames hadn't reached our end of the hall yet. We made it downstairs and outside."

She paused, as if daring him to press for details. He said nothing.

"Outside," she repeated. "I remember running across the lawn with Erin, into a crowd of neighbors in robes and nightgowns. Old Mrs. Carroway took us both in her big arms and held us, and someone else asked about our parents, and another person shushed him.

"The fire trucks arrived a minute later. I don't know how long it was before the firemen got inside, but eventually they found Maureen and Albert in the master bedroom, both of them burned so badly they had to be identified later from dental records.

"It wasn't hard for the arson investigators to reconstruct what had happened. Two gasoline cans were recovered, one in the living room, the other in the bedroom, still in Albert's hand. He must have hidden them in the garage or the tool shed. In the middle of the night he'd left the den, gotten the cans, and poured a trail of gasoline through the house, starting on ground level, ending in the bedroom, where Maureen was. Then he'd lit the match."

She looked at Walker, her eyes haunted, brimful of tears.

"He told us we would all burn. He meant it."

Walker clasped her hand. "And after that," he said gently, "the two of you went to live with Lydia, Maureen's sister, in Tucson . . . and you found out about the other murder–suicide in your family's history. Lincoln and Oliver."

"Yes." A shudder blew through her like a cold wind. "It was like the whole world was crazy. Like everyone in it was a monster. Anybody, at any time, for any reason or for no reason at all, could snap, go insane, and kill whoever he loved most."

"But it's not the whole world. There are plenty of good people."

Annie met his gaze, and he saw the hurt in her face, the lingering residue of trauma, the unhealed grief.

"My father was a good person, too," she whispered. "Once."

# 34

Annie was silent as Walker escorted her out of the community center. He wondered if he'd been wrong to ask about the fire. She had been upset to begin with, and reliving those memories might have served only to traumatize her further.

They crossed the street together. At the curb Annie abruptly turned to him and whispered, "It wasn't luck."

He blinked. "What?"

"I told you we were lucky to escape the fire. But it wasn't luck."

"What, then?"

"Erin saved me."

Their shoes clacked on the sidewalk. A robin burst out of the branches of a mesquite tree and shot into the clear, warm air. In the near distance, the bells of San Agustin Cathedral chimed ten o'clock.

"I panicked," she went on softly. "I mean, I lost it. Totally. I could hear our mother shrieking, and the flames crackling, and I started to yell and yell and yell. I couldn't stop."

He heard bitter self-recrimination in her voice, and frowned at it. "You were seven years old."

"So was Erin."

"Anyone would panic in that situation."

Annie stopped walking and looked up at him, her face flushed, candescent in the harsh sunshine. "*She* didn't."

Walker took that in. A first grader, and she had kept her cool in an arson fire.

"How did your sister save you?" he asked after a thoughtful moment.

"First she got me to calm down. She grabbed hold of me, put a stuffed animal in my hands, a koala bear. My favorite bear. I'd named her Miss Fuzzy."

Walker felt his throat catch. The mention of the doll brought it home to him—how little those two girls had been. Small enough to still cling to teddy bears for comfort.

"That shut me up," Annie went on. "It wasn't just the bear; it was Erin's attitude, her ... decisiveness. Then she took me by the hand and led me into the hall."

"Which was soaked with gasoline," Walker said, "and ablaze."

"It was the only exit. We were on the second floor, with a concrete patio twenty feet below. To jump out the window would have been suicide, and there was no time to improvise any sort of ladder, even if we'd thought of it. We had to get out fast."

Standing on this quiet tree-lined street, listening to birdsong and the rustle of leaves, Walker tried to visualize what it must have been like inside that house.

He had seen a few fires, though he'd never been in the midst of one. A house fire out of control was a waking nightmare, a riot of churning smoke and hellish flames, of windows and walls blown apart by combustible gases, of spinning clouds of soot like fallout from a bomb blast.

Even to stand outside such a spectacle could be unnerving. To be at the center of it—his imagination failed him. And to be at the center of it and only seven years old . . .

"Our mother was quiet by then," Annie said softly. "There was no sound except the fire—I can still hear it—roaring and bellowing like a dragon, and that's what I thought we were walking straight into: a dragon's open jaws."

"But you went anyway."

"Because Erin led me," Annie said simply.

Slowly, Walker nodded.

"Our end of the hall wasn't on fire yet—he hadn't poured any gasoline there, for some reason—but there was a sheet of flame across the staircase landing. Like a wall, a wall of heat, only not a wall, because it was moving, it was . . . alive."

"How'd you get through?"

"Between the fire and the banister was a narrow gap. Barely enough clearance, but we had to chance it. Erin went first, and I followed." The memory winded her; she drew a shaky breath. "It was like a circus act, you know? Like jumping through a flaming hoop."

"And you made it."

"Almost didn't. My pajamas caught fire. Erin snatched the bear out of my hand and beat at the flames till they were smothered. I was crying again, because I knew the dragon had almost gotten me, and because I'd lost Miss Fuzzy. She was all charred and mangled and . . . well, I just left her there." She hugged herself and managed a faltering smile. "Sometimes I still think about that bear. Still wish I hadn't lost her." Her voice was a whisper. "Isn't that silly?"

Walker didn't think so, and he knew she didn't, either. "Go on," he said gently.

"We got down into the living room, and God, such an awful smell, gasoline everywhere. The fire was still after us—I saw it marching down the stairs. We ran for the front door, but the fire was too quick; it beat us there. Then the whole room went up—everything flame and smoke, orange and black—whirling sparks like the dragon's eyes."

*In the belly of the monster.* The string of words ran through Walker's mind, a random fragment of thought.

"It was hard to breathe." Annie gazed into the distance, her face in profile, moisture glistening on her cheek. "Erin pulled me to the floor, where the air was cleaner. We crawled into the kitchen. No flames there yet, no gasoline trail. She helped me up on the counter, opened the window and punched out the screen, then pushed me through and followed."

Her shoulders lifted in a shaky shrug, and abruptly all the breath seemed to sigh out of her.

"Anyway, that's it," she finished. "That's how we survived."

Walker shook his head. Seven years old, hardly more than babies—yet so incredibly brave, both of them.

For although Erin clearly had taken the lead, Annie had needed courage, too, more courage then she gave herself credit for—the courage to leave the imagined safety of the bedroom and face the dragon's scorching breath.

"So you see?" She looked at him, desperate intensity shining in her eyes. "You see why I have to help her? She saved me. Now she's in trouble, and it's my turn to rescue her. *It's my turn.*"

He tried to be gentle. "You've done all you can."

"I haven't done anything," she snapped, turning away.

In the parking lot, watching her unlock her car, he looked for words of reassurance. "From everything you've told me, I'd say your sister can take of herself."

"She needs me now."

"How can you be sure?"

"SOS," she said hotly.

"Annie . . ."

Her eyes flashed at him, hard and angry. "I know you think I'm overreacting. I know you think I should forget about it. I know you think Erin is fine, just fine. But you're wrong."

"I just hate to see you so worked up over—"

"You're wrong," she said again, and then she was behind the wheel, slamming the door, revving the engine, racing out of the lot and down the street at twice the posted speed limit, daring him or any other cop to ticket her.

He stared after the car until it hooked around a corner with a shriek of tires. Then he sighed. He supposed he would never see her again.

Or perhaps he would. Once Erin turned up unharmed, sheepish about her temporary abdication of responsibility, Annie might drop by the squad room to fill him in. He hoped so.

A new thought made him frown. The seven-year-old who had kept her presence of mind in a blazing house didn't sound like the type to ever abdicate responsibility. A fire hadn't rattled her; how likely was it that she would fall victim to the pressures of work?

Standing very still, feeling the steady heat of the sun on the back of his head, Walker wondered if Annie could be right.

*He abducted her,* she'd said, *and forced her to write this phony letter, and then later he returned for the Tegretol because, without it, she could die.*

Was it possible?

Oh, hell. Of course not.

What did he have to go on? An incorrect street address on an envelope? A letter that was oddly terse and impersonal?

There was nothing to justify any further investigation. Nothing.

"Sorry, Annie," he said to the silence around him.

Before entering the station, he remembered to straighten his tie. His neck, he noticed, was damp with sweat.

The temperature must be ninety-five already; low hundreds by afternoon. Summer weather, coming early.

A real scorcher, he thought grimly, opening the lobby door.

# 35

Hot.

The sun blazed like a klieg light, painfully bright, branding a blurred red circle on her vision even through her closed eyelids.

Waves of heat radiated from the ground under her. She thought of a griddle, of sizzling meat.

Through the gag still clogging her mouth, Erin let out a choked, plaintive noise, too indistinct to be a moan.

She turned her head first to one side, then the other, trying to avert her face from the sun. The sand planted searing kisses on her cheeks.

Somewhere in the world there was shade. A cool breeze, a rustle of green leaves ... She remembered Muir Woods near San Francisco. She remembered Sierra Springs.

No shade here, not anymore. The walls of the arroyo had cupped her in shadow for only a precious hour after daybreak. As the sun climbed higher, the shadow had rolled back slowly like a receding tide, exposing first her legs, then her upper body, and finally her face.

Her eyes fluttered open briefly. From the sun's position in the eastern sky, she estimated the time at ten o'clock. She would not again be sheltered from the burning rays until evening, countless hours away.

By then it might not matter. By then, if her abductor had not returned, she might be dead.

She had been sure he meant to burn her last night. As he climbed the embankment, she struggled fiercely with the ropes, knowing that it was futile, that soon he would splash gasoline over her body and then . . . and then . . .

At a restaurant years ago she'd watched the chef prepare a flambéed dish at the next table. The flare of the match, the breath-stopping burst of flame—

That was how it would be. An eruption of agony, a final surge of terror, and then, mercifully, nothing more, ever.

He had disappeared into the night. After that, a long interval of waiting. She'd lain paralyzed, watching the rim of the arroyo, listening for his return.

The sound of hammering, distant and inexplicable, had reached her. Sometime later, the cough of an engine.

His van, pulling away. The motor fading, fading . . . Gone.

He'd left her. She would not burn tonight.

For a few giddy minutes the intensity of her relief had blinded her to the full implications of his departure.

Then gradually she'd begun to ponder his motive. Clearly he had been furious with her. He'd called her a bad girl, told her that he regretted what he was doing, but that it had become necessary.

He must have been planning to burn her, then had changed his mind. Yes, that was it. Somehow, at the last moment, he'd made contact with the better part of himself, the embryonic conscience that had taught him about remorse.

Or perhaps not.

Perhaps she had misinterpreted his purpose all

along. Perhaps his intention had never been to kill her, only to inflict punishment. To leave her here, staked supine at the bottom of the wash, exposed to the night chill and, later, to the heat of a desert day ...

Flat on her back, gazing at the cold spray of stars, she had felt relief fade, supplanted by a new dread.

He might not ever come back. Might leave her to suffer a lingering death.

Anger had made her strong, as it had in the cellar.

Her wrists twisted. The rope binding them was knotted tightly, too tight to be worked free.

Straining, she'd reached out to run her fingertips over the metal stake above her head. The edge was sharp.

Shrugging her shoulders, extending her arms a few extra inches, she had pressed the loop of rope hard against the stake. Slowly she'd begun to rub in a montonous sawing motion. Up, down. Up, down.

Within minutes, pain had radiated from her shoulder blades and neck. It had started as an ache, then sharpened rapidly to a series of electric twinges, each one contracting her facial muscles into an agonized wince.

She'd kept working. The constellations had wheeled toward dawn, and the night chill had settled deeper into her bones.

From time to time she had rested, hoping to revive muscles strained by fatigue. The worst torture was not pain or weariness, but uncertainty. She couldn't see the binding on her wrists, couldn't know if her efforts were showing results or merely wasting irreplaceable reserves of energy.

Pink dawn had congealed into a red sunrise. Astonishing how quickly the day had warmed up.

Now, at roughly ten in the morning, the temperature must be ninety degrees. By the calendar it was April, but this was August heat. Heat that killed.

Already she was severely dehydrated. Her mouth was dry; her throat ached. Cramps tightened the muscles of her abdomen and thighs. Since daybreak, sweat had been streaming off her skin; she wondered how much more moisture she had left to lose.

When perspiration ceased, her body's natural cooling mechanism would be disabled. Her temperature would rise. She would pass from heat exhaustion to heatstroke.

Untreated, heatstroke would be fatal.

And still, after hours of excruciating labor, the goddamned rope had not split. It had started to fray—when she craned her neck, she glimpsed wisps of fiber curling from the loop like uncombed hairs—but her hands remained tightly bound.

Though she kept working, she rested often now. The agony in her shoulders was unendurable for long periods, and the weakness of her arms made any movement difficult.

Perhaps she ought to give it up, conserve her strength. But she was haunted by the thought that one more try might unravel the remaining strands and set her free.

One more try. The words were a magic formula, summoning new strength. Again she lifted her shoulders to attack the rope.

A sudden wave of dizziness rippled up her spine. The world began to slide away, down a long, greased tunnel, leaving her behind. Wind chimes sang in her ears. Such pretty music . . .

With a teeth-grinding effort she retained her hold on consciousness.

When her head was clear, she locked her jaws, biting down hard on the gag as if it were a bullet, and continued rubbing the stake.

As she worked, the bad thoughts came again, the

thoughts that had been her tormentors for hours, eating at her like the vultures sent to prey on Prometheus when he, like her, had been bound to a barren expanse of sand and rock.

*If only . . .*

If only she had made it onto the interstate. If only the service station had been open. If only she hadn't set off the van's alarm.

Broiling in the sun, eyes shut and lips sealed, she pictured herself escaping from the cellar into an empty house. Swiftly she finds her way to the front door. Outside, she explores the grounds, first examining the gate and perimeter fence, then entering the barn, where she discovers her car, alone in the musty dark. The barn doors swing wide, the Ford's engine catches, and she backs out into the night, pursued by no one; and as she roars toward freedom and safety, she takes a last look at the ranch, memorizing its layout and appearance for the report she will file with the police.

Her mind lingered on that image: the ranch receding, stark in the moonlight.

Padlocked gate. Barbed-wire fencing. Horse barn and paddock. Wood-frame house with a gravel court.

Familiar.

Yes. She realized it now, for the first time.

Something about the ranch was familiar to her. Strikingly familiar, in fact.

She was almost certain she had seen the place before.

But that was crazy. How could she? And where? And what would it mean if she had?

The rush of questions brought on another slow comber of light-headedness.

Couldn't think now. The sun was too strong, the ache in her muscles too sharp.

She rested her arms and shoulders once more. Rotating her wrists, she detected perhaps slightly more give in the rope. Or maybe not. She couldn't be sure. She was tired. So tired and so very hot.

The sun beat down. The sand reflected back its heat in shimmering waves.

Water. Oh, Christ, she wanted water. Water and shade.

Her tormentor had not set her on fire. Yet in a different way, a slower and perhaps crueler way, he *was* burning her.

Burning her to death.

Though she squeezed her eyes tightly shut, she could not erase the sight of the sun's red disk, climbing relentlessly toward noon.

# 36

A surge of air-conditioned coolness greeted Annie when she opened the flower shop door.

"You turned on the A.C.," she said to Harold Gund, cutting foam at the workstation behind the counter. "Good move. It's hot as Hades out there."

He nodded in a distracted way, then looked up, remembering the reason for her trip downtown. "What happened with the police?"

"I don't want to talk about it." The words came out harsh, and she bit her lip. "Sorry. Let's just say I won't be getting any more help from the authorities. Hey, what's the story with your van? I just noticed it's all banged up."

A shrug. "Fender-bender."

"I'd say a lot more got bent than just a fender."

"Yeah, well ... I'll have it fixed."

"Your insurance cover it?"

"Sure."

"That's something anyhow."

He nodded without real acknowledgment.

Funny. Harold got this way at times—oddly detached, as if he weren't entirely present. His reliability and competence were undiminished, but the spark of personality seemed temporarily extinguished. She wondered if there was any connection between his mood and the damage to the van.

Then she shook her head, dismissing the issue. Whatever was the matter, Harold would have to deal with it.

She had enough problems of her own.

Throughout the day the feelings had been growing.

Snipping the stems of roses with a pair of florist's scissors, scraping off the lower leaves and thorns with a steel knife, he found that his fingers were tingling.

Opening the walk-in cooler, feeling the chilled and humidified air kiss his face, he noticed that the back of his neck was hot.

He knew why. It had aroused him—what he'd done with Erin last night. Carrying her into the arroyo, pounding the stakes into the ground, seeing her writhe and twitch . . . He had been unsettled ever since.

Twice during the night he'd woken from a restless sleep to contemplate returning to the ranch and finishing the job.

So far he had fought off those impulses. Erin was his lifeline to health and freedom, his last chance. She could not die until their work was done.

The day dragged on. A UPS truck delivered a shipment from a florist supplier in Phoenix, and Gund unpacked the cartons. A vendor from Nogales dropped by, hawking Mexican paper flowers. Customers came and went. Several of Annie's friends called or visited, making anxious inquiries about Erin.

Gund paid scant attention to any of it. Outwardly composed, he was struggling inside to clamp down on the feelings and hold them in check.

If he were to relax control, he knew what would happen. He would click off.

That was how he thought of it. To click off was to

relinquish control, to let his conscious mind retreat to an insignificant corner of himself while his compulsion rose to the surface and took over.

What he would do then would be shocking, horrible, yet the rational part of him would watch it without influence or authority.

He had come near to clicking off several times already. Only an iron effort of will had allowed him to maintain a degree of precarious self-mastery.

If he lost control now, alone with Annie in the shop . . . he didn't want to know what he might do.

And even if he held on until work was over, how could he possibly make it through the night?

Somehow he must. Erin could not die yet. There was much more work for her to do. Much more progress to be made.

Progress. Yes. Already he had shown progress. Perhaps he could use what he had learned to maintain control. If so, he and Erin could continue to explore his illness together until they found a cure.

At least he need not worry about any further escape attempts on her part. After a night and day staked out on the sand, she would be properly chastened and submissive, her spirit broken.

She would give him no trouble. He was certain of that. No trouble ever again.

Of course, he could never let her go.

He'd decided as much last night. She had seen his face . . . and the ranch.

He would keep her alive until his treatment was complete. Then . . . kill her. Not out of compulsion, and not by fire. He should be rid of those impulses by that time.

A bullet in the brain. That was how he would do it. Neat and quick.

The killing would afford him no pleasure. It would

be a simple matter of practical necessity. She'd brought it on herself, after all. If the little bitch had just been more cooperative—

"You going to lunch?"

Annie's voice.

He looked up from the lily of the valley in his hands, its slender stem wound in rose wire and stem-wrap tape. "Huh?"

"It's one o'clock."

"Oh. Yes."

So late already. He'd been completely unaware of the time.

Though he wasn't hungry, he had better eat. Best not to disrupt his daily routine. Normally he went next door for a deli sandwich at this hour, and Annie did likewise upon his return at one-thirty.

"See you in a bit," he said automatically as he stepped out from behind the counter.

She nodded without answer. She, too, was distracted by thoughts of Erin, he knew, but they were thoughts of a very different kind from his own.

He left the shop, emerging into the afternoon glare.

Instantly a blanket of heat smothered him.

It was like summer out here. An Arizona summer, which was a dress rehearsal for hell.

Behind him, the shop door swung shut with a rattle and bang.

He barely heard it. He was thinking of Erin. Erin, staked out in the wash under the sun.

Had it been this hot all day?

He remembered turning on the air-conditioning at nine. The duct fans rarely had stopped whirring, and the compressor's motor throbbed steadily like a pumping heart. Consumed by his inner struggle, he hadn't noticed, hadn't even thought about it.

Yet the UPS man had been sweating hard when he'd

lugged in those cartons at ten. And customers had kept making comments to Annie about the weather, hadn't they? And the paper-flower vendor from Nogales—*mucho calor,* he'd said. Hot day.

Damn it, he should have been more alert.

Blinking sweat out of his eyes, he gazed across the shopping plaza at the clock tower of a bank. Below the clock a digital board displayed the temperature: 101 degrees.

Twenty degrees hotter than yesterday's high. Well above normal for this time of year. And at lower elevations the temperature would be three to five degrees higher than in the foothills. At the ranch, the mercury must be brushing 105 on the scale.

Desert soil, absorbing the sun's heat, became hotter than the air. Erin might be roasting in temperatures of 115 degrees or more.

"My God," Gund whispered, drawing a stare from a woman bustling past with a child in tow.

He must get to Erin. Take her inside and apply first aid for heat exhaustion or heatstroke.

If it wasn't already too late.

The trip to the ranch and back would require at least an hour, twice the length of his usual lunch break. He needed an excuse.

With a glance at his van, he had one.

Annie was surprised to see him reenter the shop only a minute after leaving. "Forget something?"

"No. Well, yes. What I forgot was my van. I mean, I need to take it to a body shop, get an estimate for insurance purposes. You know."

Ordinarily he was a cool and practiced liar, but now the words kept jamming up in his mouth. It was too much to handle all at once—the compulsion rising in him, Erin cooking in the sun, the need for urgency balanced with the charade of calm.

"Okay," Annie said, puzzlement in her eyes.

"It may take a while. An hour or longer. I'm sorry."

"Use all the time you need." She gifted him with a warm smile. "How could I possibly object after you've been such a help?"

He did not smile in answer. He never smiled.

"Thanks, Annie," he said simply, turning to go.

Her voice stopped him. "Harold? You didn't hurt yourself in that accident, did you?"

"Of course not. What makes you ask?"

"You seem . . . tense."

"It's the weather."

That much, at least, was true.

Starting the van's engine, he looked at the bank tower again. As he watched, the last digit of the Fahrenheit reading flickered, and the display changed from 101 to 102 degrees.

The day was continuing to heat up. By the time he arrived at the ranch, thirty minutes from now, what would the temperature be?

Gund reversed away from the curb and pulled onto Craycroft Road, speeding south.

# 37

Erin was dying.

She knew it, in those rare moments when she knew anything.

Shortly after the sun had reached its zenith, she'd noticed that chilly beads of sweat were no longer seeping from her hairline or rolling down her arms. Her skin, having lost its sheen of perspiration, was becoming flushed and dry, as dry as her parched mouth and burning eyes.

That was when she'd understood that she would not survive until evening. Would not survive even another two hours.

The sun had wheeled westward since then, into early afternoon. Must be one o'clock by now, or later. She had little time left.

Just as well. Death would bring release. Release from thirst and cramps and fevered thoughts.

*No.*

She rallied. For the thousandth time she strained her shoulders, chafing her bound wrists against the stake.

The rope was fraying. It had to split soon. Had to.

Then she sagged, giving up. She had long since lost all strength and muscular coordination. Even if the rope did break, her nerveless fingers could not undo the knot securing her ankles to the other stake, and her legs, knotted in cramps, could not carry her to shade.

She was finished.

Her pulse, ticking in her ears, was rapid but weak—a frantic flutter that signaled imminent collapse. Nausea bubbled in her stomach. Wracking shivers, like half-hearted convulsions, shook her without warning.

She wondered how she would die, exactly. Would there be a slow gray-out, a long slide into unconsciousness, deepening to coma, ending in death? Or staccato alterations of awareness and oblivion, culminating in a few final moments of wrenching agony as her heart failed?

It didn't matter. Nothing mattered. The death she imagined was only a dream. Her hours of exposure, her captivity in the cellar, her abduction—all of it, a dream.

She had never lived in Arizona, that place of barren land and unforgiving heat. Had never left Sierra Springs. There had been no reason to leave it. No fatal fire, no inexplicable craziness that possessed a loving father, no years of post-traumatic recovery, of unanswered questions and haunted sleep.

She was a young girl again, seven years old, playing in the green yard of the Reilly house, under a maple tree's cooling umbrella of leaves. A swing hung from a low branch, and Erin climbed onto it, gripping the rusty chains. She kicked the ground away, and then she was flying, propelling herself to ever greater heights in wild, reckless swoops that carried her out of shadow and into the clear California sunlight.

Below, Annie yelled encouragement: *Higher, Erin, higher!*

Erin leaned back on the wooden seat, legs thrust out, warm air whistling past her as the chains creaked and her hair streamed like a comet's tail, and she was laughing.

Laughing . . .

She tried to laugh and choked on the wadded cloth in her mouth. The effort required to stifle her gag reflex jerked her back to this moment.

The swing was gone, and Annie, and the green yard, and there was only heat and dust and pain.

What time was it? Two o'clock? Two-thirty?

No, not yet. But if she could hold out that long, until two-thirty or three, when the sun would be behind her, not shining quite so directly on her face . . .

Then she rolled her head to one side and pressed her right temple to her forearm, pinioned over her head. She felt the febrile heat radiating from her own skin.

*I'm radioactive,* she thought with a giddy stab at humor. *Erin Reilly, the human microwave.*

Her last hope withered. No chance she could last until mid-afternoon. Another half hour, at most, was all she had.

Away again to Sierra Springs, the shaded yard. The swing described a final, reckless arc. Then her father, kind and sane, took her and Annie by the hand and led them upstairs to their bedroom. Night had fallen, although, strangely, it had been daytime only a moment earlier.

A moth beat against the window screen. Crickets chirruped in singsong choruses. Somewhere on the ground floor their mother hummed a soft, sad tune.

Albert Reilly tucked in Annie first, then moved to Erin's bed and pulled the covers up to her neck. She smelled his masculine scent, comforting in the dark. His hands stroked her hair, her forehead. Large hands. Sensitive hands.

"Christ," he whispered, "you're feverish."

That seemed an odd thing for her father to say. But she had no power left to question it.

Snug in her bed, Erin slept.

A shock of cool water on her face revived her. She blinked alert and found herself sprawled on a concrete floor, propped against a brick wall, both surfaces wonderfully cool.

The cellar. She was back in the cellar.

And the man swabbing her face with a damp washcloth, his features blurred and doubled, discolored by the red haze that hung over everything like a permanent filter ...

Him.

He had returned for her. Had saved her life.

She licked her lips, then realized that her mouth wasn't stoppered with a gag any longer, nor was it parched with thirst. Her tongue, running lightly over her gums, tasted salt.

He must have force-fed her a few sips of salt water. Standard remedy for dehydration.

The cloth moved lower, wetting her neck, her collarbone. At her cleavage he hesitated, as though debating whether or not to probe deeper. Then abruptly he rose upright and crossed the room to the sill cock in the wall.

A low hiss: flow of water from the tap. He held the cloth under the stream, then knelt by her again and began to scrub her legs.

She observed all this with blank detachment, feeling nothing except boundless relief at being indoors, and dangerous gratitude toward the man who'd brought her here.

The cloth was chilly against her ankles. Gooseflesh bumped up on her legs. She shivered.

"Cold?" he asked.

The brief, staccato chatter of her teeth was sufficient response.

"Better get you into bed."

He carried her to the foam pad in the corner, deposited her gently on her side. Eyes shut, she felt him draw the cotton blanket over her, leaving only her head exposed.

"Sleep," he whispered, and for a disoriented moment reality melded with hallucination, and he was her father, tucking her in at bedtime. "I'll be back this evening. You'll be all better by then. And we'll continue our work."

*Yes,* she thought dreamily. *Our work. Got to continue . . . the work . . .*

It seemed vitally important that the work proceed, the most important thing in the world, though she no longer recalled just what sort of work it was or why it mattered.

Her breathing slowed and deepened, and she went away again—not to Sierra Springs this time, but to nowhere at all.

# 38

Annie was rearranging her display of gift baskets, not out of necessity but simply to take her mind off Erin, when the shop door jingled open at two-fifteen.

She turned, and a sudden smile dimpled her cheeks. "Jeez, Harold, look at you. You're a mess."

Gund paused in the doorway, gazing down at himself. His pants, badly rumpled, were soiled from knees to cuffs with blotches of tan desert dust.

He blinked as if embarrassed. "Yes ... well ... there was some damage to the chassis. I had to crawl under the van to check it out."

"We'd better get you cleaned up or you'll scare away the clientele."

Briskly she rummaged in a drawer behind the counter until she found a large brush useful for cleaning clothes and smocks dirtied by potting soil.

"So what was the estimate?" she asked as she stepped to the middle of the room.

"Twelve hundred dollars."

She let out a low whistle. "That's a bundle."

"My insurance will pay for it."

She stooped and began brushing his pants with quick, vigorous strokes. "Was it the other driver's fault?"

"Yeah. He cut me off."

His answer was clipped, his posture stiff. Apparently he found her close contact uncomfortable. Funny for a man in his forties to be so shy.

Well, this would take only a minute. To distract him, she said, "If the other guy's to blame, he should pay."

"He hasn't got any insurance."

"Not even liability? Isn't that illegal in Arizona?"

"He's from out of state. A snowbird."

Annie frowned. Snowbirds were part-year residents, fleeing harsh northern winters. If this negligent motorist could afford to maintain two homes, he ought to be able to reimburse Harold out of pocket.

She was about to say as much when she noticed the belt.

A western-style belt, black leather with a snakeskin overlay and a brass buckle. Harold wore it often, nearly every day, but she'd never gotten a close look at it before.

The overlay was studded with small turquoise beads.

One of the beads was missing.

Her hand opened reflexively, and she dropped the brush.

"Oops. Clumsy me." The words were spoken by someone far away, someone who would remain composed in any crisis, someone like her sister. "Think I'm done, anyhow."

Gund took a quick step back, as if anxious to distance himself from her.

She replaced the brush in the drawer. Her mind was frozen. When she opened her mouth, she had no idea what she was about to say.

"Gotta use the powder room for a sec. Hold down the fort, will you?"

He nodded. His face seemed slightly flushed, and his eyes wouldn't meet hers.

Did he realize she'd been staring at the belt? No, that wasn't it. He was . . . aroused. Bending near his waist, stroking his trousers, inadvertently she had turned him on.

The thought left her feeling unclean. In the small bathroom at the rear of the shop, she washed her hands unnecessarily.

Then she unclasped her purse and removed the creased square of tissue. Nesting within its folds was the turquoise from Erin's apartment.

She held up the stone to the light. It might very well match those on Gund's belt.

Eyes shut, she pictured Gund in Erin's bathroom, leaning against the counter, reaching for the top shelf of the medicine cabinet, where the Tegretol was kept. His waist rubbing against the countertop's Formica edge, the loose turquoise bead coming free and dropping, unnoticed, to the floor . . .

"No," she whispered. "It can't be him. Just can't be."

But what if it was?

She sat on the closed lid of the commode, staring blankly at the stone in her hand, which gazed back like an unwinking eye. She asked herself how much she really knew about Harold Gund.

She'd hired him six months ago, when he responded to a help-wanted sign in the shop window. She almost hadn't taken him on; a flower shop seemed a peculiar place for a large, burly man, and a dead-end job at little better than minimum wage was hardly ideal for someone his age.

But Harold had explained his circumstances, quietly and sincerely. For twenty years he had worked as a custodian at the University of Wisconsin in Madison. Last September his wife had died; she remembered him fumbling in his wallet for her photo and showing it to her. Miriam had been her name.

They'd had no children. All they'd shared was each other. Now she was gone, and as autumn yielded to winter, Harold had found that he couldn't face another season of bleakness and cold.

He'd applied for a custodial position at the University of Arizona, then had come southwest with an assurance that the job was his. Through a bureaucratic bungle someone else had been hired before he'd arrived. Now he was stuck in an unfamiliar city with no employment.

The story was almost too affecting to be true. But she hadn't doubted him. He seemed incapable of duplicity, with his round, smooth face, his sad blue eyes, his large belly overspilling his belt. Though he was years older than she, he conveyed a pleasantly boyish quality, and an instant sense of familiarity, as if he were an amalgam of two old-time movie actors she liked: the face of Ernest Borgnine and the voice of Aldo Ray.

His University of Wisconsin reference had checked out. And his van, although old, was serviceable; it would be useful when he made local deliveries. Annie, feeling a stab of sympathy, had taken a chance on him. After all, she'd reasoned, he couldn't be worse than her previous assistant, a frizzy-haired nineteen-year-old named Beth whose chief talent had been devising excuses for showing up late and leaving early.

As it turned out, Harold had proved to be punctilious and diligent, the most reliable employee she could have asked for.

But although she'd worked at his side six days a week for half a year, she actually did not know him at all. He was like one of those good neighbors she occasionally read about, the person described by everyone as quiet and considerate and well mannered, until the day a cache of dismembered bodies was discovered in the crawl space under his house.

Bodies. She shivered.

Then she got hold of herself. As usual, she was becoming all emotional, letting her imagination run rampant, jumping to wild conclusions. She had nothing to go on except a turquoise bead, and such gems were commonplace in Arizona.

Besides, the whole idea was crazy. To suspect Harold—sweet Harold who made lovely bouquets of long-stem roses and worked overtime without pay and consoled her over Erin's disappearance—to suspect *him* as a kidnapper, a psycho . . .

Then she remembered how her porch light had been activated in the early hours of the night before last. The footsteps she'd heard, the chortling rumble of an engine.

Harold's van sounded like that.

Had he deposited the letter? Had it been his footsteps on gravel, his van pulling away?

No way. Impossible.

Still, she had to be sure.

He had seemed nervous about taking a long lunch break today. And something about that accident just didn't add up. And when she mentioned the dirt on his pants, he'd seemed flustered, hadn't he? Almost . . . guilty?

She wondered if he had really taken the van for an estimate, or if he had gone someplace else.

There ought to be a way to find out. Another minute of hectic, feverish thought guided her to a plan.

Before leaving the bathroom, she flushed the toilet and ran the faucet again, for realism.

In the front of the shop, Harold was on a stepladder,

hanging a basket of green camellia on a ceiling hook to replace an identical item sold earlier today.

"Looks good," Annie said, studying the plant from below. "Maybe spread the leaves a little more on this side."

He did so.

"Perfect. Which auto-body shop gave you the estimate, by the way?"

"Metzger's, at Grant and Campbell." He glanced down at her, and she wondered if it was only her imagination that caught a glint of suspicion in his eyes. "Why?"

"Just curious. I know a good place if you need a second opinion." A pause, then casually: "You know, I never did get lunch. Think I'll run next door and grab a sandwich."

Gund made some kind of acknowledgment, which she barely heard, and then she was out the door, breathing hard. The effort of maintaining a neutral facade had exhausted her.

On her way to the delicatessen, she circled around to the rear of Gund's van and memorized the license number. The tires, she noticed, were streaked with desert dust.

At the back of the deli, there was a pay phone. A battered copy of the Yellow Pages was set on a shelf below. She looked up Metzger's, dropped a quarter in the slot, and dialed.

As the phone rang on the other end of the line, she drew a deep, soothing breath and tried to calm her frantic heart.

"Metzger's," a female voice answered.

"Good afternoon." She kept her tone cool and professional. "This is Barbara Allen, calling from Allstate Insurance. I'd like to confirm an estimate for one of our clients, Harold Gund, policy number seven-six-two-three-eight." The five digits came out of nowhere; insurance people always gave the policy number, and she didn't expect the receptionist to check. "The vehicle in question is a Chevrolet Astro van, license plate . . ." She recited the memorized number.

"Hold, please."

Silence. Annie clutched the hard plastic shell of the handset and tasted a sour flavor at the back of her mouth.

Click, and the receptionist was back. "Sorry, but we have no record of any estimate on that vehicle."

Her heart slammed into overdrive. "It was my understanding"—she fought to betray no reaction other than mild consternation—"that our insured party, Mr. Gund, took his van to Metzger's for inspection earlier this afternoon. He's informed us that Metzger's provided an estimate of twelve hundred dollars."

"Well, we have no record of that."

"I see. There must be some mix-up, then. Thank you."

Even after she had replaced the handset on the plungers, Annie kept her hand on it, as if afraid to let go.

No record.

He hadn't gone to Metzger's.

Hadn't gotten an estimate.

Then what *had* he been doing? And where?

Briefly she considered calling Walker. No, waste of time; she had nothing, really. Nothing specific, nothing tangible.

For the time being, she was on her own.

Okay, then.

Erin had sent an SOS. A distress signal. A cry for help.

Annie would do her best to answer it.

Tonight.

# 39

Even after she awoke, Erin lay unmoving on the futon for long minutes, taking inventory of every separate pain.

The cramps in her abdomen and thighs had loosened their grip, to leave only a dull, throbbing ache. Rubbing at the rope for hours had taken its toll; her shoulders and arms were agonizingly stiff. When she turned her head, a hot needle lanced her neck.

The worst pain, however, was not internal but external: the searing sunburn on every inch of her exposed skin. Her gaze drifted to her right arm, lobster pink. It looked boiled.

The burn would torture her for days. Every scrape of her clothes against her skin would be a minor agony.

But at least, for the moment, she was alive.

Grunting, she propped herself on one elbow and threw back the cheap cotton blanket. A gleam of metal caught her eye.

For a disoriented moment she imagined she was wearing an anklet. A large, curiously bulky anklet glinting on her right leg.

Then her mind cleared, and she recognized what she was seeing. A loop of chain, wound tightly around her leg just above her boot, with a padlock's hasp inserted through two heavy links.

The chain snaked across the concrete floor to the wall, where a second padlock secured it to the sill cock.

Slowly she bent forward, wincing at the residue of pain in her abdomen, and studied the chain. The links were rusty and soiled, as was the padlock. They had been used outdoors.

The gate. It had been chained and locked. Yes.

And the other padlock, the one fastening the chain to the spigot, most likely had come from the rear door, which she'd tried to open last night.

While she slept, her abductor must have removed the chain and both padlocks, then brought them in here and shackled her. Christ, shackled her to the wall—like a prisoner in a dungeon.

Well, what else was she? What had she ever been?

She struggled to her feet, gingerly testing her legs. Though her knees were stiff and her balance uncertain, she could walk.

She tried reaching the door, couldn't. The chain, drawn taut to a length of six feet, stopped her when she was still more than a yard away.

He was taking no chances, quite obviously. He didn't want her escaping again.

Little likelihood of that, anyway. He'd cleaned out the room, removing all possible lock-picking tools, leaving only a bare minimum of necessities. Besides the futon, all she had left were the two chairs, a roll of toilet paper, the milk jugs and coffee cans she used for bathroom purposes, and, in the cardboard box, a few items of food—none requiring the can opener, which was gone.

Painfully she shuffled over to the sill cock. Crouching down was an exercise in self-torture so intense it was almost pleasurable. She turned the handle and cupped her hands under the lukewarm stream from the spout, drinking until she was satisfied.

A memory of the awful thirst she had known in the arroyo returned to her. It was said to be impossible to remember physical sensations, but the sandpaper dryness of her mouth, the swollen thickness of her tongue, the ache of her gums—all of it was abruptly vivid in her mind, as shockingly real as direct experience.

Not again, she promised herself, straightening up with a renewed protest of sore muscles. She would not be staked out again—to endure the elements or to burn. If he tried to take her, she would fight. She would make him kill her here.

Would it come to that? She blinked at the question, then nodded slowly. Of course it would.

She had been granted only a reprieve, a stay of execution. He would never let her go. Never.

She had seen his face.

Only dimly, it was true—in weak light outside, and through a haze of visual distortion in this room. Nonetheless, she *had* seen it.

And the ranch, too.

The ranch.

There it was again, startling as a slap—the wordless certainty that she had visited this place before.

Baking in the sun, she'd had no strength to ponder the riddle. Now she did.

A horse ranch in the desert, near the interstate.

Barbed-wire fence, wood-frame house, barn and paddock. The buildings painted green, white, and red.

Green, white, and red . . .

"Oh, my God," Erin whispered, remembering.

Her knees unlocked. She would have crumpled to the floor if she hadn't gripped the brick wall for support.

In her mind she saw it suddenly: the ranch, *this*

ranch, spread out before her, not in starlight but in the crisp May sunshine of another year, the buildings dressed in faded colors, paint peeling in strips like sunburned skin.

And at the entrance, a padlocked gate that displayed a hanging sign.

The sign was gone now. She hadn't seen it last night.

But on that spring day in 1985 she and Annie had paused before that sign, reading the inscription grooved deep in the rust-eaten iron.

A single word in block letters: CONNOR.

This was the old Connor ranch. Lincoln and Lydia's homestead, where they had spent the twenty years of their marriage.

Erin knew it, knew it with certainty, even without the sign as proof. The distinctive color scheme was confirmation enough. Green, white, red—the colors of the Irish flag.

After the deaths of her husband and son in 1968, Lydia Connor had relocated to a bungalow in town, where, later, she'd raised her orphaned nieces. She rarely spoke of the ranch, never took the girls to see it, but in her photo albums there were pictures of a house and barn, a paddock with a split-rail fence, horses grazing on a few bleached acres.

In the second semester of her freshman year at the University of Arizona, Erin had signed up for a course on the history of Tucson. At the library, hunting through the archival files of local newspapers to research her term paper, she'd come across contemporaneous accounts of the Connor case. One of the stories had given the couple's address.

The next weekend, impelled by curiosity, she and Annie had visited the ranch. The map they used had been disappointingly inaccurate, and it had taken them forty minutes of searching in Annie's old rattletrap

Dodge, with the vents blowing hot air and the brakes squealing ominously, before they finally had pulled to a stop outside a spread that matched the faded photos. The location, Erin recalled with a low incline of her head, was a side road off Houghton, just north of Interstate 10.

The Connor ranch never had been a large-scale operation, even when Lincoln's parents had run the place. By the time Lincoln himself took possession of the title, most of the acreage had been sold off; what little remained had been adequate only for the pasturage of a half dozen horses, mostly elderly animals maintained at the expense of good-hearted owners.

The developer who'd purchased the ranch and acres of adjacent land in 1968 had meant to convert the property into housing tracts, but his ambitious plans had fallen through. The Connor homestead and the land around it, remote and unwanted, had been forgotten. When Erin and Annie found the ranch in 1985, it lay in forlorn disrepair, unoccupied for seventeen years.

Well, it was occupied now. Her abductor had bought it. Bought it and taken down the sign.

But why? What would he want with it? What could this place possibly mean to him?

Nothing, obviously—unless he'd lived here himself.

But no one had lived here in years, in decades. No one had lived here since Lydia, Lincoln, and . . .

"Oliver," she breathed.

The thought was dazzling like a blow. She groped for the chair and sank into it.

The man holding her captive couldn't be Oliver Ryan Connor.

Oliver was dead.

Wasn't he? *Wasn't he?*

Eyes shut, lips pursed, Erin tried to recall what little she had ever known about Lydia's son.

Most of what she'd heard had been local gossip, circulated in school. The murder–suicide had been a noteworthy local news item in 1968, and even in the mid-'70s, when Erin and Annie were growing up in Lydia's house, it had not been forgotten. Other kids their age had heard the details from older siblings, and when they learned the two girls were living with Lydia Connor, they had talked.

From them, and later in more detail from the library's newspaper archives, Erin had learned how Lincoln Connor had tracked down his son, shot him, and turned the gun on himself.

That was the official version, at least, the one accepted by everybody. But suppose it wasn't the truth. Suppose Oliver hadn't died in that clearing of Prescott National Forest, but somehow had duped the authorities into believing otherwise.

Suppose he'd changed his identity, relocated to the Great Lakes region, only to find that his first episode of homicidal violence wasn't enough, that the same compulsion to kill would rise in him periodically, when his fingers would tingle and his ears would chime.

The aura phase. First stage of a seizure, perhaps an epileptic fugue state . . .

"Of course," Erin murmured.

He *was* Oliver. He must be.

Because she, too, was an epileptic. For both of them to suffer from variants of the same affliction could not be a coincidence.

Having studied epilepsy to better understand her own condition, she knew how rare it was. Less than one percent of the general population exhibited the syndrome. But among children of epileptics, the percentage ran as high as six percent. And when both parents had epilepsy, the percentage of affected children rose to twenty-five percent, clearly demonstrating the affliction's hereditary component.

Among the Morgans, only Lydia had shown any epileptic tendencies: occasional petit-mal seizures with retrograde amnesia. Presumably either Rose Morgan or her husband, Joseph, Erin's maternal grandparents, had carried a genetic predisposition toward seizures without exhibiting identifiable symptoms.

Both Lydia and Maureen must have inherited the trait, though Maureen never had shown any evidence of it. The syndrome had been passed on from Maureen to Erin, and from Lydia to Oliver.

"We're family," she whispered, blinking at the thought. "He and I—the same background. Same blood . . ."

And if he had bought the ranch of his childhood, kidnapped his cousin—his foster sister, in fact—then he must want something from her, something more than therapy.

She couldn't guess what it was. Perhaps he himself didn't know.

But whatever it was he wanted, she would find out soon enough. When she did, she would understand him.

And then, almost certainly, she would die.

# 40

Annie said good night to Harold Gund at six-thirty. She lingered in her shop, turning off the lights, until she heard the growl of his van's motor out front.

Peeking through the blinds, she watched the Chevy back away from the curb and swing toward the shopping center's Craycroft Road exit. The brake lights flared as the van stopped at the end of a short line of cars waiting for a break in the traffic.

She left the shop and ran to her Miata. Sliding behind the wheel, she saw the Chevy reach the head of the line and pull onto Craycroft, heading south.

She followed. A red light snared her almost instantly, and she was afraid she'd lost her quarry. But on the long, straight downhill run she caught sight of the van again, well ahead of her.

The sun hung low, westering above a spread of green treetops, as she passed over the Rillito River into city limits. At times throughout the summer monsoon season, the Rillito would be a foaming watercourse, but now it was only a dry, sandy channel, grim and barren, a gash in the landscape.

Gund's van was still in sight, though harder to track on this more level stretch of road. Annie dared to pull closer. Greater population density here, lots of intersecting streets, more chances for him to pull off.

Gund drove carefully, violating no laws. A good driver, it appeared. Annie wondered again how his van had been damaged.

Fender-bender, he'd said. She didn't think so.

As Speedway approached, the Chevy Astro eased into the turn lane, left signal winking. Luckily two other cars followed suit, providing a buffer between the van and Annie's Miata.

She made it through the intersection as the green arrow cycled to yellow, then cut her speed, dropping back slightly for safety. After a brief inner debate she switched on her headlights; keeping them off in the gathering dusk would only make her car more conspicuous.

The day's end had begun to bring relief from the unseasonable heat. The air rushing through the dashboard vents and the open window on the driver's side was mild enough to feel almost comfortable against her face.

Gund's van proceeded at a steady pace despite the crush of vehicles. Illuminated islands of strip malls glided past. A city bus groaned to a stop in the right lane, flashers pulsing.

One thing was clearly apparent. Gund was not going home—not directly, anyhow. She knew his address; it was noted on his employment application, which she'd reviewed in the privacy of her office earlier that evening. He lived west of Craycroft, near downtown. Now he was traveling east.

Erin's place wasn't far from here. Was it possible he meant to cut over to Broadway, revisit her apartment?

If he pulled into Erin's apartment complex, Annie would find a phone and call Walker.

But Gund didn't cut over. He continued east, past Pantano, heading out of town.

The sun was an orange smear in her rearview mirror, a spread of blinding candescence settling slowly below the humped backs of the mountains. Then it was gone, leaving the range outlined in fire, the western sky blushing pink. Ahead, the sky was the deep, somber blue of encroaching night, and the first stars gleamed like droplets of quicksilver.

As the edge of town drew near, traffic finally began to thin. Annie wasn't sure if that was a good development or not. On the one hand, she found it easier to keep the van in sight. On the other hand, Gund would find it easier to see her.

As a precaution she fell farther back, keeping the Chevy just within view. Its taillights burned against the dark.

At Houghton Road, Gund hooked south.

Where the hell was he going? There was nothing out this way. Nothing but the fairgrounds, and as far as she knew, no county fairs were underway this week.

She swung onto Houghton, then frowned. The road—straight, flat, and empty of traffic—mocked her efforts at concealment.

Cutting her speed, she dropped back until the van's taillights were lost to view. Then she killed her headlights and accelerated, bringing the Chevy just within sight.

She was gambling that Gund would assume the car behind him had turned off onto a side road. Without lights, the Miata ought to be nearly invisible at this distance.

Leaning forward, squinting at the dark road and the red glow far ahead, Annie wondered if she knew what she was doing.

If the turquoise really had come from Gund's belt . . .

Then right now she was alone, a mile or more out of town, speeding deeper into the desert, in pursuit of a psychopath.

# 41

Her ruminations on Oliver's epilepsy reminded Erin of the Tegretol.

Briefly she worried that he had taken the bottle of pills when he'd cleaned out the room. But no, there it was, among the foodstuffs in the cardboard box.

She washed down one tablet with a handful of water from the sill cock. Though she had missed her morning dose, a single lapse would do her no harm. Her doctor had assured her that she could go as long as twenty-four hours before withdrawal effects would develop.

It occurred to her that she must be hungry, though she hadn't noticed. She peeled and ate a banana, then a few slices of bread. For protein she scooped her fingers into the peanut butter jar and licked them clean.

Her stomach, aroused, demanded more. She went on eating from the jar as she returned to her questions about Oliver Ryan Connor.

Oliver had been eighteen in 1968; he must be forty-six now. Sixteen years older than Erin and Annie—a wide age difference between cousins, but then, there had been a similar gap between their mothers.

Lydia had been born in 1931, in the fourth year of Rose and Joseph Morgan's marriage. Maureen, their only other child, had made a much belated appearance in 1944, when Rose Morgan was thirty-nine, relatively old to be giving birth in those days. Erin had always assumed that her mother had come as a surprise.

In consequence of the disparity in ages, Lydia had been forty-two when she adopted her nieces, while Maureen, in that same year, had been only twenty-nine.

Twenty-nine. The realization was startling. She paused with a new scoop of peanut butter halfway to her lips.

Maureen had been Erin's age when she had died. Younger, in fact. Erin was thirty. Maureen had never made it that far.

Dim memories of her mother had established her ineradicably as an authority figure, connoting age and wisdom. It was somehow shocking to confront the fact that Maureen Reilly had spent fewer years on this earth than her daughters had.

She dwelled on that reality a moment longer, then pushed it away. No good letting herself get sidetracked. It was Oliver who mattered now.

In their first session he'd admitted that his mother was blue-eyed, red-haired, and Irish Catholic, a description that fit Lydia exactly. He'd made it plain that he despised the Catholic faith for its opposition to abortion; well, the Morgans had always been strict in their beliefs, almost as strict as her own father.

Her father.

Erin lifted her head, struck by a new thought.

*You'll burn,* Albert Reilly had promised, and the next night he'd set out to fulfill his prophesy.

Oliver, despite his denials, was almost certainly fixated on his mother. And his mother's sister had died in a gasoline fire. A fire set by a man who once had loved her.

The logic of the subconscious was the logic of a

dream. Identities melded; one sister blended with another; the death of an aunt could become the death of the loved and hated mother.

In the confusion of a subconscious association, had Oliver conflated Maureen with Lydia? Was that why he'd chosen burning as the method of death for the three symbolic Lydias he'd killed?

That had to be it. But why would he want Lydia dead, symbolically or literally? Why had he run away in the first place . . . and why had he killed Lincoln?

Lydia might have known the answers to some or all of those questions, but only rarely had she spoken of her past. The subject had been tacitly understood to be taboo in her household while Erin and Annie were growing up.

The two girls had been curious, though. Thumbing through old photo albums, they'd come upon more than pictures of the ranch. There had been photos of Oliver as well.

Erin closed her eyes and tried to summon up a memory of the face captured in those faded Kodachromes. A vague recollection swam into partial focus. It was a snapshot of Oliver, roughly seventeen, posed with his father at a lakeside dock.

Lincoln had been smiling, a tall, wiry man with a baseball cap tipped forward on his forehead, the bill throwing his eyes into shadow.

Oliver had worn neither a cap nor a smile. He, too, was tall, as tall as his father, but broad-shouldered and thick-limbed. His hair was blondish and long, pulled back by a tie-dyed headband; a stubble of beard salted his face.

Erin and Annie had studied that photo for a long time, staring into their foster brother's blue eyes, trying to glimpse his soul. But there was no soul to see. His gaze was blank, his features smoothed into an expressionless mask—and what made it worse was the peculiar certainty that it was no mask, that nothing lay underneath to conceal.

In that assumption, however, they'd been wrong, or partly wrong. At times, no doubt, Oliver had been as dead inside as his outward appearance would suggest. But at other moments anger must have risen in him, the blind, furious, seething anger that had driven him finally to lash out and kill. To kill the man standing beside him with his arm thrown casually over his son's shoulder, the man in the baseball cap, laughing at the day.

Anger at what—and for what? If Lydia had ever known or suspected the dark whirlpool swirling below her son's placid surface, she hadn't spoken of it.

Yet possibly she had known more than she let on. Too much, perhaps, for her peace of mind. Certainly she behaved like a woman carrying a heavy burden of anxiety.

More than anxiety. Fear.

Erin nodded. Yes. Fear, along with the unconditional love she had shown toward her two young nieces, had been the dominant motif of Lydia's personality.

She was always edgy and restless and afraid. Addicted to sleeping pills and tranquilizers, forever obtaining new prescriptions from new doctors. The variety of her nervous habits was almost amusing: her tuneless humming, her obsessive need to check and double-check every lock, the fretful attentiveness that made her look in on the girls every night, sometimes waking them inadvertently.

At the time the twins had attributed her eccentricities to the double tragedy that had scarred her life. She had lost a husband and son in the worst imaginable way; had lost a sister also, in another act of insane violence.

All that was left to her were her two nieces, and so

maybe it was unsurprising how she doted on them, fanatically overprotective, touchingly proud. *I can't believe how simply wonderful you girls are,* she would often say. *How perfect you turned out, how smart and beautiful and strong. You two mean more to me than you'll ever know.*

She loved them, and cared for them, and worriedly monitored their safety. But possibly her concern was prompted by more than a generalized fear of suffering a final, irrevocable loss.

She might have known that Oliver was still alive. Might have known that he killed Lincoln, and that he could return one day for her—and her young charges.

Erin hugged herself as a chill shivered through her.

*Us,* she thought. *That's what kept her awake at night. Not fear for her own safety. She was afraid for us. Afraid of what Oliver might do.*

They had taken his place, after all. She and Annie had been raised, in effect, as Lydia's children. And Oliver, his memory expunged, had never been mentioned or acknowledged around the house.

In the van, while she lay blindfolded, feigning unconsciousness, Oliver had stroked her hair, her face, and breathed one word: *Filth.*

He hated her. Must hate Annie also. Because they had replaced him in Lydia's heart.

*Yes,* Erin thought slowly. *He must have hated us for years.*

If Lydia had known her son was alive, then she'd been right to be afraid. He could have come after them at any time.

And now, at last, he had.

# 42

Two miles from the turnoff to the ranch, Gund became aware of being followed.

Though the sun had set, enough light remained to reflect off the windshield of a vehicle well to his rear, maintaining a constant distance from his van.

Of course, the driver might be only a commuter heading home to one of the rare, remote subdivisions along this road. But then why keep the headlights off, despite the dusk? Why, unless to avoid being seen, while holding the van just within view?

Testing his hypothesis, Gund accelerated. The other vehicle disappeared briefly, dropping below the horizon, then promptly reemerged.

Gund relaxed his pressure on the gas pedal; the speedometer needle dipped. His pursuer edged slightly closer before falling back to a safe distance.

No question now. None at all.

Someone was after him.

Pursuit implied suspicion; suspicion suggested the prospect of arrest. Of punishment.

Fear ballooned in Gund's chest and was transmuted instantly into furious anger.

"Son of a bitch," he breathed, in reference to no one and nothing. "Son of a *bitch*."

He had known punishment before. Now in a disorienting flashback he felt the awful, crippling pain again, and with it the ugly shame of his forced submission.

Random scraps of memory whirled in his mind—hiss of running water, blood running down his leg like a menstrual flow, wadded tissue paper stuffed inside him to stop the bleeding, Lydia knocking tentatively at the locked bathroom door: "Oliver . . . ? *Oliver?*" The quaver in his adolescent voice as he made some reply. The sight of his face in the mirror over the blood-dappled sink, his eyes briefly haunted, then going safely blank.

A shudder slithered through him now, breath catching in his throat.

Oh, yes, he'd had his share of punishment, of discipline, of authority's brutal lessons.

The police were only another brand of authority, offering a different form of abuse.

Yet not so very different, after all. He'd heard what went on in prisons.

If he was caught . . . sentenced . . .

Then he would not be Harold Gund any longer. He would be Oliver once more, Oliver Ryan Connor, poor helpless boy, pitiable victim.

No. He would not endure it again. He'd made that vow nearly three decades ago, in a forest clearing, and he would keep it as the sacred promise that it was.

No more punishment. Not ever.

Squinting in the side-view mirror, he strained to distinguish some details of the mystery vehicle's appearance: shape, color, markings. White T.P.D. cruiser? Gold sheriff's department car?

Couldn't tell. Night was rapidly leaching the sky of the sunset's last afterglow. He could see nothing.

But it was surely a law enforcement vehicle of some kind. Nobody else would be tailing him.

Had they tied him to Erin's disappearance? He froze, chilled by that thought.

"No," he grunted. "They don't know. There's no way they can know."

But suppose they did.

Throughout the day he'd fought the impulses rising in him, maintained precarious control. He had not clicked off. Not yet.

Now anger began to split his concentration.

*Won't do it to me again,* he thought, the words beating in measured counterpoint to the racing hammer blows of his heart. *Not again.*

The turnoff for the ranch was less than a half mile away. Just ahead, a different side road approached, running west, toward the fading memory of daylight.

He pumped the brake pedal briefly, cutting his speed only enough to take the curve without risk of a skid, and veered onto the intersecting road. Instantly he switched off the van's single intact headlight.

This area was well known to him. In his youth he'd taken many long, solitary walks, exploring the desert around his parents' ranch. He remembered the arroyo that paralleled this road, shallow and narrow, inconsequential compared with the one behind his ranch, but adequate for his present purposes.

Slowing to a crawl, he eased the van off the asphalt onto powdery desert soil, maneuvering among spiny outcrops of ocotillo and dark clumps of prickly pear.

Careful, careful. Another flat tire would be a catastrophe. He'd already made use of his only spare.

The lip of the arroyo slid into view. The pebbly bottom was no more than five feet deep, the incline of the embankment pleasingly gradual.

Shifting into low gear, he nosed the Chevy over the edge, descended to the streambed, and eased the van into hiding behind a fringe of mesquite shrubs along the arroyo's rim. He cut the motor.

Clumsily he pawed at the glove-compartment latch. The pistol was in there, a blue-steel 9mm Taurus PT.

Wait. Better idea.

Under the dashboard, a mounted shotgun. A sawed-off Remington 870, purchased from a firearms dealer in Tucson shortly after his arrival. His purpose in buying it had been purely nostalgic; the gun was an exact twin of the one found in Lincoln Connor's hand in 1968.

Gund unhooked the twelve-gauge, climbed out of the van. Ascended the embankment in darkness, then thudded down on his elbows and belly in a concealing patch of desert willow, the gun outstretched before him, the shortened sixteen-inch barrel snuffling at the road.

He worked the pump action, chambering a shell. Curled his forefinger around the trigger. And waited.

His breathing was low and regular, his pulse barely above normal. A gnat buzzed his left ear; he made no effort to brush it away.

He was a machine, reduced to a single function, his body a mere extension of the firearm in his hands, and, like the firearm, a deadly instrument. Shotgun and man were one, each capable of explosive violence, each held delicately in check. But not for long.

Nearby, a motor.

Splash of high beams through a scrim of weeds.

The pursuing car turned onto the side road, headlights on now, pace slowed to a crawl. The driver was clearly baffled. Must be wondering how the van could have evaporated, leaving no trace.

Slowly, almost lovingly, Gund tightened his grip on the trigger.

An easy kill. No need even to aim precisely. Just wait for the right moment, then point and shoot.

The spray of buckshot would tear through the car's passenger compartment like shrapnel from a bomb. Anyone inside would be instantly cut to pieces. No time even for fear or pain. A hail of shattered glass and shotgun pellets, a split second of startled bewilderment, and then nothing more for the driver, only silence and darkness vaster than the desert's desolation, forever.

He remembered what one blast from an identical shotgun had done to Lincoln's face. Of course, that shot had been fired at point-blank range.

The strip of asphalt directly before him brightened with the headlights' shine. The car crept closer, nearly alongside him now.

Not a squad car. Some low-slung, sporty model. Undercover vehicle. Must be.

Gund squinted along the barrel, lining up the sights, and prepared to shoot.

His face was calm, empty of expression. His pulse had slowed to that of a sleeping man. No slightest tremor moved through his body. Despite the warm night, no bead of sweat glistened on his brow.

A machine-man. Emotionless and efficient.

The shotgun lifted slightly, targeting the silhouetted figure in the driver's seat, less than fifteen feet away.

His trigger finger began its lethal flex.

And he recognized her.

Annie. Her face dimly outlined in the glow of the dashboard gauges.

The car—it was her red Miata.

She was his pursuer. Not a cop. *Annie.*

His superficial calm shattered. His heart sped up; his mouth turned dry.

The car was moving on. Shock had nearly cost him his chance at a clean shot.

He drew down on the trigger again.

Another ounce of pressure, that was all it would take, and Annie Reilly would be dead.

But he couldn't.

Not her.

Damn it, *not her*.

With a trembling effort, the greatest exertion of his life, he lowered the shotgun.

The Miata hummed past, the triangle pattern of its taillights shrinking, shrinking, gone.

Gund lay motionless, panting, until his pulse dropped to normal.

Then slowly he got to his feet. He stood on the roadside, surveying the darkness, dabbing distractedly at the film of sweat on his face.

She knew.

Or suspected, anyway.

But how? He'd done nothing to incriminate himself. He was sure he hadn't.

Whatever the explanation, she was on to him somehow. And that meant she could not be allowed to live.

Despite his momentary lapse of resolve, it was obvious that to protect himself, he must kill her. He simply must.

"*No.*"

The word, torn out of him, was wafted away on the warm, dry breeze.

He would not.

Yet there was no alternative. Already, Erin knew too much. Now Annie, too, had learned part of the truth.

Neither could live. Both must die.

"No," Gund said again, but his voice was softer this time, a whisper almost, and the desert did not hear.

# 43

Annie drove aimlessly for a half hour before conceding defeat. She'd lost her quarry. Gund's van was gone.

She was certain she'd seen the Chevy swing west onto a dark side road. Yet by the time she had turned the same corner a minute later, the van had been lost to sight.

At first she'd thought Gund had pulled off into the desert. But the low, sparse scrub wouldn't conceal the vehicle. And the land was flat—no hills or ridges to hide behind.

A mystery.

One thing was evident, though. Despite her precautions, Gund had realized he was being followed. And he had executed some sort of maneuver to shake off his pursuit.

His behavior was not that of an innocent person.

Besides—she thought restlessly as she guided the Miata down random roads, headlights sweeping yards of pitted asphalt—if he was innocent, if her suspicions were completely unfounded, then what was he doing out here in the gray wastes of the desert? Enjoying the scenery? In absolute darkness?

"Face reality," she ordered herself, mildly startled to realize she'd expressed the thought aloud.

Harold Gund had kidnapped Erin. Was holding her prisoner someplace in the miles of undeveloped desert land.

If he'd paid a visit to Erin on his lunch break, which seemed likely, then he'd been able to drive from the shop to the hiding place and back in little more than an hour. That meant his hideaway probably was somewhere nearby, but where precisely, Annie couldn't guess.

*So what do I do now?* she wondered bleakly as she picked up speed on a newer stretch of road, the warm night air whistling through the dashboard vents. *Call Walker?*

Sure, call Walker. Tell him she'd been playing Nancy Drew and was convinced her assistant at the flower shop was the kidnapper. Her evidence, stated objectively, was worthless. A bit of turquoise that could have come from anywhere. A van that dematerialized like a mirage. And as for Harold's lie about the body shop—did she honestly think there was an employee anywhere who'd never fibbed to the boss in order to take an extended lunch break?

Walker wouldn't listen to her. No way. Not without proof.

Well, what would constitute proof? Erin's head on a plate? Or would Tucson P.D. insist on having the whole body, no missing parts, before opening an investigation?

"Quit it," she whispered when she noticed that her hands had clamped on the wheel in a paralytic's frozen clench.

This was just like her—to lose control, become hysterical, act like an idiot. Helpless Annie. Scatterbrained Annie who never could find her keys or organize her files or balance her checkbook. She'd depended on Erin to be her anchor, her rock of stability, but now . . .

"Now Erin's depending on me." Her voice was a breathless murmur, swallowed by the engine hum.

Evidence. She needed evidence. Something to change Walker's mind, get the police involved.

Gund's apartment.

She knew his address.

He'd lived alone ever since his wife had died. If he'd ever had a wife. If he hadn't been lying about that, too.

And tonight he was out. Wherever he'd been headed, he was unlikely to be back for hours.

She could drive there now. Break in, search the place—

Break in?

"Crazy," she said with a clipped, nervous chuckle.

But it wasn't crazy. Just desperate. There was a difference.

She spun the wheel, executed a sharp U-turn on the empty road, and sped north, toward the distant lights of town.

# 44

Erin stiffened, hearing the heavy, familiar tramp of footsteps above her head.

Reflexively she looked for the blindfold before remembering that it was gone. Oliver had removed it along with most of the other items in the room. He knew she had seen his face.

But she hadn't seen it, she realized as the footfalls descended the cellar stairs. Not clearly enough to matter. She still couldn't identify him in a lineup.

Could she convince him of that? Doubtful, but she had to try.

A key rattled in the lock. She turned away and stood facing the corner like a reprimanded child.

Behind her, the door sighed open, and the short hairs on her nape prickled.

" 'Evening, Doc."

The greeting was meant to sound casual, but his tone of voice was all wrong. Strained, tense.

She might be in even greater danger than she'd realized. If he were to slip into a fugue state, she would have no chance.

"Good evening," she answered slowly.

"What's so fascinating about that wall?"

"I need my blindfold."

"No, you don't."

"You wouldn't want me to see your face, would you?"

Footsteps. Crossing the room. Closer. Closer.

His shadow expanded on the unpainted bricks, devouring her own. He stopped directly at her back.

"You've already seen me," he whispered.

From his voice, his tone, she tried to gauge his state of mind. He sounded angry, exhausted, yet still in control. Torn by conflict, fatigued by the effort of holding fast to the better part of himself.

She had no confidence in his ability to hold on indefinitely. At any moment the tension in his voice might bleed away, leaving only an affectless monotone.

"I never got a good look." Her words were barely audible above the pumping of her heart. "Last night, in the arroyo, there was only starlight; you were a silhouette. And when you brought me here, I was barely conscious. I couldn't even focus my eyes."

"That's probably true."

She waited, feeling the pressure of a suppressed hope.

"But it doesn't matter. You already know who I am."

Her heart twisted.

"How could I possibly know that?" She wished her voice wouldn't quaver.

He leaned nearer; she felt the tickle of his breath on her right ear. "You saw the ranch."

She shut her eyes. "It's just a ranch," she said desperately, refusing to turn her head, refusing to see his face and seal her fate. "Horse ranch, I guess. Like a thousand others in Arizona. So what?"

"You know this place. Even if Lydia never brought you to see it, you would have come on your own. You and Annie."

He'd mentioned Lydia. Pointless to continue her denials, but she tried anyway. "I've never been here. Really. And I didn't see your face. . . ."

The touch of his fingers on her chin startled a gasp out of her.

"You're lying, Doc. That's bad. Don't you know that the doctor-patient relationship is built on trust?"

She couldn't answer, couldn't speak, not with his hand clinging lightly to her face, weightless as a scorpion.

"Look at me, Doc."

"Please . . ."

"Look at me."

He tightened his grip, snapped her head sideways. Shock opened her eyes, and she saw him. She couldn't help but see him.

"Say hello to your cousin, Doc," he said, unsmiling. "Cousin Oliver."

Swallowing, she nodded.

He stepped back to give her a fuller view. Absently she noted the clothes he was wearing: canvas shoes, denim jeans, blue shirt, and an unbuttoned nylon jacket with a bulge in the side pocket.

*Normal,* she thought blankly. *He looks normal.* She could have passed him on the street and not even noticed him, not even suspected what he was.

He was a large man—of course, she had known that—with wide shoulders and thick arms and a spreading waistline. She wasn't surprised that he could carry her without strain, or that his footsteps shook the ceiling when he crossed the ranch's living room.

She compared him with the boy in the remembered Kodachrome, the snapshot portrait of Oliver and Lincoln side by side on a dock. Time had done its work; there were few obvious similarities anymore.

The loose cascade of long blond hair was gone, in its place a few strawlike wisps on a balding scalp. The

nose, sharp and narrow once, had been broken in a
fight or fall. He was clean-shaven now, and his receding chin, partially disguised in the photo by a fine stubble of beard, was more obvious, multiplied by folds of
fat blurring the transition between his jaw and neck.

For a long moment she went on staring, and he accepted her scrutiny, standing rigid, as if at attention.

"It *is* you," she said finally, pointlessly.

"It's me."

"I never would have recognized you. Never."

"I know. Annie sees me every day, and she hasn't
recognized me, either."

"Annie . . . ?"

"I work for her. I'm her assistant."

Erin's knees unlocked, and she stumbled backward
against the wall. The chain running from her ankle
rasped on the floor.

Annie's assistant. The new man, the one who'd re-
placed that teenager who was always late for work.
Annie had mentioned him several times in passing.
Harold something.

Gund. That was it. Harold Gund.

Erin had visited Annie's shop several times in the
past few months, yet she'd never met the new employee. He had always seemed to find an excuse to
stay out of sight.

"You avoided me whenever I dropped by," she said
slowly. "You were always in the back room or making
a delivery or out to lunch."

"A reasonable precaution, don't you think? I didn't
want you remembering my voice later on. I couldn't let
you know your kidnapper's identity."

"But now," she whispered, "I do know it."

"Sadly, yes."

"Which means you can't let me go."

His eyes closed briefly, registering his first hint of emotion—a flicker of regret. "Afraid not, Doc."

"Is that why you came here? To end it? To . . . kill me?"

A tremor rippled through the muscles of his cheek. "No. Not tonight. I won't—I *won't*—do it tonight."

The violence of his reply was a window on the turmoil churning just below his placid surface. He drew a slow, calming breath.

"Not tonight," he said again, more softly. "Not for a while. Days, weeks, whatever it takes. We'll do the work. You'll treat me. Cure me. Set me free. And then . . ." His lower lip trembled briefly. "Then it will be good-bye. But not by fire."

He reached into his jacket pocket and withdrew a blue-barreled pistol.

"This way." His voice was very small. "No pain. I promise. Quick and easy. You won't even know, it'll be so fast, so . . . clean. You won't even know."

She said nothing.

"Let's get started," he added brusquely.

He turned away from her with a jerk of his shoulders and sat in the chair nearest the door. The gun fidgeted in his lap like a small, nervous dog.

Encumbered by the chain, she shuffled over to the facing chair. Her sore muscles protested as she seated herself, and the searing sunburn on her chest cried out at the scrape of her shirt.

For a moment, as they sat watching each other like wary animals, Erin was at a loss for anything to say. She'd had no time or inclination to prepare for a second session.

Then she remembered the list of unanswered questions she'd compiled only a short while earlier.

Risky to probe Oliver's past when he was clearly on

the edge of losing his grip. Even so, she would chance it.

Because she had to know, had to understand.

And because she had so little left to lose.

# 45

"You realize, of course," she began casually, "you're supposed to be dead."

"I made it look as though I was."

He sat stiffly in the chair, one hand on the gun, the other balled in a fist, his body language expressive of rigid self-restraint. It was as if his clenched muscles and locked joints formed a barrier against the wild surge of emotion swirling in him, a dam straining against floodwaters. She waited tensely for the first fatal cracks to appear.

"But your father," she said softly. "He's really dead, isn't he?"

A brief incline of his head. "Yes."

"You killed him." Not a question.

"He deserved it."

"Why?"

He didn't reply at once. His hand stroked the pistol in his lap. Erin tried not to look at it, not to think of the explosive violence it contained.

"Lincoln Connor was a great guy," he said finally, his voice low and bitter. "Everyone said so. Always smiling and joking, and so good with horses. Believed in discipline, though. People knew that. They heard stories about how he beat his son. Well, every kid needs to learn a lesson now and then, right? Only, the discipline my father imposed didn't always stop with a beating. Sometimes he found other ways of hurting me."

"What ways?"

"Two fingers up the rectum. Then three fingers." The chair creaked as he shifted his weight, and she knew the sphincter muscles near the base of his spine were tightening involuntarily. "When I was old enough, *big* enough . . . his fist. And then . . . *not* his fist."

She felt a pang of pity, not for the killer before her but for the small boy he had been. But of course it was no longer possible to separate the two. The hurt little boy still lived within this man, buried alive somewhere deep inside, and screaming, unheard.

But the women in the woods—they had screamed, too.

"What age were you when it started?" she asked.

"Little. Maybe four."

"Did Lydia know?"

He shook his head slowly. "She never had a clue."

"How could Lincoln keep it secret?"

"He did it only when she wasn't around. Lydia was in charge of the ranch's inventory; she was always going into town for supplies. Lincoln had no shortage of opportunities. And I never told. I was scared, ashamed. And . . ."

"And what?"

"And so I . . . kept the secret," he finished lamely.

"That's not what you started to say." No reply. "You wanted to tell me something more."

Tense silence ticked in the room. She knew it was crazy, suicidal, to push further on this point. So she wouldn't, of course. She wouldn't.

She did. "In our first session, there was a point when you thought I'd implied you were gay."

"Hadn't you?"

"No."

"Then why raise the issue again?"

"I think you know why."

He said nothing.

"You enjoyed it. What your father did." Each word was a step forward into an unknown darkness strewn with lethal trip wires. "At least sometimes. At least a little bit. Didn't you, Oliver?"

His right hand closed over the barrel of the gun, clutching it tight.

"You do think I'm queer," he breathed.

"I haven't said that."

"Don't bullshit me. Don't bullshit me, you little whore."

"Oliver—"

"You *filth*. Stinking *filth*."

His hand was sliding down the gun barrel toward the handle, and she knew that when he reached it, he would lift the gun and shoot, shoot without thinking, shoot to kill.

"Oliver," she said more sharply. *"Stop it."*

His hand froze an inch from the checkered grip.

"I'm sorry if you heard me say something I didn't mean to say." She spoke softly, keeping her tone neutral and nondefensive. "It wasn't my intention to suggest that you were homosexual. I hope you understand that."

He seemed slightly mollified, but his hand remained on the gun. "Then what *were* you suggesting?"

"Only that you may still be afraid of something you felt with your father, years ago. An emotion or a physical sensation. A fleeting response, meaningless . . . but it haunts you. I think that's why you see sexual needs as threatening, dangerous—"

"But I *don't*," he cut in. "I'm not threatened. You're on the wrong track. Sex doesn't have anything to do with ... with anything."

"You believe that, I'm sure. But it may not be true."

"Are you saying I'm a liar?"

"I'm saying your true feelings are buried deep. So deep that you can't find them, can't acknowledge their reality."

"That's just stupid," he whispered, but she heard doubt in his voice for the first time.

"Don't fight me on this, Oliver," she said. "Open up to me. Please."

He didn't speak for a long moment. Then slowly he lifted the gun, as if to remind her of its presence. A shade too ostentatiously, he slipped it back into the side pocket of his jacket.

"I thought we were talking about my father," he said mildly.

She yielded, afraid to press any harder and see the pistol return. "How long did Lincoln continue to mistreat you?"

"Until I left home."

"At eighteen?"

"Yes."

"He was still abusing you at that age?"

"Not as often. But ... yes."

"Did you leave because of Lincoln?"

"No. It was Lydia. She disowned me. Ordered me out of the house."

Erin blinked, taken by surprise. "Lydia? But ... why?"

He fixed his stare on her. "That, you can't know."

Instinctively she understood that this was one territory she dared not explore, the one secret he would not share.

"All right," she said evenly. "So you left Tucson. Went to the Prescott area, as I recall."

"In a stolen car. I ditched it when it was almost out of gas. Had no money to fill the tank. Started walking, and met up with a bunch of kids my age. Hippies. My hair was long, and I looked scruffy enough to fit in. We got to talking, and I improvised a story about burning my draft card and going underground."

"You stayed with them."

"For a few weeks. We moved from town to town, keeping close to the edge of the woods. Living off the land, they called it, though really we were scrounging through garbage."

"Then your father came looking for you—"

"No. It didn't happen like that. Not like that at all . . ."

His words trailed off, and his eyes lost focus. Ordinarily she was not averse to leaving a patient wrapped in thought, even for long minutes if necessary. But not now. If he became passive, disengaged, his internal controls would relax . . . and his impulses might take over.

From experience and study, she knew that epileptic episodes were most likely to occur in that half-aware state between wakefulness and sleep. As the mind wandered, the seizure threshold was lowered, sometimes to the danger point.

She had to keep him talking and alert, without getting him agitated. Emotional stress could trigger a seizure also.

A fine line to tread. A tightrope over a chasm.

"Tell me, Oliver," she said softly. "Tell me how it did happen."

"It was evening. A summer evening. Warm day,

cooling as the sun hung lower." His voice was remote
and thoughtful, his words drifting up from a deep well
of memory. "I went for a walk in the woods with another guy from the camp. Just the two of us. He wasn't
a friend, exactly, but he'd been pleasant to me. Funny
to think he was just a kid. We both were. Just kids.
Eighteen years old. Funny.

"We found a creek, ambled far enough along the
bank to leave the camp sounds behind. In the quiet, we
sat by the water, smoking. Peaceful there, with the current forking around the rocks, and the sun setting, and
that sweet-smelling smoke.

"After a while it was dark, and we were both pretty
high. Then . . . he got rough. You know what I mean."

"He wanted to do what Lincoln had done."

A shaky nod. "I told him no. He tried to force me.
I remember him tugging at my jeans, me on my belly,
struggling, and him hard against my rear, like Lincoln
giving me some discipline, Lincoln making me bleed,
and then he *was* Lincoln. Maybe it was the dope or
some kind of sublimated revenge fantasy surfacing, I
don't know, but *he was Lincoln,* and I wasn't going to
take it from him anymore.

"Guess I went wild then. I don't remember now. But
I must have fought back, really fought, for the first
time in my life.

"When I came back to myself, there was a rock in
my hand. It was bleeding. At least it seemed to be.
Blood from a stone, I remember thinking. I touched my
face—wetness there, too. He'd broken this"—he fingered his pulped, shapeless nose—"and I hadn't even
noticed. Then I looked down, very slowly, and there he
was, on the ground, with his pants around his knees
and his dick hanging out and his skull open wide."

"How did you . . ." Erin hesitated, choosing the right
words. "How did that make you feel?"

"I didn't feel anything."

She believed him. The rare breakout of emotion must have consumed itself, leaving him empty and blank. He would have had no reaction to the body sprawled before him, the body of a boy of eighteen, killed in the woods.

Eighteen. Oliver's age. Of course.

Erin shut her eyes, making the obvious connection. "This boy's name—"

"Harold Gund."

She nodded. "You took his identity. And erased your own."

"I hadn't planned on it. But as I sat there, watching the moon rise over the trees, I worked everything out. I saw a way to cover up the murder and take revenge on Lincoln. I felt strong enough then. I'd been liberated. I was . . . free."

"How did you do it?"

"Gund was my height, my approximate build. I changed clothes with him, taking his wallet, leaving mine with the body. Used some of Gund's money to hop a bus to Tucson the next morning, then rode a city bus from the terminal to the edge of town that afternoon. At night I walked to the ranch. This ranch.

"Easy enough to sneak onto the grounds; the gate wasn't padlocked in those days. I eavesdropped through an open window while Lincoln talked on the phone. His end of the conversation made it clear he was alone; Lydia was in the hospital—nervous breakdown. Everyone assumed she was worried sick about me. Nobody guessed the truth."

Erin did not ask what the truth was.

"Once the lights were out, I broke in through the back way. The lock never was any good, which is why I installed a padlock on that door once I bought the place.

"Lincoln was snoring in bed. I clubbed him unconscious with his own shotgun. Lugged him to the carport, dumped him in the trunk of his car. Drove north to Prescott Forest. Lincoln came to around three in the morning and started thumping on the lid.

"It was still dark when I pulled into the woods and popped the trunk. At first he was crazy with rage, till I let him see the gun—his own sawed-off Remington, steady in my hands. He turned conciliatory then. Tried to make nice. Hoped I didn't hold it against him, what he'd done; it was just a father's way of showing love; sure, that's all he was, a loving father. . . .

"I let him talk as I marched him to the creek in the predawn dark. After a while the words dried up, and he started to cry. Weeping like a woman, like the bullying coward he was. But I don't think he believed I would do it, really *do* it, until he stumbled over the corpse at the water's edge.

"Fear put some fight into him. He spun around, grabbed for the shotgun, and I gave him a taste of it, right in the face."

Erin shuddered. He saw her reaction, and his eyes narrowed coolly.

"Don't look so stricken, Doc. It's not the worst way to die. He never even heard the blast."

*Just like I won't hear it when you shoot me,* she thought numbly.

"Before I left, I turned the gun on Harold. Put the muzzle in his mouth and blew his head off. Nobody was going to identify that corpse from dental records."

"What about fingerprints?"

"I'd never been arrested; my prints weren't on file. I don't know if Gund had a rap sheet. But this was 1968, remember. No computerized fingerprint searches, no nationwide data bank. If Gund had been local, his prints could have been on file somewhere in Arizona. But he'd wandered in from Oregon only a couple weeks earlier.

"Low probability the authorities would bother with prints, anyway. The case was open-and-shut, a no-brainer. Lincoln had beaten me; folks back home knew that much. He'd made a lot of noise to the press about how angry he was at his disobedient son. And just a few days earlier I'd been seen by someone who knew the family; my father could have known where to find me. Besides, it was 1968, an angry year.

"When the police found Lincoln, he had the gun in his hand; I'd wedged it into his fingers with the muzzle under his chin, or where his chin used to be. Next to him, there was the body of a boy my age, wearing my clothes, with my wallet. His hair was brown, not blond like mine, but the shotgun blast had scattered most of it, and I'd gathered up the rest and fed it to the creek.

"Lydia's hospitalization ensured that she was in no condition to view the body. The only people who looked at it were cops, coroners, and morticians, none of whom had known me."

"So you got away with it."

"Well, there was one thing that had me worried for a while. One of the papers reported that the police were trying to find a boy named Harold, last seen with me."

"You must have anticipated that."

"Not entirely. People entered and left the camp all the time. Nobody kept track of anyone. There was no organization, no one in charge. As it turned out, that's what saved me. The kids interviewed by the police knew nothing about the missing boy except his first name. They couldn't agree on his description, and they didn't even know he was from Oregon; I was the only one he'd talked to at any length. The cops had nothing to go on; there were a million long-haired teenagers named Harold. I was safe."

"Safe," Erin echoed softly.

"And free. Free of Lincoln. Free of the past."

But she knew he had never emancipated himself from his father or his childhood. And at some level, she was certain, he knew it, too.

"Gund had an Oregon driver's license," he went on quietly. "No photo on it, fortunately; that particular innovation postdates the sixties. There was only a typed inventory of physical characteristics. The one serious discrepancy between his appearance an mine was hair color, as I mentioned. When I got a new license eventually, I passed that off as a clerical error."

"Where did you go?"

"New Mexico, Colorado, Nevada . . . all over. I hitchhiked, did odd jobs, got hassled by local cops. The transient's life. Not as glamorous as it looks in the movies. Eventually I got sick of all that. I settled in Wisconsin, found myself a janitor's job at a university. Worked there for twenty years. You've read the clippings. You know what I did on the side."

"What made you relocate to Arizona?"

"You and Annie. I was looking for you."

*Stalking us,* she corrected silently. "After all that time? But . . . you never even knew us."

"Maybe I wanted to."

"Why?"

No answer.

Let it go, she told herself. She knew his reason. She had no need to hear him say it.

Except she wasn't sure. The pieces didn't quite fit.

And she had to know.

"What is it you feel for us, Oliver?" she asked, leaning forward.

"Feel? Nothing."

"That's not true."

"You ask me questions, and you won't accept my answers."

"Because the answers are incomplete. You went to a lot of trouble to bring me here."

"For help. For therapy."

"There are other therapists. Why me? Why a member of the family?" No response. "You took a risk working for Annie. There was at least a slight chance she would identify you. People don't do things— difficult things, dangerous things—without a motive. What's yours? What do we mean to you?"

"Nothing," he said again. "You mean *nothing*."

She could see the denial in his face, in the twisted pose of his body.

"You want to believe that," she breathed, "but I don't think you do."

"I don't give a damn what you believe."

She would not be deterred by his hostility. She was on the trail of something important, something hidden from her and from Oliver himself; regardless of the consequences, she had to uncover it, had to bring it into the light.

"Annie and I were born in 1966," she said slowly, "when you were still living at home. Did you ever see us as babies? Did our parents bring us to the ranch?"

"No, never."

That surprised her. "Maureen never visited Lydia?"

"Not after you were born."

"How about before then?"

A shrug. "Once."

"Was she pregnant?"

"No. She wasn't even married yet." He shifted in his seat, and his blue eyes flashed. "None of this is relevant to anything."

It was, though. She knew it was, though she couldn't see how or why.

"You remember her visit," she said. "She must have made some sort of impression on you."

"Not really."

"Did you talk with her? Spend time with her?"

"Of course not. I was just a kid."

"She was an attractive woman. Maybe you had a crush on her."

"There was nothing . . . nothing like that."

He seemed less sure of himself. Erin felt confident she was circling closer to the truth.

"Maureen looked like me in some ways," she said tentatively. "Do I remind you of her?"

"No."

"Does Annie?"

"No, goddammit."

He was lying. She was certain of it.

"You did feel something for her," Erin whispered, "didn't you, Oliver?"

He shook his head without answering.

"And what you felt for Maureen—you feel it for us, too. For Annie and me."

"No."

"You look at us, and you think of her."

"No."

"You see Maureen in us. Don't you?"

"No."

"Don't you, Oliver?"

"I . . . no, I . . . it's not . . ." He averted his face from her. Tremors shook his body. "It isn't . . . isn't . . . oh, Jesus. Oh, my God."

A change came over him then. His eyes widened in surprise, his gaze focusing inward, and Erin knew he was doing something rare and astonishing; he was looking inside himself, seeing the truth that had been long concealed from his conscious awareness.

And suddenly she was afraid. She had pushed him recklessly, almost forgetting the risk, carried away by the sheer exhilaration of an intellectual challenge.

Now she wondered how his new perspective on himself—whatever it might be—would upset his precarious equilibrium.

"My God," he said again, numbly. "My God."

"Oliver?"

"I never knew. I never even knew."

"Oliver, talk to me."

"All these years"—he spoke in a robot's monotone—"and I never knew."

His gaze shifted its focus. Suddenly he was looking at her. Seeing her with new eyes.

"You've been right all along, Doc." He nodded slowly, mechanically. "And I've been deceiving myself. Afraid to face the truth. I've been blind. For years . . . for twenty years . . . so goddamned blind."

"Oliver, I want to know how you're feeling right now. I want to know—"

"Feeling?" A catch in his voice. "How I'm feeling?"

He stood, and once again she was aware of how big he was and how very dangerous. She drew back in her chair, scared now, heart pounding.

"I'll show you how I feel," he breathed, the words gathering force as he squeezed them through gritted teeth. "I'll show you, you goddamned whore. *I'll show you!*"

He seized her by the shoulders, wrenched her upright, the pinch of his fingers painful and startling.

Her involuntary cry was stifled by his mouth on hers. A hot, searing pressure, mashing her lips, stifling breath, smothering her.

She stood rigid in his arms, every muscle locked against the instinctive impulse to twist free.

He broke away. Gasping, she stared at him, at the confusion of emotions shredding the smooth mask of his face: desire and revulsion, hatred and need.

"That's how I feel," he croaked. "How I feel. How I feel."

For some unmeasurable stretch of time they watched each other, their gazes locked.

Then a ripple of muscle spasms danced lightly over his shoulders. His body jerked toward the door.

Slam, and she was alone.

She heard the rattle of the key, the softer jangle of the chain lock, the hasty retreat of his footsteps up the stairs.

Trembling, she waited, afraid of his return, until she heard the muffled growl of the van's engine. She didn't relax until the motor noise had faded into silence.

Then slowly she sank back into the chair, wiping her mouth with her hand, trying to erase the lingering residue of his kiss. Head lowered, she fought off vertiginous waves of nausea.

Going to rape her. Christ, she'd been sure he was going to rape her.

Unquestionably he was capable of it. With his psychosis, his violent tendencies, his background of parental abuse . . .

Parental abuse.

She blinked, then blinked again, and there it was, the puzzle's final piece.

"Of course," she murmured.

Oddly, she felt no surprise. She had known already. Known without knowing. Without wanting to know.

Her analysis of his psychology had approached the truth. But at its core it had been wrong. Utterly, devastatingly wrong.

She saw that now. And something else.

The next time he visited her, she would die.

His feelings for her, liberated now after years of ruthless repression, were too intense. They cut fatally close to the heart of his insanity. They would drive him inexorably to kill.

To kill her . . . and Annie, too.

# 46

Frantic.

Gund stamped the gas pedal to the floor, careening north. He didn't look at the speedometer needle, didn't want to see it pinned to the far right of the dial.

He had no idea where he was going. All that mattered was to put distance between himself and the ranch. If he returned to it tonight, Erin would die.

Leaving her unharmed had exhausted nearly the last reserves of his willpower. Even now he wasn't sure he could hold out against the ugly impulses churning inside him, wasn't sure he could resist the urge to turn the van around.

Gasoline in the rear compartment. Two cans. More than enough to do the job.

He didn't want to think about that. But it was hard not to, agonizingly hard.

His fingers tingled and itched. His neck burned. In his ears was a faraway chiming, elusive and mysterious.

All day long he'd been on edge. And after what he'd done with Erin—the meeting of their lips, the pressure of his mouth on hers—

Until the moment when he'd pulled her close, he had never known what he wanted from her, wanted and desperately needed. He'd been blind to his true nature, blind to the origins of his compulsion ... willfully blind, afraid to face the ugly reality of what he was. Although he had tracked down Erin and Annie Reilly, although he had become part of their lives, he'd never admitted the full reason for their hold on him.

The burnings had been bad, but the twisted needs that lay at the root of his crimes were still worse.

Better to splash his victims with gas and toss a lighted match than to ... to ...

"Fuck," he whispered, testing the word, a word he had not used—not once—since he was fifteen years old.

The muttered obscenity drew the muscles of his groin tighter. He shifted in the driver's seat.

Turn around. He had to turn around, go back, fuck her. Fuck her and then burn her, *burn her*—

"I won't," he murmured, his eyes misting. "I won't do it. I *won't*."

Tension racked his body. He couldn't fight himself much longer.

But perhaps he didn't have to.

There might be a way out. A way to find relief.

His photo. His special picture.

Yes. Go home. Remove the photograph from its hiding place. And then ...

He knew what he would do.

Would it be enough? He wasn't sure. But it was his last hope.

As he swung off Houghton Road onto 22nd Street, he glanced at the dashboard clock: 8:15.

His apartment was only fifteen minutes away—ten, if he maintained this reckless speed.

And if a traffic cop should pull him over ...

He fingered the shotgun mounted under the dash, then lightly touched the handgun in his pocket.

Any cop who tried to ticket him would be dead.

Anyone who interfered with him tonight, anyone who *fucked* with him . . .

Dead.

# 47

Annie had trouble finding a parking space in Gund's neighborhood. Finally she pulled into a curbside slot on a side street, outside a used-car lot protected by a security fence and a restless Doberman. Her dashboard clock glowed 8:05 when she killed the engine.

The guard dog growled at her through the fence as she walked swiftly to the corner. She turned east and hurried past a dreary row of brick houses, their sandy lots bordered by chain-link fencing. Graffiti clung to walls and utility poles like patches of black fungus. From some homes the drone of a television or radio was audible, the voices on the broadcasts always in Spanish.

Gund's apartment was a ground-floor unit at the front corner of a two-story stucco building. His windows were dark, his curtains drawn.

No fence around the place—that was one obstacle she wouldn't have to contend with, anyway—but covering the front windows were iron security bars.

Impossible to get in that way, and she lacked the skills to pick the lock on the door. Maybe she would find some means of access at the side of the unit.

A narrow passageway ran between the apartment building and the house next door. Through the wall of the house bled the loud, insistent blare of Mexican music. Shadows of human figures flitted across the lowered window shades like drifting clouds of smoke.

Annie crept down the passage, past a wheeled trash bin and another barred window, then stopped at what must be Gund's bathroom window. It was a slender rectangle of frosted glass, five feet off the ground, sealed shut, and unbarred.

She studied the window, uncertain if it was wide enough for her to squeeze through. She thought it was—just barely.

For a moment she hesitated. Was she really going to do this?

Then her resolve stiffened. For Erin she would. For Erin.

The music from next door ought to cover the sound of breaking glass. All she needed was a way to smash the window. Should have brought the jack from the trunk of her car, but she hadn't thought of it.

She'd make a lousy burglar, she decided. She wasn't even dressed right.

A black jumpsuit would have been the appropriate attire. She was still wearing her clothes from work: a brightly colored cotton skirt and a floral-print blouse. The blouse would look good in the mug shot, at least.

The small joke made her frown. There wasn't going to be any mug shot. Everything would be fine, and there was no reason, absolutely none, for her hands to be trembling.

They trembled anyway as she rummaged through the trash bin and found someone's gooseneck lamp, the cord badly frayed. She hefted the lamp experimentally. It seemed sturdy enough to do the job.

Leaning against the bin, drawing a slow breath to compose herself, she felt a hand on her arm.

"*Jesus.*"

She swung around, instinctively raising the lamp as a weapon, and saw two green eyes staring at her from a foot away.

Cat's eyes. An alley cat, that's all it was, just an alley cat that had climbed atop the bin and touched her with its paw.

"Oh, God, puss, you scared me."

The cat sniffed her clothes, unafraid. Annie realized the scent of her own house cat must have drawn the stray's attention.

"His name is Stink," she whispered. "He's got green eyes like yours—and mine. Maybe the three of us are related."

The cat appeared unimpressed with this hypothesis.

"Okay now, scoot. Scoot."

Gently she brushed the cat away. It bounded off the bin and meandered a few yards down the passageway, then stood watching, a silent spectator.

Her conversation with the cat, one-sided though it had been, had calmed her somewhat. She always felt soothed in the presence of a feline, whether Stink or this mangy stray. Cats were good for the soul. Maybe if Harold had a cat, he wouldn't—

A new worry froze her. How did she know he didn't own a cat? Or worse, far worse, a dog? A guard dog, even, like that Doberman at the auto lot?

She might enter the apartment only to find herself pinned to a wall, fangs at her throat.

Then she shook her head firmly. "That won't happen. Come on, girl. No more procrastination."

A quick breath of courage, and she turned to face the window. Holding the lamp by its base, she jabbed the glass. The window cracked on her first attempt, crumbled to shards with a second, stronger thrust. Both sounds were largely swallowed by the wail of mariachi horns next door.

Carefully she swept the frame clear, using the metal neck of the lamp, then rolled the Dumpster under the window and climbed onto the lid.

A glance at the far end of the passageway revealed two green eyes still burning against the dark.

"Wish me luck," she whispered to the cat.

Its answering meow heartened her.

Gingerly she inserted one leg through the window, then the other. Inch by inch she wriggled in, holding fast to the sill, her feet probing until they found a smooth, sturdy surface. Resting on it, she was able to release her grip on the sill and draw her upper body, her arms, and finally her head inside.

She found herself squatting on the porcelain lid of the toilet tank. For several breathless seconds she waited tensely, until she felt reasonably confident that no German shepherd was about to charge out of the dark and savage her throat.

Then she stepped cautiously onto the seat of the commode and hopped to the floor.

She was in.

It was a strange feeling to be alone in the dark in an unfamiliar home—uninvited, an intruder, a trespasser.

She listened for sounds of movement elsewhere in the apartment. Heard nothing but the Mexican music and, overhead, a creak of restless footsteps.

Had Gund's upstairs neighbor heard the window shatter or glimpsed her sneaking in? Dialed 911? Reports of a prowler were given top priority; response time would be short.

The footsteps continued, back and forth, back and forth, registering no urgency. Annie decided the tenant was merely pacing.

It must drive Harold crazy to hear that all night, she reflected, before reminding herself that he might be crazy anyway.

Okay. Search the place. Fast.

She was in a hurry to get out. The apartment, closed up all day, was hot and stuffy; she found it hard to breathe. Or maybe it was fear that shut her throat. Suddenly her certainty that Gund would not return for hours seemed baseless, mere wishful thinking. For all she knew, he was on his way home right now. Might be outside the front door, inserting his key in the lock—

"Quit it," she whispered harshly. "Get to work."

Her hand on the wall switch, she hesitated.

Turn on the lights? It seemed dangerous. If Gund did return, he would see the lighted windows from the street.

But not this window. Only those in front.

She decided on a compromise. She would use the lights only in rooms facing the building next door. And she would turn off the light as she left each room.

She flipped the switch, and a ceiling lamp winked on, dazzling after the minutes she'd spent in darkness.

The bathroom seemed ordinary enough. Not as clean as it could be, some unpleasant smells. Towels on dented metal racks. Shampoo in the shower. Bar of soap in a porcelain dish on the Formica counter. Mirror over the sink, her reflection gazing back at her with frightened eyes.

Near the mirror, a medicine cabinet. Quickly she surveyed its shelves, looking for Erin's Tegretol. If Gund had it, the bottle would tie him to her disappearance. Even Walker couldn't dispute that.

There was no Tegretol. No medication of any kind except aspirin and antacids.

She switched off the bathroom light and emerged into a narrow hallway. Darkness in both directions. She turned left, groping along the wall until she found a door.

Pushing it open, she entered a bedroom in the front

corner of the apartment. The glow of a streetlight through the curtains provided sufficient illumination as she explored the room.

Cheap bed with creaky mattress springs. Bedside alarm clock, the dial luminous: 8:20. Clothes in the closet, but none of Erin's things. Her suitcase wasn't there, either.

Nothing suspicious so far. She returned to the hall and found a doorway to the living room. Even in darkness she could see that the place was sparsely furnished: battered sofa, a single floor lamp, an ancient television set resting on an apple crate, a dining table flanked by unmatched garage-sale chairs.

The room was most remarkable for what it did not contain. There were no books, no record albums, no paintings, no family photographs, no souvenirs from excursions to the Grand Canyon or San Diego. There was nothing.

"Harold," she whispered. "Poor Harold."

For a moment she forgot to be afraid of him. He was just a lonely man without a life.

Unless he was something worse.

Searching the living room was the work of a minute; there was nothing to see. She moved on to the kitchen, in the northwest corner of the apartment, far enough from any windows to make it safe to turn on a light.

The overhead fluorescent cast a pale, glareless glow on soiled countertops and peeling linoleum tiles. Dirty dishes crowded the sink; the water had drained away. A beetle scurried behind the refrigerator, black carapace gleaming.

She checked the silverware drawers, thinking vaguely she might find some obvious weapon—a bloodstained knife perhaps. There was only ordinary cutlery, inadequately cleaned, particles of dried food sticking to tines and blades.

In a lower drawer there was a miscellany of household hardware: cigarette lighters, manual can openers, a corkscrew, scissors of various sizes, and, lying carelessly atop the pile, a ring of keys.

The ring was tagged with a piece of masking tape marked SPARES.

Spare keys to the apartment? Or to whatever secret place Gund had been headed earlier tonight?

She examined the key ring more closely. Six keys in all, each with a bit of tape inked in the same careful hand.

FRONT DOOR. BARN. STAIRS. CELLAR. And two smaller keys, probably for padlocks: GATE. REAR DOOR.

Not for this place, obviously. These were the keys to a farm or ranch with a barn, a cellar, and a padlocked gate.

There were ranches in the desert southeast of town, where she had lost Gund's trail. Perhaps he was at one of them at this moment, with the original set of keys.

Perhaps Erin was there, too.

Annie hesitated, then slipped the keys into the pocket of her skirt, supplementing her original crime of illegal entry with a new offense, burglary.

Shutting off the fluorescent, she retraced her steps to the hall. The hall closet, overlooked earlier, was opposite the bathroom. A bare bulb illuminated shelves of cardboard cartons, apparently stuff from Wisconsin that Gund had never unpacked.

Nearly all of the apartment had been covered by now. There remained only the far end of the hall.

She slipped past the bathroom and found an open door to a small study: desk and swivel chair, file cabinet, wastebasket. The window faced the building across the passageway—safe to use a light. She fumbled for the desk lamp's pull chain, and the bulb snapped on.

Erin's stationery was not in the desk drawers. Disappointed, Annie knelt by the file cabinet, trying the lower drawer first. She thumbed through a row of manila folders, scanning the gummed labels.

TAXES. BILLS. AUTO. MEDICAL.

All marked with years ranging from 1985 to 1991. Old records, of no interest now.

Standing, she opened the upper drawer. It contained the same sorts of records, but from more recent years, with the current files foremost in line.

Nothing there, either.

Well, what had she expected to find? A file marked REILLY KIDNAPPING? Containing a helpful map to the site of Erin's imprisonment?

Angrily she shook her head. This whole venture had been a waste of time.

Her hand was pushing the drawer shut when she noticed a slim folder at the extreme rear of the cabinet, the only one that was unlabeled.

Funny how it was stuffed all the way in the back, unmarked, as if hidden.

She reached for the folder, opened it.

Its entire contents consisted of a single sheet of heavy, unlined paper, approximately eight by ten inches.

As she lifted the paper into the light, she realized that what she held was a glossy color photo, its back to her.

She turned it over, and suddenly she was shaking, shaking uncontrollably, her heart racing in her chest.

"How?" she whispered to the room, to the night. "How can he have *this*?"

Two smiling faces. Green eyes and gray. Red hair lustrous on bare shoulders.

The eight-by-ten studio portrait of Erin and herself.

# 48

The van's dashboard clock read 8:25 when Gund parked at a red curb, alongside a hydrant, yards from his apartment's front door. He didn't give a damn about a parking ticket.

The photo. That was his sole concern. He had to get the photo.

Before tonight he had never grasped its full significance. Now he knew why it had transfixed him, how he'd lost himself in the picture for hours at a time. He knew, and the knowledge sickened him.

Staring at their faces, their beautiful faces, staring hour after hour, night after night . . .

When the dream would wake him, when he found himself getting hard, then he would take out the picture and study it. He had found it soothing, or so he'd told himself.

The truth was uglier. The picture had not soothed, but stimulated.

He wondered if he had even . . .

While staring at it, had he . . . ?

No. He couldn't have.

And yet . . .

Suppose, while gazing at the photograph, lost in contemplation, oblivious to everything around him and within him . . . he had touched himself.

He had no memory of it. But he had blanked out his awareness of so much else that mattered. He had shut his inner eyes to so many truths. Why not to one more?

A shudder racked him. He threw open the van door. Crossed a strip of weedy grass to the paved walkway. Keys jingling nervously in his fingers, the flap of his jacket swirling, the gun in his pocket thumping against his hip.

Even if he was right in his supposition, even if the photo had served that ugly purpose for him, it would serve a very different purpose now.

He would destroy it. Touch a lighter to it and set it aflame. And by burning the photograph, symbolically burn the two women whose images it captured.

That might be enough—just enough—to suppress the impulses threatening to overwhelm him.

It would have to be.

He fumbled the key into the keyhole. The door swung open, and he lunged into his living room, flicking on the lights.


Annie gazed, frozen, at the photograph.

*Did he take it from Erin's apartment?* she wondered blankly. *Go back for it when he returned for the Tegretol?*

No, that couldn't be the answer. This photo had not spent the past six months in a frame, under glass. It had been handled, roughly and repeatedly. The edges were worn, the corners dog-eared.

She thought back to the day last November when she'd picked up her order from the portrait studio— multiple copies of the photo in different sizes. She'd returned to her shop with the envelope, but she hadn't had time to count the prints until that night, when she'd found only three eight-by-tens, not four as requested. The studio, apologizing for the oversight, had supplied an additional print at no cost.

But it hadn't been the studio's error. Sometime during the afternoon, when the envelope was in her office at the rear of the shop, Gund must have taken one of the prints. Hidden it, and carried it home with him that evening.

*He's had it ever since,* she thought as a wave of cold seeped slowly into her bones. *And he's been . . . looking at it. Holding it. He's—*

From the living room, the groan of a door.

The floorboards trembled.

Gund was back.

And coming this way. Coming fast.

She pushed the cabinet drawer shut, grabbed the desk lamp's pull chain, yanked it savagely. The room went dark.

Footsteps in the hall. Closer.

Under the desk. Get *under the desk.*

Groping blindly, she shoved the swivel chair out of the way, went down on all fours, crawled into the kneehole between the desk legs. Seized the chair and wheeled it back into position, then huddled behind it.

Sudden harsh glare from above. The ceiling light had come on with a flick of a wall switch.

Gund's pants brushed past the desk as he hurried to the file cabinet. She heard the slide of a drawer.

Instantly she guessed what he was looking for. The photo, of course.

The photo still clutched in her left hand.

Gund found the manila folder at the rear of the drawer, plucked it out of the cabinet, flipped it open.

Empty.

All the breath hissed out of him, and he stared at it, just stared.

It couldn't be gone. He always kept it in this folder. Always.

Unless this morning he'd forgotten. Left it in the bathroom or the bedroom . . .

No. He remembered returning it to its hiding place. Would never leave it in plain sight. After all, what if someone were to break in and find it—

Break in.

Annie.

The skin at the base of his spine tightened. The muscles of his shoulders bunched up with new tension.

She'd followed him earlier tonight. Had she come here afterward? Had she gotten in somehow and gone through his things? His most private, most personal things?

His gaze, ticking restlessly, stopped on the desk lamp.

The pull chain shivered, as if still vibrating from a violent tug.

Slowly he reached out, touched the unlit bulb.

His finger jerked away.

Hot.

That lamp had been on just seconds ago.

He shut his eyes, his last tissuey strand of self-control shredding, unraveling under irresistible pressure.

His hand dipped into the side pocket of his jacket, closed over the grip of the Taurus 9mm pistol.

He removed it. The blued barrel gleamed in the harsh glare of the overhead lamp.

The safety, when switched off, made a distinct click, loud in the room's stillness.


A sob rose in Annie's throat. She choked it back.

That noise she'd heard—it was a gun, wasn't it? She didn't know, couldn't be sure, but the sharp click reminded her of the sound a gun made on TV when the actor prepared to fire.

If he was armed . . .

Even weaponless, Gund ought to be more than a match for her, but she might have an outside chance. She'd watched Erin perform some defensive moves learned in that martial-arts class. Might be able to duplicate one or two of the simpler maneuvers.

But if he had a gun, a loaded gun—well, she couldn't fight that. Could only plead or scream, and somehow she didn't think either response would save her.

A slam of metal from the corner of the room punched through her thoughts. For a disoriented second she was sure it was a gunshot, but no, of course not, it hadn't been nearly loud enough.

The cabinet drawer banging shut. That was what she'd heard.

Then silence, filled only with Gund's rapid, shallow breathing, audible to her even under the desk.

He must have discovered that the photo was missing.

What next? Would he search for it? And if he did, would he start here or in another room?

Uselessly she pressed herself tighter against the desk's rear panel.

A soft thud. The floor shuddered.

He'd moved the file cabinet to look behind it. Which meant he *was* searching the den first.

The desk was the only other hiding place in the room. He would look here next.

She didn't want to cry, didn't want to cry, but suddenly she was certain she would die in a few seconds.

Gund's shoes marched into view, directly before the swivel chair.

The chair was pulled away.

Teeth clenched, eyes squeezed nearly shut, Annie watched through a blur of tears as Gund began to kneel.

From the bathroom next door, a shatter of glass.

Gund grunted—a subhuman interrogative sound— then bolted upright and pounded out of the room.

Annie started breathing again.

A reprieve. She didn't understand it, but she'd been granted a reprieve.

She dived forward, wriggling out from under the desk.


Gund had her now.

Hiding in the bathroom, the stupid bitch. The next place he would have looked.

His hand was hot, the pistol icy against his fingers.

Two quick strides, and he pivoted into the doorway, hit the light switch.

On the floor, a bar of soap and a spray of glass shards.

Perched on the counter, fur bristling, an alley cat.

No Annie in sight. Just some damn stray that had jumped through the open window and knocked the glass soap dish off the counter—

The open window.

But that window didn't open, ever. It was sealed shut.

Gund blinked, then realized the glass had been removed from the frame.

Annie had gotten in that way. Maybe escaped that way, too. Maybe heard him coming and left as he entered via the front door.

With a snarl he lunged for the window. The cat hopped onto the toilet tank with a frightened screech, then slipped outside.

Gund thrust his head into the passageway, glanced up and down its length, the pistol extended before him and ready to fire. He would shoot her regardless of the consequences, shoot to kill even though the noise would bring a dozen cops to the scene.

In his mind he pictured himself placing a single, perfectly centered bullet between her wide, terrified eyes.

"Filth," he whispered through gritted teeth.

But she wasn't there. No one was there. The passage

was empty save for the cat, gazing up at him curiously, a furred ink spot with a green luminous gaze.

Gund swung the pistol toward the stray, almost enraged enough to waste a shot on that worthless target, and the cat, sensing danger, wheeled abruptly and vanished into the shadows.

Gone. Like Annie herself. *Gone.*

Annie struggled to her feet, stuffed the photo in her pocket—evidence, she thought vaguely—then padded to the window of the den.

She unlocked it, tugged it open a few inches. The friction of the stiles against the casting produced a teeth-jarring squeal that froze her in terror.

Helpless, she waited for Gund to pound back into the room, drawn by the noise.

He didn't appear. Hadn't heard, obviously. But if she forced open the window any farther, he was sure to come running.

The only other exit was the door to the hallway, and Gund was out there.

But maybe the hall was clear. She had to chance it. No alternative.

Soundlessly she crossed the room, then peered past the door frame, shaking in expectation of the gunshot that would take her head off like a clay target in a shooting gallery.

No shot. No Gund. The corridor was empty.

In the bathroom, a snarl of anger.

That was where he'd gone.

All right, then. Down the hall. Now, while she had an opportunity.

She stepped fast but lightly, urgency balanced with caution. The hallway was carpeted—some cheap short-nap stuff, but thick enough to muffle her footfalls.

A screech from Gund's lavatory. Cat noise. Absurdly

she wondered if Stink was in there, if he'd come to rescue her, like Lassie.

Not Stink, of course. The alley cat. Must have slipped in through the window, broken something, diverted Gund.

At the bathroom doorway now. She would have to cross in front of the open door. That was bad, very bad. Gund couldn't help but see her.

Risking a peek inside, she felt a rush of hope. Gund's back was turned to her as he stared out the window into the passage.

Go.

Past the doorway in a silent flash of motion, and then she was safely on the other side, hugging the wall.

From the bathroom another enraged growl, terrifyingly close, followed by an explosive crackle of glass.

Thud of footsteps. He was coming out.

Ahead of her, an open door. She ducked into Gund's bedroom and prayed he wouldn't come this way, prayed he would return to the den and give her time to escape.

Gund spun away from the window, animal growls erupting from his throat, fury and shame overriding a last effort at restraint.

He struck out with his fist. Smashed the bathroom mirror. Cymbal crash of impact. Cascade of silvered shards. A hundred reflections of himself spilling to the floor.

Out of the bathroom, bellowing. Down the hall to the den. Was she under the desk? No.

Where the hell *was* she?

Wait. The window. Open a crack.

It had been closed a half minute ago, when he'd left the room.

She must have tried to get out that way while he was

distracted by the cat. But she hadn't succeeded, obviously. She was still somewhere in the apartment.

"Boss?" he whispered, a chilly, feral gleam in his eyes.

The answering silence mocked him.

He left the den at a run.

Annie considered escaping through a bedroom window, but it would take time to go out that way, and time was one thing she was sure she didn't have.

The hallway was empty again, Gund back in the den. The doorway to the living room was two steps away.

Chance it.

She dashed across the hall, into the living room, brightly illuminated now and somehow rendered more dismal in the glare.

Gund was a sad man with a sad life, but she felt no twinge of pity.

Behind her, a bestial roar.

*Insane,* she thought as she darted among the sparse furnishings on her way to the front door. *He's completely insane.*

And he was coming this way.

From the hall, the mounting racket of his footsteps. He would be inside the living room in seconds.

She reached the door, fumbled for the knob, her hand slippery with perspiration, fingers sliding on the smooth metal.

*Get a grip, Annie,* she ordered, unconscious of any pun.

Her hand found purchase. The knob turned, the door popped open, and she was outside, shutting the door behind her, then sprinting down the paved walk, into the street, the macadam a dark blur under her racing feet, the corner straight ahead.

Backward glance: Gund wasn't behind her, not yet. She'd been sure he would see the door swing shut.

But maybe he hadn't gone directly into the living room. Maybe he'd looked in the bedroom first.

Gasping, she turned the corner, flew past a line of parked cars, and then her Miata was beside her and she was digging in her skirt pocket for her keys.

Abruptly the wire fence of the auto lot clanged with a violent impact—the Doberman, leaping at her, slavering wildly, releasing a crazed volley of barks.

"Shut up!" she gasped, hating the dog, its insane ferocity reminding her of Gund.

She found her keys—no, wrong ones; those were the spares she'd taken from Gund's kitchen. Thrust her hand into her pocket again, the dog howling, a banshee wail.

Was Gund in the street by now, seeking her out? Would he hear the noise, connect it with her? Was he running here at this moment?

She fished out the right set of keys this time, unlocked the car, flung herself inside.

Which key was it? Too many on the ring. House key, mailbox key, shop key, office key . . .

The dog attacked the night with long ululant wails. Gund must have heard it, must be on his way.

Garage-door key, storage-locker key, luggage key . . .
Car key.

She tossed a split-second glance in the rearview mirror, expecting to see Gund round the corner, but the street remained empty and still.

Key in the ignition. Twist of her wrist, the engine firing. Headlights on, and she spun the wheel hard to the left and tore free of the curb.

Her foot slammed down on the gas pedal. The Miata shot forward, outracing its own headlights.

Shaking all over, fighting for breath, Annie sped north, toward the lights of downtown—and the police station.

# 49

Eyes shut.

Jaws clenched.

A bead of sweat traveling slowly down her cheek, her neck, the curve of her breast, disappearing finally inside the waistband of her shorts.

Erin, kneeling on the floor, naked from the waist up, gripped the central coupling nut of the sill cock in the cellar wall and tried again to loosen it with a counterclockwise turn.

Her leg was chained to the spigot. She had no hope of defeating either of the padlocks securing the chains, not without tools or the means to make some. And Oliver had removed everything useful.

Her only chance at mobility and self-defense was to disassemble the sill cock. If she could detach the spout-and-handle component from the horizontal pipe feeding into the wall, one end of the chain would fall away, and she would be free.

But the job was hard, maybe too hard. At first she hadn't even found purchase on the nut. Her fingers had slipped, as if greased, over its smooth contours.

That was when she'd stripped off her shirt and removed her bra, the bra Oliver had so thoughtfully packed for her. She'd unhooked one of the adjustable straps, an inch-wide ribbon of Lycra, and wound it around the nut, forming a tight rubber skin.

The wrapping improved her grip considerably. Even so, the nut continued to resist her efforts.

She bore down harder, straining with both hands to rotate the damn thing counterclockwise. The muscles of her arms and shoulders, still painfully sore from her ordeal outside, screamed in protest.

"Come on," she whispered through gritted teeth. "Come *on*."

She felt an instant's slippage.

But was it the nut that had moved or only the bra strap, sliding on the metal?

She wasn't sure. She tried again.

And again she felt it. Unmistakable now.

The nut was turning.

Only a fraction of an inch at a time, each small victory costing her an agony of effort, but it *was* turning. It could be loosened. Given time, she could unchain herself from the wall.

And then . . . ?

She didn't know. She would still be locked in a windowless room, behind an impregnable door. But at least when Oliver returned, she could fight.

Fight—and die, almost certainly.

But fight nevertheless.


"May I help you?"

The sergeant on duty at the lobby desk studied Annie with a cool, level gaze.

"Yes, please. I need to talk to Detective Walker." Annie spoke rapidly, struggling to keep her voice under control.

"This some kind of emergency?"

"Life and death," she blurted out, then wondered if it sounded melodramatic.

The sergeant showed no reaction. "Walker's gone home," he said with irritating matter-of-factness.

Of course he had. She should have assumed as much, but fear had rattled her; she wasn't thinking clearly.

"Could you give me his home number?" she pressed.

"We don't normally give out that information."

"Please."

He hesitated, then flipped through a Rolodex file and produced a card. "Use that phone over there. Press nine for an outside line."

"Thank you. Thank you so much."

She hurried to the far end of the desk, stood leaning against it as she turned an unused telephone toward her and dialed.

Two rings ... three ...

What if Walker didn't answer? What if he was out of the house? It would take too long to explain everything to some other cop. She—

The fifth ring was cut off. "Walker."

"Michael, it's Annie. Annie Reilly."

"Annie?" Concern in his voice. "What's happened? How'd you get this number?"

"The desk sergeant gave it to me. I'm at the station. I need your help."

"Are you all right?"

"I'm fine, don't worry about me, it's Erin, I know who's got Erin!"

"Slow down, Annie. Take it easy."

"I can't take it easy, *he's got her,* don't you understand?"

"Who's got her?"

"My assistant at the shop. His name is Harold Gund."

"Gund?"

She spelled it. "I hired him six months ago. I

thought he was okay. He's not. He's crazy. And he's got a copy of our portrait—the photo you looked at—the photo of Erin and me."

"Where?"

"It was in a file cabinet in his apartment."

"How do you know that? Did he show you?"

"Of course not. I broke in, I searched—"

"You *what*?"

"Damn it, just *listen* to me."

"You broke into his apartment?"

"Yes. I broke in."

She glanced behind her to see if any of the cops had overheard. No one was paying her the slightest attention.

"I broke in," she said again, more softly. "Searched his apartment. Found the photo, which I guess he stole from me when I had the prints at my shop. Don't you get it? He wanted her picture. He's *obsessed* with her."

"I don't understand. What made you suspect this man Gund in the first place?"

"He lied about where he went on his lunch hour. So I followed him after work. He drove into the desert. He's got a ranch, somewhere southeast of town—I found a spare set of keys."

Vaguely she realized she was not relating these events in any logical order, but she couldn't seem to organize her thoughts. Panic kept squeezing her throat shut, making it difficult to speak.

"A ranch?" Walker asked, sounding dubious.

"Yes. A ranch. I've got the keys. He's keeping Erin there."

"You don't know that. You didn't see her."

"I saw the photo. I have it with me. His fingerprints are probably all over it. What more do you need?"

"Annie, you're in the photo, too."

"So?"

"Maybe it's you he wanted a picture of. Maybe he's got a crush on his boss. Nothing more sinister than that."

"Oh, Christ . . ." Disappointment thudded down on her like a deadweight. "You don't believe me."

"That's not what I said."

"You *still* won't help me. *Still.*"

Suddenly she was crying, though she hated herself for it. Crying, her back turned to the cops, hoping they couldn't see.

"Annie," Walker said gently, "what do you want me to do?"

"Arrest him. Arrest Gund."

"He's not charged with any crime."

"There's the photo," she said desperately. "It's my property. He stole it, didn't he?"

"And you stole it back. After breaking and entering."

"Then arrest me, too, I don't care!"

"I can't do it, Annie."

He couldn't do it. Naturally. He couldn't do anything. Except tell her that she was a paranoid head case and Erin was fine, just fine.

Annie wiped her eyes, straightened up. All right, then. If he wouldn't help her, then she would handle things on her own.

"Annie?" Walker's voice was curiously tinny. She noticed that she had lowered the telephone handset to the desk. *"Annie?"*

She cradled the phone, then walked briskly out the door into the warm night.

The cop on duty at the glassed-in cubicle outside nodded to her as she passed by. She didn't notice.

A pickup truck had parked next to her Miata in the visitors' lot. Her car door banged the truck's side panel as she slipped behind the wheel. She didn't notice that, either.

Cough of ignition, squeal of tires, and she pulled into the street.

Her mind was only marginally focused on the details of driving. She was mapping strategy.

Erin was at Gund's ranch. Had to be.

The ranch was probably in the general vicinity of Houghton Road.

Annie had a set of keys to that ranch.

Simple enough, then. She would retrace the route Gund had taken this evening. Search the side roads for a ranch whose gate and doors would open to the keys in her pocket.

Of course, there was a chance Gund would go there, too. Might be on his way already. Presumably he knew she was on to him. He might panic, decide to end it all.

If he was there when she arrived . . .

Well, maybe he wouldn't be. Maybe he was looking for her at her town house or the shop. Or fleeing across the state line, or getting on a plane to Mexico.

Anyway, she would have to risk it. She had no choice.

There was no one to help her, not this time. No one to take charge and spare her the responsibility of action. No one to lead her by the hand, out of the flames.

"Annie? *Annie?*"

Walker stabbed the reset button on his kitchen phone and used the memory feature to dial the station.

In their first meeting, Annie Reilly had told him she was impulsive and emotional. She might be wrong about Gund, about Erin, about nearly everything, but on that particular point Walker had to concur.

Ringing on the other end of the line.

"Hackett." The desk sergeant.

"Ed, this is Walker. That woman who phoned me—is she still there?"

"Just left."

"Send someone after her. Bring her back."

"Right."

Walker waited on hold, the fried eggs on the stove beginning to burn.

He was worried. Annie already had done something crazy when she broke into Harold Gund's apartment. Now, distraught as she was, she might do something still crazier.

Smoke from the frying pan wafted toward the ceiling. It would set off the smoke detector in the hallway before long. He reached across the kitchen, turned off the burner, then picked up the pan and placed it in the sink.

No eggs tonight. Just as well. His doctor had warned him to watch his cholesterol.

Hackett came back on the line. "Sorry, Michael. She's gone. Whipped out of the visitors' lot like a smoking fast ball."

"Okay, Ed. Thanks."

He thumbed the reset button again. Then stood motionless, staring out the window at the night sky, thinking hard.

A ranch in the desert, Annie had said. Southeast of town.

If Gund had bought the place, a record of the purchase would be kept at the county tax assessor's office.

The office was closed for the night. But Walker had a friend who worked there. A friend who owed him for some hard-to-get playoff tickets to a Phoenix Suns game a few years ago, tickets obtained from a former Tucson cop, now part of America West Arena's security detail.

It would take his friend less than a half hour to drive to the office and find the file, if it existed.

Probably unnecessary. Probably Erin Reilly had left of her own volition, as her letter had stated. Probably Annie was imagining the worst, and this Harold Gund was just a lonely man infatuated with his attractive boss. Probably.

"Oh, hell," Walker whispered.

He dialed his friend's home number and called in the favor.

# 50

Gund, driving fast on Interstate 10, heading southeast.

He would keep going until he crossed the state border into New Mexico. In Las Cruces he could ditch the van and steal a car. Afterward, he would get off the main highway and take the back roads. In Dallas or Houston, he would buy new ID.

Did he have money? None. He'd packed nothing, taken nothing. Panic must have chased all practicalities from his brain.

It didn't matter. Along the way he would steal whatever he needed.

His grip on the steering wheel tightened. He pushed the speedometer needle to eighty as the concrete miles blurred past.

The engine throbbed, and his head throbbed with it. But at least the tingling of his fingers had faded, as had the unnatural heat at the back of his neck and the distant, unreal chiming in his ears. Those symptoms had vanished sometime during his search of his apartment. He had no idea why.

He wondered how much time he'd wasted in that search, exploring every possible place of concealment, the pistol shaking in his hand. Hatred and humiliation had made him sloppy, the search feverish and inefficient. Frequently he'd found himself checking the same closet or cubbyhole for the third or fourth time.

Finally he'd understood that she was gone, had been gone for many minutes, and worse—that she must have driven directly to the police.

She would talk to the detective who'd looked into Erin's disappearance. The man would believe her this time. He would want to ask Gund some questions. Might already be on his way over.

Fear had seized him. He'd run from his apartment, not looking back, then gotten on the interstate and floored the gas pedal, barreling past semi trucks and sticker-festooned campers traveling at sixty-five.

Now he was beyond city limits, coming up on the Valencia Road exit, passing it, with Wilmot Road two miles ahead.

Soon he would leave the Tucson area behind. Christ, he never should have come here in the first place. Never.

"Never," he murmured under his breath. Distantly he noted how peculiar the word sounded, slurred and indistinct, as if he had been drinking, or as if he were mumbling in his sleep.

The thought skipped lightly along the margin of his awareness, leaving him before he could quite grasp it. Unimportant anyway. What was important was to keep driving, get the hell out of here, never come back.

Shouldn't have left Wisconsin. Things had been all right there. He had been safe there. Safe and empty inside.

For twenty years he'd worked as a janitor at the university, the lonely monotony of his life interrupted only by the periodic need to kill and the anguish afterward.

Perhaps he could have continued that way for another twenty years . . . if he hadn't seen the article.

It was a scholarly monograph on fire setters, appearing in the *Journal of Consulting and Clinical Psychology*. Some professor had left the slim, glossy publication on a coffee table in the psychology department's faculty lounge. Gund had found it while cleaning up on a winter night in 1992, a few months after the third woman, Deborah Collins, had burned.

The title, printed on the cover, had hooked his attention at once. "Fire as Rage: Pyromania and the Antisocial Personality."

Below it, the byline: Erin Reilly, Ph.D.

Erin Reilly.

A biographical note appended to Erin's article had said she'd recently established a private practice in Tucson.

After that, he'd checked each new issue of every psychology publication as it had come in. Over the past four years he had found several other articles by Erin. All concerned the same issue: fire as a weapon, fire as an instrument of rage.

He wasn't sure exactly when it had occurred to him that she could treat his problem. At first he'd dismissed the idea; in order to undergo therapy, he first would have to confess, and there had never been any chance he would do that.

Then, last year, the possibility of kidnapping her had entered his mind for the first time. The plan had exercised a peculiar hold on his imagination. He couldn't shake free of it. He'd found himself rehearsing it mentally, examining his strategy for imperfections, revising it again and again.

Last October he'd quit his job at the university. He had sold his ancient station wagon and replaced it with a used Chevy Astro. Had packed his few belongings into a U-Haul trailer, hitched it to the van, and driven to Arizona.

Money was not a problem for him. In his twenty years of custodial work, he had saved nearly all of what he'd earned, spending next to nothing for the studio apartment he rented. The surplus had accumulated week after week, month after month, in a simple savings account. The total had been $126,295.32 at the time of his departure.

He had not been putting away a nest egg for his retirement; he merely had never found any use for money. His plan had given him a conscious purpose for the first time in his life.

Erin advertised her practice in the Tucson Yellow Pages. The day after his arrival, Gund had watched the office complex where she worked until she emerged at noon.

He'd recognized her immediately—her red hair was still the same—but the sight of her slender, long-legged figure had startled him. At some level he hadn't quite accepted the fact that she was an adult now.

She'd gotten into her Ford Taurus and driven to a restaurant downtown. At the restaurant she'd met Annie.

The two of them, together. Dining on a sunny veranda. Through binoculars he had studied them.

Beautiful. Both so very beautiful.

After lunch, the women had separated with a hug. Gund had tailed Annie to her flower shop, where he'd caught sight of a sign in the window: HELP WANTED.

It had been crazy to apply for the job. If she'd recognized him as Oliver . . . or if she simply had checked out his phony story about a mix-up at the University of Arizona that had cost him a promised custodial position . . .

But he'd risked it. To improve his chances he'd invented a mawkish story about his late wife. The wallet photo he had showed Annie was actually one he'd found among Deborah Collins's belongings. Deborah's mother, probably.

Annie had fallen for it. He'd gotten the job. Later he had tailed her to her home; on a weekend afternoon he'd spied on her and Erin as they played tennis, then shadowed Erin to her apartment complex.

Once he'd known where Erin lived, he had begun to finalize the preparations for her abduction and captivity. His last step had been to purchase the old Connor ranch, the ranch of his boyhood, depleting nearly all of his twenty years of savings to make a single payment of $119,000 in cash. The ranch, isolated yet convenient to town, had been ideal for his purposes.

An impeccable strategy, faultlessly implemented. He was sure of that. He had planned and executed every stage of the operation without a single misstep.

And yet here he was, speeding out of town, abandoning his possessions and his very identity to pursue a life on the run.

A freeway sign alerted him to the next exit. Houghton Road.

His foot eased up on the gas pedal, and the van's speed began to drop.

Odd.

Why was he slowing down? He'd been making good time, and there was nobody ahead of him.

The steering wheel turned under his hands. The beam of his one headlight crossed over the white line as the van pulled into the right-hand lane.

The exit lane.

The off-ramp for Houghton Road lay a hundred yards ahead.

A flick of his hand, and the right turn signal flashed.

He dropped his gaze. Nerveless, paralyzed, he stared at the small, flashing arrow on the dashboard for what seemed like a very long time.

He got it now. Of course he did.

There would be no trip across the state line, no change of identity, no fugitive existence.

None of that ever had been his purpose. He'd merely imagined that it was. The idea had been only a twitch, a last, feeble spasm of rational thought; it had not moved him.

Because he had clicked off. Become unplugged.

Sometime during that episode of rage and frenzy in his apartment, when he'd been hunting Annie, he had slipped into this altered state of mind without even realizing it.

Since then he had been operating on automatic pilot, thoughts running on one track, actions proceeding along another.

At forty miles an hour he left the interstate, then swung north on Houghton Road. He passed the gas station where Erin had tried making a 911 call last night.

There were reasons, sound reasons, for returning to the interstate and continuing his drive east. But those arguments held no force. They had long since folded under the pressure of the beating needs in control of him.

Only one impulse motivated him now.

He would kill her. Kill Erin. Take her out to the arroyo and stake her to the ground and burn her.

Next, Annie. Sooner or later she would return to her town house. When she did, he would be there. He would tie her to a chair or truss her on the floor, and then . . .

The van thumped and rattled, and he realized with mild surprise that he had turned onto the side road that led to the ranch. He hadn't even been aware of slowing down or steering to his right.

Ahead, the gate of the ranch was open, the padlock

and chain removed this afternoon to serve as Erin's shackles.

He guided the van through the gate, to the barn. The barn doors, too, had been left open in his hasty departure. Careless—the wreck of Erin's Taurus was dimly visible within.

He parked alongside the car. From the van's glove compartment he took his flashlight and the stun gun.

The flash would be helpful in the arroyo. And the stun gun might be necessary to get Erin there without unduly harming her.

He wanted her conscious when he struck the fatal match.

Funny how calm he felt. Calm outwardly, of course; he always was, once his plug was pulled. But the strange thing was that he felt the same tranquillity within. There was none of the turmoil that had accompanied his other killings. No inner witness who looked on aghast.

He was at peace with himself. In memory the words of that smug TV expert came back to him: *This is not a tormented person. This is a man who's quite comfortable with what he does—and what he is.*

That never had been true of him before. Had been the furthest thing from reality. But not tonight.

Tonight the burning felt good to him. Felt *right*.

Flashlight and keys in hand, the side pockets of his jacket stuffed with the pistol and stun gun, he strode out of the barn. He shut the main doors behind him, then crossed yards of brittle grass to the house, his legs cutting space with mechanical efficiency, his gaze focused straight ahead.

Felt right, he thought again. Well, of course it did. Why wouldn't it?

It *was* right.

The burnings in the woods up north had been wrong.

He saw that now. The three women he'd killed had meant nothing to him. They had been mere random strangers, surrogates for the two he'd really wanted. Symbolic sacrifices, that was all. Their deaths, satisfying him only briefly, had served no lasting purpose.

But these two were different. These were no strangers, no stand-ins. These were the two who had ruined his life. Who had haunted him, obsessed him, poisoned his mind with unclean thoughts.

Everything he'd done—it was their fault, entirely theirs. They had been the source of all his troubles and afflictions right from the start. They had been the unhealed sore in his soul.

He reached the front door, turned the key in the lock. As he entered the house, he nodded in silent assent to his own thoughts, then went on nodding, nodding, the slight incline of his head repeated like a programmed routine.

It was right, so right, that he do this. There could be no hesitation, no doubt. Not this time.

Never could he be liberated from the torment that plagued him—never—until Erin and Annie Reilly were dead.

# 51

With a final twist of her wrists, Erin wrenched the coupling nut free.

As she separated the two halves of the sill cock, she heard the familiar rumble of the van's engine.

Oliver had returned, as she'd known he would.

He wouldn't expect her to be unchained. There was a chance she could take him by surprise.

Quickly she shrugged on her blouse and buttoned it. She tossed the bra and its unhooked strap into the cardboard box containing her provisions, then slid the box in front of the sill cock.

Footsteps overhead. The stairs drummed as he descended.

The sill cock's detached spout would make a serviceable weapon. She tucked it into the waistband of her shorts behind her back.

Then she seated herself in the chair facing the door, one end of the chain still padlocked to her ankle, the loose end snaking behind the cardboard box, out of sight.

A key rattled in the lock. The door opened, and Oliver was there.

Yet not there, not really. She could see that.

His face was expressionless, a mask of slack flesh.

He stepped forward into the glow of the bare light bulb on the chain. The shadows lifted from his eyes, and she saw his dull, glazed stare.

Fugue state, she thought with a ripple of dread.

The pockets of his jacket were bulging—she glimpsed the checkered grip of the pistol, and the stun gun's metallic gleam—but his hands held only a set of keys and a flashlight, switched off.

" 'Evening, Doc." His affectless monotone matched the emptiness of his eyes.

"Hello, Oliver."

"I've come for you." He moved nearer, then stopped behind the other chair. "She's on to me. Your sister. She knows."

He said it so simply that Erin needed a moment to grasp the significance of the words.

Annie *knew*.

She kept her own voice safely casual. "Does she?"

Oliver nodded. "Don't know how she guessed. I must have slipped up somehow. But it doesn't matter. It's over."

He was standing more than six feet away. Too far. He had to be within reach.

"We still have work to do," she said, hoping to draw him closer.

"No more work. That's done now."

"We were making progress—"

"Uh-uh. I'm discontinuing therapy, Doc." He stepped around the chair, advancing on her. "We're going outside now. Out to the arroyo."

"You don't want to do that."

"Oh, yes." A yard away. Half a yard. "I do."

He reached for his pocket. For the stun gun.

*Now*.

She twisted sideways, seized the chain, then shot upright, swinging it in a wide, looping arc.

Instinctively Oliver stepped back.

The loose end of the chain flashed past his face and found its target.

The light bulb shattered in a tinkling rain.

Darkness. Intense and absolute in the windowless room.

Even as the bulb exploded, Erin sidestepped away from the chair. A heartbeat later the wooden legs scraped noisily on concrete. Oliver had lunged blindly at the spot where she'd stood.

Her right hand fumbled behind her, prying the spout free of her waistband.

To her left, the flashlight snapped on, its pale beam dissecting the dark. The circle of light whipped toward her, sudden glare dazzling her vision.

She raised the spout and brought it down, knife-quick, aiming just behind the flash.

The pipe chopped Oliver's wrist. Gasp of pain, and the flashlight fell free.

It struck the floor and rolled, its beam painting yellow spirals on the cellar walls. In the blurred half-light Erin saw Oliver again reaching for the stun gun.

She lashed out with the spout a second time.

Oliver sensed the attack, dodged to one side, then seized her right forearm, his grip painfully tight, squeezing a gasp out of her.

Involuntarily her fingers splayed. She had time to think that the pressure of his clutch had paralyzed her radial nerve, and then the spout dropped from her hand like a discarded toy. She heard it clatter on the floor.

No weapon. But she could still fight. Months of self-defense classes must have been good for something.

*Don't think.* The voice in her mind belonged to Mr. Sanders, her tae kwon do instructor. *Thinking is too slow. Let your reflexes take over.*

Oliver, still holding her right arm, jerked her toward

him. His face rushed at her, his eyes sparkling in the dimness.

Reaching across her body with her left hand, she grabbed the wrist of her captured arm, then snapped her upper body back and tore free of his grasp.

She retreated a step, and then his two hands closed over her throat.

Brief panic shook her—she couldn't *breathe*—before habits more deeply ingrained than she'd suspected, habits that mimicked instinct, dictated the correct response.

She raised her arms fast, over Oliver's forearms, then swung sharply to the right, bending at the waist. Her left elbow came up, and she whipped back to an upright posture, using the momentum of her upper body to drive the elbow savagely into Oliver's jaw.

Stunned, he released her throat.

Her right hand wasn't paralyzed anymore. She curled it in a tight fist, the first two knuckles projecting slightly, and directed a reverse punch at Oliver's ribs, pivoting as she delivered the blow.

He gasped but didn't go down. With her left hand she executed a crippling palm-heel strike to his groin.

Grunt of pain, and he staggered backward, then dropped to his knees.

She'd done it. She'd beaten him.

Erin spun away from him, her next moves fully formed in her mind. Simply get out of the room, bolt and chain the door, then lock the door at the top of the stairs also. He might be able to shoot his way out, but not before she'd fled the ranch.

These thoughts crowded her brain, borne on a cresting wave of triumph, as she lunged blindly for the door frame, found it, began to step through—

The chain fastened to her right leg was jerked taut.

She lost her balance, slammed down on hands and knees.

Oliver, still sprawled on the floor, gave the chain another tug. Erin slid on the smooth concrete, dragged closer to her adversary.

She rolled onto her side, bent her left leg at the knee, and aimed a punishing snap kick at Oliver's head.

Crack of impact. She ripped the chain free of his grasp, then scrambled to her feet.

She'd hoped the kick would immobilize him, but no; he was rising, too, his recovery so rapid as to be almost instantaneous. He seemed impervious to pain. The thought flashed in her mind that the same neurological wiring that had suppressed awareness of his deepest feelings might have cut him off from unwanted bodily sensations as well.

For the moment she'd forfeited her chance to escape through the doorway. She had to put him on the floor again.

Turning to face him, she lashed out with another kick.

Her intention was to disable him with a fractured kneecap, but he stepped into the kick, catching the blow on the side of his calf, then locked her in a crushing bear hug.

Pain shot through her ribs. She smelled his breath, sour and close.

Proper defensive move: knee strike.

Her left leg shot up. Simultaneously Oliver pistoned out both arms, shoving her away.

Caught off balance, she tried to find her footing, failed, and thudded down on her side with a gasp.

Impact shocked all the breath out of her. She tried to rise, couldn't. Her legs and arms wouldn't work. For a long, helpless moment she just lay there, wheezing, until her lungs sucked air again.

Then slowly she looked up, and there he was: Oliver, looming over her, a yard away, the stun gun in his hand, the flashlight on the floor throwing his huge, distended shadow across the ceiling like a great black stain.

*Sparring session's over, Erin.* Mr. Sanders sounded faintly disappointed. *Better luck next time.*

Dazed, she crawled blindly backward, away from the weapon, the chain rattle-clanking in her wake.

Brick walls bumped up against her shoulders. She had retreated into a corner. Nowhere to go.

Oliver took a step forward, closing the short distance between them. His mouth worked soundlessly for a moment, and then he remembered speech.

"You filth," he muttered. "Stinking *filth*."

He switched on the stun gun. Electricity crackled between the prongs in a blue arc.

"Oliver." She coughed, then found the strength to speak. "You don't hate me enough to kill me. You know you don't."

"Wrong, Doc." Still no emotion in his voice, no expression on his face. "I do hate you. You and your damn sister. I wish the two of you had never been born. I wish—"

He stopped himself.

"You wish Maureen had had us aborted," Erin finished for him.

His eyes narrowed, the lids sliding shut as if with sleep. Slowly he nodded.

"But she didn't," Erin said, "because she was a Catholic, and it would have been a sin."

"There are worse sins."

"Like your sin." Tick of silence in the room. "Incest."

Oliver said nothing.

"Lincoln molested you for years. And when Maureen visited the ranch, you did the same to her. You raped her, because she was your mother's sister, and incest was the only form of intimacy you'd ever known."

From between frozen lips, a faint sleepwalker's murmur: "Shut up."

"And she got pregnant. With Annie and me." Erin gazed up at his face, searching for a response. "You're our father."

Something flickered in his eyes. A hint of personality, of human consciousness.

He switched off the stun gun. The hiss of current was replaced by the labored rasp of his breathing.

"Yes," he whispered. "God damn you, yes."

# 52

At the eastern end of the side road where she'd lost Gund's trail at nightfall, Annie found a ranch with a padlocked gate.

Brief excitement shook her. But the duplicate key marked GATE would not open the lock, and neither would any other key on the ring.

Disappointed, she doubled back to Houghton Road and continued south.

Already her quest was beginning to feel hopeless. It was one thing to assume that Gund had a ranch in this vicinity; it was quite another to search every side street, every dirt road, every unmarked lane intersecting with Houghton for miles.

For all she knew, Gund's ranch was far south of here, perhaps south of Interstate 10 and the Pima County Fairgrounds. Or—a grimmer prospect—it might be nowhere in the area at all.

It Gund had known all along that she was following him, he might have driven out of his way deliberately, in order to give no clue to his true destination, before performing whatever mysterious maneuver had made him disappear.

There were so many possibilities, and the desert was

so dark, so vast. She could very well be wasting her time.

Another side road passed by, this one on her left. Unmarked, barely visible. She nearly missed seeing it.

With a squeal of brakes she cut her speed and executed a skidding U-turn, then pulled onto the narrow dirt lane.

The Miata bounced lightly on the rutted surface. To the north, barbed-wire fencing glided by; beyond it lay the dim shapes of a house and barn.

She stiffened in her seat as a distant memory snapped into focus.

"Can't be coincidence," she whispered, unaware that she was voicing her thoughts. "Can't be."

Her headlights picked up an obstruction ahead.

A gate.

The Miata slowed to a halt. Annie sat in the driver's seat, very still, barely breathing.

The twin circles of her halogen beams played on the gate. Unlocked, it creaked lazily on rusted hinges.

If the labels on the key ring meant anything, then the gate of Gund's ranch was padlocked.

This couldn't be it, then.

But she knew it was.

Because this was the old Connor place. The ranch she and Erin had tracked down on a spring day in 1985.

There had been no reason to think of that visit in years. She'd forgotten all about the ranch, forgotten its location, its very existence.

Until now.

Now she knew—she *knew*—that this was the place she was looking for.

Harold Gund owned the ranch . . . and Erin was inside.

Switching on her high beams, she scanned the

grounds. Part of the fence, she noticed, had been torn apart as if by a speeding vehicle. She thought of the damage to Gund's van.

His van. If he was here, it ought to be within view. Parked in the carport or on the gravel court at the front of the house.

It was nowhere. And the house was dark.

Apparently Gund hadn't returned. Perhaps he really had fled, as she'd hoped.

Or perhaps he was on his way here right now.

She killed the high beams, using only her parking lights. Cautiously she eased the Miata forward and nosed open the gate. The car hummed over yards of stiff brown grass and came to a stop fifty feet from the house.

When she shut off the motor, the night's sudden stillness pressed in on her, squeezing her chest, making it difficult to breathe.

She left her key in the ignition—her experience in Gund's neighborhood had alerted her to the advantages of a quick getaway—and got out of the car, being careful not to slam the door. The warm night wrapped itself around her, dry and dark.

Her shoes crunched loudly on the gravel, an oddly hungry sound, like the grinding of some large animal's jaws, as she walked to the house's front door.

It was locked. Searching the key ring, squinting at each hand-labeled tag in the starlight, she found the key marked FRONT DOOR.

Even before inserting it in the keyhole, she was irrationally certain it would fit.

It did.

The door glided open under her hand. She stepped into a spacious living room, unfurnished, empty except for a potbelly stove bolted to the floor.

No light was apparent, other than shafts of feeble

starlight lancing through the broken windows. No sound was audible save the hum and whistle of the wind.

Annie moved forward, into the dark, and found her voice.

"Erin . . . ?"

# 53

"It must have been the summer of 1965," Erin said softly as the stun gun wavered in Oliver's shaking hand. "You would have been fifteen."

"Fifteen," Oliver whispered, memory dulling his gaze.

"Maureen was twenty-one."

"And beautiful." The flashlight on the floor shined up at him, casting weird shadows over his face. The hollows of his eyes were deep wells of ink. "So beautiful."

Erin squeezed more tightly into the corner. The floor under her was cold. The bricks at her back—cold. A trickle of sweat ran down her spine like an icy finger.

"How did it happen?" she asked, fighting to hear herself over the pounding of her heart.

He looked away, toward the open door, but she knew he wasn't seeing it, wasn't seeing anything around him.

"In July of '65," he said quietly, "Maureen came out from Sierra Springs, alone, to celebrate Lydia's birthday. One afternoon she set up a lounge chair out back. I sneaked through the arroyo to where she was sunbathing. And spied on her.

"She took off her shirt. Squeezed suntan oil onto her

breasts. Touched herself. I heard her moan. Skin wet with oil, legs twisting . . ."

Erin felt it was wrong somehow, a violation of some ancient taboo, to picture her mother touching herself so intimately.

She blinked the thought away. "How long did you watch?"

"Until she was finished. Then I returned to the house. Lincoln saw me as I entered. And he saw the stain. On my pants. A big, dark stain.

"I didn't even know I'd . . . done that. Hadn't felt it. Hadn't felt anything at all."

She understood. He must have survived the years of abuse by disconnecting himself from his emotions, even from physical sensations—and from sexual feelings most of all.

"Lincoln said he knew what I'd been up to. I'd been peeping at my Aunt Maureen. That kind of behavior demanded punishment. A boy needed to learn discipline.

"Lydia was in town, and Maureen was still outside. Nothing to stop him, so he did it right then, on the living room floor, near the potbelly stove.

"Afterward, I locked the bathroom door, scrubbed my pants and underwear. I didn't think about Lincoln. I thought about Maureen."

He lowered his head, the flashlight's pale radiance brightening on his face like a flush of shame.

"I wanted her. Before, it had been enough to just watch, but now I had to have . . . had to prove . . ."

Erin knew what he'd felt the need to prove.

"Next morning, Maureen was up before dawn; she liked to walk when it was cool. I found her by the barn. Said I'd hidden a birthday present for Lydia in the tack room.

"She went in with me. Trusted me. I was only a kid,

after all. But I was taller than she was. And in my back pocket I had a knife.

"Her eyes got big when I popped the switchblade. I was going to stick something in her, I said: the knife or my cock. Her choice.

"She was crying, saying I couldn't mean it. Good hard slap shut her up.

"We did it there, on the floor, with the knife at her throat and the horses restless in their stalls on the other side of the wall."

On the floor. The same way Lincoln had abused Oliver. The same pattern of perfunctory violence, repeated.

The son had learned from the father, but it was not discipline that had been taught.

"Once you let her go," Erin whispered, "she didn't tell?"

"No. She was scared. I let her know that even if I served time, I'd be out in a couple of years. That was all I had to say.

"She left later that day, even before Lydia's party. Made some excuse. Drove back to Sierra Springs. And not long afterward . . ."

"She found out she was pregnant."

"That's right, Doc. I got twin girls started that morning in the barn. I gave you life." He switched on the stun gun again. "And what I gave, I can take back."

Erin stared at the ribbon of current as Oliver guided it slowly toward her throat.

Upstairs, the groan of a door.

Her glance ticked upward. Oliver cocked his head.

They listened, frozen, breathless, wax figures in a tableau.

Softly, footsteps.

Someone in the house.

An emotion so intense as to be unidentifiable swept through Erin and set her body shaking.

*Oh, God*—the words in her mind began as a plea, ended in a silent shriek—*let it be a cop, please, let it be a cop!*

The footsteps stopped directly overhead.

In the sudden silence, in the motionless air, a voice.

"Erin . . . ?"

Annie.

Recognition jerked Erin half upright. All the breath rushed out of her lungs in an urgent, warbling cry.

*"Annie, get away, he's got a gun, he's—"*

The pincers slammed into the soft skin under her jaw, and she fell instantly into a lightless void, pursued by the echo of her scream.

# 54

Annie raced across the gravel court, her shoes scattering a fine spray of stones.

The echo of Erin's scream rang in her memory. A scream from the cellar, abruptly cut off.

After that, footsteps drumming on the stairs. Gund, ascending at a run.

He was here, after all. He was here, though she hadn't seen his van, hadn't seen any lights in the windows of the house. He was here, and if he chased her down, he would kill her. Kill her and Erin, too. Annie was sure of that.

The Miata was just ahead, the driver's window open, the door unlocked. She reached the car and fumbled for the door handle, Gund's key ring slipping free of her grasp to land somewhere on the ground with a distant, barely noticed clink.

The door swung open. She threw herself into the bucket seat, cranked the ignition key, and the motor caught.

Her high beams flicked on. Gund exploded out of the ranch, loping into the headlights' twin funnels, flashlight in one hand, pistol in the other.

Of course, Annie had not the slightest intention of fleeing.

Run away? Abandon her sister to a psychopath's mercies?

She never would. It wasn't a question of bravery or loyalty or commitment, but of simple self-preservation. To flee and leave Erin to die would be as good as committing suicide. She couldn't live with herself after that.

He had a gun, all right. But a car could be a weapon, too.

Annie hunched low over the wheel and floored the gas pedal.

For a heart-freezing second the Miata's tires spun uselessly, chewing gravel.

Gund stopped, twenty feet away, pinned in the high beams. Threw aside the flashlight. Lifted the pistol in both hands.

Annie had time to think she made a perfect target, stationary and at close range, and then with a squeal of rubber the tires caught.

Sudden acceleration punched her backward, hard against the seat.

The pistol bucked in time with a sharp crack of sound.

She jerked to one side as the windshield puckered. Crumbs of tempered glass showered her, gummy fragments seeding her hair.

She didn't slow down. Refused to be intimidated.

Gund was ten feet from the Miata's front end. Five. Annie braced for impact.

At the last instant Gund leaped.

Timing the jump perfectly, he flung himself onto the hood, landing spread-eagle on his belly.

The car left the gravel court, bouncing on mounds of dirt and patches of stiff, dead grass.

Gund extended his left arm, smashed through the windshield, and thrust the gun at her face.

The blued barrel gleamed, catching the spectrum of colors from the dashboard gauges. The muzzle was a hungry, sucking hole, a lamprey's mouth.

Annie spun the steering wheel.

Gund slid sideways, his aim thrown off as he squeezed the trigger.

The report deafened her. The bullet screamed past her face and clawed a hole in the convertible's top. A tongue of black cloth flapped wildly over her head, inches away.

*Close,* Annie noted, strangely unmoved despite the nearness of death.

Gund's pistol swung toward her again, the barrel compressed by foreshortening until it had disappeared and there was only the muzzle, inches from her right eye.

She stomped on the brake pedal.

The Miata screamed into a skid. The world blurred. The night sky, the barbed-wire fence, the ranch buildings all melted together in a giddy smear, like the view from a carousel.

Inertia yanked Gund halfway off the hood. He clung to the windshield frame a heartbeat longer, his knuckles squeezed bloodless, then let go and was gone, vanishing in the dark, rolling somewhere in the brittle grass.

The Miata pirouetted, completing a full circle, and shuddered to a stop.

Silence. Sudden and absolute.

The engine had stalled.

Annie heard a soft, plaintive whimper and realized it was her own.

The unreal calm that had armored her a few seconds earlier was gone, replaced by fear—pure, uncomplicated animal fear that choked her in a breathless stranglehold.

What to do? Start the car again. Yes. Get it moving and find Gund—injured, maybe unconscious—find him and mow him down, crush him under the wheels like roadkill, finish him, finish the bastard *now*.

Feverish thoughts and images beat like bat wings in her brain as she twisted the key in the ignition.

The motor coughed, died. Coughed, died.

*"Start,"* she hissed, tossing frightened glances at the rearview and sideview mirrors.

She jerked the key again. The engine feebly cleared its throat, then expired with a chortling death rattle.

Movement on her left.

She turned, and a gasp hiccuped out of her.

Gund.

At the open window on the driver's side.

In his hand, the pistol—or something like a pistol. Sleek and metallic and coming at her face.

Instinctively she recoiled.

Too late.

Pincers bit her neck in a vampire kiss.

Crackle of static, and pain clamped down on her, every muscle clenching.

Vision faded. Reality receded. Awareness broke up, flying into fragments like the Miata's windshield, plans and memories and speculations shattering in a mist of crystal dust.

*Erin*—it was her last thought before her mind was lost in a haze of glistening white—*I'm sorry.*

# 55

He picked up the phone on its fourth ring. "Walker."

"Okay, Mike. I got what you wanted."

The slightly whiny voice on the other end of the line belonged to Roger Dickinson of the county tax assessor's office.

It was 9:25. Walker hadn't expected his friend to get back to him so quickly. "Fast work, Rog."

"Yeah, well, you try hanging out in the County Administrative Center when the place is deserted. It's giving me the creeps."

"You still there?"

"Sure. In my office. Got the info you wanted right in front of me."

Walker uncapped a pen and flipped open a memo pad. "Shoot."

Papers shuffled. "Harold Gund did purchase a ranch outside town. Two and a half acres in an unincorporated area of Pima County. Escrow was recorded on the ninth of February this year. Place must be in piss-poor condition; it was assessed at only $119,000—a bargain for a parcel that size."

Even so, Walker wondered how Gund could have afforded the down payment on a clerk's income, much less qualified for the financing.

"Address?" he asked, pen poised over the pad.

"One hundred East Ravine Road."

As he wrote it down, Walker found himself frowning. The address tickled his memory, though he wasn't sure why.

"Mike? You there?"

"Sorry, Rog. Just thinking. Look, thanks a lot for your help. I appreciate this."

"We're even for those Suns tickets." It was not a question.

"All square. Thanks again."

Walker killed the phone, got out a spiral-bound map book, and looked up Ravine Road in the index.

Flipping to the appropriate page, he surprised himself by stating the address aloud.

"One hundred East Ravine Road."

Suddenly he remembered.

In the clutter of papers on his dining table were the two *Tucson Standard* articles Gary had given him. He found the one on the deaths of Lincoln and Oliver Connor.

First paragraph. Almost the very first words.

. . . *Lincoln Connor, 46, of 100 E. Ravine Road in the Tucson area* . . .

The Connor family had lived there. At the ranch. The ranch Harold Gund had bought just two months ago.

Fear crawled in Walker's gut, slimy and cold.

The fact that Gund had purloined a copy of Erin and Annie's photo portrait might indicate nothing more alarming than an adolescent infatuation with one or both of the women.

But someone who'd sought out and purchased the old Connor home, paying more to acquire it than he possibly could afford, was in the grip of more—much more—than a harmless schoolboy crush.

Annie might be right about this man Harold Gund. Walker blinked.

Harold . . .

The loose end in the Connor case. A missing teenager. First name Harold. Last name unknown.

The same Harold? Harold Gund?

No, couldn't be. Made no sense.

But Annie's assistant spending a small fortune to purchase the Connor ranch—that didn't make sense, either.

Or maybe it did. Maybe it all fit together perfectly in some subtle way Walker couldn't quite see.

He shook his head. Didn't matter. Time to puzzle it out later. Now he had to get hold of Annie, tell her what he'd learned.

He dialed her number. A message machine answered.

Not home. Damn. Where would she go?

He remembered her telling him how she'd followed Gund into the desert. Had she gone back, looking for the ranch?

Walker didn't want to believe that. Wanted to think she had more sense.

But somehow he knew better.

He returned his attention to the map book. Ravine Road was a minor dead-end street, southeast of town, off Houghton.

Didn't appear as if there were too many roads or ranches in that area. If Annie had gone looking for Gund's place, she might well have found it.

And if Harold Gund was there, he might have found *her*.

"Christ." Walker grabbed his car keys and his walkie-talkie. The ranch was outside T.P.D. jurisdiction, but it would take too long to explain all this to the sheriff's department.

Out the door. Sprinting to his car, a blue Mustang, parked in the driveway. The engine turned over instantly. At the corner he hooked south.

The Mustang, his personal car, had no siren or light bar. He exceeded the speed limit anyway. He would run red lights if he had to. What the hell. He was a cop.

As the Mustang skidded west on Fort Lowell Road, speeding toward Interstate 10, Walker was speaking into the portable radio microphone, requesting backup.

# 56

Tramp of shoes. Air moving past her face.

Erin blinked, coming back to herself. For a disoriented moment she was a small child, and her father was carrying her up the stairs to bed.

Sleep would be good. She was tired, so tired . . .

No.

It *was* her father, but not Albert Reilly.

Oliver was climbing the cellar stairs, and she was slung over his shoulder, a sack of trash, a bedroll. The chain trailing from her leg clanked after her, the padlock at the other end bouncing noisily.

Groaning, she tried to squirm free. Useless. The effects of the stun gun hadn't fully worn off. Though her mind was clear, her limbs were numb, her movements uncoordinated. She flailed and kicked without strength, landing soft, random blows.

Top of the stairs now. Into the hallway.

She wanted to speak, to argue, to plead, but her mouth wouldn't work right. The sounds she made were not words, not even wordless protests, merely unintelligible grunts and gasps, expressions of blind, consuming panic, panic of phobic intensity, panic that set her heart racing rabbit-fast and thrilled her with a roar of blood in her ears and a high electric whine in the bones of her skull.

She thought of the arroyo. Of flame.

Faint ambient light. The living room. Starlight spearing through the broken windows.

Hard to breathe. No air in her lungs, and her throat had closed. She remembered choking on fumes in a burning house, twenty-three years ago. That had been like this. Like this.

He stopped in the middle of the room, near its sole furnishing, the potbelly stove.

Alongside the stove, a shapeless heap of hair and clothes.

Annie.

Limp and still. Unconscious or dead. Propped in a seated position, her legs stretched out on the hardwood floorboards, her back resting against the stove's round belly.

Oliver hadn't simply deposited her there. He'd arranged her in that pose, as carefully as he would have arranged a bouquet in the flower shop. He'd made a display of her.

Erin saw all that, and abruptly she understood what he was about to do.

Not the arroyo.

Here.

He would burn them here, in the house of his childhood.

"*No!*" she screamed, fear finding a human voice at last.

Oliver flung her down.

She hit the floor hard. A groan racked her.

He crouched by her side. She wanted to scratch his face, gouge and claw, but still her body would not respond to her will. She could only thrash weakly, gasp-

ing in inarticulate protest, as he shoved her up against
the stove opposite her sister.

Snap, and the padlock securing the chain to her ankle was released, the chain pulled free.

The ribbon of heavy welded links was drawn across
her waist, her arms, then wound around the stove,
encircling Annie also, before its two ends met, a snake
swallowing itself.

With a jerk of his wrists Oliver yanked the chain
tight, chokingly tight across her midsection, crushing
her arms to her sides, pinning her to the stove.

Snap. The padlock was again engaged, joining the
two ends of the chain.

Erin moaned, struggling for speech and failing.

Oliver moved away, his back to her, and then he was
out the door, lost in the darkness of the night.

She stared blankly after him for a long moment.
Then with a spasm of violent energy she shook her
head, twisted her body, clenched her fists, reviving
dulled nerves and spent muscles.

She could not afford numbness and lethargy, not
now. She had to fight. Fight for survival—her own and
Annie's, too.

Blinking rapidly to clear her vision, she gazed down
at the padlock nestled in her lap, its steel shackle glinting at her like a smiling mouth. The chain extended on
either side of it, binding her and Annie to the stove.

If she could raise the chain a few inches, to the point
where the stove's belly narrowed in diameter, she
might be able to slip free.

Breathing hard, she contracted the muscles of her
lower back, pressed her palms to the floor, and struggled to push herself up.

The chain wouldn't budge.

But why not? Why the hell not?

Craning her neck, peering at the front of the stove out of the corner of her eye, she saw the reason.

Oliver had carefully looped the chain under the handle of the loading door and snagged it on one of the pin hinges. It could be neither raised nor lowered.

All right, then, how about the stove itself? Could it be moved?

A downward glance gave her the answer. The stove's legs were bolted to the floor.

There had to be something she could do. Free her arms, at least.

But she couldn't. The chain was wound too tight, jamming her elbows hard against her ribs.

No hope, then. No chance for her. For either of them.

Licking her lips, dispelling the last of the numbness that had frozen her mouth, she called her sister's name.

"Annie?"

She heard no answer. She had expected none.

Maybe Annie was dead already. It might be best that way.

Her gaze moved to the front door, hanging ajar, letting in the warm night breeze.

Oliver still had not returned.

But he would, of course.

Soon.

With gasoline.

# 57

Walker picked up two T.P.D. patrol cars at the interstate's Miracle Mile entrance. As he passed the Valencia Road on-ramp, he collected a sheriff's department
cruiser also.

The patrol cars activated neither sirens nor light bars
on the freeway, a standard safety precaution. Walker,
still in the lead, used his horn to scare slower traffic
out of the fast lane.

On a tactical frequency the other units were asking
questions, and he was doing his best to fill them in.
But his best, he had to admit, wasn't very good.

All he really knew was that a suspect in a possible
kidnapping might be at a ranch on Ravine Road, with
a hostage.

Or two hostages.

Driving with one hand, he put down his walkie-
talkie, switched on his car phone, and punched in Annie's number.

A recorded voice came on, as it had the last time
he'd called. "Hi, this is Annie. I'm not home right
now, so if you're a burglar, I'm in trouble—"

He turned off the phone. Swallowed hard.

*I'm in trouble,* the message had said.

A joke, of course. Recorded days or weeks ago, irrelevant to this situation.

*I'm in trouble.*

Ridiculous to dwell on those words, the mock plaintive tone of voice.

*I'm in trouble.*

Leaning forward, Walker pushed the Mustang to eighty-five.

"Annie?"

Still no response from the other side of the stove.

Though it was futile, Erin struggled against the chain, as if believing that by sheer force of will she could crack open the welded links.

"Dammit, Annie, *answer me.*"

"Sorry, Doc. She can't."

Erin jerked her head toward the doorway, where Oliver stood motionless, watching her across yards of darkness.

His arms hung straight at his sides, his hands wrapped around the handles of two bulky metal canisters.

Gas cans.

"Did you . . . shoot her?" Erin whispered. "Is she dead?"

"Unconscious." He spoke in a monotone, all emotion drained from his voice.

"Let her go. Please. If you want one of us"—she sucked in a sharp, shallow breath—"take me."

"I'm taking you both."

He set down the gasoline cans near the door, knelt, and calmly unscrewed the lids, his actions controlled, deliberate, robotic.

Nothing she said could move him. Even so, she had to try.

"Oliver." She held her voice steady, fear channeled

into her madly shaking hands. "You can't do this. Can't keep on killing."

"I won't. You two will be the last. Once you're gone, I'll be free."

He picked up one can, tilted it, and began to pour.

The gurgle of fluid from the spout set Erin's heart racing still faster. Her legs twisted, knees bending and straightening, boot heels dragging on the floor's hardwood planks.

In her mind a stranger's voice kept up a manic, witless patter: *I'm afraid, so afraid, so very afraid* . . .

But when she spoke, her own voice was calm and reasonable, the voice of a therapist doing her job. "You'll never be free that way."

"Yes, I will." Oliver walked with the can, pouring as he went, staying close to the living room wall. "Once I'm through with you . . . once you're out of my life . . ."

"We've been out of your life before. After 1968 you weren't Oliver Ryan Connor anymore. You could have stayed away from us forever. You didn't."

"No."

"You waited until August of 1973. And then . . . Well, you know what you did then."

No response.

"It was you, Oliver. It had to be. Albert Reilly never set that fire. You did."

Still nothing.

"Why? Oliver, tell me why."

Even now he was silent. She feared he had slipped still deeper into the fugue state, to the very bottom of the abyss, where no voice could reach him.

Then, without looking up, he spoke one word.

"Revenge."

Not much of a reply, but something. She had to capitalize on it, maintain a dialogue. "Revenge—for what?"

"I'd warned her. Warned Maureen never to tell."

Erin understood. "She waited two years—but in the summer of '68 she told Lydia at last. That's why Lydia disowned you."

"Yes."

He reached the corner, then continued along the adjacent wall, methodically laying down a trail of fuel along the room's perimeter. The smell of gasoline, the smell Erin hated more than any other, rose to her nostrils. Nausea coiled in her stomach.

She forced herself to continue her charade of disinterested professionalism. "Tell me about it."

The noise he made was intended as a chuckle, but came out stillborn, a croak of pain. "An ugly scene. Lydia called me names. Terrible names. I told her she could say the same about the man she'd married. And I told her why."

Erin nodded. It wasn't fear for Oliver's safety that had put Lydia in the hospital with a nervous breakdown, as everyone assumed. It was the double shock of learning the truth about her son and her husband.

The five-gallon can dribbled out its last drops. Oliver tossed it on the floor with a hollow clang. He walked past her, toward the doorway, where the other gas can waited.

Desperately Erin tried to keep him talking, fighting to reinforce the fragile connection she had established. "So you waited five years, then went to Maureen's house—our house—for revenge?"

"But first I visited Albert at his office." He hoisted the can by its handle. "He'd thought I was dead. I straightened him out about that . . . and other things."

"You told him you were our real father."

Remorselessly Oliver began wetting down the opposite side of the room. "Came as kind of a surprise," he said mildly.

"Weren't you afraid he'd go to the police?" Erin wished the sound of her voice would cover the low, insidious murmur of gasoline escaping from the can. "You were confessing to rape and murder—"

"There was no risk. If I were arrested, the truth about you and Annie would come out."

The truth. That they were products of an unnatural union, products of incest. Sideshow specimens. Freaks.

Oliver was right. Neither Albert nor Maureen would have willingly brought that fact into the light. Especially not in a small town like Sierra Springs, where everyone would talk.

He reached the doorway to the hall and continued past it to the living room's rear wall. The thread of fuel was lengthening, inexorably boxing her in.

"What was Albert's reaction?" she asked slowly.

"Shame. Grief. Most of all, anger. But not at me alone."

"Who else?"

"Maureen."

"My mother? She was the victim in all this."

"Was she?" Another lifeless chuckle. "I told you, Maureen wasn't married when she visited the ranch. Wasn't even engaged."

"Then when she found out she was pregnant—"

"That's right, Doc."

Erin shut her eyes. Her mother, panicky, unwilling either to abort the babies or have them born out of wedlock, had lied to Albert, convinced him that whatever precautions he'd taken had failed, railroaded him into a hasty wedding.

She remembered that nightmarish summer evening when Albert, drunk, wild with rage, had railed at his wife, rejected his children, and finally, in a fit of bellowing fury, had promised they would burn, burn, *burn*.

"In hell, he meant." Her voice was a whisper, the words spoken half to herself. "In hell."

The gasoline gurgled to a stop, the can empty. Oliver threw it aside.

"I let him suffer awhile," he said. "Maureen, too. They might have assumed I'd done my worst. Then on the night of August eighteenth . . ."

"You broke into the house."

"Yes. Found Albert asleep in the den. Clubbed him unconscious. Soaked the ground floor first, then carried Albert upstairs and finished the job."

"In the master bedroom. That's when Maureen woke up."

"She saw me, screamed. I gave her a good hard slap, just like I'd done in the barn. She was pleading with me when I tossed the match."

The floorboards shivered under his slow, heavy tread. He moved to the stove and stood before her, staring down.

"You two got out that night." Cold words. "But not this time."

Erin gazed up at him, his face as round and pale as a full moon, his gaze still blank, void of compassion, empty of self.

"You're lying," she whispered.

Puzzlement flickered briefly in his eyes. "What?"

"Revenge wasn't your motive. You had another purpose. A purpose you've never been willing to consciously acknowledge."

"Too late, Doc. Therapy's over." He began to turn away.

"That wasn't a fatherly kiss you gave me, Oliver." The words stopped him.

"In Sierra Springs," she said, "you did more than

visit Albert in his office. You spied on Maureen. Found out where she lived and observed her from hiding."

He blinked. "How did you know that?"

"It's what you always do. When Maureen visited the ranch, you spied on her from the arroyo. And when you came to Tucson, you must have followed me to learn where I live. I've got an unlisted address."

"All right. I watched her. With binoculars."

"And while you were observing Maureen's house, you saw her two little girls—*your* girls. *You saw us,* didn't you?"

"I . . . saw you."

"And you wanted us."

A muscle twitched in his cheek. He said nothing.

"Even though we were little, only seven years old, you wanted us, just as your father had wanted you, just as you'd wanted your mother's sister. Love and incest—you've never been able to separate the two. You wanted us."

"If I did . . . so what? *So what?*"

"That's why you set the fire. Not for revenge. You meant to wipe out all three of us—Annie and me and Maureen—so we wouldn't be there to tempt you anymore."

"It would have worked. If you'd died—"

"Nothing would have changed. You still would have had the same needs, and you would have responded the same way—by burning other women. Women who reminded you of us, because they were Catholic or they were young or they had the same color hair. The details wouldn't matter. You would have gone on killing no matter what."

"I wouldn't. Dammit, it wouldn't have been like that."

"It would. It would have to be. It always will. You think that by killing the object of your desire, you can kill the desire itself. You're wrong. What you're trying to destroy is within you, not outside you. It's part of you. It *is* you."

"It's not." He shook his head blindly in a last, desperate effort at denial. "You're the problem, not me. You and Annie. Filth. Whores. I'll get rid of you, and then I'll be free, God damn you, *I'll be free.*"

"You can never be free that way—"

But he wasn't listening anymore. A ripple of spasms in his shoulders, and he pivoted away from her, moving fast toward the front door. Helplessly she called after him. "Oliver? *Oliver?*"

At the door he turned. Something trembled in his hand.

A matchbook.

"I'll be free," he said once more, his voice muted and faraway.

He took a backward step, removing himself from the flash zone. A wisp of orange light flared between his fingers.

Flick of his wrist, and the match traced a slow arc through the darkness.

The gasoline vapors ignited even before the match hit the floor, triggering a split-second chain reaction that engulfed the lower portion of all four walls in a flexible sheet of flame.

*"Oliver!"*

Her scream didn't reach him. Nothing could reach him now.

Cymbal crashes of shattering glass. Every window in the room disintegrated simultaneously, blown out by the rapid expansion of superheated air.

*"Oliver!"*

Still no response, though he must have heard her. He had not moved from the doorway.

Erin had spent her life studying fire and fire starters. She understood what happened next only too well.

The upward rush of intense heat kindled the walls, boiling off the wood's most volatile contents. In a heartbeat the mist of outgassed turpentine, resin, and oil achieved its flash point, feeding the flames even as the gasoline vapors were consumed.

Convective updrafts teased the fire relentlessly toward the ceiling. Indrafting air from the front door and the broken windows flung exploratory firebrands across the floor.

"Goddammit, Oliver, *talk to me!*"

The fire cast a ruddy, wavering glow on his face. He stood motionless, gazing transfixed at what he had done, what he had finally brought himself to do after so many years.

His eyes were wide and glassy. The sparse hairs of his head rustled in the fire's hot wind.

Flames reached the first of the rafters, caught hold, then hopped from beam to beam. Churning fumes collected along the ceiling, forming a noxious mushroom cloud.

The smoke was what would kill her and Annie. That, or the stinging heat, or the collapse of the roof.

*"Oliver!"* She had to make him hear her. "Oh, Jesus, Oliver, don't leave us here, please *don't,* for God's sake, *don't*!" Each breathless shout seemed to jerk the chain tighter around her midsection, the wicked links chewing hungrily at her stomach, her lower ribs. "Don't let us burn, it's not the way to solve anything, *it's not the way!*"

The noise around her was thunderous, the Niagara roar of the flames competing with the moans of tortured wood, the pops of metal fixtures springing free of bolts and screws, the sizzle of sparking wires, the whoosh and howl of eddying air currents that spun pinwheels of soot and embers across the room.

Oliver shambled backward, still watching spellbound.

*"Oliver!"* she called for the last time.

Abruptly he turned, and then he was running, running into the night.

Gone.

Erin struggled with the chain, knowing she could not free herself, knowing she would be dead very soon, as the lethal heat pulsed around her and the roof beams began to groan.

# 58

"I did it."

Gund spoke the words between gulps of air as he sprinted to the barn.

He threw the double doors wide, climbed into the Astro, started the engine.

As he backed out into the open, as he swung the van toward the open gate, as he pulled out onto the side road, he felt strange tics and twitches in his face, peculiar muscular contractions at the corners of his mouth—and in his eyes, beads of dampness, blurring his world.

In the sideview mirror, the receding ranch house glowed with a red, feverish light.

Anther ripple of his facial muscles, and the shape of his mouth changed. It took him a moment to understand that he was smiling, really smiling—the first smile he had worn in years, decades—almost the first he could remember.

This, then, was happiness. That word he so often had heard and never comprehended.

"I did it," he said once more as he eased his foot down on the accelerator pedal.

The smile remained fixed on his face even while the

water in his eyes spilled over, warm droplets tracking slowly down his cheeks.

Walker led the three backup units off the freeway at Houghton Road. He headed north, maintaining a steady speed of seventy.

Behind him, the patrol cars switched on their light bars, red and blue dome lights pulsing. The sirens stayed silent.

Ravine Road must be directly ahead. Walker pumped the brake pedal, slowing in preparation for a sharp right turn.

Gund reached Houghton Road, and abruptly the newfound smile faded from his face.

To his left, three squad cars, rooftop flashers twinkling, with an unmarked Ford Mustang in the lead.

Arrest.

Punishment.

*No.*

With a snarl of rage he steered the van hard to the right.

As the Chevy swung onto Houghton, Gund reached under the dashboard with one hand and released the sawed-off Remington from its mounting.

Walker had run a D.M.V. check on Harold Gund during the drive to the ranch. He drove a Chevrolet Astro van.

The same make and model as the van that now squealed out onto the road, directly ahead.

"That's our guy," he said over his walkie-talkie.

Three sirens blared at his back.

He sped up, closing on the van.

* * *

Gund thrust the shotgun out the driver's-side window, muzzle pointing backward.

Under these circumstances he couldn't possibly aim. Fortunately, he didn't have to. The wide spray of shot would cut apart anything in its path.

He spun the steering wheel, barreling onto the shoulder, leaving the Mustang completely exposed in the middle of the road.

A single blast would tear the driver to pieces. With luck, the careening coupe would wreck one or more of the other pursuit cars in a deadly pileup.

He wedged the shotgun's stock against the windshield pillar and pulled the trigger.

Walker saw the van slide to the right, glimpsed a flash of metal near the driver's window.

Gun barrel.

He swerved onto the shoulder as the gun bucked with a booming report.

His windshield starred but didn't shatter.

Shotgun. He'd caught only a couple of stray pellets.

Accelerating, he rammed the rear of the van.

Damn.

The other driver had been too quick for him.

Now Gund couldn't see the unmarked car. It was directly behind the van's windowless cargo compartment, out of the side mirrors' field of view.

He released the steering wheel momentarily to pump another shotgun shell into the chamber.

Impact. From the rear.

The wheel spun crazily, the van skidding out of control.

He dropped the gun in his lap. Seized the wheel.

Too late.

The Chevy screamed off the shoulder, through a

waist-high wire fence, and plunged down, the front end tilting almost vertically, the lone headlight beaming into a sandy pit ten feet below.

The arroyo.

He was a hundred yards north of Ravine Road, at the point where the dry wash passed under Houghton. With the fence ruptured, there was nothing to stop the van as it plummeted headfirst into the gully.

Rushing up at him, a dry parcel of ground, pitted and whorled like the surface of some wind-scoured alien planet. For a timeless moment there was no sense of distance—the scarred landscape might be a yard away or a mile—and he was conscious only of inertia shoving him roughly against the seat as a high, keening protest escaped his open mouth.

With a howl of metal, the front of the van met the ground and crumpled in a mist of sparks and sudden smoke, the windshield exploding, the dashboard popping free as the lights of the gauges went dark, steering wheel wrenched loose, horn jammed, its blare earsplitting and continuous.

Gund waited for the van to tip over, to crash down on its roof or on its side.

Nothing happened.

Dimly he understood that the chassis still leaned on the roadway above, propped against the overpass like a ladder against a wall.

He coughed. Something harsh and foreign scratched his throat.

Smoke.

Clouds of it. All around.

Red glow from the ruined engine. Heat underneath the floor.

The van was on fire.

"Hell," he whispered dully. He groped for the door handle, turned it, but the door wouldn't open.

Wedged shut.

He remembered how the door frame had buckled slightly in last night's crash, how he'd had to hammer it back into shape. This new trauma had undone his work, sealing the door again.

Out the window, then, or through the shattered windshield.

But he couldn't. The dashboard, punched backward by the crash, trapped his legs.

Hotter now.

He coughed again, and this time found it hard to stop.

Smoke rose on both sides of him, billowing up from under the driver's seat.

He had seen people burn.

Couldn't die that way. Not him.

Wildly he pounded the dashboard, fighting to shove it free, like an animal clawing at the metal teeth of a trap.

Pain in his feet, his legs.

Downward glance. Caldron of black smoke where his lower body ought to be. Glinting in the smoke, malevolent pinpoints of fire.

The blare of the horn went on, and for a moment he didn't even hear the new sound overlaid on it, the piercing wail of his own scream.

*Get it off me,* he begged without voice, as if the fire crawling up his pants were some kind of ravenous animal. *Get it off, get it off, get it off—*

He was beating his pants with both hands, trying to slap the fire down, and screaming, screaming, screaming.

Had it hurt this much for the others? Were his daughters screaming with the same agony right now?

Impossible. There never had been this much pain before, not in all the world.

He was drowning in smoke, being eaten alive by flame, and now he couldn't scream anymore; he had swallowed too much smoke and could only wheeze, light-headed with pain and fumes, as he writhed and twisted, head whipsawing frantically, arms flapping, and then his hand touched hot steel, smooth and cylindrical, the barrel of the shotgun, thrown onto the passenger seat in the crash.

He thought of Lincoln Connor, of the real Harold Gund, their bodies sprawled together in the woods, a sawed-off Remington 870, like this one, clutched fast in Lincoln's hands.

Clumsily he turned the gun toward his own face.

The muzzle brushed his cheek, his chin. Mouth open, he swallowed it.

Somewhere at the end of the sixteen-inch barrel was a trigger.

He groped for it as the back of his seat erupted in flame and his scalp began to crisp.

Twenty feet from the van, Walker was slip-sliding down the embankment, carrying his Smith .38 and a dry-chemical fire extinguisher from his car, when he caught sight of Harold Gund.

The man couldn't be alive, certainly couldn't be conscious, not in that hell of folded metal and spurting flame.

But he was.

Walker saw movement. A gleam of steel.

The shotgun again.

For a wild moment he thought Gund was trying to take another shot at him. Then the barrel swung toward Gund's own face and the muzzle disappeared into his mouth.

A sharp crack, a viscid spatter.

The fire still burned, but Gund didn't feel it anymore.

Walker turned away from the van, then stopped, staring along the length of the arroyo toward a distant radiance.

Another fire. Larger than this one. A house or some other structure.

"Christ," he hissed. *"Annie."*

He scrambled back up the slope to his car, praying he wasn't already too late.

# 59

Annie knew what this was.

Her familiar nightmare.

Smell of smoke and gasoline. Whisper of flame. Heat on her face. The house in Sierra Springs ablaze.

She roused herself, eyelids fluttering, vision swimming into focus.

Around her, a blazing light show. Showers of sparks. Blooms of flame.

She wasn't awake yet. Couldn't be. The nightmare was continuing, taking a new and more vivid form. . . .

A wave of heat pulsed over her. The stench of gasoline bit her nostrils. She choked back a cough.

No dream. Reality.

She remembered her last waking moments. Gund at the car window. Voltage coursing through her body.

Comprehension hit her like a punch in the stomach. *"Erin?"*

From directly behind her, less than a yard away: "I'm here, Annie."

Though her sister's voice was ragged, her tone— measured and steady—gave an impression of something close to calm control. An illusion, certainly, because no one could be calm here, calm *now*.

"What the hell's he doing to us?" Annie heard raw terror in her own voice. "Christ, *what's he doing?*"

"Don't panic, Annie. Please don't."

The words made no sense. Panic? Of course she would panic. Who *wouldn't* panic, for God's sake? Didn't Erin understand what was going on? Didn't she *see*? Gund had set the house on fire, they were going to burn, burn to death—

No. Quit it. *Quit it.*

With trembling effort she forced down her rising fear.

As a child in a blazing death trap she had yielded to terror, become hysterical; but she was not a child any longer.

Head lowered, she looked herself over for the first time and found that she was seated on the floor, chained to an appliance of some sort, a water heater or a furnace or something. Stubby metal legs, bolted in place, held the base of the contraption six inches off the floor.

Potbelly stove. That's what it was. She remembered it from snapshots in Lydia's photo album.

She strained against the chain links, trying to release her arms. No use.

"Isn't there any way to get free of this thing?" she yelled.

"Chain's wound tight. And it's—" A spasm of coughing interrupted Erin's reply. "It's padlocked."

Padlocked.

Annie blinked.

Twisting her right arm, she thrust her hand into the pocket of her skirt, and yes, there it was: the key ring she'd taken from Gund's apartment.

As she pulled the keys free, it occurred to her that there was something funny about her having them, something that ought to disturb her, but there was no time to think about it now.

"I've got his keys!" she shouted.

"What?"

"Gund's *keys*. Can you reach the padlock?"

"Think so." Now it was Erin's voice that quavered, not with fear but with barely suppressed hope.

"Okay," Annie said. "I'm gonna slide 'em to you."

"I'm ready."

She placed the keys on the floor, took a breath, and flicked them backward, between the stove legs.

For an endless moment there was no response, and she was sure she'd blown it, *blown it,* hadn't pushed the key ring far enough, and now it lay somewhere under the stove, out of her reach and Erin's, useless to them both, their last chance wasted.

"Got them!" Erin called.

*Thank God.* "Do they work? Does one of them work?"

"Give me a second."

Annie waited, tasting smoke, trying to be brave.

Fumbling one-handed, Erin found two small padlock keys on the ring. She wedged the first one between two fingers and lifted the key to the padlock at her waist.

Hard to keep her attention narrowed to this tight focus when everywhere the smoke was thickening, the heat rising to a murderous intensity.

Little time left. Couple of minutes at most. Combustion was entering its second, still more deadly phase.

The wood of the walls, ceiling, and floor, dried out after years in an arid climate, could not feed the flames for long; already the fire was fading in patches to a dull glow as it burrowed into the timber, snouting out the carbon still trapped inside. The heat would further weaken the cellulose and lignin that gave the wood its structure and strength, until the roof beams and wall panels simply fell apart, collapsing the house on top of Annie and herself in a cascade of burning debris.

The smoke might get them sooner. It was a witches' brew of carbon monoxide and outgassed toxins from the walls: vaporized varnish, paint, glue, and insulating material. The fire was rapidly consuming the room's remaining oxygen; before long there would be only poison to breathe.

Her hand shook, and she nearly dropped the key ring.

*Come on, Erin. Concentrate.*

The keyhole wasn't visible from her angle; she had to stab the key at the bottom of the padlock case several times before it slid into the plug. She twisted her wrist.

Nothing happened.

Wrong key, then. Try the other one. Hurry.

She rotated the key ring, isolated the second padlock key, inserted it.

Clockwise turn, and the padlock released.

She stared at it, stunned, then tried to laugh and hacked out a ragged cough instead.

"Annie, it worked! It *worked*!"

Another spasm of coughing racked her as she kicked free of the chain. She crawled around the stove and found her sister untangling herself from the heavy links.

"This way!" Erin yelled. "Front door!"

Smoke had turned Annie's eyes to water. "Can't see."

"Take my hand."

Annie obeyed.

Erin crawled toward the doorway, guiding Annie through the inferno, just as she had led her sister through another burning house so many years ago.

Char and soot and white mineral ash whipped around them in a swirling haze. Clouds of sparks like fireflies singed their hair.

The door wasn't far, less than twenty feet away, but it was separated from them by a river of gasoline a yard wide, its surface webbed with kinetic ripples of flame.

*Have to jump across,* Erin thought. *If we can.*

Behind them, an echoing groan.

She glanced back and saw the rafter directly above the stove splitting cleanly in the middle, raining sparks and splinters.

Close. Too close.

*"Move!"*

She yanked Annie forward. At their backs the ceiling beam pitched down in a rush of charred timber.

Thunderous impact. The house shook. The rafter disintegrated into a vortex of burning brands. The last of the wood's stored energy ignited in a monstrous shout of flame, exploding like a bomb at their backs, the pressure wave hurling Erin flat against the floor, and for a second she was certain a seething comber of fire was about to surge over her and Annie and consume them both.

It didn't. The flame contracted and winked out, its fuel supply devoured in an instant, leaving only a tempest of smoke and, rising above the background roar, Annie's screams.

Erin spun toward her sister and saw her writhing on the floor as flames crawled over her skirt and blouse.

*"Help me, oh, Jesus, help me!"*

With her bare hands Erin slapped the flames, trying desperately to smother them. In her mind she was seven years old again, in the stairwell of another fiery house, beating her sister's flaming pajamas with the stuffed bear called Miss Fuzzy.

Pain. Pain in her left arm.

Embers had drifted from Annie's clothes to her own, setting the sleeve of Erin's blouse ablaze.

She broke free of Annie, pawing at herself, smacking wildly at the bright blemish of flame, but even as she did, new hot spots erupted on her skirt, her blouse, her hair, and she was burning, *burning*—Oliver had won—after twenty-three years he'd had the last word, God damn him, he'd murdered them both.

Dragon hiss.

Jet of chemical spray.

An arc of aerosolized powder, soaking her and Annie in a white drizzle.

Fire extinguisher. It was a *fire extinguisher*.

Erin lifted her head, glimpsed a dark figure in the doorway—a man struggling toward them, sweeping the canister from side to side, cutting a narrow swath in the river of fire along the room's perimeter.

"Michael?" The hoarse, whispery voice was Annie's.

Over the threshold, a shuddering creak.

Anther ceiling beam threatened to give way.

Erin grabbed her sister's hand and pulled her upright.

Sparks rained down as the beam weakened. The man called Michael took a last step forward, reaching out to them.

Erin's fingers locked on his wrist. He pulled her, stumbling, through the doorway. Annie clung to Erin's hand and followed.

Inside the house, a sudden wrenching groan.

Erin looked back in time to see the rafter above the threshold plunge down in a curtain of fire, engulfing the doorway in a roaring shower of debris.

Together they staggered across the gravel court. Fifty feet from the house they stopped, safely distanced from the waves of blistering heat and the torrent of smoke.

Erin's knees unhinged. She sank into a crouch. Annie knelt beside her, coughing weakly.

From the direction of the gate came the squeal of tires, the pulse of dome lights—police cars arriving at the scene.

Erin looked at the man kneeling beside her. "Who . . . who are you?"

"Michael Walker." He forced out the words between harsh gasps. Sweat streaked his face and neck, pasting the open collar of his shirt to his skin. "Tucson P.D."

"Got here . . . just in time."

"Should have been sooner." He looked at Annie. "Much sooner."

Annie rubbed the smoke from her eyes. "Well"—she managed a smile—"better late than never."

Walker's startled laugh died in a wheeze.

Erin had one other question, but almost no strength to ask it. She tugged Walker's sleeve, met his gaze, and voiced one word.

"Gund?"

"Dead."

Slowly she looked away, toward the burning house, and nodded.

"Good."

# 60

In darkness, the buzz of an intercom.

Blinking awake, Erin leaned on one elbow and stared at her bedside clock.

12:03 A.M.

*It's happening again,* she thought groggily. *Oliver is back.*

Crazy notion. Insane.

Even so, she was trembling as she threw off the covers and padded into the living room.

She thumbed the Talk button. "Yes?"

"Erin? It's me." The voice was Annie's. "Sorry to come over so late, but . . . I need to talk."

*Need to talk.* Even the same words as last time.

"Annie? *Is* that you? Is it *really*?"

"Of course it is. . . . Oh, I get it. I—I didn't think of that. Maybe I shouldn't have stopped by, huh?"

Oh, hell. "You're here, so come on up."

Pressing Enter, she buzzed open the lobby door.

It would take Annie a minute or so to ride the elevator to the fourth floor. While waiting, Erin returned to her bedroom and put on her slippers and robe.

Which was exactly what she'd done that other night, she reflected grimly, then shook her head in self-disgust.

Stupid of her to entertain such a blatantly irrational fear—especially after Detective Walker had explained precisely how Annie's voice had crackled over the intercom on the night of the kidnapping.

Nothing mystical about it. Oliver had owned a tape recorder with an attachment that let him tape directly off his phone line. He had called Annie's number while she was out and recorded her answering machine's outgoing message.

*Hi, this is Annie. I'm not home right now, so if you're a burglar, I'm in trouble. If you need to leave a message, please wait for the tone and then talk. Bye.*

Then he'd edited the tape, leaving in only certain words. The spliced audiocassette had been found during a thorough search of his apartment.

*This is Annie. . . . I'm in trouble . . . Please . . . Need to . . . talk.*

The doorbell rang. Annie was here.

If it really was Annie, and not Oliver once again returned from the dead.

At the door Erin flipped the wall switch, illuminating the living room. Before retracting the dead bolt, she checked the peephole. The face in the fish-eye lens was her sister's.

She opened the door. "Annie. You okay?"

"Okay?" Annie stepped inside, smiling blithely at the question. "I'm perfect. That's what Lydia used to say about us, you remember? That we were perfect."

Her words were strange, her smile oddly fixed. A worry flitted through Erin's mind that her sister might be having some sort of breakdown.

*Never should have told her,* she reproached herself for the hundredth time.

Though she'd given the police most of the details of Oliver's past, Erin had withheld one crucial part of the story: Maureen's rape and pregnancy. That secret had been shared only with Annie.

It had seemed only proper. Her sister, after all, had every right to know. But Annie had taken the news hard, terribly hard.

And why not? Such an ugly word, redolent of ancient taboo: incest.

Erin felt it, too—that crawling sense of unfitness, of impurity. Had felt it ever since she'd grasped the truth about Oliver and his relationship with Maureen. In the two weeks since the fire at the ranch, she'd tried to rationalize the problem out of existence. When those efforts had failed, she'd found herself taking long baths and too many showers, hoping illogically to wash away the physical sensation of corruption.

No use. There were some things water couldn't cleanse.

She was tainted; they both were. Contaminated.

*Filth.* She heard Oliver's voice in her mind. And, deeper in memory, Albert Reilly raging: *Abominations.*

She pushed away those thoughts and gestured toward the sofa. "Why don't we sit down?"

"Not there." Annie was still smiling, smiling, an unnatural glitter in her eyes. "The dining table. Light's better there."

Though Erin had no idea why the light would matter, she complied, seating herself across the table from her sister.

"Sorry to drop by so late," Annie said. "You were asleep, I guess."

"It's all right." Erin kept her tone neutral.

"I couldn't sleep myself. Came back from a date with Michael around ten o'clock."

"A date? How long has this been going on?"

"Oh, I don't know. This was—let's see—our third

date. He's a nice guy, as it turns out. But I mean, it's not real serious."

"Think it will be?"

"Too early to tell. Anyway, that's not what kept me awake." Annie fumbled open her purse, exposing a remarkable clutter of junk inside. "I was doing some research."

"Research?"

"Going through the family records—the stuff Lydia inherited from Maureen. Found a few interesting items." From the purse she removed a thin sheaf of folded papers, then unfolded one and gave it to Erin. "First thing ... Maureen and Albert's wedding license."

Erin accepted the faded document with a frown, intellectual curiosity beginning to override her concern.

"September 2, 1965," she said thoughtfully. "Seven months before we were born. Two months after Maureen's visit to the Connor ranch."

"And two and a half months after June 15. That was when they officially celebrated their anniversary."

Erin had forgotten that. She nodded slowly. "Keeping up appearances. The whole family must have played along."

"Sure. They all believed they were covering up some premarital indiscretion on the part of Albert and Maureen. Even Albert himself believed that. At least until 1968, only Maureen knew the truth."

"Interesting." She gave her sister an inquisitive look. "But not what you came here at midnight to discuss."

"I found a couple of other things. Here's one."

Annie handed over a second sheet of paper, older than the first, the creases deeper, the corners more badly dog-eared.

Erin smoothed it out. Maureen's birth certificate, dated April 22, 1944.

Mystified, uncertain why this would matter, she looked expectantly at Annie.

"And last," Annie said softly, with an odd note of triumph, "there's this."

She pushed a third folded document across the table. The oldest of all, yellow and brittle, specks of mold like liver spots dappling one corner.

Some intuitive presentiment of the document's substance set Erin's hands shaking as she unfolded it.

The paper was a certificate of adoption, dated August 30, 1931, for an infant girl born six weeks earlier, named Lydia Aileen O'Hara.

"Adopted," Erin whispered. "Lydia was *adopted*."

"You got it."

"She was never related to Maureen by blood."

"Nope."

"So we . . . we aren't . . ."

"Oliver was guilty of plenty, but not, as it turns out, of incest. He only thought he was. Maureen and Lydia thought so, too. Neither of them ever knew about the adoption."

Erin stared at the certificate until the words before her blurred with a rush of tears. Then she lifted her head to see Annie's broad grin—not a tight, strained smile any longer, but a laughing expression of release.

She knew her own face looked the same. She could feel the tension sighing out of her body, the dull ache of her burden lifting, leaving her weightless and free.

"But . . ." she began, then had to steady herself before continuing. "But Lydia had all these papers. Inherited them after the fire in '73."

"Had them, but never looked at them, any more than she looked at her photo albums. Just locked them away untouched. The past—any part of the past—was too painful for her to face."

"She could have saved herself so much grief. . . ."

Annie's smile dimmed slightly. "I know. But she didn't. And it's too late now—for her. But not for us."

"Not for us," Erin agreed, her voice unexpectedly hoarse. She gazed down at the thin sheet of paper shivering in her hands. "Oh, God, Annie. It's . . . it's a miracle."

"Maybe not the only one," Annie said cryptically. "Actually, it shouldn't have come as a total surprise. We always knew Maureen was an accident; she was born thirteen years after Lydia. The way I figure it, Rose and Joseph Morgan tried to conceive a child, but had no luck."

"So they adopted Lydia secretly and raised her as their own. Then when Rose was thirty-nine . . ."

"Surprise." Annie beamed. "Here comes baby Maureen, defying the odds. I'd say that's one trait we inherited from her, wouldn't you?"

*Inherited.* Erin's mind seized on that word, the last of the pieces falling into place.

"Maureen never had seizures." She was thinking aloud, putting it together as she spoke. "None of the Morgans did, or any of the Reillys, either. It was Lydia O'Hara who carried that gene. She passed it on to Oliver, and he passed it on to me."

"You don't have to keep convincing yourself, Erin." Annie's tone was gentle. "It's for real."

"I know it is, but . . ."

But it was almost too good to be true. Childishly she was afraid of saying so and perhaps jinxing their good luck somehow, voiding the miracle.

Miracle . . .

"Wait a minute." Erin frowned. "What did you mean when you said this might not be the only miracle?"

"Oh. Well, there is one more thing."

"More? More than *this*?"

"Yeah, but . . . I don't know how to feel about it.

You see, when you told me the truth about Harold—
about Oliver, I mean—there were some things that
didn't make sense to me."

"Like what?"

"Take the way he set the fire in 1973. He poured
gasoline everywhere in the house . . . except our end of
the hall. He left a clear path from our bedroom to the
stairs."

Erin shrugged. "An oversight."

"Then he left us alone for twenty-three years. He
killed other women, but never came near us, though
he could have tracked us down at any time. And when
he did come looking for us, what did he do? He got a
job with me. He became my assistant."

"And kidnapped *me*."

"He went to a lot of trouble to prevent you from
guessing his identity, as if he really intended to let you
go. Even after you escaped, he didn't kill you."

"He wanted therapy. He needed my help."

"But the truth is, he could have snatched any therapist. It would have been less risky to pick a total
stranger. What he specifically wanted was to work with
*you*—and, in a different way, with me. He wanted to be
close to us."

"Because he was obsessed with us. And when he realized what lay at the heart of his obsession, he wanted
us dead."

"Part of him did."

"You're saying there was a conflict?"

Annie reached into her purse again. "Look at this."

She removed the key ring taken from Oliver's apartment, the keys charred and melted now.

"The firefighters found it when they were sifting the
rubble. Michael gave it to me tonight." She handed the
key ring to Erin. "And I remembered something."

Erin ran her fingertips along the serrated edges of

the two padlock keys, one of which had saved their lives. "The other miracle?" she asked quietly.

"Might be."

Erin waited. When Annie spoke again, her voice was a whisper.

"I used those keys to open the door of the ranch house. They were still in my hand when you shouted from the cellar. I ran to my car. And somewhere along the way . . . I lost them. Dropped them on the gravel. Dropped them and never picked them up."

A beat of silence in the room.

"Later, in the fire, when I grabbed for the keys, it was just reflex. They shouldn't have been in my pocket. But they were." Annie looked across the table, green eyes sparkling faintly. "You see what I'm saying?"

Erin sat very still. Only her hand moved, fingering the ring of keys like the beads of a rosary. "Yes. I see."

"He put them there. He put the keys back in my pocket. He gave us a chance, just like in 1973. Not much of a chance, but enough. Both times—just enough."

"I guess he did."

"But what I don't understand is why. He was a killer. He murdered Maureen and Albert, Lincoln Connor and the real Harold Gund, and those three women up north. So why not us? What was special about us?"

Erin gazed into the shadowed corners of the room. Slowly she smiled, a thin, sad smile of wisdom and pain.

"We were his daughters, Annie."

Nothing more to say after that. They sat together, lost in private thoughts; and sometime in that long silence, Annie reached out slowly and took her sister's hand.